CELTIC WAR ON TERRORISM

CELTIC WAR ON TERRORISM

Eagle Ross

The Book Guild Ltd
Sussex, England

First published in Great Britain in 2002 by
The Book Guild Ltd
25 High Street
Lewes, East Sussex
BN7 2LU

Typesetting in Baskerville by
SetSystems Ltd, Saffron Walden, Essex

Printed in Great Britain by
Antony Rowe Ltd, Chippenham, Wiltshire

A catalogue record for this book is
available from the British Library

ISBN 1 85776 692 X

*This book is dedicated to
the author's
faithful wife
and
four children.*

Many thanks are given to everybody who has participated in some way to make this book possible. Special thanks are given to anonymous sources that have contributed with secrets and official facts.

The Scottish independence fight has been proceeding for hundreds of years. Many incidents may recently have taken place. One will never know, as such matters will remain secret and will never become public.

Eagle Ross – 1998

Life is too short to
be spoilt by only a
second's lapse in
concentration.

Eagle Ross
– from *Independence Fight*

PROLOGUE

The flames heaved into the sky and thick smoke covered the whole area. It was an army depot in the neighbourhood of Kursk, Russia, which was on fire. The local Russian army's fire brigade was fighting a loser's game. They kept a good distance from the fire because of the extreme heat. The weapons in the depot that were threatened by the fire also prevented any closer contact. None dared to stay close to the fire, which might suddenly reach the explosives. It seemed as if the fire must burn out by itself, and there was nothing to do. The fire fighters looked like supernumeraries in an old third-rate movie. Their absence would have made no difference to the circumstances.

Suddenly the air was filled with a war-like sound. The fire had finally reached the weapons. It was as if thousands of New Year celebrations were going off at the same time. The exploding weapons led to a massacre. All the fire fighters nearest to the explosion were killed instantly. The rumour afterwards was that more than three hundred men were killed.

The Russian authorities had adopted some of the old Soviet Union's political habits of not stating the real situation when disasters happened. The public would therefore never know the real figures of casualties, if they got any information about a disaster in the army at all.

Rumours spread that there were also tactical nuclear

weapons in the depot. Everybody ran desperately away with great fear for their life, leaving dead and injured comrades behind in the inferno. The destruction of the nuclear weapons might cause a much greater catastrophe than Chernobyl many years before. The survivors of the fire fighters and the people staying in the surrounding environment would die from cancer in the years to come. Therefore, everybody's thoughts were suddenly only to get away as quickly as possible. Superiors, still clear thinking, shouted orders to deaf ears. It was an entirely panic-stricken situation.

1

Nearly a year before the fire catastrophe at the weapons depot, the depot's superior, Colonel Igor Salnikov, had been on vacation in western Europe. When he afterwards talked eagerly about his vacation, he said it had been the journey of a lifetime. He had never been out of the Soviet Union before, not counting the times he had been ordered by the army to participate in tragic wars, which the *Politburo* in the Kremlin had engaged in, connected with their ongoing wish to include more of the world in the communist block. Salnikov said he had used all his savings on this particular journey that had included Italy, France and Spain, and that he believed he never again would get the chance to see the Western world. Sorrowfully he had also added that for the rest of his lifetime he probably only could afford to eat dark Russian bread and drink cheap, weak vodka.

The journey had purely been possible because of the new democratic facilities for Russian citizens, which had allowed the population to travel freely abroad.

The fifty-year-old colonel was very typically Ukrainian, in both conduct and appearance. He was stocky, had broad shoulders and a thick neck. His hair was dark, straight, unruly and close-cropped. Salnikov had climbed the most important steps of military rank in Afghanistan, where he had been a hero. His military career accelerated rapidly and he had been promoted from the rank of lieutenant to major after he had saved his entire platoon from certain death by showing extreme shrewdness and courage. Army colleagues said he had been entirely loyal, even risking death for his soldiers, but his superiors never considered him loyal to the Soviet. They had correctly believed he had been absolutely against the Soviet's involvement in the Afghanistan war from the very start.

Salnikov's ancestors came from Ukraine. During the last part of the Second World War the family had been forced, by Stalin's liberation troops, to move from Kiev to Perm, a city by the river Kama in central Russia. Afterwards, they had not been allowed to return home. The colonel's patriotism, if he had any patriotism at all, belonged for this reason, exclusively to his ancestors' Ukraine.

Salnikov had also served two long years in Chechnya until the Russians had been forced to pull out of the conflict. He had always, like any loyal soldier and perfect army officer, obeyed all orders, although they often seemed completely against his personal will. He had, without protesting, executed all the killings and seen his troops and enemies blown to pieces. As compensation for his loyalty to the army, he had received the rank of colonel, but he considered there would be no future opportunities for further promotion.

After his participation in the Chechnya War, Salnikov had been ordered to serve his last years in the army as the commander-in-chief of a weapons depot in the neighbourhood of Kursk, a town near the Ukrainian border. He felt very dishonoured by this order which would positively be his last task in the army. Afterwards, as a Russian army officer, he could only foresee a depressing life. Retired and living on a scanty pension in a small, army retirement flat, among similarly dispossessed colleagues, he would be waiting for the release of death. He could not accept this prospect for the future.

The plane carried Salnikov directly from Moscow to Linate airport outside Milan in Italy. He could read the enormous Grappa poster on one of the hangars at the airport, when he descended the steps from the plane. He felt as if he was in another world.

The Hertz car rental company, with a desk by the exit door, had accepted his Russian driving licence and he became the driver of a four-wheel drive, aluminium Audi for the first time in his life. The taste of Western luxury made him feel really good. He had never felt more strongly that he had missed something in his former life. He studied the map and was soon driving eastwards on the motorway, in the direction of Padova.

The traffic was heavy and the speed was slow. However, he considered this only as an advantage because he had to get used to the new monster of a car before he drove any faster. It was quite different to drive a new four-wheel drive Audi with more than 130-horse power, compared to his old Lada back in Russia.

He had observed the frighteningly high speed of the cars in the westbound lane at the other side of the green, dense row of shrubs that divided the road. The traffic was not as obstructed on that side, as on his. It was seven p.m. and the whole of Milan's work force seemed to be on the road at the same time and travelling in his direction. The Italians were on their way home for dinner, probably consisting of pasta or pizza, covered with a thick layer of Parmesan cheese. He had been told the Italians mostly ate these dishes and he had himself several times eaten pizza with great delight in the new Italian restaurants in Moscow. He had also frequently eaten Russian meals containing pasta and Italian cheese. Thoughts about food made him suddenly hungry and he stopped at the first motorway restaurant – a Motta Autogrill.

The restaurant was a self-service one, which bridged the motorway and could be entered from both sides of the road. Salnikov impatiently loaded his tray with dishes he had barely heard of. It looked fantastically delicious. He sat down at one of the tables with a view towards the cashier's desk. He wanted to look at the people around him and to feel the atmosphere. He wanted to feel what it was like to be a free man in a free country – at an Italian self-service restaurant by a motorway.

Salnikov noticed a furtive-looking man in his late thirties. The stranger did not look as if he belonged to the blissful, bawling Italian crowd. The stranger looked extremely Russian and he glanced around for a couple of seconds like a youngster for the first time on a dance-floor, before he finally bought a Coca-Cola. He glanced again carefully in ' Salnikov's direction while he walked across to a table by the wall, where he could sit in the shadows and view the entire restaurant unnoticed.

A woman with three children tried to load several trays with different dishes, accompanied by their protesting and demanding cries. An old man took a pre-cooked dish with *mozzarella* cheese and was slowly pouring oil and vinegar over it, and then sprinkling on some salt and pepper. One of the crying children ran into him and the plate fell to the floor and broke. The old man angrily shouted something to the child that Salnikov did not understand. Afterwards, he started again on the same slow procedure with another pre-cooked dish. The incident looked extremely comical and Salnikov chuckled silently.

Well fed and in a superb mood, Salnikov turned off the motorway half an hour later, in the direction of Lake Garda. He drove along the straight country road between the green fields, into a small town called Sirmione. The hectic tourist season had not yet started and the traffic in the town was light. He stayed at the first tiny hostel he stopped at.

The next morning Salnikov woke up to an amazing view of Lake Garda. The lake was glittering in the slowly rising sun. He felt relaxed and sovereign. He ate a delicious breakfast, fried eggs and *prosciutto*, the very tasty Italian ham, in the hostel's breakfast room, before he checked out.

Salnikov had previously read about the Roman ruins in Sirmione. The ruins were near the hostel. He left his car in the hostel's car park and walked. He took the narrow path to the ruins along the beach of Lake Garda, in line with other tourists who also had been able to get their bodies out of their warm beds early in the morning. He found the ruins astonishing. While his ancestors had lived in caves and hit their neighbours over the head with clubs, the Romans had lived in houses with bathrooms not far from Italian standards of today. The mosaic on the floor was especially impressive.

When he returned on the narrow path towards the car he suddenly recognised the same fellow, who had separated himself from the crowd at the Autogrill the day before.

From Sirmione, Salnikov followed the country roads towards Verona. He arrived just after noon and drove into the old town looking for the five star hotel Due Torri. This old hotel in Verona was well known to him from tourist brochures. It was built in the fifteenth century. All the rooms in the hotel were different and were equipped with old-fashioned furniture.

He found the hotel almost by accident, as he was driving down a narrow one way road, which ended in another narrow road, passing a small square. The hotel was situated just off this square. An antiquated church, with two towers, was to the left of the hotel. The church's two towers explained the hotel's name. The hotel had a very unpretentious facade. If one did not know it, it would be easy to pass it by looking for a more prestigious facade. He parked his car in the small square in front of the hotel. The square could only accommodate a maximum of ten cars and there were plenty of parking restrictions all around. He concluded that the hotel's guests must be pedestrians only.

He entered the hotel with his suitcases and was suddenly standing in an enormous hall, which was almost as large as the parking square outside. The vaulted ceiling was ten metres above the glistening marble floor. Two rows of thick, Roman marble pillars carried the ceiling. Old fashioned, exclusive, leather sofas and chairs were spread around in groups. There was nobody in the hall except for a very polite middle-aged man in a black suit, who stood quietly behind the reception desk to the left of the entrance and looked enquiringly at Salnikov, while he politely waited for him to speak.

"Is it always this empty here?" – Salnikov asked in broken English with his marked broad Russian intonation.

"Most of the time," the Italian receptionist replied in perfect English. "The hotel is a very quiet place mostly chosen by adult tourists and business people visiting the town. Verona is a Trade Fair city, you know, but there is no Fair going on at the moment. The last one was the Agricultural Machine Fair, and the tourist season has not yet fully started so we do have some rooms vacant."

The receptionist spoke as if he was repeating a lesson that he had learned when he got his job. Obviously, to impress and make the obligatory marketing for the hotel, the receptionist continued: "Very often the same people return year after year, especially those visiting the Trade Fairs."

Salnikov listened diplomatically and silently to the receptionist without any interruption. When he finally considered the receptionist had finished his defence of his doctorate thesis, he asked quietly for a nice suite.

He checked in, slept for a couple of hours and then took a shower. Afterwards, he put on the new black suit that he had bought in one of the new shops in Moscow, which sold solely expensive western European makes. The suit had the latest Western look and he would not be any different from most people in the town. He completed his outfit with a white Van Heusen shirt, a dark blue and white spotted English silk tie and Italian hand-made shoes.

Salnikov usually had absolutely no interest in clothes at all. He only wore them because he needed to. However, he did not want to stand out from the crowd. That was the only reason he had equipped himself with these rather expensive Western clothes when he travelled to western Europe. He could easily see the main difference between a Russian-made, and a Western-made suit. The Russian authorities considered this knowledge of great importance to someone in his position, however ridiculous it sounded. This was because high ranking Russian officers had to attend one of the Russian Military's Secret Intelligence Police spy schools – GRU institutes. Salnikov had stayed in such an institute for six months as a part of his military education. To detect an enemy spy's identity by clothes and behaviour was one of the subjects at the institute. Anybody was a potentially dangerous enemy of the dear Motherland and the Third World War could break out at any minute, the officer students were told at that time. Salnikov considered afterwards all this to be nonsense and completely absurd brainwashing.

Salnikov went down to the reception desk and asked for directions to the famous Arena of Verona. He had bought a ticket for a concert six months ago in Moscow. The Three Tenors, José Carreras, Placido Domingo and the great Luciano Pavarotti were to sing in concert. This could purport to be one of the main reasons why he had included northern Italy in his travels to western Europe. Anyway, he adored opera music greatly.

He seated himself in his place in the ancient Arena an hour before the concert started to avoid the crowd. While waiting, he observed the audience. Again he suddenly caught sight of the same man he had seen at the Autogrill near Milan, this time with another man of about the same age. Both men were wearing black suits and grey ties. He could immediately see the suits were Russian-made. Both men had detectable, typical Russian behaviour. He was quite sure now, the men had actually followed him. And they were obviously amateurs. No professional spy would show himself to the victim three times within a short interval. The victim needed no statistical education to calculate that this was a completely impossible random incident.

Salnikov shook fearfully. The Russian Secret Police must have had me under observation for a long time. It is more than six months since I ordered the tickets in the Italian tourist office in Moscow, the only place where the tickets could be ordered in Russia. The tickets had probably been completely sold out for at least five months. Suddenly he felt calmer. However, this might not be such a strange situation. The Russian Secret Police had obviously not realised that the Cold War had ended, and were still suspicious of all unusual behaviour. He was a colonel in the

Russian army. He was travelling alone to western Europe. That must be considered as very uncommon behaviour. In addition they knew he was Ukrainian and not a real Russian. This must have made them especially suspicious. What was the damned colonel's real purpose in travelling to Northern Italy alone? They would of course doubt the purpose was his great interest in opera music and ancient architecture. They just had to send investigators, hopefully to be correctly informed, Salnikov concluded with a relaxed smile. He had still not yet done anything that might create suspicions for the Russian Secret Police. He decided to ignore them and made up his mind to enjoy the concert even more.

After the concert Salnikov walked around for a while and looked at the town. Old Verona had heavy, five-storey buildings. One got a very typical view of the buildings when looking away from the Arena to the right side of the large square. The old city was surrounded by an ancient Roman city wall, which twisted itself between old and new buildings. One could easily see it was centuries ago since the town had grown beyond the ancient wall. The traffic was not too heavy. It was still possible to breathe without yearning for oxygen in the clouds of exhaust gases and to smell the special aroma of a living Latin town.

The amateur spies followed Salnikov at a distance, but he was very careful not to give any sign that he had seen them. He found a nice *ristorante* where he was sure the spies had no chance of following him without revealing themselves. The spies had to gaze from outside, while he was enjoying a splendid dinner. The restaurant was a small, rebuilt church forced in between two other buildings. All the buildings were probably from the fourteenth century. The restaurant was just one large room and all the guests had a full view of each other. There were only about twenty tables, but at least seven or eight waiters served the guests. All of them were dressed similarly in black livery, white shirts and black bow ties.

The headwaiter appeared as soon as Salnikov came in and asked him politely in English: "Are you Scandinavian, sir?"

"No, I'm Russian!" Salnikov replied militarily and brusquely, as if to show that the Russians were a lot better than the Scandinavians.

"Are you alone, sir?" – the headwaiter continued, completely ignoring the brusqueness of Salnikov's reply.

However, he did not wait for an answer to his new question, but led Salnikov to a table with a thick, white tablecloth and a vase of fresh red roses.

Three beautiful women in their early forties were sitting at the next table. They were laughing and were obviously in excellent spirits. Salnikov nodded politely to them, as only a Russian army officer can, and got wide, inviting smiles in return. The contact was established.

"Would you like an aperitif, sir?" – a waiter suddenly asked.

The waiter had soundlessly approached Salnikov's table, while Salnikov was engaged with the women.

"Yes, anything you might have, please," Salnikov replied politely.

"Do you want an English menu, sir?" – the waiter inquired graciously, just like a waiter must have sounded in an English upper-class club a hundred years ago.

"No, thank you," Salnikov replied determinedly, and continued: "I want to select a complete meal including *antipasto, pasta.* A main dish composed of *manzo* or *bistecca.* After the main dish I would like some *formaggio – formagetto sott'olio,* if you have any. As an end to the meal a tasteful *dolce* – a *spungata* would be nice. The wine must be red and full-bodied – a *Valpolicella* vintage would be fine. – And an *espresso caffé* after the meal with *Drambuie* or *Amaretto* liqueur. Afterwards, I would like a double whisky instead of the traditional French cognac," Salnikov said, as if he ordered such meals at restaurants every day.

"Very well, sir," the waiter replied and disappeared, over-whelmed, as he could not believe that a Russian could be so well informed about Italian food. He whispered, very impressed, to his colleagues who glanced discreetly towards Salnikov.

Salnikov was no specialist on Italian food; he had only been sitting on the Alitalia aircraft on the way to Italy reading an article in the airline's magazine about Italian food, because there was nothing else to read. He had tried to memorise some names. He just bluffed the waiter to impress the women at the neighbouring table.

He ate and became a bit drunk although he had more than thirty years' experience with vodka in Russian army officers' bars. The women at the nearby table were contin-uously making advances towards him, and they toasted him repeatedly. When he had finished the meal he joined their table. All of them were extremely amenable. The women obviously had plans for their new companion.

"A Russian army colonel. That must be very exciting," the youngest of the women gushed more than once.

She was wearing an expensive, pastel green, strapless dress. The dress seemed only to be fastened to her luxuriant bust and ample curves. Her bust seemed all the time to be trying to get out of its jail behind the dress. She wore no bra. Her lips were full and painted red. Her hair was the brown you only find on Italian women. She had deep, large, brown eyes, which easily could swallow your whole soul. Her skin was tanned, and she had long, beautiful legs and was as thin as a model. Her name was Gina. There was absolutely no doubt about Gina's intentions for Salnikov later that night.

All the women came from Venice and had also been to the concert at the Arena. They all seemed to be well educated and spoke English fluently, with a very sexy Italian accent.

"Do you want to come to a night-club with us, dearest?" – the woman, who might be the oldest of them, suddenly asked very sexily. Her name was Claudia and her attributes were equal to her friend's. Her hair was fair and her eyes bright blue. She looked Scandinavian, although she was a genuine Italian. She was wearing a short, ice blue dress, which covered little, and a beautiful pearl necklace. She also had tanned skin and was about the same height as her younger friend, Gina.

"Sure, ladies," Salnikov answered and lifted his glass in a toast, "I'm a tourist and want to experience as much as possible while I'm visiting Italy. I can sleep when I get home."

The three Italian beauties and Salnikov hired a taxi to a night-club, which was situated on the hillside high above the town. Salnikov was too drunk, and too surrounded by beautiful women, to observe exactly where they went. Anyway, it did not matter, because he was sure the two Russian pursuers were tailing them, and he could just ask the Russian Secret Police to tell him where he had been, if he ever needed to know.

Sofia, the third lady, had jumped onto his lap in the taxi. They all sat close in the back seat. Sofia twisted herself continually towards him, with all her weight. Salnikov could swear that Sofia was wearing no pants. Luckily he was too drunk to be fully affected by the situation.

Sofia was a couple of years older than Gina and maybe a little shorter. She had dark hair and brown intelligent eyes. She had beautiful, round curves and a huge firm bust. She was wearing a red dress that must have been designed by the same Parisian fashion house as Claudia's. She had light brown skin and looked oriental.

All the three women danced, drank and enjoyed themselves with their Russian companion at the night-club. They did not seem to be interested in other males at the establishment. Salnikov noticed one of the non-professional, Russian spy-tails in a dark corner. Because of that, he celebrated more than he normally would have done. He had to give the young spy the chance of writing an exciting report to the dull and dark offices back in Moscow. The spy though, had sense enough to disappear after someone close to him started a fight.

The women wanted to go with Salnikov for a drink at the hotel Due Torri. The night porter in the reception also functioned as bartender at a tiny bar in the back corner of the reception hall. They sat in one of the leather sofa groups.

The women said they had been friends for many years. They had all previously studied art and other academic subjects, including English and French. Only one of them had been married, but for a very short period, many years ago.

Sofia was 45 years old and had come to Venice from Rome twenty years earlier. Her mother had been Arab and married to an Italian businessman.

Gina, who was 43 years old, had come from the Italian speaking part of Switzerland to Venice seventeen years ago.

Claudia had lived in Venice all her life, but had studied and worked in Rome, Florence and a couple of other places. She was 46 years old and had known Sofia since her arrival in Venice. She told Salnikov that her Scandinavian looks were not uncommon in northern Italy.

Suddenly, Gina, the woman with no hidden intentions concerning the Russian colonel, said: "I have read about the hotel Due Torri and want to see if the rooms in the hotel are as special as they are reported."

They all left soon afterwards for Salnikov's suite on the third floor.

Gina undressed immediately she arrived in the room and angled down on the bed in posing array. Her friends took no notice. They were used to her behaviour. Anyway, ten minutes later they were all undressed. The women had torn all the clothes off Salnikov. He was shocked. He had never before had sex with more than one woman at the same time. He felt great.

Gina was over him at once, like a wild tiger. She hardly gave the other women any space before she was satisfied, which she was only for a very short time. Sofia rode Salnikov like a camel, while Claudia tried to strangle him with the most exotic part of her body. At the same time Gina was standing with her bottom in the sky for Claudia to taste her wet, intimate fruit, while she herself alternately tasted the same fruits of her friend and Salnikov's risen lord, meanwhile her friend rode Salnikov, like a rider at the rodeo. He was brutishly and intensely released from years of accumulated sexual desire. They all reached a climax at the same time. The women were screaming like Caesar's army must have done when they attacked an enemy. Salnikov believed nobody could have slept at the hotel that night.

Salnikov considered ironically that he would have liked to read the Russian Secret Police's report on his visit to Italy. He presumed the two pursuers were guarding him from a car parked in the small square outside the hotel. They must have been aware of the excessive screams from the women during the night.

The party woke up at noon the next day. Salnikov felt exhausted and completely empty. He had told everybody that he considered his travels to western Europe as the experience of his lifetime. The night's experience did not fall short of his expectation. He also knew now why the women had kept together, as very close friends, for nearly twenty years, but he was more than satisfied.

They all showered and went down to the breakfast room on the mezzanine floor, beside the large reception hall.

"Good morning sir, you might really need a large breakfast," the waiter said discreetly to Salnikov, while he glanced obliquely at the women.

Without hesitation he continued loudly, for everybody to hear: "Do you want tea or coffee, sir?"

"Tea, please," Salnikov replied quietly and confidently.

Salnikov felt momentarily twenty-five years younger. The waiter's reaction was similar to the receptions he could remember from the officers' mess on mornings after successful hunting nights for the women living in the billeting area around the military barracks – receptions, which immediately stopped after he got married.

"You want to serve yourself from the buffet, sir, or shall I order something special from the kitchen?" – the waiter asked smilingly.

Salnikov looked hastily at the women before he replied, also smilingly: "From the buffet. The ladies seem to be very hungry today."

Sofia asked Salnikov: "Are you ending the visit to western Europe after the visit to Italy?"

"No," Salnikov replied, "I have planned to continue my

journey to southern France and further along the Spanish Mediterranean coastline to Gibraltar."

"It must be nice to take a break from your job?" – Sofia asked and continued without waiting for any reply. "What are you really doing in the army?"

Salnikov did not consider the question to be anything other than normal conversation. He believed there would be no harm telling the woman what he did.

He replied smilingly: "I am the superior at a Russian army depot."

But he was to become more suspicious after Sofia's next questions. The woman was actually examining him.

Sofia asked him quickly and eagerly: "Where is this depot, and what does it contain?"

Salnikov did not, of course, want to disclose military secrets, and replied diplomatically: "It's situated in the middle of Russia and contains all the equipment which a weapons depot normally would contain."

To change the subject, he quickly asked Claudia: "Are you all travelling back to Venice today?"

Claudia did not have time to reply, before Sofia asked: "Do you have access to all the equipment at the depot?"

Claudia was obviously not as experienced an interrogator and Salnikov answered calmly: "If you mean the kitchen, I'm permitted to enter, but god damned if I touch anything. I would be thrown out directly by the chef, I'm quite sure – I really am."

Sofia took the hint, and she did not ask any more. It seemed as if she was for a while immersed in her own thoughts. The meal continued without further questions about Salnikov's occupation, but when the women were about to leave the hotel, Sofia spoke in the sexiest way she was able in this situation.

"I want to show you Venice before you leave Italy. Nobody can leave Italy without seeing Venice – it's *a must.*"

Salnikov considered the situation for a while, whilst pretending not to have heard her.

However, Sofia did not give up, she continued to get Salnikov's attention and said softly: "My mother was Arabian."

Salnikov thought quickly and replied loudly: "I would be very pleased to visit you in Venice. I will extend my Italian visit by one day."

"Make it two days, dear love," Sofia said, again as sexily as she could, but loudly so her friends could hear.

"OK, I will – love," Salnikov replied shortly.

2

Salnikov's real purpose for travelling to northern Italy was to meet a Scottish colleague, whom he had met during a UN conference, concerning the Russian withdrawal from Chechnya. The meeting with the Scotsman was planned to take place in Verona, but the Russian secret agents that he had discovered were tailing him, prevented all contact. Therefore he had to continue to the next alternative meeting point, Saint Tropez in southern France. This small town was chosen instead of a larger town, because foreign tourists crowded it in the summer season, and it was also reckoned to be a very normal destination for a Russian tourist. In addition, the Scottish representative considered the town to be easier to control concerning potential spies, because only one narrow road led to the town.

Saint Tropez was an old, small, fishing village situated at the end of a confined three kilometre long road that twined under green trees from the coast road to the right of the bay not far from Saint Maxim, between Nice and Marseille. It was a very picturesque town and it had, for decades, been a playground for the European jet set in the summertime.

A famous French movie star has also contributed to making the town well known. Salnikov could remember her with great pleasure. Her name was Brigitte Bardot and she was a fair sex idol with a large bust. Her movies had been shown some nights in the barracks for the officer recruits on army exercises in Siberia, many years ago. It had been during Salnikov's first years in the army. The exercises took place hundreds of kilometres from the nearest inhabited areas. The troops joked there were only two grams of woman per man in the camp. The women in the camp were only a few, now very old ladies, who had been deported to Siberia during the Stalin period and worked in the kitchen. The movies had therefore been especially welcome and had been popular entertainment in the dark cold winter nights. After Bardot ended her movie career, she moved to Saint Tropez, where she lived for many years together with her cats, dogs and other animals, as animals and their rights had long been her main interest.

Salnikov took the motorway to Padua in the evening. He proceeded further to Mestre and out to the large concrete parking lot on the shore side of the canal, dividing old Venice from the mainland. He pulled out a parking ticket from the ticket machine and drove in. He found a vacant parking place on the third floor. The Russian amateur spies followed him. They parked on the top floor. Salnikov ignored them completely. He went down the staircase to the ground floor and spent a while pretending to admire the famous view, while he observed the spies who also came down and desperately tried to hide themselves in the shadows. Salnikov chuckled over their pathetic behaviour and went towards the mahogany coloured taxi boats along the pier in front of him. One of them took him the short distance to the exclusive hotel Gritty, highly recommended by the three lovely women of Verona.

Salnikov was by now used to the fact that old, exclusive hotels in Italy did not always give the right impression from outside. This was also true of the Gritty, but the hotel's site was really excellent. From the window of his suite on the third floor, he could see on the other side of the canal, the famous fifteenth century Gothic style church of San Giovanni in Bragora. He knew he was not far from the famous Saint Mark's Square, situated at the other side of the hotel, with Saint Mark's Cathedral, which was built a thousand years ago.

Salnikov had been very doubtful about including the visit to Venice. He did not know if it would be an intelligent move, because of the spies who were following him. Anyway, it was also necessary to think about a manoeuvre to get rid of them, because he otherwise could not make contact with the Scottish lieutenant colonel in Saint Tropez. He was besides convinced that Sofia had another reason for asking him to come to Venice, except for her obviously immense desire for sex. She had invited him to Venice after she had questioned him about his activities in the Russian army. She looked very oriental and Salnikov wondered if there might be a connection. Sofia had mentioned something about an Arabian mother, but he had been too distracted by the two other women to be quite certain he had heard her correctly. Nevertheless, in only a few hours he hoped to have an adequate answer to that question. Meanwhile he had to get something to eat and to make an obligatory visit to Saint Mark's Square.

Salnikov was very well informed about Venice's history. He had read a lot. What else could he do during all the free time he had spent in the army barracks? Ancient history had also been the only politically safe literature in the Soviet, where nobody could read what he or she wanted. It was the authorities who exclusively directed which literature was correct for the people to read.

*

According to tradition, Venice was founded in the year 452, when inhabitants of Aquileia, Padua and other northern Italian cities had escaped the Teutonic tribes that invaded Italy during the fifth century. The refugees took shelter on the twelve islands of the lagoon, between the mouths of the Po and the Piave rivers. In the year 692 the refugees created the Republic of Venice. Venice was a leading maritime power in the Christian world for more than a thousand years, till Napoleon Bonaparte invaded the city-state in the year 1797 and laid it under Austrian sovereignty.

Sofia came to Hotel Gritty alone, just before dinner.

"Oh, how I've missed you," she said, in such a way Salnikov felt he must have been away for many years.

"I love you so," she continued and kissed him all over his face and pressed her entire body, sexy and soft, towards him, as though to test if he reacted physically to her presence.

Salnikov was not used to such hot, clinging women and reacted of course, at once. He was suddenly at a complete loss for words and said nothing, only cleared his throat carefully, while Sofia forced him towards the elevator.

"What's your room number," she whispered in his ear.

While he was being pushed towards the elevator he regained some of his ability to speak.

He answered quietly: "317 – my love."

When they entered the room, Sofia whispered quietly: "I had to pretend an especially huge sexual appetite when I came in because there are Russians outside the hotel spying on you."

"I know," Salnikov confirmed quickly. "When we took the elevator I saw one of them enter the hotel foyer. By now they are probably in the corridor outside our door."

The couple had not been in the room half a minute

before Sofia was without any clothes and was occupied in undressing Salnikov at a particularly high speed. As soon as Sofia was finished, she placed Salnikov roughly on the bed and forced him to enter her directly without any foreplay. She roared loudly with great delight as she pressed him inside herself. After a quarter of an hour, at exceptional speed and with loud grunts and cries, they finished the first round together.

"By now I believe the Russian in the corridor will have been convinced about your intentions in visiting Venice," she whispered tiredly.

"Surely, my love," he replied, equally as tired.

Later they had a delicious meal in a nearby restaurant. Sofia was dressed in a short, green dress, showing her long tanned legs and most of her large bust. She never asked about Salnikov's profession or anything else concerning the Russian army. She was only the sexy girl who had her lover at the other side of the table. She touched him shoeless under the table, hidden by the tablecloth. She seemed only to be getting ready to be his delightful, sexy mistress of the night.

The turtledoves left the restaurant, arm in arm, pleasantly satisfied by the marvellous Italian food, just before midnight, and went straight to Salnikov's suite. There she gave him another very extraordinary night of experiences in love.

Sofia left early next morning and told Salnikov to meet her at noon, at a nearby café by the canal.

Salnikov was in the café at the agreed time. He could not see Sofia, but he sat down and ordered a *café espresso*. He looked at an elderly couple sitting at one of the tables nearby. They looked like tourists, but they did not speak together. Salnikov thought they had probably nothing to talk about after at least fifty years of marriage. The old man only stirred his cup of coffee and looked around seemingly at nothing. Maybe he was thinking about all the girls he did not get in his youth. Salnikov smiled at this thought. The old woman only blinked her eyes and just looked tired. She seemed to have accepted this as near the end of her stay in the living world, but she would see Venice before she died.

Suddenly a speedboat appeared with a loud roar. Sofia was aboard together with another beautiful girl with black hair that shone blue in the sun. Sofia held the steering wheel with one hand and waved enthusiastically with the other. Salnikov jumped onboard the boat in seconds. They made a violent turn and left immediately at high speed in the direction of the airport. The boat arrived at a small pier half a kilometre to the left of the small passenger ferry pier from which the old-fashioned ferry continually shuttled people back and forth from the old city of Venice to the airport.

Salnikov was introduced to Mustafa, a short, hairy Arab in his late thirties. Mustafa kept himself away from the pier – out of sight.

Mustafa asked quickly: "Did you like the boat ride?"

Salnikov did not reply to this question. The Arab's English sounded perfect, but with a slight accent. Mustafa continued after a short break, as if he had expected a reply from Salnikov.

"I don't want to waste your time or mine. I am going to catch an early flight. You can call me Mustafa. This lady here," he pointed quickly at the girl who accompanied Sofia, "we will only call her Cleo. She is a good friend of Sofia, but Sofia does not know her real identity. Our names are of course fakes. Sofia has told Cleo that you are a Russian colonel and chief of an army weapons depot. Is that correct?"

Salnikov nodded, confirming.

"I'll go directly to the questions, which are the only reasons why we are here today."

Mustafa took another short pause, as if loading his fast-speaking mouth, before he started on another speedy speech, obviously prepared beforehand.

"As you already must have understood, we are looking for weapons. Your solo trip to northern Italy is very suspicious and you are obviously here to locate a potential market for your private weapon deliveries, otherwise you wouldn't have joined Sofia here in Venice. You might be horny, but not that horny. We will pay you very well because we know everybody can be bought at a price. You need only tell me your price. I am quite sure we will be able to agree on an acceptable arrangement."

Salnikov was not surprised at all at the situation, because he had expected it to occur. He had reflected about a possible connection between the Arabian world and Sofia. That was also one of the reasons why he had changed his planned route to include Venice. He hoped Sofia would set up a meeting with a wealthy Arab weapons customer. He was of course not at all unwilling to sell weapons at an acceptable price, which was the only real reason why he was in Western Europe, but he considered his reply very carefully before he spoke. He knew he had to give the Arab a positive reply, otherwise he would probably end up in seconds as fish-food, with a knife between his shoulder blades. He had observed four of the Arab's assistants, who were spread around on watch in an easily recognisable army style. Salnikov understood at once from his previous experience, that those men were hardened guerrilla troops, probably also heavily armed.

As he would rather not give the Arab the impression he was too eager to sell, he diverted the question to test his counterpart: "How do you know I have access to any weapons?"

The Arab laughed artificially loudly and answered: "We have had time for some investigation since we received Sofia's message about you. You must know we wouldn't have travelled from Cairo to Italy just because Sofia had met a horny Russian."

Mustafa chuckled loudly and looked disapprovingly at Salnikov with a pair of black protruding eyes before he said: "We can assure you that we know you are the commander at the army depot at Kursk. That very weapons depot contains the full range of army weapons. It is also a depot meant for export of Russian weapons. Somebody has also whispered in my ear that the depot might contain nuclear weapons."

"Then the whispers must lie," Salnikov replied quickly. "We are not storing nuclear weapons in peacetime, so close to the border."

"I don't believe that nonsense," Mustafa replied. "Don't tell me you have changed your atomic storage policy in Russia since you wanted to store atomic missiles only a hundred kilometres from Miami, during the Cuba crisis in the sixties."

"That was very special," Salnikov replied. "The shipment of atomic missiles to Cuba was only a demonstration, to gain a deal with the Americans. Do you believe the Americans would have accepted a communist regime on their doorstep, if the Russians hadn't interfered? Everybody must have understood the Soviet's intentions with the shipment of atomic missiles to Cuba. Why do you think the Soviets shipped the missiles on the deck of a ship, fully visible for everybody to inspect and photograph?"

"Anyway, President Kennedy made a great political show of it," Mustafa said, demonstrating some political know-how.

Salnikov smiled and said: "That was before your time, my dear friend. It is correct that Kennedy made a lot of political show of the incident. The Americans were afraid he would

27

force America into a serious disaster in the short time he was not occupied in fucking all the women around. That's probably why they killed him."

"It was Lee Harvey Oswald who killed Kennedy," Mustafa added, still demonstrating that he knew something.

"If you believe that, you must only be one of very few who do," Salnikov added smilingly. "First of all, they registered shots from several directions when John F. Kennedy was killed, and do you really believe a night club owner like Jack Ruby could have carried a weapon inside a police office undetected. I will tell you why. He had to shut Oswald's mouth forever, ordered by somebody who was able to get him inside that very police office. Ruby knew he had cancer and had only a few months left to live. He had nothing to risk. He only became famous in his last days – or maybe he hadn't money to pay for medical treatment and hoped that the nation would do whatever was necessary to keep him alive." Salnikov chuckled quietly while he spoke. "How he or his group were rewarded after his successful job is a question probably never to be answered."

"What you say sounds actually very reasonable. I have never considered such a view of the incident," Mustafa concluded. "You are sure the Russians did not kill the American President?"

"Positively," Salnikov replied and waved his hands to make clear his pronouncement. "The Russians were afraid of Kennedy because he was not considered stable, but they reckoned that there were reliable Americans in the leadership of the United States, and that they would finally clear the situation, which they did. A president who was more occupied in fucking women than ruling the country was not to be considered seriously. Somebody also suggested that together with his brother Robert he was responsible for the death of the movie star Marilyn Monroe. She had threatened the Kennedy brothers the night before she died, that she would expose facts about the Kennedy's connection with the United States' criminal Mafia organisations. The Kennedy brothers had obviously to act quickly."

"Whom do the Russians believe killed Kennedy?" Mustafa asked impatiently.

He appeared to have totally forgotten the real reason for the meeting.

Salnikov considered this side-tracking was very good for his business, to make contact with his customer. He had registered that Mustafa had shown himself to be a young fellow with few or simply no alternative opinions to what he heard. He seemed to have absolutely no ideas of his own. Salnikov knew such people very often were extremely dangerous, as they always acted irrationally and impulsively without any deep consideration of the consequences.

Salnikov replied: "This information is of course secret, but the KGB's analysis concluded that it was the supporters of Vice President Lyndon B. Johnson who killed Kennedy. Many questions are raised. Why did Johnson accept the relatively unimportant vice-presidential post when he was a lot more experienced as a politician than Kennedy? Could it be that Kennedy's ability to win the election was considered greater by strong hidden forces within the Democratic Party, than Johnson's, but Johnson was, however, the man they actually wanted to be the leader?"

"But the Americans loved Kennedy," Mustafa added, "They treat his death like that of a hero."

"Of course," Salnikov replied very indulgently. "The people who killed him would be the first to make him a hero. A dead body would of course not cause more trouble, but the information, which probably will be accessible in the future, will unquestionably tear Kennedy down from his throne. History will often give a more objective view of the facts than the present time. Why do you believe the British Scotland Yard closed the case on Jack the Ripper for another hundred years? There can only be one reply to that question. That will be to delay the true information about the Prince of Wales, Queen Victoria's son, later King Edward. The information would have been very unfavourable for the English Royalty at that time, and would obviously also have been as unfavourable today, because of the Royalty's continuing declining popularity. History though, will hopefully give true information. That, one who lives will see. We just have to wait another hundred years."

Salnikov took a small break, while he chuckled loudly, before he added: "But I am not here to discuss ancient politics."

"Sorry," Mustafa replied. "It was interesting to listen to a Russian's point of view."

"I am definitively not able to deliver nuclear weapons, even if they had been at the depot," Salnikov said strongly. "Such weapons would be guarded by different security systems, out of my range. I would have to be a general to get access to that kind of equipment. The depot is intentionally for export and contains no nuclear weapons. As you must know, the Kremlin has signed the *Non-proliferation Treaty for Atomic Weapons*, and therefore never exports nuclear weapons."

The Russian's teacher-like attitude greatly irritated Mustafa and he said rather wildly: "OK, I believe you. You are not able to deliver atomic weapons, but which kind of bloody weapons are you able to deliver, and what are your damned prices? I have not come all this way to Venice just to listen to lies and fairy-tales."

Salnikov decided resistance in the discussion battle was over. It was time for him to collaborate fully and get the best price out of the young, inexperienced Arab. The delivery to the Arabs would not cause him a lot of extra trouble. It was a deal that could easily be handled in parallel with the deal he had actually come to Italy to make. He felt greedy and needed money – a lot of money. After a short pause for thought he said in a very businesslike way: "OK, I can deliver you reasonable quantities of almost any conventional hand weapon you might require. What do you need specifically?"

Mustafa told him what he wanted without unnecessary hesitation. He seemed to be a real professional when talking about weapons, although having an infantile mind concerning other things. They finally agreed on a price of three million American dollars for the trade.

Mustafa suddenly handed Salnikov ten thousand American dollars in small, used bills and said: "This is a small prepayment for you to taste being rich and to show our seriousness. Half of the purchase price will be transferred to an account in the Central Swiss Credit, for your immediate disposal to cover your expenses. You will have access to that account in one week. The remaining half of the price will be transferred when the weapons are out of Russia and handed over to us."

He gave Salnikov the necessary identification numbers for access to a numbered account in the Swiss bank.

Afterwards, he said threateningly: "I suppose it will not be necessary to tell you, that if you don't fulfil our deal, we will kill you wherever you are, and in the most horrible way you might imagine."

Salnikov did not comment on Mustafa's altered expression, as he undoubtedly believed him, but he said: "Two spies from the Russian Secret Police are following me."

Mustafa replied amusedly: "We know, and we are convinced the spies must be ridiculous amateurs. I have seen spies operate more professionally in comedies at theatres. You must know a Russian colonel travelling abroad alone will always be watched. We suppose the Russian Secret Police has not changed its behaviour since the KGB operated during the Soviet period. That is why we used the speedboat to bring you here. They could of course not follow you at such short notice. What are your plans for the rest of the trip?"

Salnikov did not want to disclose his plans, but he had no choice in the situation.

He replied quickly to appear more convincing: "I am returning to Russia from Barcelona via Vienna in one week."

He did not explain about his plans for spending the time before returning.

"OK," Mustafa said thoughtfully, after a short consideration. "You must take the motorway to Bologna and further in the direction of Florence, but you must stay one hour in the motorway restaurant before you reach the intersection for Florence. We need this time to make some arrangements. When you are on the Florence stretch you must drive as fast as possible and we will arrange a small accident for your ardent Russian friends. When it happens, don't stop. You can be quite sure the pursuers will never bother you again. It will take some time to replace these pursuers with others. If you start your journey towards Florence immediately, the spies will not have time to make a report about losing you today while we had this meeting."

The meeting was finished. Mustafa and Cleo went quickly in the direction of the airport departure hall. Sofia and Salnikov returned to the café. The meeting had lasted approximately half an hour. When arriving in front of the café, Sofia again pretended being the lustful woman, squeezing and kissing Salnikov for a long time to be quite sure that the spies fully observed them. The spies might have believed the couple only had been out in the boat fucking.

Salnikov immediately checked out from the hotel, hired a taxi boat back to the parking lot and entered the motorway in the direction of Ancona. He stopped at the first gasoline station to fill up and to give the Russian pursuers sufficient time to pick up his trail. Their grey BMW was soon detected creeping along the road. Salnikov maintained a very moderate speed for a couple of hours until he reached the motorway intersection of Bologna and Milan. He stopped and waited at the appointed motorway restaurant, exactly as the Arab had instructed him. The Russian spies sat in their car outside the restaurant and ate chocolate they had bought from the tiny retail store beside the petrol pumps.

Was it their last meal? – Salnikov thought melancholically and felt some pity for them. He could see his pursuers from the restaurant window. However, he was a soldier and had seen many men die before, and the predicable destiny of those irritating Russian watchers did not destroy his appetite any more than the killing of an unwanted insect.

Salnikov returned to his car after an hour in the restaurant and continued on the motorway with the Russians permanently approximately three hundred metres behind. After a short while he was passed by a Milan registered large, black Mercedes. Four young men, who were undoubtedly Arabs, waved carefully to him when they passed. Salnikov nodded just as carefully back. The Mercedes with the Arabs drove into a gasoline station ten minutes later. Salnikov and the following BMW passed it. At once Salnikov speeded up. In the rear-view mirror he could see the BMW followed him. He turned off the motorway in the direction of Milan and onto the motorway in the direction of Florence. The BMW was following him like a shadow.

The landscape had been quite flat all across the Po Basin. South in the direction of Florence, the landscape changed radically. The motorway changed from being monotonously straight to a series of bends as it twisted down the hills. There were many places with steep, frightening drops down into stony hills below. It was quite impossible to keep the car at full speed on the winding road, but Salnikov drove as fast as he dared. He could feel the outer wheels leave the road surface on the curves. He congratulated himself for having chosen a car equipped with four-wheel drive. It was absolutely certain that his old Lada back home would have reached only half the speed. Even then, Salnikov thought in terror, it would probably have changed from being a car on the road to a steel bird in the air on its way down to certain death, smashed in the stony hills below. He could see in the rear-view mirror that the BMW, equipped with only two-wheel drive, followed him with great difficulty.

Suddenly, he saw the black Mercedes with the Arabs approach rapidly behind the BMW. The huge Mercedes, with its very powerful motor and wide tyres, had a higher speed than the two cars in front. The Mercedes passed the BMW on the outside of a bend. When it had overtaken, it suddenly cut in front of the BMW, only a few metres ahead of it. The two Arabs in the back seat of the Mercedes suddenly stuck two machine guns out of the rear windows and pretended to shoot at the BMW. The BMW driver saw the guns, became stiff, choked and panicked. He stepped apprehensively on the car's brakes. This was exactly what the Arabs had planned. The machine guns might have been made of plastic. It would not have mattered, as the Arabs had no plans to shoot at all. They did not want to leave any evidence. The BMW had absolutely no chance at all. When the brake pedal was pressed, the high-speed car swerved uncontrollably across the road and rolled over several times before it hit the barrier, where it reared up and tipped over. It described a large curve, continually spinning, before being entirely smashed when it hit the rocks nearly two hundred metres below.

3

Lieutenant Colonel John McPride had served under the Union Jack in all corners of the world. He had participated in the Falklands War and been military attaché at several British Embassies for many years. He had served as a United Nations' representative in many conflicts and been in Africa many times, as well as Kashmir, Lebanon and Bosnia Herzegovina. In the Chechnya conflict with Russia he was a UN observer. He was fifty-three years old, of medium height, was fair and had a red moustache like so many other Scottish army officers.

For the last three years McPride had been the second-in-command of the Black Watch infantry regiment in Scotland. The British army raised the famous Scottish regiment, officially known as the Royal Scottish Premier Regiment, in 1725 to control clan uprisings in the Scottish Highlands. The regiment had distinguished itself greatly in later wars – the Napoleonic Wars and the First and the Second World Wars. The regiment was, from the outset, a tool for English oppression of the Scottish people.

"My regiment, the Black Watch, was an element in that damned English system – *divide and rule!*" McPride always maintained angrily among his close Scottish friends.

*

McPride sniggered as he drove from Verona to Saint Tropez, the appointed alternative meeting place with the Russian colonel, Igor Salnikov. He sniggered, satisfied, because he knew the colonel was on route, as they had seen each other at the Arena in Verona.

They had walked around pretending they were only looking at the town. Salnikov had made no contact. The only reason for that could have been there were certain factors that prevented contact. The Russian must have detected he was being tracked by someone – probably the Russian Secret Police. However, McPride had considered that a likely possibility even before he had travelled to Verona. Spies on Salnikov's trail only confirmed that the colonel had important status in the Russian army, McPride thought contentedly, while he geared down, turned into the left-hand lane of the motorway and speeded up. My Scottish organisation has never before been so close to the target. He believed the Russians did not send delegations of spies after every bloody officer who travelled on vacation to western Europe.

During their meeting in Chechnya, Salnikov had agreed with McPride to use Saint Tropez as an alternative meeting place, three days after Verona, if any situation should make it necessary to utilise an alternative. Salnikov said it was necessary to have a gap of at least three days to dodge possible trackers, as the Russian Secret Police were very clever.

McPride had met him for the first time in Chechnya when he was a UN observer. Salnikov had been one of the Russian watchdogs, which continuously covered the UN delegation, and had been chosen for this assignment mainly because he spoke almost perfect English. They had become good friends. Salnikov had often repeated that he was no Russian, but a Ukrainian who would take the first possible opportunity that might occur to get out of damn Russia, where his parents had been interned by Stalin's brutal regime, after the Second World War.

McPride switched on the radio and listened for a long time to Mireille Matieau while he permanently drove in the left-hand lane of the motorway's two lanes heading westward. The British always feel more at home on the left hand side of the road, he thought ironically as a yellow Porsche flashed irritably behind to pass. It seems that I don't have the right machine to stay in this fast lane, he considered, but did not react immediately. He lit a Camel cigarette with his old Zippo lighter and blew blue smoke tranquilly into the air. The lighter, with his name neatly engraved, had been like a shadow for almost twenty-five years, since he received it on a memorable day from his wife in Saint Tropez. It always awoke good memories.

Behind him, the Porsche's lights continued flashing and it had driven dangerously close to him. He turned, somewhat humiliated, to the right-hand lane, while the woman driving the Porsche gave him an ugly grin as she passed, accelerating her speed. He did not take much notice of her, only adapted himself better into the car seat and relaxed, while he again wrenched the car back to the left lane.

Matieau's songs might sound pretty old fashioned to the younger generation, but how intensely and beautifully she sings. She really touches a man's inner feelings and fantasies, McPride thought while he felt fascinated and heightened by the music. Her prickling voice, accompanied by an excellent full symphony orchestra, reminded him of unforgettable moments in his past.

Suddenly, he was brutally awakened from his harmonious dreaming, back to hard reality. At high speed a red Ferrari had approached him imperceptibly. Its horn sounded behind him. In pure irritation because of the damned Sunday driver that occupied the fast lane, it had driven its front bumper nearly into the rear of McPride's car, intending to frighten the driver. Where in hell did that car come from? McPride took a few seconds to realise that they did not drive on the left side of the road on the Continent, as in the United Kingdom. When his mind was fully aware of the real situation, he turned his car slowly and carefully over to the right. You never see such exclusive cars on any other stretches of road in the world, he thought ironically, as the Ferrari passed him with a loud metallic thunder. Its passenger sneered at him and gave him the finger.

"Bloody Italians," McPride said out loud to himself, when he saw the Italian numberplate on the rear of the rapidly disappearing Testarosa. But what cars they build, these damned bastards, he thought with a slight touch of jealousy. To own such a car, I would even have given away my dear old Zippo. But a short time later he had reconsidered completely. Oh no – I am probably too old for that kind of life. It's better to keep my Zippo and drive my car in the right lane.

McPride was driving on the motorway between Genoa and Ventimigla towards the French border. He drove alternately through tunnels and over bridges, high above narrow valleys between the tunnels. He was as impressed as everybody else when driving on this stretch of road for the first time. He crossed the border and soon was through Monaco, Nice and Cannes. He expected to be in Saint Tropez in about two hours, after half an hour's intense negotiation of the narrow, curved country road from the motorway towards the town. Previous experience had taught him to select the narrow country road, to avoid the heavy traffic caused by the tourists on the coastal road through Saint Maxim.

*

Salnikov had observed in his mirror that the assassins' Mercedes had left the motorway at the first exit after the dispatch of the two Russian agents. There had been, as he had noted, no other witnesses to the incident and it would probably only be registered as an ordinary traffic accident, caused by too high a speed. He believed the Russian Secret Service had used only a single car on his track, although it was more normal to employ several cars to track one. With several cars in action, the pursuers would constantly be able to change the car nearest to the car being tailed. The tailed car would, in this way, have problems identifying the pursuers. Salnikov thought that if the Russians had had more than one car behind him, these would eventually have been hindered by the traffic jam which occurred at the scene of the accident. He believed also that it would take a considerable time before Russian headquarters would receive any information about their dead colleagues. This would surely prevent any possible rapid replacement by new followers, who might tail him, for instance, when he crossed the French border at Ventimiglia.

To be quite sure of this, he decided to drive only to Genoa and then take the train to Nice. He therefore delivered his car to a Hertz office in Genoa and took the train, renting a new car at an Avis office in Nice. In this way he broke the connection with the previous car rental company. He hoped that this would make it even more troublesome for the agents to get back on his track, if they had to search out another car rental company. From Nice he drove directly to Saint Tropez for the appointed meeting with his next weapon customer, Lieutenant Colonel John McPride of the United Kingdom.

McPride arrived in Saint Tropez, according to his schedule, after the long drive from Verona. He had been in the town many times before, as an ordinary summer tourist with his family – four children and his lovely wife. He knew it very well. That was the main reason he had chosen it for the meeting.

McPride drove up the hills behind the town to the Hotel Belle Vue. The hotel was located out of the way, and guests had to know of its existence in order to find it. From the hotel he had an attractive view of La Plage Ramatuelle – the beach which made Saint Tropez one of Europe's most popular summer resorts. The beach was situated behind the hill, three kilometres south-west of the town centre.

He remembered with great pleasure when he had visited Saint Tropez for the first time, thirty years ago with his newly wed wife. The town did not have so many visitors at that time. More of a small French coastal village's atmosphere remained. There was absolutely no rush and tranquillity completely dominated the town. His wife became tanned all over. She had laughed and played in the sand as if nothing in the world concerned her. She was united with nature like the natives in the jungle of Brazil must be. She was naked like Eve in Eden's garden. He could remember her breasts vibrating and shaking with stiff nipples when she ran into the azure-blue water. Nudity was normal on a large part of La Plage Ramatuelle. McPride remembered how it had been impossible to determine the difference between the rich and the poor. It was nearly impossible even to recognise the most famous movie stars, when they were totally nude.

It was popular and considered the in-thing with society to visit Saint Tropez and always a lot of famous film celebrities were to be seen on the beach. This was a marvellous time. His first child had probably been conceived in the grasses, which covered the dunes of the long yellow beach. He could remember, as if it were yesterday, that his wife, tanned and constantly wanting sex, time after time, day after day, during the whole vacation, swung her legs around him and kept him inside her till, weary from exertion, they fell asleep. He could still feel the taste of Salade Niçoise and the well-rounded French red wine on his tongue. He could still smell the suntan oil and the sweat from the surrounding people. He could still hear the sound of the chattering, the laughing and the virile cries from happy people.

In the evenings, McPride, at that time a young Scottish lieutenant, and his young wife had dinner in the town, at the restaurants which surrounded the port. They sat in front of the large leisure yachts. The yachts were pitching in the quiet water while the owners and their guests, many obviously newly rich, were acting out what they assumed was the role of the wealthy, while desperate bankers probably awaited their return.

Most of the people ashore, who walked along the pier, smiled at the yacht owners' artificial and affected behaviour. These comedians played an amusing part in the town's special atmosphere. The really rich leisure craft owners had anchored their craft discreetly outside the port better to slide into the mixed international sphere and not separate themselves from ordinary people visiting the town.

The young lieutenant and his wife visiting night-clubs and other establishments, really felt the throbbing life of the town. In the years to come he and his wife returned again and again, later also with their growing children, to their own summer paradise – Saint Tropez.

"Those were the days my friend, I thought they'd never end . . ." McPride hummed softly while he was remembering.

Salnikov arrived in Saint Tropez late in the evening and rented a room with a shower in one of the many small boarding houses with a little restaurant on the ground floor.

41

He avoided the big hotels even though he had never been so rich before, as he felt it was safer to keep a low profile. When he touched the large bulge of American dollars received from the Arab in the inner pocket of his jacket, he felt intense satisfaction. The next day he would meet the Scottish lieutenant colonel – a meeting that would give him an additional unthinkable amount of money. He grinned like Fagin must have done in Charles Dickens' book *Oliver Twist*, as he thought that he must have become extremely greedy, but this evening his only desire was to get a hot meal and go to bed.

At eleven o'clock the next morning Salnikov placed himself discreetly at the small out-door restaurant called Tante Anna with a cup of *cappuccino*. The restaurant faced the port, along the pier. Half an hour later he saw McPride approaching. He waited restlessly for a couple of minutes and looked carefully around for possible tails, who might be following the Scotsman. Then he got up and sauntered in the same direction as McPride.

He saw him walk into one of the narrow pedestrian streets and enter a small fish restaurant. Salnikov passed the fish restaurant and looked into a nearby shop window. He pretended to be an ordinary tourist, but the window acted as a mirror and he could inspect the street behind him completely unnoticed. He walked into another narrow street. He checked and double-checked the surroundings for anyone following him or McPride. In this way he walked around the whole row of buildings and appeared again outside the fish restaurant McPride had entered. He studied the menu beside the door for a while before he walked in.

Inside, the restaurant was dark compared to the bright sunlight outside, so Salnikov needed a couple of seconds to adjust his eyes. He observed McPride at a table for four, in the shadows by the far wall. He was dressed in a beige shirt and brown trousers. There were only two other rather old couples in the restaurant. They were sitting at tables by the window. Salnikov heard them speak French as he walked towards McPride's table and he sat down as if they were old colleagues from work, and had eaten lunch together every day for years.

A waiter appeared at once. They ordered tomato salad as starter and *filet sole* with a raw lemon dip, diced carrots and boiled potatoes as a main dish, together with a bottle of local white wine of an unknown brand and two small bottles of Perrier mineral water.

"Sorry I couldn't meet you in Verona," Salnikov said quietly and smiled, when the waiter had disappeared. "I suspected correctly there were Russian Secret Service agents who tried to mix the salad."

McPride smiled back and said in the same quiet manner: "You're here now, that's what matters. Everything else is going according to plan I hope?"

"Yes, everything is going exactly as planned," Salnikov replied. "You only have to describe precisely your requests concerning weapons and I will try my best to deliver."

McPride quickly itemised his requests. Salnikov became quite astonished, but it was very difficult to see that from his face. Salnikov simply answered in a business-like way, like that of an experienced assistant in an ironmonger's shop.

"At the moment I'm able to deliver modified versions of small tactical surface-to-surface, portable, self-propelled, guided missiles, with a small atomic warhead. You can choose missiles guided either by remote control or by an internal mechanism. The weapon handles similarly to an ordinary bazooka. The user just has to direct the missile on the target and press the button. Easier than launching fireworks on New Year's Eve."

Salnikov continued inquiringly: "I presume you have had some time to learn more about tactical nuclear weapons since we last met at the UN conference on Chechnya? Anyway, I believe tactical missiles and nuclear weapons must have been part of your training during your long service in your country's army, so you might be very well informed."

McPride did not comment. He only listened quietly. Salnikov poured more white wine into his glass and looked suspiciously around. Seeming satisfied with what he observed, he kept on talking quietly in a monotone.

"Guided missiles consist of three separate systems – power source, guidance and control mechanism, and warhead. The power sources can be self-contained rocket motors, or air-breathing jet engines. The rocket can also, of course, be powered with outside booster charges from ramp or tube launchers."

Salnikov took another mouthful of white wine, nervously examined the surroundings once more and said: "The type of the guidance and control system depends on the type of missile and the target. Remote control missiles are linked to a human or mechanical target locator through trailing wires, wireless radio or some type of signal system. Internal guidance mechanism has radar, optical, infrared or sensor systems that can detect heat, light or electronic emissions from the target."

The colonel took a break and a gulp of Perrier to rinse his mouth before he tasted the white wine again. He kept the wine in his mouth for a while and let it roll over his tongue before he swallowed. He restarted his monologue after a deep, sonorous breath.

"The missiles I am offering you, will have movable fins which can be used to direct the course of the missiles against targets in flight. The same missiles can, of course, be used against stationary targets, if that is your purpose."

Salnikov looked nervously around again, as if he expected

someone to storm through the door firing a machine-gun. McPride quickly hid a smile, as he registered that Salnikov obviously had seen nobody and therefore subsequently continued a little more quickly than before.

"Missile velocity, pitch, yaw, and roll are sensed by internal gyroscopes and accelerometers. Course corrections are made mechanically by altering the thrust of the rocket exhaust by means of movable deflectors."

Salnikov seemed a little more relaxed now. He must have realised that nobody was going to burst through the door during the next few minutes. He took another break in his lesson, another gulp of water, some of the wine, and then he suddenly smiled, surprisingly, for the first time since he had started on his missile lecture.

He said: "The most important thing for you might be the missile's pay-load or warhead?"

McPride smiled too, but he still did not reply. He only nodded inscrutably.

"The warhead of the missiles is a small, clean neutron bomb, also called a fusion bomb. This type of bomb is preferable because it is relatively clean. It will destroy the target completely, but without producing the radioactive fallout which endangers people or structures kilometres away. I will explain for you simply how a clean atomic bomb functions. On average half the power of an H-bomb results from thermonuclear-fusion reactions and the other half from fission, that occurs in the A-bomb trigger and in the uranium jacket. Fusion does not produce any radioactive products directly. It is the fission that produces the radioactivity. The warheads of the missiles are made with no uranium jacket, but with a fission trigger. Less than five per cent of the total explosive force comes from the fission and more than ninety five per cent is from the fusion. The warheads of the missiles can therefore be considered as completely clean. After you have fired the bomb in the morning you can put up your breakfast table in the detonation area and eat your toast, bacon and egg with English blended Earl Grey tea. You will only be exposed to the same quantity of radioactivity as if you were sitting in front of your own television."

Salnikov became silent while the waiter again appeared and took away the plates from the main course.

The waiter asked, in the way of waiters all over the world: "Would you like cheese or some dessert, gentlemen?"

McPride looked at Salnikov for a few seconds waiting to be informed of his wishes, but Salnikov said nothing, only waved his hands in a gesture that indicated, order whatever you want.

McPride therefore said, distantly, like an English aristocrat: "We will first have some *brie* and afterwards you can serve the famous yellow *gateau Tropézien* cake with vanilla cream and icing sugar. – American coffees without sugar and Larsens cognac."

After the waiter had vanished, Salnikov continued indefatigably his lesson in nuclear physics.

"The missiles that I can deliver will be based on a line-of-sight guidance system, which relays corrections in the flight path by infrared signals. A laser beam will mark the target. The missile can be launched several kilometres from the target, and it searches for the marked target while in flight. It can be launched thirty kilometres away from the target without problems, if that is necessary. The distance depends only on the topography of the area and the level of launch position of the missiles in the terrain. Of course the nearer the launch position is to the target, the more sure you are of accuracy."

Salnikov seemed finished with his clarification and wiped some beads of sweat from his forehead and again looked nervously around in the room. McPride had become used to this behaviour by now and waited in silence till he had made his periodic, systematic sweeps of the restaurant.

Salnikov suddenly started to talk again.

"I almost forgot the specification of the missiles. It is SSF98. From now on we will only use a code for the specification. I suggest we call the armed missiles *vodka bottles.*"

He laughed a neighing laugh.

McPride, who had been sitting listening quietly without interrupting, now laughed loudly at his remark.

He did not want to give Salnikov the impression that he had not previously checked out the subject properly, so he said diplomatically: "You obviously know what you are selling. You would have been an excellent salesman of technical equipment if you had been employed by a private Western company."

And to flatter Salnikov even more, he added: "Or maybe rather run a technical company yourself."

Salnikov had observed, correctly, during his monologue that his customer did not know a lot about the equipment he was going to buy.

He replied politely: "Thank you – I hope my sales pitch has been instructive, but you obviously knew everything well beforehand."

After a small pause for thought, he continued: "The main thing is that these missiles can be operated by anybody who has been trained in the use of a standard bazooka. To be sure that no accidents happen when using armed missiles, which I believe never will, I will dispatch a number of missiles without warheads for training purposes. As a code name for the unarmed training missiles, I suggest *wine bottles.*"

For a second time Salnikov's neighing laughter could be heard. McPride laughed with him, more at the neighing laughter, than at the joke.

"The *wine bottles* and the *vodka bottles*," McPride repeated and laughed even more, as if the remarks were funny.

Russians must have a different sense of humour to Western Europeans, he thought ironically.

"I believe you wonder why I call the armed missiles *vodka bottles* and the unarmed missiles *wine bottles*," Salnikov said, still neighing like an old horse.

"I really do," McPride replied and sounded quite interested.

"I don't think the humour is so different in Russia compared to western Europe," Salnikov said coughing slightly, "but situations that occur in Russia can be quite different from situations which occur in Western countries." He took a gulp of water before he continued laughing with tears in his eyes. "It was some years ago, at a Red Army training base in the Verkhoyansk Range of mountains, five hundred kilometres north-east of Yakutsk in eastern Siberia. The officers had their usual Saturday vodka party – the younger officers at one end of the camp and the older senior officers at the other. Some of the younger officers proposed to send an unarmed missile, similar to the type you will purchase, to destroy a small cabin near the building where the older officers were celebrating. We will send them a *wine bottle* to liven up their atmosphere, the younger officers shouted and ordered two of the youngest inexperienced recruits to execute the assignment. Shortly after, the recruits launched a missile towards the cabin and scored a perfect hit using an infrared laser indicator. A court-martial was held afterwards. One of the recruits, who had executed the launching, said sadly in the court: You see, we were ordered to launch a *wine bottle*, but we chose wrongly and instead sent a *vodka bottle*, which was really strong, and half the camp just vanished."

"That remark probably saved the young officer's life," Salnikov added. "The court members had to laugh, and all the young officers involved were condemned to life in prison instead of the expected death sentence. Afterwards, these missiles were simply called *wine bottles* and *vodka bottles* in the Soviet army and later the Russian army."

McPride was quite silent for a moment while he was thinking about the Cold War. They must have been close to an atomic inferno many times, but nobody in the West knew how the Red Army had handled their nuclear weapons.

He asked: "How many missiles could you possibly deliver? – And when can you deliver? I suppose we need three times as many for training purposes as armed with warheads."

Salnikov replied after a short hesitation: "To answer your estimate first. Yes – I believe it is right to have at least three times as many for training purposes as loaded with warheads."

He hesitated again for a moment.

McPride said: "The . . ."

Salnikov raised his hand to stop him, but he excused himself at once when he realised what he had done.

"Sorry – to interrupt you, sir, but the time for delivery will be approximately a year and you can determine the quantity yourself – of course, within reason."

"The price?" – McPride asked. "The price is of course very important."

This time Salnikov replied without any interruption, though he spoke as if he expected one.

"The price will be one million US dollars per missile with its warhead, and a minimum of twelve units. The training missiles will cost you an additional three million US dollars altogether."

McPride was noticeably astonished at the high price and had to think for a short while. That son-of-a-bitch has obviously planned to live well for his remaining years. He really will be well paid for stealing these rockets from his damned employer – the Russian State. But Salnikov has no competitors, and he knows it. On the other hand, you cannot buy rockets with atomic warheads from hot-dog stands. Our cause is worthy and this payment means nothing by comparison, but it will be a considerable problem to raise such an amount of money without causing suspicion.

McPride said, very diplomatically: "The number was exactly what I wanted, but your price seems a bit high. Is it possible to lower the price?"

Salnikov knew he had made the chance deal with the Arabs in Venice. The situation was quite different at the moment compared to what it had been when he left Russia. He already had enough money for the rest of his life from that deal. He did not need to do this risky business at all. But opportunity knocked.

He replied: "The deal is at a very risky level and it will be very expensive to carry through. It is quite impossible to reduce the price."

McPride knew after Salnikov's reply that there was no discount to be had and he asked quickly to get the discussion immediately away from the price question: "How are we going to pay you and how are you going to deliver?"

The waiter came with the cheese. Both were silent while he served. He asked his guests politely if they would like anything else, but received a negative reply.

Salnikov had learnt from the trade with the Arabs and replied at once, when the waiter had vanished.

"You must open an account in a Swiss bank, and give me the identification number. You have to transfer two and a half million American dollars into the account within one week. Within two months you have to transfer another five million. The rest on delivery. In half a year from today, we will have another meeting in Geneva. At this meeting you will be informed precisely about the delivery. By the way, do you have access to the information received by military intelligence satellite surveillance on Russia?"

McPride nodded. He had access to all the information received by the military satellites. One of the members of the group of Scottish conspirators was a high-ranking officer at the Royal Army Satellite Centre.

He said: "The payment can easily be arranged and I have access to all information from the military satellites."

The two officers agreed on a meeting in Geneva in February. The business part of the meeting was ended. The two gentlemen had agreed and the deal was settled. The waiter served the remaining order. They had coffee, finished the dessert cake and toasted each other in cognac, while relaxedly talking about the marvellous small town of Saint Tropez and other subjects of common interest.

4

Immediately after the meeting with McPride, Salnikov picked up his rental car at the large municipal parking lot by the sea, at the entrance to the town. He started his journey to southern Spain, feeling rather satisfied, like an ordinary businessman who had just accomplished an agreement on exceptional orders from his customers. In just two days I have made the astronomic amount of eighteen million US dollars – three million from the Arabs and fifteen million from McPride, whomever he might represent, he reflected while grinning foolishly in self-satisfaction. The total amount of money is so large that I can't even convert the amount into Russian roubles. Anyway, it's of no interest because not a penny can ever be utilised in Russia. I would have to work for thousands of years to earn the same amount on my low salary, as colonel in the Russian army.

"By the way," he said out loud as his foolish grin was transformed into an energetic vulgar laugh. "I really have to thank the Arabs – or rather the Arab woman I accidentally met in Verona, for the fabulous result of a delightful fuck."

Salnikov lit a Marlboro cigarette, took a long, deep draw and blew out the smoke calmly. He did not smoke a lot, as the Russian hemp tobacco did not encourage too much smoking. He had almost stopped smoking ten years ago and had later only smoked socially, or so he said, when asked why he still smoked. What a profitable fucking, Salnikov thought again and felt like a gigolo must feel in the morning waking up beside an ugly, but rich and generous woman.

After the deal with the Arabs was closed, Salnikov certainly had enough money to live as a rich man, without working, for the rest of his life. Suddenly he was not dependent on the deal with McPride at all, and could therefore confidently triple the price he had planned. If the Scottish officer did not accept, it would not matter. McPride, however, had no choice if he wanted the weapons, because he could not purchase them elsewhere. He was simply forced to accept any price without complaint.

Because of all the money at my disposal, the delivery can now also be accomplished much more safely, Salnikov considered, – as complete silence and co-operation in such business, of course, costs a hell of a lot of money.

Who is McPride's employer? Could it be a crazy criminal gang, or could it be a crazy political organisation? Either way, they have to be completely crazy. Who else would spend fifteen million US dollars in such a stupid way? Who wants to buy atomic weapons but guerrillas in third world countries, now that the desperate German Bader Meinhof Group has finally been destroyed? A serious British army officer would surely not represent any neo-nazi groups in Germany or Scandinavia. Could it be the IRA? Salnikov doubted it. He tried to analyse the situation seriously. It was not their style. The IRA always used conventional bombs with good results and would presumably not change their methods. Anyway, the Russian government might quickly get rid of their national debt by selling their atomic weapons at such high prices.

What was the purpose of the trade? What in the hell was the purpose when they needed atomic weapons?

Unanswered questions weighed heavily on Salnikov. He wondered deeply and rather confusedly for a long time, without any clear answers to any of them. Conventional weapons must have fulfilled most assignments effectively. Had his customers planned to blow up Fort Knox to steal the American gold stock or something similar?

Salnikov suddenly realised the atomic weapons' purpose. The weapons must obviously be planned for some kind of pressure to gain political end. What else could it be? He thought for a long time, over and over again considering all other possibilities of the weapons' utilisation, but he did not come up with another rational solution. The purpose is surely to use the atomic missiles for political pressure. That means that only the buyer, and the government exposed to the pressure, will have any information about them. Finally he decided to base his delivery plans on this conclusion. This will make it a lot easier for me to fulfil a successful delivery and there will be a lot fewer problems to consider afterwards, he concluded with satisfaction.

When Salnikov later reached Perpignan, near the Spanish border, he exchanged his rental car – a discreet, grey medium sized Peugeot, which he had rented from Avis in Nice. Instead he rented a brand new red convertible BMW equipped with four-wheel drive, from Hertz. Such a car is just right for a proper dollar millionaire like me, he thought happily. However, the car was as expensive as hell to rent. I must work at least half a year in the Russian army for that bloody price.

The rental contract made it possible for him to return the car at Barcelona airport in ten days. He hoped that the exchange would create additional problems for any possible Russian hunters to relocate him, although it did not matter a lot at this moment, as he had completed his business. Anyway, he reckoned with being ordered to make a detailed report, completely confirmed by receipts from hotels, restaurants, car rental companies and so on, to his superior, the Region General, about his journey, when he came home. Of course, only necessary receipts would be used in that report. Before he left Russia he had borrowed money from a colleague to justify the spending. However, he found a great deal of pleasure from the thoughts that he might have created insuperable problems for his Russian hunters. Perhaps they would not track him down at all before he returned to Russia. Many officers in the Russian Secret Police would lose their positions thereby. Salnikov happily indulged himself in these reflections.

Salnikov crossed the Spanish border and made up his mind to continue as long as possible before he stopped for the night. He passed Barcelona, then Valencia, but had to make a stop to rest when he reached Benidorm.

Benidorm seemed to be a very active tourist resort. There were people all over. He chose the first hotel he saw when he entered the town from the highway, one kilometre away. The name of the hotel was the Cimbel. He parked at one of the vacant parking places outside the hotel. He did no security inspection of the surroundings for possible trackers because he was too exhausted after the long day behind the wheel. The success he had achieved during the last couple of days had drained him completely of normal and trained security habits. He just opened the luggage compartment, snatched his suitcases, walked towards the hotel reception and checked in. He was extremely tired and fell asleep immediately he swung down onto the bed for the short rest he planned before dinner and a look round the town.

He slept long, woke up late into the evening, dressed and went down for dinner in the hotel's restaurant. After an excellent *filet mignon* with a bottle of acceptable rioja vieja, an ordinary *crème caramel* and *café Americano*, he asked one of the receptionists, where he would advise him to spend the evening.

The receptionist, a younger man, looked at him for a short while, as he took his measure.

He grinned, as if telling the man before him he was too old to be anywhere else than in a retirement home, but then said rather gallantly: "I believe Sunset will be a suitable place for you. There you might meet people of your own age. If you walk to the left along the main street towards the old post office, you will find the place to the right before you reach the roundabout – you can't miss it."

Salnikov did of course not know where the old post office was, but headed to the left along the main street and found the place by luck, after having asked a taxi driver.

The night-club Sunset was a discotheque without live music, a rather small and narrow establishment in the basement of an apartment hotel. To make the room feel larger, mirrors covered the walls and the pillars. A lot of people swarmed around as always in such places. Salnikov bought himself a whisky at the bar and found himself a vacant stool to sit on, at a small table. In a good mood as he was, he came at once in contact with the people around the table. It was a noisy couple of German friends, who, rather high on strong liquor, were painting the town red together. One was large, fat and fair, the other, dark and small. Salnikov was at once put in mind of Laurel and Hardy from the movies he had seen in the Russian army barracks many years ago.

A good-looking, fair woman in her early forties had also joined the table, but she was not in the company of Laurel and Hardy. She looked like a lonely soul, hunting desperately for men.

The good looking woman whispered at the first chance she had, exchanging winks with Salnikov, that she knew the noisy German couple from gossip. The bigger one was presently occupied in checking out an unwilling young girl and the smaller had left for the lavatory. She said that many

Germans lived on the Costa Blanca. There had for many years been a very high standard of living in Germany, especially in the Bavarian part, in the south. Many Bavarians had therefore turned their backs on the cold German winters, to enjoy a carefree life under the hot Spanish sun.

She looked at Hardy and whispered gruffly as she pointed unobtrusively: "That ugly, fat fellow tries to check out girls young enough to be his granddaughters, though he is married to a nice, ordinary woman. He tries to make out he is an important playboy, but comes across as a completely ridiculous pig – a pig that has definitely no chance of impressing serious older women. People say he has built a few small, cheap apartments, which he is trying to sell at extremely high prices to unsuspecting old Germans. The bank believes he has no real assets, but lets him run the business although it knows it has made a big mistake, but cannot go back."

The woman suddenly bent slightly forward, this time pointing briefly at the smaller German who had returned.

"The small, dark one is a printer's assistant who has inherited his father's printing shop, which he is letting out. Women avoid him, as he looks rather ugly and unpleasant," she concluded with a rather arrogant expression.

The smaller, dark one might have heard her as he grinned nervously before hastily making for the bar, without a single word.

Salnikov smiled when he looked at the attractive gossip-monger. What the woman so anxiously talked about was of absolutely no interest to a stranger. People certainly do live a harmless life in Spain; there are few weighty matters to think about, so they seem, instead, to run around spreading wicked rumours about each other.

The woman suddenly asked: "You don't say a lot, dear. Where do you come from?"

"I come from Ukraine," Salnikov lied.

"By the Black Sea," the good-looking woman confirmed knowingly. "I've never been there. It must be a very beautiful place in the summertime. Isn't Crimea in Ukraine, where Churchill, Roosevelt and Stalin met during the Second World War and held the well-known Yalta conference? You know, the place where they agreed about the world's shape after the end of the war, like Poland's new borders, the sectioning of Germany between the Allies, the Axis' payment of war indemnity, and where the Americans appealed to the Soviets to join the war against Japan."

"Yes, that's correct," Salnikov confirmed, rather impressed by the intellect the woman showed. Such historical knowledge is not customary, he thought. This must be a very remarkable woman.

The beautiful talking-machine saw he was impressed and smiled contentedly before she started to chatter again, like a machine-gun.

"I have once been to Romania. That must be close to Ukraine. I was on vacation at a tourist resort called Mamaya, near the town of Constanza, not far from the Danube delta. It was during the time the communists ruled the country and I saw dreadful poverty."

Salnikov hastily put in to prevent the woman starting on a lecture about the dreadful poverty in Romania: "Where do you come from, my dear?"

"I'm from Denmark," the woman answered. "Oh, it is an extremely beautiful country in the middle of the summer," her eyes nearly swam for a short moment, "but the summer is, unhappily, very short," she concluded quickly and twisted her head as if to make an additional confirmation.

"What's your name," Salnikov asked quickly, to steer her conversation in a happier direction.

"My name is Brigitte Caroline Aalrup, but everybody just calls me Brigitte," she replied and pouted her red mouth sexily and invitingly.

"That's a nice name," Salnikov said trying to keep the conversation light. "Have you been on the Costa Blanca long?"

"Nearly ten years," Brigitte replied eagerly. "I was a guide for Spies, a large Danish travel company, but I fell in love with a Spanish doctor, who later exchanged me for a younger model."

Brigitte paused, while her eyes for a moment became reddish and then suddenly filled with tears that trickled slowly down her cheeks. Salnikov could not decide if the tears were real or fake.

"Now I am working for a travel agency, and only receive complaints from angry and irritated tourists all day," Brigitte said and tried unsuccessfully to look desperately sad.

She is very beautiful and attractive, but too talkative. I must invite her for the night, and I'll give her something else to do but talk me deaf, Salnikov planned rather lustfully.

The small night-club suddenly filled with a loud noise from a group of guests who had just arrived.

"It's the damned Russian Mafia members who've arrived," Brigitte whispered quietly, but truly resigned. "They occasionally visit all night-clubs in the area. These newly rich Russians have bought many large villas around here, from Calpe twenty kilometres further north to La Nucia, just above here. They behave absolutely irresponsibly, just like Western playboys did in the sixties. The Spanish police avoid them, because they bring in a lot of desperately needed money to the area."

A group of fifteen, young middle-aged, visibly drunken Russian men impolitely forced their way into the establishment. Some of them stopped at the bar, others moved inside.

One of them stopped at Salnikov's table, pointed at Laurel's empty chair and asked in inadequate English with an unmistakable Russian accent: "Is that hell of a chair free?"

Salnikov did not reply, but the talkative Brigitte had already pulled the trigger on her speedy talking cannon, and chattered a white lie: "The chair is occupied by a man who is at the lavatory – I believe he probably soon will return."

"He has not bought the chair, I presume," the Russian responded impolitely as a man with a bowler hat and brief case might say when entering a first class compartment on a British train. "Ivan, pull over that free chair to this table, we will join these people, or they might let us have that one," he continued laconically in Russian, pointing towards another free chair by the next table and hoped none of the other guests understood him.

Brigitte's rapid-cannon must have developed functional problems, as she suddenly said absolutely nothing. Salnikov grinned with amusement for a short moment.

Both the Russians sat at the table and one of them said, insultingly, to Hardy: "You fat man – you must be too old for that young girl."

The Russian pointed at the young girl who tried to become invisible and at the same time made eye contact with the newcomers like the experienced hooker that she also might be.

Hardy did not reply. He only rose quickly and walked straight out of the night-club without looking back. Laurel followed him from the bar like an obedient dog. Hardy's girl remained at the table and immediately turned her inviting eyes on Ivan, the youngest Russian. She blinked sexily to signal that she was free and prepared for a younger mate than the one who had hastily vanished without a word.

Brigitte suddenly woke up from her temporary lethargy. She said abruptly, like a teacher who was talking to a naughty child: "That was a very impolite way to behave, young man."

"Shut up old grandmother. The girl was too young for that old, fat, dirty pig," Ivan said brusquely.

Salnikov agreed with the Russian concerning the dirty pig, but parried immediately, rather irritated at his impolite appellation of Brigitte: "Please talk politely to the lady."

"Don't get involved grandpa, or you will regret it," the Russian said roughly. "By the way, are you Russian – you sound exactly like one?"

"No, I am from Ukraine," Salnikov lied for the second time that night.

"I don't believe you, you son-of-a-bitch. You sound like a damned Russian without any accent," Ivan remarked in Russian. "You are surely one of these bloody police spies they send to investigate us in Spain."

The night-club had become more crowded. A group of guests with dark hair and brown eyes – very Arabian look-ing, had arrived and stood in the corner, not far from Salnikov's table. Another three Russians arrived from the bar with vodka drinks for their comrades. They also sat at Salnikov's table. Guests at neighbouring tables, who sus-pected trouble, had moved away and freed chairs.

Ivan raised his glass and said in Russian: "A toast for the bloody Russian police spy!"

Salnikov decided it was time to go, but as he tried to rise up he was pressed down into the chair again by a huge Russian, who had arrived behind him.

"I hope you haven't planned on leaving us already – you fucking police skunk? That would be rather impolite, don't you agree, Boris," Ivan said sarcastically with an ugly grin and blinked towards Boris, who was the Russian behind Salnikov.

The other Russians laughed maliciously and sounded exactly like hungry hyenas over a cadaver.

61

"We have proper treatments for people like you. Inform your bosses in Lubianca headquarters in Red Square, that their spies are not welcome in Spain," Boris declared ceremoniously and brutally gripped Salnikov's right cheek.

Salnikov immediately hit Boris' arm with great force and Boris squealed loudly like a stuck pig. Salnikov quickly made another effort to rise, but was gripped by several other Russians. Igor raised his arm holding an empty vodka glass ready to crush it down on Salnikov's skull, but one of the Arabian looking guests, standing strategically near, grabbed his hand and another Arabian started to hammer his face with a knuckle duster just like a jack hammer.

Brigitte screamed like a girl cast onto a bonfire during the Holy Church's medieval witch-hunt. The Arabs immediately surrounded Salnikov's table and professionally pounded down on the drunken Russians. Other Russians, who came running and mixed into the fight, got the same treatment. The whole establishment seemed like a Hell's Angels' battlefield. Chairs, tables, bottles and glasses were being used as weapons.

"Come on Brigitte," Salnikov roared loudly. "We must run like hell."

He gripped Brigitte by the arm and pulled her after him. They were soon on the street and could hear the sound of approaching police sirens as they jumped into one of the many taxis, which desperately hunted for passengers during the hours before anybody really needed one to get home after a night on the town. Salnikov and Brigitte drove directly to the Cimbel.

"I need a drink," Brigitte whispered desperately in the lift. "I was so frightened, I have never seen such violence. Benidorm has always been a quiet town."

Her tears flowed down her cheeks. Salnikov kissed her hastily to prevent her starting up the talking cannon, which he feared would accelerate as the shock gradually left her.

Her tears tasted salty and Salnikov suddenly felt an indescribable tenderness for her, like he had not felt for anybody in years. Had she manipulated him? No, – he decided not. He had simply fallen in love at first sight with the attractive Danish woman.

The hotel's room service arrived with champagne and canapés, shortly after they arrived in the suite. Salnikov had placed the order when he had passed the reception desk and had paid the receptionist over the odds, to prevent them asking questions about the woman he brought with him.

Salnikov considered the incident in the night-club, but he could not find any suitable answer. He decided he probably had been extremely lucky to escape the event unharmed. It must have been a local rival gang, which by coincidence had helped him out of the precarious situation and used the opportunity to deal with the Russian Mafia. He did not get any further in his silent consideration because Brigitte swung her arms around his neck.

She pressed her body tightly against him and kissed him deeply on his mouth, while whispering dreamily: "I have such a fanatical need for love, to calm my nerves."

Brigitte had not understood a word of the Russians' conversation and was quite ignorant of the Russians' accusations against Salnikov. She started to undress him hurriedly, without asking for permission, and of course talked continuously. Salnikov resigned and let her do what she wanted.

He only replied at intervals: "Yes – yes", without actually listening to her.

She pushed him down on the bed before she pulled her dress over her head, placed one of her legs on the bedside and started slowly rolling down her nylon stockings like a professional striptease dancer. She smiled as she noticed he grew physically, as if synchronised with the advancement of her striptease show. When Brigitte tore off her small, white briefs with a broad, sexy smile and showed her large wide open well-rounded secret, prepared to wear the slightest of bikinis, a part of Salinkov looked like an imitation of a moon rocket just before launch.

"Have you had a hot Danish girl before, my love?" – the ample-bosomed woman said wonderingly, while she took the moon rocket firmly in her hand and slowly lowered her wide-open hungry mouth.

Salnikov did not reply. He only enjoyed the experienced Danish woman's ministrations. At least, he thought sarcastically, she doesn't talk when she pretends to eat my pulsating cream-machine in one mouthful.

It was the Arabs who were tracking Salnikov that had rescued him at the night-club. He had never spotted any of them while they had followed him closely, in the most professional way, from Venice. Their tracking cars had constantly, at certain intervals, altered position to be closest to him. No less than three cars had been on his track. The cars too had been exchanged as they passed through different towns along the journey down the coast. In this way, the cars had almost always local numberplates. This security feature had probably no meaning to a Russian colonel along the coast of the Mediterranean for the first time, but the pursuers did not know the identity of their target. They only operated strictly according to orders. For security reasons they never received more information than absolutely necessary and they worked in a kind of closed cell system. Unfolding of one of the cells would not affect the others. To use local cars when pursuing was a part of the organisation's normal security system. It had previously proved very successful in similar assignments. Anyway, this time the pursuers were ordered to look out for and detect other potential trackers of the subject. This was very important, they had been firmly told. If something unforeseen happened, they had been ordered to protect the subject, if necessary with their lives.

All the cars contained Arabs, who were members of Mustafa's organisation and who lived in different towns along the route. The organisation, which Mustafa belonged to, was very large and had members all over the world. All were professionals, well educated and highly trained. They had all been sworn to die for the organisation. If they were killed, they would reach Paradise directly as heroes of the revolution. However, there were no stupid suicide candidates among the organisation's members and few of them really believed in the childish Paradise propaganda. The men, and the few women, in the organisation were all very serious and loved their life, especially the men who lived along the Mediterranean coastline. They always had plenty of money in their pockets, continuously transferred from the organisation. Most of their time they could act as playboys, daily hunting for eager and fair Nordic tourist women and other pleasures. It was only for a very short time that they were in action on assignments on behalf of the organisation, but they were constantly in a state of readiness, always fully prepared for action.

Every year they attended courses at secret military training camps in northern Africa. Their visits to these training camps abroad were always covered up as vacations, and they never travelled directly to the final destination, but always via different tourist spots around the world. They were constantly at the peak of fitness, both physically and psychologically and never asked unnecessary questions. This time they tracked and possibly protected one of their weapon suppliers, with no knowledge of it.

The Arabs had followed Salnikov to Benidorm and later in the evening, to the night-club. Some few of them had followed Salnikov into the establishment, while the others had remained outside as guards. When the drunken Russians had appeared, more of the Arabs had entered the establishment and they had discreetly taken up positions around Salnikov, to protect him if anything should happen.

When the trouble started, the experienced Arabs had no difficulty in sorting out the situation rapidly. They had vanished long before the police arrived. All the Russians who were involved in the fight had been collected by ambulances, and taken with sirens howling to the hospital in Villajoyosa, the nearest town south of Benidorm. The repairs on the Russians created work and foreign income for the local medical staff and society for months afterwards.

The Arabian tails had also noted Salnikov's meeting with a British gentleman in Saint Tropez. Conditions made it impossible to discover what the meeting concerned, but they were sure that the information would be revealed later.

The Arabs had made a report to local superiors, which quickly reached the main office in Cairo. There the leaders decided the Briton should be observed until the question as to why he had met the Russian colonel received an acceptable explanation.

Salnikov woke up early in the morning with Brigitte's naked body twisted tightly around him like a snake. They had slept well and Salnikov was in a splendid mood. After a quick repetition of some of the different acts of the physical performance from the night before, they ordered breakfast from room service.

They ate by the window with a marvellous view over the Mediterranean. Salnikov noticed that the sea was more blue here than on the Côte d'Azur, where it had a special green-blue colour when the sun was shining – the azure blue colour. He looked at the wide, yellow Levante beach.

"It's one of the cleanest beaches on the Mediterranean," Brigitte boasted proudly. "It has the European Community's blue flag and the beach stretches approximately one kilometre in each direction from here."

Further to the right there was a headland, with picturesque old town buildings, which stretched out into the sea. Fifty metres further into the sea could be seen a fountain spraying water more than thirty metres into the sky. Salnikov had seen photos of the fountain before in tourist leaflets. At the other side he saw another wide yellow sandy beach, considerably longer than the Levante beach.

Brigitte said it was the Poniente beach. He saw an enormous crowd of people streaming down to the beaches. It looked as if the people were going to work. He realised that Benidorm was a mass tourism resort. Everything was cheap in Benidorm, Brigitte said, and the quality was often better than in more expensive resorts. During a year there were millions of tourists in Benidorm.

Benidorm is obviously not the place for me, Salnikov reflected smugly. As a real dollar multimillionaire, I must stay at a place with people of my own standing and I do not find them in Benidorm. Salnikov was greedy. He just adored his new role of a multimillionaire. Mustafa had made a very astute move when he gave him the ten thousand American dollars as pocket money – money he gave him with the sole intention of involving him so deeply in the affair that it would be impossible for him to withdraw later.

However, this money made it possible for Salnikov to test his future role as millionaire – and he decided he really would play the millionaire, as it was safest to spend the money before he returned to Russia. He believed there would be no problem spending it, as there were plenty of women, night-clubs and other pleasures to be examined thoroughly. Nevertheless, now he was going to Marbella, which he had read was the place for Europe's really rich scoundrels, and he was now one of them for sure – one with millions of American dollars in the bank.

Salnikov checked out of the Cimbel and rushed to the car together with Brigitte. Brigitte lived in Altea, a small town next to Benidorm. He drove her home and like two teenagers in love, they agreed to meet the following weekend. Later, he thought that bringing a woman to Marbella must be like bringing fish on a fishing trip, but he was in love and love surely makes one blind. The Scandinavian woman was an attractive and beautiful mistress. Her only fault was her constant chatter, but that was no worse than the sounds he had experienced in the killing fields, he thought resignedly.

Salnikov decided to drive on the inland roads after passing Alicante. They looked a lot better on the map than the coastal roads. He followed the motorway till it ended at Murcia, and then took the country road towards Granada. He drove slowly and relaxed, stopped for meals, and acted just like an ordinary tourist.

However, the Arabs were still hanging on his tail. They kept a good distance from him, especially on the country roads after Murcia, so as not to be detected, and they were not.

From Granada to Torremolinos by the coast the road was excellent, and Salnikov soon passed through Malaga and drove into Marbella at dusk. He checked in at a hotel, the El Fuerte, a four star hotel in a very central situation in the town – an excellent headquarters for planned attacks on night-clubs and women. He gave generous tips to all the staff and acted just like a really rich playboy. He occupied the best suite on the hotel's top floor.

Salnikov had some marvellous days in Marbella. He adored the pleasant international atmosphere; the hot sun and beautiful surroundings with mountains rising in the north and the west towards a sky that always appeared blue. Life seemed to be completely without any concerns. Nobody thought about the days to come, but concentrated on living for today. Salnikov enjoyed the willing women as he tested a different one each night. At Puerto Banus, the famous yacht marina, he inspected large yachts and told himself that one day he also would have his yacht here.

Fifteen minutes distance by car from Marbella in the direction of Gibraltar, was the Aloha golf course. White houses were spread around the green golf course. It looked like a fairy-tale, he thought, and decided to choose this place for his nice white house with a large pool. He looked forward to dining among the anonymous rich people at the golf course's restaurant, after he had finished the 18 holes. In the evenings, he would jump into his convertible Mercedes and drive to his new home and his always waiting wonderful wife, the Danish woman he had met, or another one – also fair – with a wonderful large bust.

Salnikov suddenly felt a stab in his heart. He missed his wife, who had died at a young age without leaving any children. Perhaps the new wife would give him children – possibilities to live after death. He felt lonely and outside society. He realised that he actually hated his present situation, which he considered himself more or less to have been forced into. The hate was intense against the former Soviet. A young man had few or no possibilities if he had no family with political positions to smooth a future career through the corrupt system. Therefore he had to choose the army, although he would rather have been an architect.

To live at Aloha would be his dreaming political refugee soul's future. However, Russian army officers were normally not able to move abroad, after they had finished their service. They could never move out of Russia, first of all because of economic reasons, as the Russian army retirement pension could hardly cover food costs, even in Russia. Secondly, there were strict restrictions on army officers because of their knowledge of Russian army secrets. Salnikov considered therefore the difficult situation for retired army officers in Russia as a defence for his behaviour. In his own eyes, that made his conscience completely clear. He could have sold all the weapons in Russia and it would have made no difference. He was no betrayer, as he actually was a pure Ukrainian with only questionable connections to Russia. His family had been forced to stay in Russia after the Second World War completely against their will, and could not return to their beloved Ukraine because Stalin needed people to rebuild the country after the war. There was no system for taking into consideration the special needs of the people. They were considered to belong entirely to the Soviet Union – slaves of the system. His family's continuous applications to move back to the Ukraine were just as continuously refused.

Salnikov was more or less fed up with the jet-set life when Brigitte arrived the following weekend. She gave him what he considered to be the perfect ending to his travels. By the time he returned by plane from Barcelona to Moscow, he was deeply in love with the talkative Danish woman.

5

A short time after Salnikov returned to Russia from Spain, he received peremptory orders from his superior, Regional General Vladimir Martjuk, to make a complete report on his entire journey to the Mediterranean countries. The general had personally told Salnikov that he wanted a very exact and detailed report.

"Reports about travel to foreign countries must be strictly in accordance with the army's rules and regulations – especially when high-ranking officers make journeys to Western countries – our potential future enemies," the general told Salnikov informatively and somewhat brusquely at their first meeting after his return.

Martjuk had afterwards determinedly added: "This of course also applies to vacation travel."

Salnikov had anticipated such a report ahead of his journey and could easily reconstruct a detailed description of his travels, which would match the Secret Police's template exactly, as far as he believed they had one. The receipts confirmed all his activities. He had receipts from restaurants, hotels and car rental companies. To divert the readers' attention, he wrote at length about the small town Sirmione with the ancient Roman ruins, Verona with the old town, the old Hotel Due Torri and the ancient Arena. He specially gave a very detailed description of the three tenors' concert at the Arena, as he knew Martjuk was an enthusiastic opera fan.

71

The concert was magnificent and the sound effects in the old Arena were really superb, almost impossible to describe, he wrote. He also described his trip to Venice and did not forget to mention his journey on the motorway towards Tuscany. As he vividly described the wonderful scenery in this part of Italy, he forgot to mention the two Russian pursuers who found their death among the rocks of the hillside, after their car had dived off the motorway.

When he described southern France, he did not forget the marvellous picturesque town of Saint Tropez. "It is a remarkable place that I recommend everyone should visit," he added, without mentioning the outstanding business he had made for himself in this exceptional little coastal town. He described Benidorm and Marbella, included the famous yacht harbour of Puerto Banus, but did not mention Aloha – the place where he had decided to make his future home. Neither did he mention his great Danish love, Brigitte.

General Martjuk always smiled, but sometimes with extremely cold eyes. He had been told to be very wary, even slyer than an old wolf. The general was a small, stout man with blue, piggy eyes and blunt fingers. He was sixty-five years old, florid and bald. From a distance, he was extremely like the Politburo's former First Secretary after Stalin, Nikita Sergeyevich Khrushchev, but rumour had it that the general was considerably more brutal and bestial. He was *nekulturnyj* – impolite, they said.

Martjuk was informed by the Secret Police that their evaluation of Salnikov's report was positive. Their final conclusion had been that Colonel Igor Salnikov was absolutely tried and true. *Nullum crimen, nulla poena* – no crime, no punishment.

Approximately two months after Martjuk received the report, he met Salnikov at the obligatory drinking party following the annual tactical meeting for superior officers in the region. Martjuk was extremely drunk after too many cocktails and vodka, and Salnikov simulated being very drunk. Salnikov wanted to take advantage of the informal meeting to gain even more trust from the general than he had gained with his report. Information about the positive evaluation had already leaked to him through an old colleague.

Salnikov knew Martjuk probably was very well informed about the women he had accidentally met in Verona. However, Salnikov pretended he believed the general knew nothing.

He said, snuffling, acting, as if severely befuddled: "I had an unforgettable experience in Verona in Italy, which really refreshed the heart of an old man."

To pretend being even more drunk and to give his story the appearance of a conspiracy, he added, almost whispering: "You should really have been there with me, old comrade."

He grinned and constantly blinked eagerly, looking like a real, lecherous, drunken fool.

"At a small restaurant I accidentally met three women, who sat at the next table." Salnikov cleared his throat a couple of times before he grumbled crossly: "What marvellous women – I'll tell you they really had all the right things in all the right places. You should have seen their busts."

Salnikov waved his arms, to indicate large ones, while at the same time he pronounced a sound, which seemed to come deep from his stomach: "Oho – oho."

Martjuk hid a grin, by coughing behind his hand, while he chortled silently.

"Their dresses could hardly keep their horny tits inside," Salnikov said, pretending lust, while he carefully studied Martjuk's reaction.

"I established contact with them," he added, this time very matter-of-factly, "and all four of us ended up in my hotel room – in the very same bed."

He paused deliberately in the telling, to increase Martjuk's anticipation. Martjuk expected him to relate sexual stuff, which the police could not have known. Martjuk was known to have an immense sexual appetite. He looked sceptically and very doubtingly at Salnikov for a short while before he moved closer, like a kid who was invited to hear about his pal's last raid on the neighbour's fruit garden.

Salnikov satisfyingly noticed the old pig's great interest and made a grimace and belched like only a very drunken person can, before he continued whispering into Martjuk's red, sticking-out ear.

"We kept on till the morning. It was the perfect fuck – I was completely exhausted. You know – none of the women had a single hair on their bodies except for that on their heads."

Martjuk's piggy blue eyes rolled, as he obviously had fixed his mind on the hairless women.

Salnikov raked his mind to find enough horny superlatives to describe the situation. Meanwhile, he tried desperately to hide his laughter, which was becoming increasingly difficult to cover.

Salnikov ended his story by recommending to the general to try more than one woman at the same time himself. He knew also that the general probably would do so, because it was well known among the officers that he was an enthusiastic and regular user of the Pigeons.

The Pigeons were call girls who operated on behalf of the Secret Police, to treat foreign diplomats and people they wanted to put under pressure. The superior officers had always had the right to utilise these women for their own purposes. In the same way they also had the right to have luxury cabins – *dachas* – in the pine forests around Moscow and to shop in special retail stores – *sakrytye raspredeliteli* – containing products the ordinary consumer could not obtain. Although the system-change in the country had reduced many of these special advantages, the Pigeons still were at their disposal.

As Martjuk's wife's unpleasant appearance did not attract anybody to sexual actions, Martjuk's meetings with the Pigeons were fully accepted and understood by his colleagues.

Salnikov also told Martjuk he had extended his trip to include Venice, to meet one of the women again, and that her extreme sexuality had nearly killed him in the space of a morning.

"She – she was really hot, dear comrade," Salnikov chuckled drunkenly and gave Martjuk a friendly slap on the shoulder.

Martjuk, who previously had been informed about these incidents, knew the Secret Police had examined the back-grounds of the three women. Nothing suspicious had been found. One of the women had afterwards travelled to Lebanon on holiday, as her mother was Arabian and where she had some relatives. She had previously lived in Venice for about twenty years.

In September she had made a phone-call to her friends, telling them she was going to be married in Arabia some-where. Therefore she could not risk having any more connections with them because of her husband and his family, as the women were openly known as lesbians. The police report had therefore tersely concluded, as a business-like matter of fact, that Salnikov must have been one of the first men in their entire lives and that he therefore probably had not contracted any venereal diseases.

As this was a reasonable clarification, the Secret Police later dropped all examinations concerning Salnikov, as a waste of time and money. He was, after the inspection, considered a hundred per cent reliable and trustworthy.

Martjuk sat quietly with his own thoughts for a long time after Salnikov had finished his confession, before he suddenly returned the friendly slap on his shoulder. Martjuk grinned widely and sympathetically with his blue, pig-like eyes and chuckled drunkenly. The colonel smiled contentedly, but the general was too drunk to notice.

Salnikov planned the transport of the illegal weapons from Kursk to Odessa and further to Istanbul. There was very close official contact between the army in Ukraine and the depot in Kursk. The former Soviet republic imported considerable quantities of weapons from Russia and as the depot was near the border, it was usually chosen by the Russian authorities to arrange exports. The depot sometimes delivered complete goods trains of weapons. The trains went directly to Kharkiv in Ukraine via the small Russian town of Belgorod, on the border.

Salnikov intended to send two separate container wagons, loaded with the weapons for his private customers, coupled to one of these goods trains. He planned to separate his wagons from the train at Kharkiv. Afterwards, he would send them to Mykolayiv and on to Odessa. In Odessa the weapons would be transferred, by trucks, to the harbour to be loaded onto a small part-load vessel, that would cross the Black Sea directly to Istanbul. There the weapons for the Arabs would be divided from the weapons for the Scotsmen. At this point Salnikov considered he would have executed his part of the deliveries according to the agreements. The customers had to arrange the transport from Istanbul themselves. The plan was worked out with military precision and Salnikov believed nothing could fail. To direct the delivery process Salnikov would use his subordinate, Major Pavel Lapin – the only person who had his complete trust.

*

Major Lapin was quite a different person from the colonel. He was a head taller than the norm. He was black-haired and first impressions convinced everybody he was a very violent and stupid man. Uniforms never fitted him, they always seemed to be too small, but he was said to be very popular among the women, without any uniform at all. Plenty of stories circulated among his colleagues about his brave adventures on the women front. They said he just harvested women wherever he went, like a farmer would harvest his crops. Lapin's eyes were angular and there was no doubt that he was a genuine Mongolian. He always boasted he was a direct descendant of Genghis Khan. Many men had, through the years, realised that they should never contradict or express any doubts about his origins. Rumours were also in circulation about men who might have tried to express some doubt, but they all needed another day to wake up – usually in hospital.

Lapin was promoted to the rank of major only because of exceptionally brave actions in battle. The promotion was honourable and had no logical military basis. Lapin was not a parade soldier, although his parade uniform looked like a decorated Christmas tree. He had one of Russia's largest collections of distinctions and was an official Russian hero. This had saved him many times from problems with the army authorities, especially when he had reconstructed the faces of men who had expressed doubts about his Mongolian descent, or had raised objections to him in discussions, after he had consumed a few bottles of vodka. His superiors and judges had looked away in the cases that had been brought before courts-martial. They would never dare to punish a Russian national hero.

However, sober, Lapin was known as a fair and friendly fellow. He played chess and was rather sporty. He usually won when he was playing chess and was undoubtedly very intelligent, though by looks he did not appear so. Lapin was completely loyal to his superior, Salnikov. Only a few knew Lapin had been in the platoon that Salnikov had saved from certain death in Afghanistan. Lapin considered he owed Salnikov his life.

During the Afghanistan War Salnikov had led the forward guard of a company consisting of four hundred men into a narrow valley, three hundred kilometres west of Kabul. The company was mainly equipped with T72 combat tanks and BMP armed vehicles. The force also had two Mill Mi 24, known as Hind, helicopters for air defence. The company moved in the usual Russian formation with flank reconnaissance platoons on each side, in the front, a forward detachment, followed by a forward guard, before the main force, secured on each side and behind.

The force had moved more than fifty kilometres into the narrow valley when ground-to-air missiles suddenly shot down the two Hind helicopters. Afghan guerrillas attacked between the main force and the forward guard and effectively split the Russian company. The main force's only alternative was to turn and escape or be completely annihilated. The forward formation was effectively trapped.

Suddenly, their only choice was to remain in position and accept losses from constant heavy guerrilla bombardment, or force their way forward and possibly sustain even larger losses, until help could be received from helicopters. Everything happened very quickly.

The Afghan guerrillas bombarded the Russian force with bazooka missiles, while their machine-guns chattered and caused a large number of casualties. The guerrillas had a higher position in the terrain, and were situated on both sides of the narrow valley. They controlled the situation entirely. Salnikov, who was the commander of the remaining Russian force, consolidated and split the forward guard in two halves.

With one half he managed to capture the right side of the valley, while the other half sheltered in the valley bottom. This was possible mainly because of natural shelter on the hillside, which protected the climbing soldiers from the left side of the valley. When Salnikov had cleared the right hillside he ordered the other half to attack the left side, meanwhile he bombarded the guerrillas continuously from the right. The guerrillas, who mainly used the hit-and-run tactic, soon withdrew and fled.

The Russian forward detachment was still trapped in the valley bottom by heavy gunfire from the guerrillas in positions on both hillsides. Salnikov moved the two parts of his front guards along both hillsides and effectively saved the forward detachment from certain and complete destruction.

Violent gunfire was still heard from approximately one kilometre further up the valley. It was from the battle between the reconnaissance platoons and the guerrillas. There was one Russian reconnaissance platoon consisting of fifteen men on each side of the valley.

Salnikov considered it was too risky to move a large part of the remaining force to assist them, especially as he did not know the situation exactly. He therefore decided only to send one rescue-group consisting of fifteen men on each side of the valley to assist. He ordered the rest of the force to take cover until helicopter assistance arrived from Kabul, hopefully within one and a half hours. He determined to lead one of the rescue-groups himself. He chose the one on the right side, as they had no radio contact with the platoon there.

Salnikov's rescue-group had not moved more than half a kilometre up the valley before their first casualties were registered. Afghan snipers were posted high in the terrain to prevent any assistance to the trapped platoons. A sniper killed a sergeant only two metres behind Salnikov, with a perfect shot through the skull, just below the helmet. Another soldier further behind was fatally wounded. Bullets whistled around and ricocheted off the stony hillside.

Salnikov, together with the remaining men, threw themselves flat down taking cover from some large rocks. The sweat poured down his face and the wind blew sand and dust into his eyes and nose. He felt a moment's pity for himself as he thought he had never been closer to the end of his life. It had only been chance that the sergeant had been chosen by the sniper and not him.

However he was quickly brought back to reality and determined that they must climb higher up the slope, if possible without being detected by the enemy. At this level they would simply be slaughtered like sheep in a butcher's shop. The enemy certainly expected them. Salnikov instructed his men to move back quickly and quietly about one hundred metres, before they crept silently upwards, covered from the snipers' guns by a crack in the hill-face.

They reached an area of overhanging rocks three hundred metres higher and carefully progressed further up the valley, protected from the enemy's sight by the rocks. After only two hundred metres they saw the first sniper, lying in cover, about a hundred and fifty metres below. The sniper was cautiously monitoring the terrain below.

Two men were posted to deal with the sniper, while the rest of the Russians moved forward. Several snipers were detected. Salnikov divided them among his men, so they could be knocked out at exactly the same time, not to disclose their position too early.

The snipers were equipped with different precision guns, while the Russians were armed only with ordinary AK-74 battle guns, except for one soldier, the group's sniper, who was equipped with a precision gun mounted with a telescopic sight. The AK-74 was not a gun for precision shooting, but it had the great advantage of firing 600 shots per minute and thirty bullet magazines. Faster shots therefore effectively substituted for the precision of a sniper gun.

The execution of the Afghan snipers started when Salnikov fired his first shot. Some Afghan victims were nearly cut into two by the fast Russian guns. The execution was perfect. The snipers were not warned ahead and died like flies before they knew what had hit them from an unexpected direction.

The rescue-group moved silently further up the valley, along the hill-face, and kept about the same height above the valley floor. Six hundred metres later they were just above the battle raging between the reconnaissance platoon and the guerrillas. The fighting platoon was entirely trapped in a strategically completely closed position. The guerrillas fired from three sides and controlled the only possible retreat down the valley. The Russians had no chance at all to combat their enemies and could only keep their heads down and wait for probable assistance from the helicopters, which they hoped would arrive soon.

This would have been an acceptable strategy if the efficient guerrillas had not used gun grenades. They bombarded the Russians randomly with the gun grenades and caused heavy losses, as the Russians crept frantically around and tried desperately to hide behind large boulders. They also had to change their positions constantly in hopes of confusing the guerrillas.

Salnikov decided to use the same tactic as he had successfully used against the snipers just minutes before. He moved his men another two hundred metres further up the valley sides, before he let them sneak towards the guerrillas, from an unexpected direction. The Russians were greatly outnumbered. There were probably at least three guerrillas per Russian, including those who were trapped.

Salnikov's men spread like a wing with him in the middle, to achieve optimal communication. Because of the loud noise from the constant gunfire and exploding grenades, Salnikov risked taking his men as close as only fifty metres from the enemy's upper right flank before he signalled attack on their selected targets.

The attack came as a complete surprise to the guerrillas and the Russians spread effectual and conclusive death. The enemy hit only one of Salnikov's men, who unfortunately had overlooked a nearby guerrilla fighter. A guerrilla threw a hand grenade towards the Russian who had just killed his comrade, and killed him instantly, but only seconds later the guerrilla was peppered by other Russians' bullets.

Afterwards, Salnikov moved his men towards the next sections of enemies as if they were harvesting a field. This time he had not the advantage of surprise. Therefore he ordered two of his men to move up the hillside to inspect and prevent possible restructuring of the guerrillas' upper flank and to prevent them moving to higher ground behind the rescue-group. The guerrillas in front of the trapped platoons were, by now, themselves effectively trapped by the Russians. The Russians' main problem became suddenly not to kill each other in the crossfire aimed at the guerrillas in the middle. Salnikov decided, therefore, primarily to use hand grenades.

As the rescue-group were situated above their enemies, they could easily throw their hand grenades downwards. The enemy was not able to throw grenades effectively upwards, though some desperate enough among them tried, but could not obtain sufficient thrust. The grenades were received in return. As they rolled back down the steep slope towards their point of departure, they killed the thrower.

To use the gun grenades from hidden positions at such a short distance was practically impossible. The guerrillas who tried, had to stand up and disclose their positions, and were immediately picked off by the Russians from either side, like figures in a shooting gallery. The guerrillas were rapidly outmanoeuvred and the remaining few left alive hid themselves among the boulders.

It had been very shrewd of Salnikov to cover his back against any potential regrouping enemies. Soon after they had reached their positions further up in the hillside, the two Russians observed several guerrillas, who were climbing eagerly up the slope to gain a position behind the rescue-team. With calm precision they targeted them wherever their heads appeared between the rocks.

The gunfire ceased, then only sporadic fire could be heard. Salnikov considered it was too risky to move towards the reconnaissance platoon to examine their condition, because of the remaining guerrillas. He therefore decided to let his men remain in their newly obtained, relatively safe positions and to make the risky attempt to creep more than two hundred metres towards the trapped platoon, himself.

He left his AK-74, which would hinder his necessarily quiet movement, as it was dragged along the ground. He filled his pockets with hand grenades and in addition carried only his officer's pistol and a bayonet. His men fired and threw hand grenades continually to divert the enemy's attention from him, while he crept forward.

He did not see any guerrilla until he had crawled nearly a hundred metres on his sore elbows and knees. The guerrilla fighter had not detected Salnikov because of the distracting fire and exploding hand grenades. Salnikov passed ten metres behind him and turned towards him.

The guerrilla must have thought Salnikov was a colleague as he approached from behind. The guerrilla pointed, without looking at him, while whispering something to him, which he did not understand. Salnikov crept up to the guerrilla with his bayonet raised and saw the white in his violent eyes as he turned just at the moment Salnikov's bayonet slashed into his neck. He screamed harshly like a mule stuck by a sword. Another guerrilla only a few metres away suddenly rose astonished and directed his gun against Salnikov. Salnikov had not seen him and momentarily he was quite sure he would be killed.

Suddenly the guerrilla fell forward, as he was shot in the back by several of Salnikov's men. The Russians had seen the guerrilla stand up among the rocks, a perfect target, and all of them had fired at the same time. Salnikov sent his observant men many thanks as he advanced again.

It was as Salnikov rounded a large rock, fully alert, with the pistol ready in his hand, that he saw a grotesque sight that made his stomach turn.

He saw two huge, black-bearded guerrilla fighters about to behead two wounded Russian soldiers that lay helpless on the ground. A massive machete swung through the air while the guerrilla uttered a barbaric cry. Salnikov believed he heard the sound of the machete through the air before it hit the soldier, sounding like a pumpkin being halved. The soldier's head rolled across the ground like a football, while the blood splashed from his wide-open neck. The other guerrilla's machete was swinging towards the second soldier's neck when Salnikov shot. The guerrilla tumbled forward and the razor sharp machete missed the neck by barely a millimetre. The first guerrilla was taken by complete surprise and was not able to react before Salnikov placed a bullet in his skull.

The second Russian soldier was the giant sergeant Lapin. He had been struck twice by bullets and by a large quantity of fragments from grenades. A considerable amount of blood covered the ground. He was completely unable to move, but he was still remarkably conscious. Lapin looked with an ironic grin at the loose head of his colleague and the dead guerrillas lying in a bloody mess that resembled the gory deck of a universally hated Norwegian whaler.

"Sir, you saved my head, but a lot of excellent vodka seems still to have been wasted in my blood on the ground," he suddenly said sarcastically.

A squadron of Hind helicopters arrived shortly afterwards and quickly finished Salnikov's job with their speedy machine cannons and air-to-ground missiles. The helicopters also cleared the situation at the left side of the valley where the other rescue-group had been caught up in positional warfare with the guerrillas.

It was from Lapin that Salnikov had borrowed money before he went on his trip to the Mediterranean. Lapin felt he owed Salnikov his life and had unquestioningly given him all his savings – or all the money he cautiously had not invested in vodka, he had said tersely.

Lapin had been only 17 years old when he started his regular army career. "I started on this foolish career only to become a professional killing machine without a brain and with only irrational feelings, before I was dry behind my ears," he used to say, although sometimes he would add nostalgically, "I really had no other choice." There were not many other alternatives for a poor, homeless, young boy, apparently without any future other than remaining in poverty, perhaps mixed with criminality and prison.

Except for the expense of the vodka, Lapin had always saved all his wages during the 30 years he had been in the army. He had no family and he had never been married, so no wife had spent his money, which anyway had never been of any importance to him.

What's outside the army camp's borders doesn't matter except for women and vodka, was another of his regular remarks. Lapin got everything he needed in the army – food and accommodation. He was very popular among the man-hunting women, who fought for his favours and were therefore always available for him. To get Lapin horizontal was a popular goal of the boasting women in the sauna.

Lapin did not ask for more details concerning the weapons delivery than he considered absolutely necessary to accomplish his part in the assignment, and he completed everything perfectly in accordance with Salnikov's instructions.

"The less I know the better," he once said to Salnikov. "Less would be exposed if anything goes wrong and I'm detected."

For his own part, Lapin gave full assurance that he would never disclose anything, even if he was exposed to physical torture, but he was not sure about all these drugs they used to make reluctant people talk. Because of this, he had obtained a cyanide capsule, which he always carried with him – just in case.

Salnikov had in Lapin a remarkable partner and together they made an exceptionally dangerous, but effective team.

Lapin had been in the Ukraine several times for reconnaissance, preparation and organisation of the weapons transport route. As a cover-up, Salnikov often sent him to the Ukraine concerning legal weapons exports and training assignments on these weapons. He had made connections with reliable railway workers and even a couple of lorry drivers, during these visits. To be sure all the people chosen were totally reliable, Lapin had simply chosen people who hated the Russians with their whole heart, and had relatives or ancestors who had fought on the German side against communist Russia during the Second World War. These were people, if they survived the war, that Stalin deported to Siberia or simply shot, as he did to more than twenty million other Soviets.

Lapin had also been in Geneva and Istanbul. In Geneva he had arranged bank accounts for his new partners in Ukraine. The journey to Switzerland had been made by car during one of the instructional periods for the Ukrainian army.

As a Russian hero, he did not have to worry about being pursued by Russian police agents, although he always carefully took all necessary precautions against such. The Russian Secret Police probably believed he was too stupid to represent any political risk, and the fact that he might take part in a large-scale sale of the depot's weapons never entered their minds. If he was out of their control for a while, they only believed he was desperately hunting for women to fill up and vodka bottles to empty.

Lapin brought a considerable amount of US dollars back to the Ukraine from Switzerland, hidden in his car. The money was used to prepay his new partners. Each partner also received half a number code of an account in the Central Swiss Credit Bank. On completion of their assignment, the remainder of the code would be made available to them, in order to withdraw their payments. All the bank accounts contained the necessary money for the partners to live the rest of their lives in any Western country. Some of them already dreamed of palm trees, beaches, rum bottles, steel drums and the coloured, limbo dancing, prurient women of the Caribbean.

The partners received no information about what kind of goods were to be transported. They did not want any information either, because they knew the risk would increase proportionally to their knowledge.

Lapin had also informed the partners he had formed death squads to kill anyone who did not fully co-operate, or who tried to get unnecessary information or give information to third parties or the authorities. For safety reasons, the partners were fully convinced they would be watched very closely till the business was accomplished. They were also completely convinced the huge giant of a man in the Russian major's uniform, entirely covered with highly prized decorations, was an extremely dangerous person to cheat.

It was quite correct that Lapin had formed two independent death squads to kill all potentially unreliable staff members. The death squads had very soon eliminated two people. Lapin told the squads to take care of these people who had made suspicious movements, but had no connections directly to the weapon transport. This assignment was given to the squads primarily to test them and to secure their total reliability. He informed all the other partners about the elimination of the two people to show what would happen to them if they did not follow his orders.

From Geneva, Lapin had made a return flight by Swiss Air to Istanbul in Turkey. He was not used to travelling like a free man in a free country and behaved somewhere between a lunatic maniac and a horny tourist, in addition to acting like an experienced businessman. He fucked at least five dark-skinned, lustful, Turkish women. Still, he managed to visit the ancient sultans' residence with the harem section, to look at the sultans' treasures, to visit the famous Istanbul Bazaar, the large Blue Mosque and other attractions.

Lapin contacted a small shipping company, which regularly transported goods between Odessa and Istanbul. The shipping company was situated on the European side of the Bosporus Strait. He ordered a shipment consisting of two containers, which he wanted to dock in Istanbul, without any customs clearance either at the Odessa or Istanbul ends. He said he would travel himself, incognito, with the goods. The cost, of course, rose greatly because of his conditions, but he believed it would be a fairly safe arrangement.

In connection with ordinary business, he also made

agreements with six different warehouses, spread around both sides of the Bosporus Strait. The Scotsmen's goods would be stored on the European side of the Strait and the Arabs' would be stored on the Asian side. He needed four different warehouses because he would transport the goods from one warehouse to another with lorries from different companies to cover his tracks if something unforeseen should happen.

6

The telephone rang shrilly in William Wallace's modern office complex, on the top of the new office building in Glasgow's business centre. Wallace was working as a self-employed consultant on economic and legal inquiries from trading and industrial companies. He had established his company, Wallace Consulting, nearly fifteen years earlier. Today, thirty-five skilled people were on the company's pay roll. The employees were mainly experienced economists and lawyers. The company had prospered and Wallace was working day and night.

Wallace was forty-seven years old and married to the woman he had met during his first year as a student at Cambridge, where they both took their degrees in business and administration. Since then they had had five children, three boys and two girls and were still surprisingly deeply in love, their friends said.

After graduating from Cambridge, Wallace studied for two years at Harvard in the United States, where he gained an excellent Masters Degree in economics. Later he went to the law school at the University of Edinburgh to obtain the right to act before the Inner House and the Outer House of the Court of Session, the civil parts of the Scottish judicial system. At the same time he worked part time as economic consultant for a local finance company.

Wallace was dark blond and a couple of inches taller than

the average. From his behaviour and attitude the first impression was of a much younger man than he was. He had a full beard and was a little grey at the temples. That made him look a lot more distinguished and skilled, which was excellent for business, his colleagues said. He was muscular, but not fat, although his wife sometimes remarked that he had some kilograms to spare around his stomach. To which he always replied laughingly that they were muscles that had dropped as a normal part of the ageing process.

In his youth Wallace had been very athletic and he boasted he could still easily lift a six stone weight above his head without any trouble. He was a lot quicker than the average for his age at running and he participated enthusiastically in different Japanese fighting sports. He also practised gun and pistol shooting frequently, activities he had started when he had been in the Special Air Service – SAS. Wallace had been injured and decorated with the Victoria Cross as a hero during the Falklands War. He left the SAS afterwards and was enlisted as a major in the unit's reserve force.

When the Argentinians invaded the Falklands on the second of April 1982, the Argentinian Marines and Special Forces met almost no resistance from a rather small force of British Royal Marines, stationed on the islands. The British governor of the islands took the most logical and practical alternative considering the superiority of the invading forces. He surrendered quickly and unconditionally. Afterwards, the Argentinians prepared the defence of Port Stanley and the largest settlements on the islands against possible future British counter attack.

Troops from the British Special Boat Squadron, called the SBS, and the SAS to which Wallace belonged, landed secretly on the islands only three days after the invasion with the intention of reconnoitring and carefully investigating all Argentinian movements. These special troops had only light hand weapons and were completely dependent on their field-expertise to operate and survive. They looked for suitable targets for future British actions, for instance, targets where cannon fire from Harrier planes and warships could later be aimed. They also studied alternative locations for the British landing forces. Wallace participated in this action as captain and as one of the leaders from the very beginning.

The reports from Wallace and his companions led the British landing forces to select the beaches by San Carlos Water as a landing site – a place where the Argentinian forces had not anticipated an attack nor had made any preparations for defence against one. The British quickly gained the necessary bridgehead for further advancement in the battle, even though the Argentinians constantly attacked them from the air during the first few days. The British further knew it was vital to destroy the Argentinian air force and therefore the SAS was commanded to destroy the enemy air base at Pebble Island.

It was dark when the SAS force approached the base. The Argentinians had posted guards surrounding it. These guards were supposed to be constantly on full alert to protect the base from sudden attacks, but the rainy weather and the dark night of late autumn in the southern hemisphere greatly blunted their alertness.

The SAS forward attack squad advanced with great caution towards the parking area of the Argentinian Mirage fighter planes. Captain Wallace crept close to his colleague, Captain McPride. They were both considered by their superiors as outstandingly skilful and were therefore specifically chosen to take part in this very important British commando raid.

"Don't you see the bloody half-hidden machine-gun entrenchment or something like that over there, to the left – at two o'clock?" – the exhausted Wallace suddenly whispered to McPride and pointed, as they wriggled along towards their previously agreed attack positions. "I can clearly observe something odd there – against the horizon."

McPride placed his night binoculars to his eyes and studied the terrain cautiously. The night binoculars magnified the scanty light forty thousand times.

After a short silence he whispered apprehensively: "You are damned right, William. You must see like a hawk in the dark. I can see one helmet moving, but there seem to be at least another four helmets just above the sand walls. They must be sleeping. They have a machine-gun. Hell – I advise not disturbing them – these bloody bees – they are too well tactically situated. If they start to sting with that buzzing machine-gun, the entire base will be awake and we will all probably be killed immediately. I therefore suggest we move further to the right with lightning speed."

The squad moved quickly and silently to increase the distance between them and the newly detected machine-gun entrenchment and to establish alternative ground for fast withdrawal, after the mission was completed.

If the detected entrenchment were still in operation when they retreated, they would be in big trouble. Therefore two soldiers were sent back to destroy it from the rear with bazookas, simultaneously with the commencement of the attack.

Fifteen minutes later the squad arrived at the planned attack location, within reachable distance of the parked fighter planes. They arranged themselves in horizontal positions on the ground, spread at about ten metre intervals and utilised the terrain as best as they could to obtain some cover. Each of them instantly aimed his bazooka towards the dark shadows of the French produced Mirage fighter planes on the airfield. Wallace, on the left flank, targeted the left plane and the rest of the planes were allocated successively among the men, to the last one on the right side. All the men carried several bazookas. They extended them and raised their sight equipment ready for immediate launch when the attack signal was given.

Around the air base other SAS squads had also taken up positions to create diversionary activity to aid the forward squad's escape after they had finished the attack. All the British SAS troops were by now established in their planned positions and waited restlessly and apprehensively for the appointed time for the attack to start. The attack would start when Wallace fired the first bazooka.

The SAS soldiers, Duncan Moore and Steve Bryce, who had been ordered to demolish the newly detected machine-gun entrenchment, had moved effectively, completely silent and undetected, into a well-covered position higher up the slope and could look directly into the entrenchment approximately three hundred metres below.

The entrenchment was dug into the muddy ground and was almost invisible at that distance. It must have been dug that evening, after dark had covered the landscape, otherwise it would obviously have been detected during the British reconnaissance of the area.

If the Argentinian soldiers in the entrenchment had fulfilled their duty completely responsibly and correctly, kept awake and guarded with care, as they were supposed to do, they would doubtless have prevented the entire British raid against the air base.

The machine-gun entrenchment was an enormous threat

to the forward squad. Therefore it had to be destroyed immediately the attack started, because it could, theoretically, reach nearly the complete squad ranged about in the open terrain.

It was also not known what types of weapons the Argentinians had in the entrenchment in addition to the machine-gun that had been observed. If they had, for instance, ordinary gun grenades, RPG-7's or something similar, their threat would undoubtedly be tremendous.

One British SAS squad was allocated especially to an attack on the air base buildings and the neighbouring Argentinian defence arrangements. Other squads were in withdrawn positions to cover the forward squad's retreat. Everybody was in place and only waited anxiously with their fingers on the triggers, for the first bazooka to be launched.

Wallace suddenly pressed the trigger. The bazooka fizzled from the aluminium catapult towards the Mirage and rammed home perfectly. The fighter-plane exploded instantly in a sea of flames. The black night's silent peace was broken. Lights from the weapons and the explosions immediately lit up the scene like fireworks on New Year's Eve in New York. The bazookas destroyed plane after plane in only a few seconds. Eleven Argentinian fighter planes were completely destroyed and the flames licked into the black starless sky.

It was after the planes were destroyed that Wallace became aware of splintered stones that hailed down on them as streams of bullets hit the surrounding ground and ricocheted.

"Keep down and stay under cover. The machine-gun entrenchment on the left is still operational," McPride cried loudly.

Wallace thought in sheer disbelief that McPride must

have cried impulsively. He could not believe anyone would not take cover automatically, regardless of orders or warnings, when deadly bullets whistled over their heads.

The Argentinian machine-gun operator in the entrenchment saw none of the British attackers, because of their low positions in the surroundings as they tried to avoid making silhouettes against the horizon. He only aimed randomly in the direction of the enemy as he observed the launch of the bazookas. He fired desperately, in an extremely fast tempo and seemed just to puke bullets hoping some of them might find a useful target. It was a very dangerous situation for the British.

The Argentinian machine-gun position gained precious seconds to execute its deadly task, only because of a fatal malfunction of the bazooka that should have destroyed it simultaneously with the commencement of the attack. It was quite impossible to stop this strategically well-placed machine-gun with hand weapons alone. The distance was too great and the Argentinians had taken cover in the bottom of the entrenchment. Maybe the Argentinians, in addition, also had some kind of underground cover.

Moore prepared another bazooka and launched it towards the entrenchment, while Bryce targeted the entrenchment as quickly as possible with his sniper rifle, but without any success. The missile missed the target by many metres. The detonation could be observed to the left of the entrenchment, as it threw stones and dirt into the air, lit up by a red and white flash. Nevertheless, it at least made it impossible for the machine-gun operator to continue the bullet stream towards the British, as he lost his night vision. The squad was spared for some seconds, but then the first gun grenades left the entrenchment in the direction of the British. The situation suddenly became even more precarious.

Wallace, McPride and their comrades in the forward squad, pressed their heads against the cold, muddy ground and hoped for a miracle to happen. Men with Christian beliefs prayed what they believed to be their last prayer. Others only hoped that fortune might smile on them once more. Everybody's thoughts went to their families and life back home, to incidents and unimportant matters.

I should have painted the bedroom before I left for the Falklands; the colour is dreadful. The damned gears of my son's mountain bike should have been repaired. Oh, I hate that neighbour because he cut down the oak between our houses.

Many wonder what is a man's last thought and as many are surprised to hear what the research psychiatrists reply. Absolutely non-important matters can be a man's last thoughts.

The squad had no chance to move or to make any positive attempt to resolve the desperate situation. They were completely trapped and entirely dependent on their colleagues' success in destroying the machine-gun entrenchment to get out of their desperate position.

Wallace had also frighteningly discovered that the gunfire did not come from only one direction against their exposed position. They were in addition under heavy fire from another machine-gun entrenchment on the right side. He did not see the muzzle flame on that side, because a low rock in the terrain luckily protected him. It was about half a metre high and approximately four to five metres from him. He could, however, feel the hail of stone splinters, dust and mud every time the bullets hit the top of the rock.

Therefore he concluded the enemy's position to the right would eliminate all the squad's possibilities of withdrawal, even if their machine-gun entrenchment to the left had been destroyed. He knew the men lying to the left of him were entirely exposed to the Argentinian machine-gun entrenchment to the right and would be wiped out once the enemies got sight of them. He also knew there was nobody to destroy that enemy position.

Moore and Bryce, who he had commanded, if they still were operative, could possibly destroy the enemy position on the left flank. Maybe they had been killed? Terrible thoughts suddenly filled his mind with great fear, but in the depths of his soul he still hoped they only had been delayed. He had observed the explosion of the bazooka in the neighbourhood of the machine-gun's muzzle flame. It might have been they had only missed the entrenchment. If they had been killed, or prevented from finishing their assignment, the exposed squad had surely only seconds, or at best minutes, until their certain deaths.

If Moore and Bryce had somehow been delayed in destroying the entrenchment on the left flank, Wallace considered the squad's only chance would be if he could destroy the other, on the right. He was the only one of the squad who had the slightest chance of moving from his position, but he did not know for how far.

It was Moore's third bazooka, which finally destroyed the machine-gun entrenchment in front of him and stopped the deadly chattering machine-gun and the constant fire of gun-grenades. The enemy's entrenchment had, until then functioned long enough for it to have had the possibility of killing all the British in the forward squad.

*

Wallace, satisfied, observed the demolition of the entrenchment, as Moore's bazooka missile touched down perfectly and exploded with a bright flash. He thanked his lucky stars at least a couple of times, before he started, without any further hesitation, to move forward. He did not know how many of his men had survived the Argentinian bombardment until now, but he waved with his hand to signal he was moving towards the other entrenchment and that they had to remain quietly in their positions. He did not wait for any reply as this might possibly disclose their positions, if they waved in return or gave any physical signs.

Wallace crept forward about fifty metres before he reached an old fence, which ran parallel with the landing field. He made himself as inconspicuous as possible and moved along it quickly, all the time aware of not creating any silhouette against the horizon or lighter background – a silhouette which could be seen from any direction. He could possibly be detected from both the entrenchment, which he planned to capture, and by all the Argentinians deployed around the area in various defence facilities constructed during the two months since they had arrived on the island. He had to choose a middle way considering the risk of being detected, and move as quickly as possible. It was like balancing on a knife-edge with potential death on either side if he in some way failed. He had to take cover twice and wait for some minutes, when the Argentinians sent up magnesium flares.

Wallace had moved four hundred metres along the old fence when he met a ditch in the ground, which crossed the fence at right angles. It was not deep and it had probably been abandoned by a stream which had found a new course thousands of years ago.

Wallace followed the ditch upwards for about a hundred and fifty metres, when he suddenly realised he was forty metres behind the entrenchment. There was now nothing to hide behind. It was a quite open stretch to where the Argentinians had hastily dug in. They had chosen the site with the utmost care. Wallace understood immediately that if the enemy had kept better watch, the British would never have had a chance of completing the raid. The Argentinians' officers were obviously smarter than their private soldiers. The soldiers were probably fed up with being on this goddamned cold, deserted island in the middle of the southern Atlantic. They were probably only too pleased when the British finally came and threw them out so they could return to their tango bars and big beef oxen on Argentina's huge pampas.

The Argentinians had traditionally never been interested in what happened in the rest of the world, and that habit would not change overnight because some crazy politicians had suddenly decided that the Falklands should be their country's property. However, these same politicians probably were more concerned about the partition of the Atlantic, and the islands' territorial rights to the ocean in accordance with the international regulations, than the cold, unpleasant, bleak islands themselves.

Wallace was presented with a very difficult choice. Should he run openly towards the entrenchment firing his small M16A1 machine pistol with only thirty shots in the magazine, or should he try to creep towards it and throw a couple of hand-grenades? The first choice would obviously lead to certain death and it was possible he would not succeed at all if the Argentinians were observant and quick on the trigger. The other choice would give him a chance of survival if he was lucky and was able to creep close enough to throw hand-grenades without being detected. If he was detected before he came close enough, his attempt would be completely useless and he would lose his life without helping his comrades at all.

He chose the latter, because if he succeeded, he would

be quite sure his comrades could easily escape from the trap. The first alternative gave no guarantee at all because he would immediately be detected and the entire result of the action would depend on how many Argentinians he could kill before he was killed himself. Without wasting any more time, Wallace crept as silently as possible towards the entrenchment with a split-drawn hand-grenade in his right hand and the unsafe machine pistol in the other hand.

The Argentinians seemed to have detected something in the other direction. To Wallace's unexpected luck, that eagerly occupied all of them. A soldier with night binoculars in one hand pointed and directed the machine-gun operator with the other. He must have been the entrenchment's commanding sergeant. Gun-grenades were fired continuously by two soldiers at the edge of the entrenchment. One soldier talked on an old-fashioned field telephone.

Wallace was by now only about twenty-five metres away from the entrenchment. – Not a great distance for a hand-grenade thrown from a standing position, but much too far to throw from a lying position. Wallace decided to chance some additional metres before he threw the grenades.

He had reached nearly three metres further when the Argentinians at the airfield fired another magnesium flare. Wallace saw it as it was on its way up into the sky, where it would turn and light the whole area with an intense bright light for several seconds, while hanging from a small parachute as the magnesium burned. The flare was shot in the direction of the trapped squad. It would expose both him and his comrades who lay completely wide open on the wet, unpleasant plain. There was now no more time to hesitate. They would undoubtedly all be killed within a few seconds, if he did not act quickly.

Wallace rolled silently onto his back, placed the machine pistol on his chest and speedily removed the split-pin from another hand-grenade. He carefully removed the handgrips from both grenades to be sure they did not fall to the ground and make a noise when he threw them. He counted slowly, one, two, three, four, before he threw both the grenades as hard as he was able backwards over his head. He made a noise when he threw, and more noise when he rolled back around and pressed his face against the ground protected only by his helmet.

Suddenly he heard the hammering of an automatic weapon. The bullets peppered the ground around him and he felt a searing pain in his left arm and shoulder, before he heard the hand-grenades detonate. He was hit in his left thigh by a fragment from one of his own hand-grenades. One of them had detonated on the ground just in front of the entrenchment, but the other detonated in the air above as planned. His wounds did not prevent him moving towards the entrenchment for an inspection, although the blood poured from his arm, shoulder and thigh. He could confirm with satisfaction that his grenades had fully completed the task. He thanked his lucky stars once more, and without any waste of time drew the signal pistol, which was fastened to the back of his bandolier and shot a green coloured signal.

All the SAS commando soldiers recognised the special colour and withdrew immediately from their positions as soon as the Argentinian magnesium light had dimmed.

Wallace was badly hurt, but he managed somehow to force his way back to the appointed assembly point, where he was taken care of. He confirmed the success of the raid. Not a single British soldier had been killed and only three men including himself, had been wounded.

His comrades carried Wallace the three kilometres to the Sea King helicopter's pick-up point. He was flown directly to a hospital-ship and afterwards sent back to England, where he recovered completely after a couple of months.

Later, he was awarded the Victoria Cross for his honourable, unselfish and exceptional service, saving his colleagues from certain death with little regard for his own safety. Half a year later, he was discharged from the SAS with honour as a British hero.

The history of Scotland had always been an extremely strong passion of Wallace since he was a young schoolboy in primary school, running around in a blue blazer, grey trousers and the red and blue striped tie of his school uniform. It might have been his ancient Scottish name *William Wallace* that had started this life-long passion.

Sir William Wallace had been a Scottish patriot who led the struggle of a combined Scottish nation against England in the last years of the thirteenth century. He destroyed an English army at Stirling in 1297 and reinstituted Scottish rule after John de Baliol's army was completely crushed at Dunbar by the English King Edward, two years before. King Edward led a large army into Scotland the year after Wallace's victory and destroyed the Scottish army at Falkirk. After his defeat, Wallace started guerrilla warfare against the English, who finally caught him in 1305 and executed him.

Nearly seven hundred years later it seemed as if Wallace wanted revenge for the English killing of his Scottish namesake. He passionately wanted to throw the English out of Scotland and to see his country completely separate and independent. Wallace considered himself a Highlander of pure Celtic blood and he retained a strong feeling for his clan. He could speak the Scottish form of Gaelic fluently. Not many Scotsmen had a complete command of the ancient Gaelic language. As a true nationalist, he wanted

Hadrian's Wall, constructed by the Roman emperor Hadrian in the second century, to be Scotland's border with England. The rampart was constructed as protection against Caledonia, the old name of Scotland. Hadrian's Wall runs from the Solway Firth to the mouth of the River Tyne. Wallace considered his company only as a cover for his real activities. He had been working secretly for a free and independent Scotland from the time he left secondary school.

The switchboard's redheaded, young, female operator answered the shrill telephone politely: "Wallace Consulting – can I help you?"

"This is Mister Smithfield, and I'm calling concerning a loan," a voice said sharply at the other end of the line.

The voice wanted to talk to the managing director William Wallace immediately. It was very important. The switchboard transferred the telephone call that came from London to Wallace's personal secretary who listened to the repeated story, before she put the call through to Wallace, who was alone in his office. The voice presented himself again as Mister Smithfield, a code Wallace knew.

"The financial problem can be solved, if your client accepts an increase on the annual interest by one per cent over the top rate."

Wallace did not know the voice, but as he knew the code, he asked: "Are you really sure?"

"Not really sure, but eighty per cent," the voice answered quickly.

There were further safety procedures to avoid any mistakes, and Wallace asked: "How much of the necessary loan is offered, and how is it separated?"

"Sixty five per cent at the lowest rate and another twenty

at the top rate. That should be exactly ninety per cent," the voice stated.

"No, that makes only eighty five per cent," Wallace replied quickly.

"OK," the voice said, "I just had to inform you."

The voice was disconnected without further ado and Wallace was left holding a droning telephone receiver in his hand. He knew he had to travel to Geneva at once.

To travel to Geneva was an ordinary affair for an economic consultant. He would apparently visit the Central Swiss Credit Bank in Geneva concerning the loan he worked with for the Scottish Standard Group – the SS Group, the one he had not succeeded in obtaining from banks in the United Kingdom. The Swiss bank had a different way of calculating their risks to cover loans. To take a loan in Switzerland would of course be more expensive and risky than one from a British bank. There would be a considerable risk of loss, dependent on the future exchange rate between British and Swiss currency, as the debtor had its income mainly in British currency while the creditor had to be paid in Swiss currency.

The SS Group was a very old, large Scottish industrial producer of steel castings for large buildings and for the offshore oil industry. The oil industry in the North Sea had, since the middle of the seventies, created more than a hundred thousand jobs in Scotland. The Group had been responsible for the creation of many of these jobs.

Sir James Smollett had established the company ninety-five years ago, as a small building assemblage, in Glasgow. During the following years the company had taken over and started up small shipyards in Scotland and in various British territories around the world. Although many of these shipyards had been sold during the years after the Second World War, the company still ran shipyards in Edinburgh, Malta and Singapore. After the discovery of oil in the North Sea, the company had grown to be one of the largest offshore suppliers in Scotland.

The English bank, National London Bank – NatLon, which boasted in the media of being the largest bank in the United Kingdom had refused to extend their involvement in the SS Group. The Group's free assets did not provide the necessary collateral for the loans. The bank's main office in London had so replied to Wallace Consulting's exact and complete application for a loan. The bank's local representative had explained the refusal in another way. The bank was mostly concentrating its financial activity on small businesses and wanted to spread its risks on many small businesses rather than on a few large ones. The SS Group was too large to be considered as a small business.

The bank's local representative did not say what Wallace thought: English banks' unofficial policy was not to spill money into Scottish industries. Their policy was to keep the money in England and only run minimum activities in Scotland for the sake of appearances. English banks were only working hard to get Scottish saving accounts. This was to drain Scotland of capital to be used in capital hungry England.

Wallace also knew an additional reason concerning the refusal of the application for the loan. One of NatLon's other customers, an English company, was the SS Group's biggest competitor in a particular part of the off-shore market. Therefore Wallace considered the English bank's refusal was pure sabotage against Scottish industry.

The SS Group employed more than seven thousand people, mainly in the Aberdeen, Edinburgh and Glasgow areas. The company was one of the fundamental enterprises in these areas. The board pretended to consider itself betrayed by English banks, especially because of the company's local importance. Similar applications had also been made to other English banks, but all of them had refused. For that reason the board had come to a conclusion which they intended to make public in all the largest Scottish newspapers through an interview with the company's chairman, about the future of Scottish industry. The chairman, Sir Walter Bruce, stated that the English banks did not care at all about Scottish industry or Scotland's part of the United Kingdom's total economic development. Even the Scottish part in recent years had grown considerably more than England's and Scotland had become more and more important for the United Kingdom's economy.

The oil activities in the North Sea were, of course, the main reason for the high growth in Scotland compared to that in England. Scotland alone could easily develop a strong economic situation, similar to that in Norway, just two hundred miles away – on the other side of the North Sea.

All members of the SS Group's board were members of different Highland clans. They all had pure Scottish backgrounds and they were all co-conspirators in William Wallace's Scottish independence activity.

The company did not need any more capital for its activity. The company had one of the most brilliant economies of all Scottish industry. For years there had been a considerable under-valuation of the company's assets. The concealed assets were enormous. The real value of the company was unknown by anyone, except for the initiated. The refusal from NatLon to give a loan, though the bank had been the company's main backer for more than twenty years, made it necessary to change bankers. That was the real intention for the unrealistic loan application.

The SS Group was going to put up an amount of fifteen million US dollars. The company was, in fact, the financier of the weapons deal in Saint Tropez with Colonel Salnikov. For that reason, the company needed to change its main financial partner. It would be too large a risk to have a financial partner with access to the company's accounts, who knew its historical background. Although NatLon mostly used young, inexperienced economic experts, they might accidentally detect and question any serious alterations in the economic structure of the company in the course of their continual analysis.

The company also had to contrive a believable reason to explain to the shareholders the drastic change of structure in addition to the exchange of financial partners. The reason for the company's turnabout was concealed beneath the loan refusal and consequent necessary adjustments.

The economic adviser, William Wallace, had devised a perfect plan to complete the arrangement. The twelve members of the board owned fifty-one per cent of all shares in the SS Group. They therefore controlled the majority of the shares.

Three of the company's board members established a new holding company, which they called the Scottish Standard Holding – the SS Holding. All members of SS Group's board bought shares in SS Holding according to their percentage of the shares in the SS Group. Afterwards all the members of the board sold all their shares in SS Group to SS Holding. The three founders of SS Holding had, after the transaction, in addition, forty nine per cent of the shares of SS Holding unnecessary for controlling the company. These forty nine per cent were sold to third parties at beneficial prices.

In this way, the company board of the SS Group raised nearly half of the value of their shares in cash without losing any control of the company and retained original ownership. To cover the utilisation of the money, and to prevent tax losses, the three founders of SS Holding moved to Spain.

According to the Common Market's rules, a member of a company board in a company registered in the United Kingdom could live within any country of the Common Market. In Spain the company board members did not register as ordinary residents. They only registered a *Número de Identificación de Extranjero – n.i.e.* In this way they were not liable to pay taxes in Spain or to declare the amounts received for the sale of their shares. They had to live in Spain for a maximum of six months a year, less a day, and they had to live a minimum of two days in a third country, the rest of the time they could live in the United Kingdom as usual, if they wanted.

The money the founders of SS Holding received for the shares was deposited in different Swiss banks. From these banks they transferred fifteen million US dollars to an account in the Central Swiss Credit Bank. From this account they transferred money to Salnikov's account in accordance with the agreement on the delivery of the weapons entered into by their representative, McPride.

7

The autumn and winter had been windy and bitterly cold in Russia that year. In the colder parts of Siberia the temperature had already been close to minus forty degrees Celsius.

Salnikov prepared another journey to western Europe to collect the necessary money for the weapons delivery and to agree the final arrangements with his customers. This time he had decided to travel entirely incognito on a false passport, so as not to risk any further investigations. He considered a second journey would be highly suspicious and quite impossible to cover with any reasonable excuse, and would therefore automatically lead to a full investigation by the Russian Secret Police.

On the first day of February, Salnikov left for Geneva. He chose to stay in a small hotel, about two hundred metres above Lake Geneva, in the neighbourhood of the well-known Hilton hotel. It was a cheap, anonymous hotel. He could see only dirty back yards of the neighbouring old houses from his window. He had registered in the hotel as an ordinary Russian tourist, on his false passport.

Geneva was not presenting itself at its very best at this time of year. Cold winds swept down from the Alps and made everybody feel frozen to the bone. White frost mist rose from the lake. Snowflakes whirled in the air, fastening onto the clothes of everybody who moved around in the frozen streets of the commercial Swiss city. The buildings had a white hoarfrost cover, which made the city ghostly and strange. Only those who had to be, were out in this dreadful weather.

Salnikov hastened, shivering and red in the face from the extreme frost, with his coat collar wrapped tightly up to his ears, while his breath showed white – like smoke from a large Havana cigar. He was on his way to the Hilton hotel, alongside Lake Geneva. Constantly he looked suspiciously and nervously around to ensure there were no possible pursuers hanging on his track.

He had travelled by car to Odessa, where he had caught a plane to Bucharest. There he had changed planes and approximately an hour later, arrived in Geneva.

The same false passport he used at the hotel had brought him through the border controls. He had bought it from the rapidly growing Russian Mafia at an extremely expensive price. He knew it was dangerous to have any contact with these Mafia gangsters, but it was, however, the safest way to get a completely reliable false passport and he therefore had no alternative.

Salnikov did not know, but the passport was a real one. It was issued in the name of Dimitij Bubka, a Russian structural engineer, of about the same age and the same height as Salnikov. Bubka also looked very much like Salnikov and had the same hair colour. There was, therefore, no need to change the photo, because the chances of the border inspectors detecting any difference between Salnikov and the passport's original owner were completely unlikely.

Salnikov did not know either that Bubka had disappeared just days before he had received his false passport. Only the Mafia alone knew that Bubka had vanished completely and forever. Before Bubka had left home he had informed his wife that he must make an important business trip to eastern Siberia for his misguided company. He had told her he would not return for several weeks, and had left in a hurry. Just before his departure, Bubka had made a deal with the Mafia to lend them his passport for a large sum of money. The Mafia had, however, given Bubka quite a different fate than the one he had planned. His body would never be discovered.

Once Salnikov had landed in Geneva, he had made a telephone call to a certain number in London, one he had received from McPride during their meeting in Saint Tropez. He only repeated an agreed code and hung up. Salnikov did not know that the recipient immediately called Wallace's office in Glasgow and presented himself as Mister Smithfield, the code for Wallace's instant departure to Geneva. Salnikov did not know who he was going to meet at the Hilton hotel.

Salnikov entered the hotel's lobby and sat down against the inner wall, near the ventilation opening from which delicious hot air streamed out with maximum effect. He was still shivering visibly as the temperature of his body gradually rose. He took from his attaché case *The Financial Times*, which he had bought in a paper shop on the way to the hotel and read, or more correctly pretended to read. He did not know anything about business and hardly recognised a single name of any of the companies mentioned in the paper. He did not understand the graphs, or anything concerning the stock markets around the world. The news in the paper was for him just like something that belonged to another strange planet. He decided this would change dramatically, when he began his new role as a dollar millionaire in Spain. He was, for a while, completely occupied with these thoughts about his future and hardly noticed the man who walked across the room and suddenly sat down beside him.

Wallace had, after he received the coded telephone call in his office, immediately booked a ticket to Geneva with British Airways. The flight left early the following morning.

Wallace's body tingled as the plane approached Geneva airport. He had never felt closer to his target – a free Scotland. He would effect the cessation of the Act of Union of 1707. The Act of Union that had been created as an inappropriate result of many miserable circumstances at the time, not in accordance with the Scottish people's wishes.

The Scottish Parliament had voted itself out of existence in 1707, acclaimed by the nobility. Those were bought by the English, and did not represent the people. This resulted in the Jacobite Rebellions in the eighteenth century. First there was the rebellion led by James the Second's son, James Francis Edward Stuart, called the Old Pretender. He had surrendered to the English, after losing the battle at Preston in Lancashire.

Afterwards, his son, Charles Edward Stuart, known as the Young Pretender or Bonnie Prince Charlie, was defeated at Culloden Moor, though he previously had won three battles against the English enemy. It was the Highlanders who supported the rebellions.

After the battle at Culloden Moor, the English brutally killed all their wounded, defenceless enemies lying spread around the battlefield. They hunted the escaping, defeated, private soldiers who had survived, and killed them like flies. Afterwards, they sentenced another thousand men to death. Most of the Jacobites were Highlanders. They considered the rebellion a way to independence.

Many of the Highlanders killed were family members of

Wallace's ancestors. The story about the battle had afterwards passed from father to son. Wallace had heard about it from his father when he was only a small child. Afterwards he had hated the union with England with all his heart.

In 1934 the Scottish Nationalist Party had been founded. In latter years the party has become a significant political force in Scotland. Especially after the discovery of the enormous oil reserves in the North Sea, more and more demands for independence have been registered by the members of the party. They claim an independent Scottish Parliament. British governments had clearly refused to consider the possibility of such a one. Thus Wallace did not see any possibility of political solutions to the creation of an independent Scotland. He recognised it as a standard English habit to take advantage of other people. This was so deep-rooted, that the English even believed they had the legal right to do so.

Wallace took a taxi at Geneva airport and half an hour later he walked quickly into the Hilton's hot lobby from the cold weather outside. He could see a man sitting alone against the inner wall. He seemed to exactly fit the careful description McPride had given him before he travelled. The man was reading *The Financial Times*, which was one of the instructions agreed to make recognition possible.

Wallace sat opposite the man at the other side of the lobby for a long time, observing if there were any suspicious elements in the surroundings. After a while he decided to make contact. He went towards the man, sat down beside him and pretended to look outside at the traffic along the lake.

He said very quietly, as if he spoke to himself: "It's a lot colder in Geneva than on the Côte d'Azur."

Wallace could see the man reacted immediately. Satisfied,

114

Wallace rose without a word and left for the hotel's restaurant.

Salnikov observed the code. He waited quietly for some minutes and continued to pretend to read the paper with the utmost care, while he studied the lobby carefully to establish if anyone followed his contact. Then he also rose and headed for the restaurant. He gave his coat to the man in the cloakroom and entered the rather crowded restaurant. The hotel guests probably preferred staying inside, to running around in the cold weather to find other places to eat.

Salnikov observed the man from the lobby seated discreetly behind a large green plant arrangement, well inside. He stopped for a minute and looked around expectantly as if he were looking for a table or somebody he knew. He found nothing unusual to be afraid of, and moved further on, straight to the table behind the plant arrangement.

Wallace followed him with his eyes as he approached his table and rose politely with a broad smile and stretched out his hand for a handshake.

"Mr. Ben Ironside, I presume," he said politely, as if meeting a business partner. "I'm Willie Copperfield. I think we have a mutual friend. Do you know Mr. Antonio Gremlin?"

"Yes, I surely do. Antonio told me that the Eiffel Tower is 331 metres high," Salnikov answered smilingly with his special Russian accent.

"No, I suppose he didn't. He rather told you it is 327 metres high," William added quickly.

"That must be six metres higher than it actually is," Salnikov replied smilingly.

That was the rest of the agreed code for the meeting. Both men were now sure they had the correct man across the table. The business could begin.

Salnikov informed Wallace that everything was going

exactly according to plan, and Wallace informed him that he wanted some additional conventional weapons included in the trade.

He needed five hundred kilograms of plastic explosive and two fast machine cannons with loose, ground-based attachments, quick and easy to install, with six thousand ammunition rounds. In addition he needed thirty bazookas and fifteen AK-74 machine-guns with thirty thousand rounds. If it were possible he would also like to have fifteen pistols, each with three extra magazines and one hundred rounds.

Salnikov did not consider Wallace's request for additional conventional weapons for long before he positively confirmed, because he knew this extra delivery would not present any problem at all. The ordinary legal export to Ukraine was always loaded from the warehouses containing conventional weapons. He would need to load the wagon for the Arabs from such a warehouse and the Scottish atomic missiles had to be loaded via one of them.

Salnikov only smiled and said immediately: "These extra small candies will be delivered to you quite free, as an extra discount if you pay the bill for this lunch."

Salnikov then said he would deliver the weapons in Istanbul at an estimated date in June. He also said that the weapons would be stored in an ordinary warehouse on the European side of the Bosporus Strait and that there would be no problems in respect of tolerance about the date regarding collecting the weapons. The collectors had only to pay for additional storage time. Salnikov said he would pay for fourteen days storage when delivering the container.

"The risk of course, will increase considerably as the storage time extends. Istanbul is not a very safe city, you know," Salnikov said distinctly and smiled nostalgically.

They agreed about the place for the meeting in Istanbul in June. Their representatives would meet in the Sultan's

Palace at a certain showcase containing some of the ancient sultans' treasures.

Salnikov made a one-way flight with Swiss Air from Geneva to Cairo the day after the meeting with Wallace. He was going to meet Mustafa at the airport.

Mustafa belonged to the organisation Formation of the United States of Arabia. The organisation simply called itself the Formation. They worked establishing a close union between all Arabic Muslim states, from Syria in the east to Morocco in the west. The United States of Arabia would be equivalent to the United States of America. The Arabic world would appear together in all foreign affairs and be a power to be reckoned with.

The United States of Arabia would control seventy per-cent of all known oil reserves in the world, and be an economic super power. The planned development in the union was almost incredible. There would be no poverty, as a social security net for the population, similar to that of Scandinavia, would be established. Hospitals, schools and universities would be built and the entire population would be eligible for welfare.

Arabic banks would stimulate private enterprise with all the money necessary for the creation of new companies and improvement of old ones. Increased oil prices would secure the banks sufficient money. The intention would be to transfer some of the present industrial world's welfare to the Arab World. There would be some of the world's best-educated technical and economic people available to the companies. Foreign enterprises would be attracted to the United States of Arabia like flies to a dead dog in the heat. The union would have competitive advantages compared to

117

other parts of the world. It is a short transport distance to Europe, the world's largest market. It is also a large advantage that the time zones are similar in the union and Europe. In the future the best computers, the best television sets, the best refrigerators and the best cars, would be Arab made products.

At the moment the Formation consisted mostly of university graduates. The organisation was originally established by academics at the University of Cairo. Soon it spread to employees and students at different Arab universities. Prosperous Arab companies and private people supported the organisation strongly.

The leaders of the Formation were considered very realistic, and they were non-violent, which was unique among Arab political organisations. The leaders worked mainly for a political climate to be created that would later automatically transform the Arab world into the United States of Arabia in a peaceful way. The organisation also had members spread all over the European, American and Asian continents working secretly for the organisation's aim.

However, a violent extremist group had developed within the peaceful organisation, which often happens. The extremists were fighting for the same ideas, but they considered violence as the only possible tool to gain their aims. A consortium of five young leaders led the extremist group. Mustafa was one of them.

Mustafa was the only son of Haji Abdul, the leader of a small village south of Beirut near the Israeli border. Mustafa had attended the University of Beirut, but the civil war in Lebanon had interrupted his education, and he had instead become a full time guerrilla soldier. At university he had been turned on to the idea of the United States of Arabia and he had joined the Formation.

The civil war and the struggle against the Israelis, who

had incorporated his village in their security zone against Lebanon, had turned him into an extremely experienced and cunning fighter. He had no respect for life. He had several times narrowly escaped and survived the Israeli Army, said to be the best in the world. Once he had been the only member of a large guerrilla group to survive.

About five years earlier the Israeli Army and Airforce had undertaken a clearing sweep of their security zone following continuous Palestinian guerrilla attacks.

Mustafa and his guerrilla group, consisting of nearly thirty-five well-trained soldiers, were taken totally by surprise by Israeli fighter planes minutes after dawn on a cold, clear morning. The planes suddenly dived towards their hideout and fired dozens of air-to-ground missiles before they vanished as quickly as they had appeared. The whole incident took only a few seconds and created complete chaos among the guerrilla group. Eight of Mustafa's men were killed immediately and another four were severely wounded having no chance of survival without proper medical care, which they, of course, could never obtain.

Only minutes after the planes had disappeared, the first bazooka targeted the guerrilla group without any warning. It just seemed as if the bazooka missile came out of nowhere. It rammed the group immediately after the planes had disappeared. By now the group was completely paralysed with shellshock. Although the guerrilla group was trained how to react against such physical circumstances, no training could ever prepare for the shock effect of such a tremendous bombardment. The bazooka missile killed a further two of Mustafa's men instantly. The remainder of the men spread out immediately, and took cover, as best as they could, in the rocky terrain, surrounding the old, stone, shepherd's cottage, where the guerrillas had gathered for training.

The Israeli machine-guns started up at the same time,

rattling like hundreds of concrete mixers partially filled with stones. Under cover of darkness the Israelis had approached the cottage and settled in excellent positions. They had remained in complete silence in their hidden positions until the air attack had terminated. Then systematically and calmly they executed the terrorists whom they believed were responsible for the killings of their innocent fellow citizens, defenceless elderly people, women and children. The Israelis wanted to respond to the terror in a way the Arab terrorists knew only too well.

The Israelis did not know that Mustafa was never responsible for any attacks against children and women. Mustafa was as barbarous as the next man, but he was still equipped with a certain modicum of common morality. Mustafa was no war criminal like the Nazis, Stalin's communists and the previous Yugoslavian civil war lords. He was only a brutal, inconsiderate fighter for the future establishment of the United States of Arabia. In addition, Mustafa desperately wanted the Israelis out of Lebanon and his ancestors' village. He had, however, always accepted the Israelis' presence in Palestine. He saw the Israelis' presence as an important element of the future Arabian union's strength. The Israelis would certainly maintain the significant influence, which they held at the moment, in various Western countries, including both Europe and the USA. He believed this would strongly assist the regional economic interests and development. He was not against the idea that the Israelis had an absolute right to their own country, from which they had been driven through thousands of years of pursuit by different political and ethnic groups. The Arabian Palestinians had rights also, but they had to learn to live in peace with the Israelis.

Mustafa was convinced that only through education of the Arabs and the elimination of the large difference in living standards between the two ethnic groups could such circumstances be established. Even then there would be large problems, as there would always be illogical extremists. He determined the only solution to end the Israeli-Palestinian problem was to meld the two ethnic groups entirely together, but he understood that religion would probably create too large a difference for centuries ahead. Education and high living standards had, however, extended the tolerance levels and he maintained that intense development of education might create an improvement in the short term. To express clearly and simply his opinion about the Israeli-Arab question for some of his naive friends, he had once proclaimed in a speech that Israeli cunts tasted as well as Arab cunts. The only difference was that the Arab cunts were always bald, but he did not say if he had tested any Israeli.

The Israeli machine-guns and bazookas killed and mortally wounded another nine Arab guerrilla soldiers before the Arabs had reached adequate cover. Then suddenly the Israeli fire stopped completely. Nothing happened and the Arabs lay in anticipation, waiting for the Israelis' next move. The Israeli machine-guns, which a moment before had vomited death over the terrified Arabs, seemed to have disappeared completely, or been moved to another location.

The Israelis' next step could hardly be heard. The only sound was of high-speed bullets forcing their way through human flesh. An unknown number of Israeli professional snipers had, from positions above the cottage nearly half a kilometre away, using silencer and telescopic sights on their precision guns, picked off five more Arabs before the Arabs knew what was happening. The Israeli snipers had carefully observed the escaping Arabs when they took cover and easily targeted them.

Mustafa and two of his men had been inside the cottage when the fighter planes appeared. The first missile had exploded outside and given the men inside the cottage a second warning. The trapdoor to the basement tunnel, where weapons were hidden, was open. Mustafa knew at once the reason for the unexpected explosion outside and jumped directly down into the basement, the two other men following. He ran into the tunnel, but the last of the following men was not quick enough. The explosion of the missile that hit the cottage a few seconds later caught him. Mustafa and the other man were relatively safe in the tunnel for the next few minutes. The ruins of the cottage covered the tunnel's entrance.

There were two different escape exits, both of which ended in the hillside some fifty metres below the cottage and about forty metres apart. The tunnel's hidden escape exits could not be observed from each other. Mustafa chose the left one and his comrade the right. The escape tunnels were low and Mustafa had to crawl through most parts. He frequently lit his Ronson for orientation. He had stolen the lighter from an enemy he had previously killed. He did not smoke, but the lighter was useful, and therefore, was always in his pocket.

The escape exits had never been used before. Because the tunnel had been dug entirely from the opening in the cottage's basement, the exits could not be detected from outside. Only a small, narrow hole beside a big stone, well-hidden behind dried vegetation was at the end of Mustafa's tunnel. The hole functioned as a ventilation channel for the tunnel system. It was about ten by twenty centimetres and Mustafa had to dig himself out with a small pick that was placed just inside the tunnel opening. A barrier of tight chicken wire prevented rats and other small animals entering.

Mustafa reached the chicken wire and again lit his Ronson. He immediately saw, in the flickering gleam of the lighter-flame, a large snake's nest at the other side of the wire, in front of him. The nest seemed to be filled with dozens of dangerous poisonous snakes. Mustafa felt hopelessly trapped.

It had been silent outside the ruined cottage for more than ten minutes, but the Arabs could not move because they did not know the snipers' positions. As soon as they altered position they would clearly expose themselves to the snipers' bullets. Three of them tried to slide discreetly away, but were targeted and shot dead before they had moved more than a few metres.

A rumbling noise approached from the south. Suddenly five Israeli US made Hughes AH-64 combat helicopters rushed over the nearby hill. Seconds later the sound of the helicopters' rapid machine-guns mixed with the roar of their large rotors. The air vibrated, and the sound level increased gradually as the deadly steel birds came closer. It had become the Day of Judgement for the few remaining Arabs, who were spread across the terrain with no cover. They were as easy to target as ducks on a farmer's pond.

Naturally, some of the Arabs would not lie still just waiting for the final execution bullet. They rose, swore loudly and desperately and tried to flee. At the same moment as they rose, they became easy game for the hidden snipers, waiting like ghosts behind stones and bushes for new targets to appear in their telescopic sights. The few bushes around were all on fire and the Arabs were killed one by one. The whole area was soon cleaned of living Arabs and the helicopters swept over the area several times to look for any other life, before four of them landed, only a hundred metres away.

At the same moment as the helicopters landed, thirty camouflaged Israeli commandos rose up from their hidden positions and slowly approached with their guns trained on the execution site of the guerrilla group. When they reached the first dead Arab body, which lay with its head down, two Israeli soldiers turned him with the toe of their boots, guns at the ready. In this way they examined all the Arabs.

From one of the helicopters two Israeli soldiers came with two Giant Schnauzer dogs. One of the dogs was led to the demolished cabin. The dog soon discovered, under dust and stones, the body of the Arab who had failed to reach the tunnel opening before the missile hit the cottage. The Israelis expected a tunnel system to connect with the cottage and sure enough, only five minutes later the tunnel opening was discovered. Seconds later, five tear-gas grenades were shot into the tunnel, quickly followed by five smoke grenades issuing red smoke. The tunnel opening at the cottage had been concealed. The red smoke would soon indicate the tunnel's hidden exits. All the Israeli soldiers then waited on full alert, weapons ready for Arabs to appear from them.

Ten minutes later red smoke could be seen faintly from two spots on the hillside. More minutes went by and the smoke became thicker. Suddenly an Arab came roaring out from a hole like a bull from a burning byre. He had a chopping machine pistol in his hands, but he had no chance, and was taken out immediately by deadly bullets from at least ten Israeli guns.

*

124

Mustafa knew the Israelis would sooner or later, find the tunnel opening under the cottage. Their experience warned them of the existence of such tunnel systems in houses used by the guerrillas. Therefore Mustafa had to get out at once, before the Israelis approached, otherwise he would have absolutely no possibility of escape. He had to take a chance.

As he reckoned that most of the bushes around were on fire after the bombardment, he lit the snake's nest with his Ronson. The smoke would be seen outside, but would hopefully not be noticed among the smoke of the burning bushes and continual explosions. The poisonous snakes swarmed out of the hole immediately the dry nest flared. The smoke from the burning nest drifted into Mustafa's nose, his eyes were filled with tears and he coughed as if he were dying of pneumonia. But he tore down the chicken wire and desperately dug with the small pickaxe to widen the hole to his body size.

It took only a couple of minutes before he pushed his body through the hole into the fresh air. He did not stop but crept on down the hill like a snake, hiding under anything to hand. When the Israeli helicopters arrived he was more than five hundred metres away from the ruin of the cottage. The tears ran freely down his cheeks as he looked behind him at his comrades' desperate situation. He knew they had no chance at all. They would all be killed. The world's most effective army had made another magnificent commando attack, operating as ghosts without even showing themselves to the enemies they killed. Mustafa observed the Israelis leave southwards half an hour later in the heavily armed helicopters.

As agreed six months earlier in Venice, Mustafa met Salnikov in the arrival hall at Cairo International Airport on the evening that Salnikov arrived from Geneva. Mustafa looked more businesslike this time. He could easily be taken for an ordinary Arab businessman, who was meeting a European colleague. Salnikov was greeted like an old friend and Mustafa at once took him into Cairo Centrum traffic.

Salnikov had never experienced anything like it before. It was as hot as a baker's oven and he sweated like in a Finnish sauna. The impression of the sounds and colours was remarkable. Among the traditionally dressed old Arab women, swung modern beauties in Parisian fashions. Men were dressed in the Arabian way. Old, unshaven, toothless men sat on the pavements in dirty clothes, with their hands outstretched begging for money. More fortunate men passed them by, in suits not out of place in Wall Street in New York, or in the City of London.

Mixed with the local population were numerous tourists, who stuck out from the rest of the masses, dressed in typical tourist clothes, as they pointed and waved apathetically with their arms. Old-fashioned, rusty cars in all colours blew their horns constantly as they slowly tacked through the streets. The street sellers and shoeshine boys shouted their wares loudly. Some boys ran dangerously into the streets with rags to clean the windows of cars that stopped at traffic lights.

Mustafa and Salnikov sat in the back of a large black Mercedes, driven by a huge man with a brutish, violent look, who was silent during the whole trip. The men in the back did not talk a lot either, as their language of communication, English, was not their mother tongue.

Suddenly Mustafa said informatively: "We are finally at the end of our journey, dear friend."

The car crossed the pavement and stopped under a canopy, in front of an elegant swing door. Two commissionaires, dressed in black livery, opened the back doors on either side of the car and politely welcomed their guests to the Hotel International. A liveried porter opened the boot and took Salnikov's suitcase to the reception desk. Mustafa had ordered a suite for his Russian business partner. The two men met in the hotel's air-conditioned restaurant an hour later after Salnikov had showered off his sweat in the suite.

"Do you like the city?" Mustafa questioned.

That must be the most standard phrase every stranger hears from locals, Salnikov thought tiredly.

"Yes, but it seems very crowded and extremely hot," he replied politely.

After they had exchanged some further politenesses, Mustafa then changed the subject.

"Our trade is proceeding in accordance with the agreement, I presume?"

Salnikov smiled as a reply, and said softly: "You can reckon with collecting the delivery at the Asian side of Istanbul in June, as agreed."

The two men discussed the delivery down to the last detail for half an hour, and they agreed about how to make contact in Istanbul, while waiters ran to and from their table with delicious local dishes. After the dessert and a French cognac for Salnikov, as Mustafa did not drink alcohol, Mustafa suggested taking Salnikov to a real Arab night-club, to see professional belly dancers. Mustafa knew after receiving reports from his men who had pursued Salnikov in Spain, that the Russian was an extremely active woman hunter. Salnikov immediately accepted Mustafa's proposal with great delight.

The night-club turned out to be more like a brothel than a night-club. Mustafa had paid some of the waitresses beforehand to provide extra services to Salnikov.

"If you are in Egypt you must have a harem, don't you agree?" – Salnikov shouted to Mustafa through the smoky establishment's loud noise of talkative voices and shouting guests, mixed with the monotone of Arabian instruments playing for the lightly clad, wriggling female dancers.

The constantly woman-hunting Salnikov left the brothel with three women and experienced another delightful evening completely surrounded by beautiful, lustful, hairless Arab flesh.

After they had taken Salnikov and his load of beautiful night work to the hotel, Mustafa said quietly to the driver: "The bloody colonel's enthusiasm for women might one day be his downfall."

Salnikov bought a ticket to Rome at the airport, late the next day. When he arrived in Rome, he bought another ticket to Vienna, where he stayed the night. Next day he took the morning flight from Vienna to Odessa, where he changed back to his own identity and returned to Russia in his own old Lada. His car had been parked near Kharkiv, in a garage owned by one of his relatives.

8

Spring arrived early that year. The birds of passage had been late although they had arrived fairly close to the normal time. The Russian farmers had started the spring work in the fields half a month earlier than last year. Rusty, old Belarus tractors, with impatient farmers behind the wheels, drove back and forth on the flat fields day and night. Some older farmers used horses in their work, as their ancestors had done for centuries. They walked slowly behind the horses and seemed to have plenty of time available for their annual assignment. These farmers would probably not die of stress. The birch trees had once more become living green. The people's melancholy winter mood had changed to the optimism and confidence of summer.

At the weapons depot in Kursk, there was hardly any difference between the seasons. One day was like another. Officers and privates, who worked at the depot, often felt they rolled a rock to the top of a mountain and afterwards let it roll down again, only to roll the same rock once more to the same top, and let it roll down again – perpetually. This boring existence assisted Salnikov and Lapin during their preparations for the weapons delivery to the Arabs and the Scotsmen. Boredom had blunted the workers' common sense and they became completely unable to detect anything unusual that might occur. The different weapons, which were wanted by Salnikov's personal customers, were collected together in the same warehouse, ready to be loaded into containers on railway carriages – everything at the same appointed time.

The most difficult assignment, though, had been to get the nuclear weapons into the special stock for export, because Russia never exported any nuclear weapons.

For extra protection, the nuclear weapons were stored in very well guarded tunnels in a separate part of the depot, deep below the surface. Lapin had, on a false requisition issued by Salnikov, simply ordered three army trucks into the guarded tunnels, with three privates to drive and six others to load. They had passed through three different checkpoints, each with large, strong, steel doors and five guards. Lapin and his privates had easily loaded the trucks with missiles, warheads and separate target indicators, and afterwards returned through all the checkpoints, without any control or questions.

The difficult and dangerous assignment had been carried out as if it were quite an ordinary operation, and that was probably one of the reasons why it had been so successful. Also, not a single person at the depot would have believed that such a famous Russian hero as Major Pavel Lapin, would be a traitor to his beloved motherland. Furthermore, nobody asked Lapin any questions on days he seemed to be in a bad temper. On this day, especially, Lapin seemed to be in a really bad temper. The whole depot had heard rumours about a violent and noisy drinking party in the officers' mess the previous night. The threatening behaviour of the gigantic major just told everybody to keep far away, otherwise, they had better be prepared to wake up in the hospital, some days later, with a terrible headache.

During a later visit in the tunnels, Lapin had discreetly placed several small boxes containing plastic explosive to be activated by special remote control. Because of the protected atmosphere in the tunnels, he had made another visit there some days later, to create a link to a portable remote control unit, for detonation from outside. Lapin had also placed similar small boxes, with explosives, in the different warehouses at the depot from where they had stolen the equipment.

A goods train containing weapons for Ukraine was loaded on Saturday morning. It was loaded from the warehouse Salnikov and Lapin had chosen as their transit store. It was Saturday, and a day off for a large number of the employees. Lapin, who had no life outside the army camp, supervised the loading. He had ordered some of the most imbecilic privates to participate in the loading. He had also brought a large quantity of beer from the officers' canteen, which he distributed generously among his workmen. He had told them it was Saturday and just the time for a drink and it was an extremely hot day.

The soldiers followed Lapin's strict orders and drank deeply. The more they drank, the better their humour, though they loaded the goods perfectly, while they reduced the pile of beer bottles. The workmen handled the electrically driven loading trucks among the explosives, like circus artists.

Lapin divided the cargo between the buyers. The weapons to the Arabs were loaded in two large containers and the cargo to the Scots was loaded in a smaller container. Salnikov had issued fake consignment chits with different destinations for the three railway carriages with the stolen arms, than for the other twenty-five wagons. The three carriages would be disconnected from the rest of the train in Kharkiv. Additional fake papers were issued. These would be carried by Lapin, who would follow the cargo. Lapin would use his new partners in Ukraine to change consignments several times and lead the carriages carefully through Ukraine to Odessa, on the Black Sea.

The train left the depot at five o'clock in the afternoon.

At seven thirty a fire broke out. The fire started in a small warehouse filled with explosives. Building parts and weapon fragments leapt towards other warehouses and set them on fire when the first warehouse exploded. The other warehouses exploded, and a raging fire spread quickly through the depot. For a time the fire was considered as possible to control.

Lapin had taken cover in the shadows, behind some vehicles, and was directing the fire with the remote control.

"What the hell are you doing?"

Two sergeants had come upon Lapin from behind. He did not reply, just spun round and pulled a twenty-five centimetre long needle – a sharp screwdriver – from one of his riding boots. The sergeants were paralysed as he grabbed the nearest one by the neck and pressed the needle between his ribs. It all seemed to have happened in a single movement. The sergeant made some rattling sounds and fell dead on the ground.

The other sergeant was so astonished by the incident that he did not react fast enough. Lapin's needle hit him from beneath, under his chin and forced its way into his brain, where it moved around a couple of times, like a soup being stirred. The second sergeant was dead at once, without uttering a sound.

The needle was Lapin's favourite weapon. With it he had dispatched dozens of enemies in commando raids in previous years. He had really become an artist in handling it.

Lapin quickly carried the two bodies into the nearest warehouse, which he later blew up. The bodies were cremated and disappeared forever. The whole incident took just a couple of minutes. Then he continued his destructive work, completely unaffected by the incident.

The situation around him was absolute panic. People ran around on fire from burning objects, which had hit them from the exploding buildings. Some, entirely covered by napalm from grenades, rolled around like pigs in the mud, in completely hopeless attempts to put out the fire on their clothes and skin. Lapin stood calmly under cover from the explosions and the fire's intense heat. He continually changed the frequency of his remote control and pressed the button. Every time he pressed, another warehouse blew up. It could not be worse in hell, he thought sardonically, with a lunatic smile.

Lapin moved onward and sent the main warehouse to heaven, as a last assignment. Then he was discovered again, this time by the Lithuanian lieutenant, Dmitriy Andrianov, who had hated him deeply since he had demolished his face in a drinking bout a few months before. Andrianov was aggressive and nearly as tall and heavy as Lapin. He was a karate expert who had been forced to leave Lithuania just after the dissolution of the Soviet, because he was of Russian origin, and a known violent fighter. He stood with a large red axe in his hands and a furious grin on his face.

"I knew it had to be you, – you bloody Mongol – who is responsible for the inferno. I'll cut off your damned head."

Andrianov rushed towards Lapin with the axe swinging above his head, while he roared like a wounded lion. Lapin was quick and moved away just before the axe chipped his shoulder. Andrianov turned and raised the axe again for a second attempt. Lapin narrowly escaped again, moving around like a ballet dancer, as Andrianov swung the axe again and again, all the time roaring loudly.

"I shall kill you, you damned bastard. – I shall kill you."

As Andrianov became exhausted, Lapin got the chance that he had waited for. Andrianov swung the heavy axe slower and Lapin moved quickly aside and hit his upper arm. The axe dropped to the ground. The men immediately ran at each other, to fight for life or death. Lapin took the needle from his boot, but he was tired and losing his concentration and therefore was too late. Andrianov was an experienced fighter and executed a karate kick that hit Lapin's hand and forced the needle to drop to the ground. Andrianov's next kick hit Lapin in the stomach and, as he wavered for a moment another kick hit him in the face. Lapin fell to the ground and Andrianov kicked again, but this time Lapin managed to grab Andrianov's foot. Lapin twisted Andrianov's leg around and he fell to the ground.

Awkwardly he scrambled up and ran off crying: "Lapin is sabotaging! – It's Lapin that is responsible for the destruction of the entire depot!"

Nearly as quickly Lapin got on his feet and picked up both the axe and the needle and chased after the yelling Lithuanian. He reached him too late. Andrianov had caught up with two other officers and told them about Lapin. Lapin knew he had to kill all of them to be safe. He checked around, saw nobody else in the vicinity and ran towards the officers with the axe lifted.

They ran in different directions, like fish when a stone hits the water. Lapin had to choose, and he chose the nearest. The officer was running as if he had The Grim Reaper behind him. He probably had – but this one had a wide-bladed axe, and not a scythe. The result was, however, the same. Lapin threw the axe through the air. It spun round several times before it hit the running man in the neck. The head was chopped clean off, as if the officer had been guillotined.

Lapin turned and ran towards the second officer, the needle in his right hand ready for action. Andrianov had seen the execution of the first officer. It made him shudder. He had, however, observed that Lapin did not have the axe anymore, and he therefore ran towards the second one, to help. The latter realised he was to get help from the Lithuanian and that it was useless to try to outrun the speedy Mongol major. He stopped and took up a defensive position, like a boxer in the twenties. Lapin grinned when he saw the officer's ridiculous position. He decided not to stop, but ran towards him at full speed. The officer faltered then took a better foothold to receive the attacker. He had not read his physics lessons too well and did not know the force of an object on the move, increases with the square of its speed. Lapin maintained a phenomenally high speed. He jumped like a long-jumper and hit the officer with both his feet. The officer was thrown to the ground, as if kicked by a horse. He tried desperately to rise, but Lapin kicked his head backwards breaking his neck. The officer was suddenly joining his headless colleague, wherever he was.

Lapin had not managed to turn around after kicking the officer, before Andrianov's heavy body, also at full speed hit him. He tumbled over on the ground a couple of times before he saw Andrianov's foot trying to give him the same final kick that he had given the officer. Lapin rolled immediately backward and gripped Andrianov's foot as he kicked. Andrianov fell to the ground. Both men fought a desperate fight to get up. Lapin won. He threw himself towards Andrianov, with the needle in his hand. Andrianov was too quick. He twisted around and received the huge Mongol with both his feet in the Mongol's stomach. Lapin was thrown backwards and Andrianov now had time to regain his footing. He gripped an iron bar, which had been thrown to the ground by one of the explosions. He raced towards Lapin with the bar raised for action. Lapin sprang up, like a gymnast, and started the same ballet dance he had performed previously in avoiding the axe.

Andrianov cried out loudly and desperately: "I'll kill you – I'll kill you, you damn bastard!"

Nearly the same thing happened again. Andrianov became more and more exhausted, so when he finally hit Lapin, there was no force in his stroke. Lapin grabbed the bar and pulled it away. Andrianov was forced to let it go and the bar fell to the ground. At the same moment Lapin's needle hit Andrianov in the arm. Andrianov cried desperately, as Lapin gave him a final stab in the chest and twisted it around to mess up his inner organs. He died instantly.

Nobody had seen the incident under the cover of the burning buildings and smoke. Lapin immediately carried the bodies into the burning ruins, where they quickly would be cremated. Afterwards, he mixed with the people who desperately tried to escape the inferno.

He found the army truck where he previously had parked it. The truck could not be moved by anybody else, because he had removed the ignition distributor. He quickly installed it again and started the vehicle, drove quietly and carefully away, like a father on an ordinary Sunday outing with his family.

He stopped on a hill, where he had a clear sight of the depot, approximately ten kilometres away. As he looked at the flames and the heavy black smoke rising into the sky from the weapons depot, he calmly changed the frequency of his remote control. He pressed the button and immediately a large mushroom shaped fireball rose a kilometre into the sky. It was the remaining nuclear weapons cache, stored in the depot's tunnels, which had detonated. Lapin studied the effect, only for a moment, before starting the truck and driving in the direction of Ukraine, as if the catastrophe at the depot did not concern him at all.

Salnikov had discreetly left the weapons depot when panic ensued, during the first phase of the fire. He had an ancient Togelatti parked in the neighbourhood of the depot, which he had bought second-hand, under a false name, a week before. He changed from his uniform into civilian clothes and buried the uniform in a deep hole, after he had torn off all his decorations. If the uniform were ever discovered there would be absolutely nothing on it to be connected with him. Later, he burned the decorations elsewhere. Afterwards, he headed in the direction of Ukraine, as he had planned, for a new life of luxury.

He had a brand new false passport and a driving licence that he had bought from the Mafia. The border was crossed, unnoticed, on an old farm road. Ukraine had been a member of the Soviet Union some years earlier and the border was not so strictly guarded.

He and Lapin met, later, at an appointed site, just outside Kharkiv. They did not celebrate the dreadful events at the depot. Too many people had died. They discussed why it had all gone so wrong. The destruction had been planned to happen on a Saturday, to reduce possible casualties. The two weapons robbers had therefore, only estimated a small number of victims, hopefully none at all.

Salnikov assumed the main reason for the disaster was that the depot's fire brigade had been poorly led and organised. The leaders had been unaware of the types of explosive that were stored at the depot and therefore led the fire fighters to certain death.

"Maybe the reason for the fault was inappropriate experience and training," Salnikov said sincerely and sorrowfully to salve his rather painful conscience. "Not one of the members of the fire brigade had ever taken part in any army actions. They had probably never seen weapons in real action and therefore were justifiably terrified about them. If we had been more lucky, and everybody had undertaken their assignment properly, nobody would have been killed at all."

He did not mention, or even consider, that he had been the depot's most senior officer and was responsible for all matters, including the training of the depot's fire brigade. Lapin knew, but did not comment. Both were silent for a moment as they activated their consciences and remembered the disaster and deaths. However, death and brutality had often been experienced by both of them. Their long, rough army life and training had taken away all normal feelings and made them extremely hard and unscrupulous. The army had taught them that only the clever and competent soldier would survive. The army system was responsible for their actions; Salnikov consoled himself with these thoughts.

The two weapons thieves had previously agreed about how to follow the carriages and secure the transport to Odessa. Lapin would constantly keep in contact with the planned transport partners, while Salnikov would keep in the background and only assist if necessary. But he would have direct access to both independent death squads. Any trouble, disloyalty, or even the slightest suspicion of disloyalty, would lead immediately to execution of the transport partners without any hesitation, so as to prevent, or limit, eventual damage. The partners were kept fully aware of this constant threat, in order to secure their absolute devotion and obedience to orders. Similar procedures would also terminate anybody else who might show up and represent a potential risk concerning the transportation.

The transport went exactly according to plan, without any problems, as far as Mykolayiv. The partners worked correctly and efficiently as expected. The carriages had, unfortunately, to remain one night at the railway station in Mykolayiv, because goods trains going on to Odessa were already full that day. The carriages had, as normal, been parked at the end of the station's goods terminal. This was readily accessible to everybody. The only protection was the station's ordinary security guards that patrolled frequently.

Salnikov knew this protection was absolutely insufficient. By its very nature, routine reduced the guards' attention and any burglars could adjust their activities in accordance with the guards' regular routines. The guards could also, quite possibly, have been paid to look away, while professional thieves emptied overnight-parked carriages.

Salnikov had, therefore, discreetly parked his car in a gateway directly above the carriages. Lapin had chosen another position for his car. The two death squads were easily accessible, nearby. The two Russians had divided up the time into watches.

They had agreed to use walkie-talkies, but only for strictly necessary, and then coded, communication. They had equipped themselves with strong coffee, in thermos bottles, to aid staying awake, and so they believed the carriages were properly and carefully guarded.

In the middle of the night, just after three o'clock, Lapin suddenly observed movements around the carriages. It was completely dark, because the railway station's arc lights did not cover this part of the goods terminal sufficiently. He could observe at least six men. He watched them for a while. Then suddenly one of them tried to open one of the carriages, while the others kept watch. They seemed to behave very professionally. The men were, without any doubt, skilled burglars on nightly stealing raids on the overnight-parked carriages at the terminal.

Salnikov had correctly foreseen the possibility of this happening, and not only because this was quite normal in Ukraine. He knew it was common in almost all countries in the world, and particularly in countries with a high rate of unemployment and a difficult social situation. I bet the guards don't show up before the burglars are finished, he thought cynically.

Lapin acted at once. He made the agreed signal on the walkie-talkie to Salnikov and to the first death squad waiting closer to him, in a car only a short distance away. The second death squad, under the command of Salnikov, was in a different position, beyond the outer perimeter.

The four men in Lapin's death squad immediately climbed out of the car. Lapin only nodded in the direction of the carriages, and placed his finger on his lips, to indicate complete silence. Then he moved a finger demonstratively across his throat, to indicate killing.

It was a very hot night. The shirts stuck to their bodies and the sweat streamed from the dark-clothed professional killers, who were led by Lapin. They moved silently and quickly towards the intruders.

The death squad's members were not selected at random by Lapin. He knew each of them from his army service in Afghanistan. He had once trained them and he knew exactly how effective, and innovative, each member was. He also knew it was quite unnecessary to give an order to them in detail.

When they arrived by the carriages, one of the death squad's participants suddenly whispered to the nearest burglar: "Over here!"

The burglar believed it was one of his companions who he had heard, and moved quickly towards the death squad. He would never get the chance to know the real truth. His throat was quietly cut, while a hand completely covered his mouth. Another burglar got the same treatment, but there were still four others left. These had been too busy breaking the strong locks of the carriage to notice anything irregular.

One of them used a wrecking bar on the lock, but had not yet managed to open the heavy iron doors. Another stood impatiently with an iron saw in his hands, only waiting to start on the lock, if the man with the wrecking bar did not succeed. The man nearest to Lapin stood expectantly watching his comrades' work, like a spectator at a wrestling match or other exciting sporting event. Lapin carefully touched the back of his neck with a finger and the man turned rapidly, believing it to be one of the other burglars with something to tell him. Lapin quickly and brutally forced his needle, used last time at the weapons depot, directly into the burglar's heart. He twisted the needle a couple of times, so as to be quite sure the burglar was dead. The man was taken completely by surprise and was probably dead before he knew what was happening.

At the same time the four men in the death squad silently, professionally, cut the throats of the remaining three burglars. Just one of them managed to let a weak cry pass over his lips before he joined his comrades presumably already, efficiently installed in Hell.

Salnikov, who slept over the wheel of his car, while Lapin was on watch, had been woken up by Lapin's short, coded, walkie-talkie message and he observed Lapin's actions around the carriages. He was greatly impressed by Lapin's activity, but at the same time intensely concerned, in case anyone else also saw what happened. He had, at once, alerted the second death squad, which was ready for action, if necessary. They all kept close watch for possible witnesses, but nobody was seen until two guards, dressed in the railway company's uniforms, suddenly appeared out of the dark. The guards gesticulated, but did not really seem to know what to do at all. It was incomprehensible that they neither used their guard whistles nor their hand weapons. They only hesitated, apparently not fully understanding the situation. Salnikov had no choice. He quickly waved with his hands to his death squad, who were already silently on the way towards them.

This death squad had also previously been trained by Lapin, and Salnikov knew they were experts in dirty work. Salnikov was sorry for the guards when he saw them die, only a few seconds later. Afterwards, the guards' bodies were thrown into the boot of the death squad's car.

The next problem was what to do with the dead bodies of the burglars, which were spread around below the carriages.

141

Lapin twisted his brains for minutes before he whispered an order: "Find some steel wire and tie the damned bodies up under one of the other carriages at the terminal, far away from our carriages. Send the burglars' bodies, as rail-freight, elsewhere."

He hesitated a second before he continued with an ugly grin: "With luck, nobody will discover where the additional rotten flesh cargo has come from. Anyway, the discovery will not concern us because our cargo will soon be well away from this morbid place."

He hesitated again: "By the way, don't forget to eliminate carefully all tracks on the ground after the bloody execution."

The death squad looked around among the parked carriages at the terminal and found an old Russian carriage with the destination of Moscow. The bodies were tied up below the carriage, and nobody could possible detect them, without knowing they were there.

The remaining railway transport to Odessa was accomplished without any other incident. The containers were offloaded from the railway carriages at a goods terminal, in the north of the city. The carriages were not taken directly to the harbour, in order to reduce the risk of detection by the authorities.

The railway company's huge crane lifted the containers directly onto three waiting container trucks. After exchange of trucks at a transit storehouse, the containers were, later the same day, transported to a small, antiquated Turkish cargo ship in the harbour. As it was already issued with convenient, false Bills of Lading – properly stamped and signed, the containers were taken directly on board. On the other hand, the customs inspectors had been very well paid to look in another direction when the containers were handled. Lapin boarded the ship anonymously, just after sunset, and the ship left the harbour in the direction of Istanbul, without any delay.

Salnikov waited in the neighbourhood of the harbour, to see the ship off. He scanned the sea till the ship faded in the far-off heat haze. When he was satisfied, he turned his car and left Odessa on his way to Vienna, via Hungary. From Vienna he took a plane to Istanbul and was there when the old cargo-ship arrived with the containers

About four months later a memorial service was held for the people who had died in the great disaster at the weapons depot.

Most of those killed were never identified. They had been reduced to dust, and some of them had also vanished into the atmosphere as atoms, when the tactical nuclear weapons had blown up.

It was completely impossible to examine the depot's ruins. Rescuers, who went into the ruins, could only stay for a few minutes, because of the heavy radiation. They received their lifetime dose of radiation and could not enter a radiation area again. Many of these people had, in spite of strict safety regulations that had been developed after the accident at the power plant in Chernobyl, accumulated too large a radiation count and would die of cancer in the near future. The whole area, where the weapons depot had been, was completely closed by the authorities and it became illegal to approach within three kilometres of the area.

In the memorial service, General Vladimir Martjuk gave a moving speech for the two Russian heroes, Salnikov and Lapin. He said that they had been great men and exceptionally resourceful officers. They had lost their lives in the course of duty for their dear motherland and would be remembered forever. Both of them were posthumously decorated with the highest Russian army awards and each received large memorial tombstones.

9

Wallace and McPride sat relaxed on the sofa on the fly
bridge of a motor yacht, each with a glass of Scotch whisky
in his hand, and glanced disinterestedly over the Marmara
Sea, while they discussed the assignment of the days to
come. The chairman of the SS Group, Sir Walter Bruce
owned the yacht, which most of the time was moored in
Puerto Banus, Marbella. Sir Walter had put the yacht at
their disposal for the transportation of the weapons bought
from Salnikov, from Istanbul to Scotland.

The boat had a crew of fifteen, including Wallace and
McPride. Four of the crew were women, who were married
to four of the crewmen. The crew were all between thirty
five and fifty five years old. They were all Scottish Highlanders and veterans of different units of the British Forces. In
addition they were all members of the secret Scottish Independence Organisation's underground group, the Highlanders' Commando's operation section. They were all well
trained, military professionals, hand-picked for this special
assignment by McPride and by Sir Walter, the leader of the
Highlanders' Commando.

The yacht was a brand new exclusive Sea Champion, 125
feet in length, with a fly bridge on the top and pilothouse
or cockpit on the hardtop level below. Under the hardtop
level was the upper level that contained a saloon, a dining
room, an entrance and the galley. In addition there was, in

the bow, a very luxurious cabin for the owner of the craft. The cabin section was below, on the lowest level with the engine room in the stern. The yacht was equipped with three Detroit Diesel engines of which two were in action and one in reserve. These gave the craft a cruising speed of twenty-one knots. The top performance speed was approximately twenty-three knots. The craft was not very fast, as Sir Walter had bought it only for leisure purposes, long before he knew that it would be used for such an important assignment as this. Sir Walter had, when he ordered the boat, only considered the western Mediterranean, including Spain, France and perhaps sometimes Italy and Malta, as the craft's normal operating range.

The yacht was about to approach Istanbul, the old capital of the ancient Byzantine, and later the enormous Ottoman Empires. Previously called Constantinople after its founder, the Roman emperor Constantine the Great, who founded the city in the year 334, the name was officially changed to Istanbul in 1930. The Golden Horn, the narrow inlet to the Bosporus Strait, divides Europe from Asia and is the only entrance to the Black Sea. This gives the city its important strategic position that has caused political trouble throughout the centuries. The city lies on both sides of the strait connected now by a new, very long bridge.

Constantinople was, like Rome, built on seven hills and in the Byzantine era it greatly influenced the development of Roman law, Greek philosophy and art, as well as Christian theology and church history. The city rivalled the cultural contributions of Athens, Jerusalem, Paris and Rome. Constantinople had been the capital of the Ottoman Empire since 1453, until the Empire faded from the map in 1923 to become the Turkish Republic, after the Empire had chosen the wrong side during the First World War.

The Islamic Ottoman Empire had, by then, been the longest existing empire in the Western world, outstripping that of Rome and later Britain. It had for centuries controlled all Arabic territories from Algeria in the west to Iraq in the east, the Balkans, Bulgaria, Greece, Hungary, Romania and a large part of Ukraine.

Expansion in Europe had been stopped by the Empire's failure to conquer Vienna in 1529. It started to split in 1832, when Greece became independent. During the following years most of the European territories were lost. The Balkan War, four years before the First World War, took away the remaining European territories, except for a small part of Europe included in Turkey today. France took Algeria in 1830 and about fifty years later, Tunisia. The Empire's financial situation collapsed in 1875, after gradually worsening conditions from the middle of the nineteenth century. The Empire had to accept some degree of European financial control from 1881. The British took advantage of the economic situation and occupied Egypt in 1882. After the Balkan War, Italy annexed Libya in 1912.

Earlier the same day, the Scottish yacht had passed through the Aegean Sea, and at the moment it was cruising steadily through the Sea of Marmara. The sea was as calm as it only can be before a storm. The sun was about to set behind the yacht. Marvellous colours were blinking on the water's shiny surface from the reflection of the low sun. The yacht's steadily throbbing engines were the only things to disturb the idyllic peace.

One of the crew operated as the yacht's pilot. The rest, who were not nodding or sleeping on the saloon's sofas or in the armchairs, sat on the hardtop level outside the pilothouse or outside the saloon and talked quietly together.

The yacht had the most up-to-date satellite navigation system, and the machinery was conveniently accessed from

147

the cockpit. One man could therefore easily handle the yacht alone. All the crew were trained to handle it and they had all seen service as pilots, during the long voyage across the Mediterranean Sea.

McPride had received a report from his contact at the Army Satellite Centre before departure. The report told him that there had been a large explosion at a weapons depot in Kursk, and therefore he knew the delivery was just around the corner. The Scottish yacht had left Puerto Banus less than two days later, heading for Istanbul.

Mustafa had not received any information from satellite centres. Access to that kind of equipment was still many years away in his part of the world. Salnikov had said that the delivery would take place in Istanbul during June. Therefore Mustafa had arrived in the city the first day of June, ready to load his weapons cargo.

The shipment would be carried by a small, old, rusty cargo craft, which had been rebuilt to carry containers on deck. A small Arabian shipping company in Algeria owned the ship and it was planned to transport the containers to Tunisia for reloading. Mustafa had planned to follow the cargo ship in a special motor yacht – a rebuilt British motor torpedo boat.

The MTB had been bought from an Egyptian demolition company a couple of years previously and was pretty old. The British Royal Navy had left it behind when they left Egypt in the fifties. The Egyptian navy had, for many years, used the boat on the Red Sea as a patrol boat, before they had withdrawn it from service. Afterwards, it had been docked for many years in Suez, until an Egyptian admiral had wanted to clean up the harbour, and sold it to a demolition company in Port Said. The demolition company had later sold it to Mustafa at a reasonable price.

The boat had been rebuilt and painted white to look like an old private yacht. It looked really nice at a distance, although it was no luxury boat. Inside it was still as it always had been. Mustafa did not waste money on what he considered to be unnecessary. The crew and passengers of the MTB must remember it was not a pleasure voyage they were on when they were on a raid with the boat.

The MTB had a great advantage over a private yacht, because its maximum speed was more than thirty-eight knots, but at that speed the engine fumed like an old steamboat on full steam.

It was armed with an old, heavy, but very functional, American Browning 12.7 millimetre machine-gun. The machine-gun was hidden under a special cover in the keel of the boat. It could easily and quickly be prepared for use. The crew's personal weapons were also hidden in the same store. The crew had Austrian Steyr 5.56 millimetre attack versions of automatic army rifles and were equipped with 40 millimetre Mecar high-explosive shells. The shells had a range of 100 metres. They also had some Israeli Galil short attack rifles, of the same calibre as the Steyrs.

The MTB had a crew of seven experienced seamen, in addition to Mustafa and twenty relatively inexperienced, young guerrilla soldiers. The boat was therefore completely overcrowded and the Arabs slept anywhere they could.

The reason for using the MTB was not just that Mustafa wanted to follow and protect his cargo while in transit. Some of his men would join the cargo on board the cargo ship and Mustafa did not expect there would be any particular problems.

However, his agents had detected the meeting between Salnikov and a British gentleman in Saint Tropez, the previous summer. The agents had afterwards pursued the

Britisher back home. He had proved to be the Scottish Lieutenant Colonel John McPride. Mustafa's agents had not discovered the real reason for the meeting. Therefore he, together with other leaders of his violent group, had carefully considered the information received about the Scotsman.

They had decided that it was impossible that Salnikov was a British spy in Russia, or the Scottish lieutenant colonel was a Russian spy in Britain. Salnikov could not be a spy, because he could have no useful information for the British Intelligence Service, as a second rate superior of an army depot outside Kursk. Neither could Salnikov be a leading officer of the Russian Secret Police, from which he had allowed Mustafa to kill two agents on the motorway in Italy. The only reasonable solution left was that the Scotsman probably was another of Salnikov's weapon customers, and it was very likely that the delivery of this customer's weapons would be done at the same time Mustafa received his weapons in Istanbul. Mustafa believed that the Scotsman sold weapons to a guerrilla organisation or something similar. What, otherwise, could be the reason for a Scotsman to buy weapons?

Mustafa knew the only acceptable and relatively safe transport possibilities from Istanbul for those kinds of goods were by sea. He had decided to try to take over the Scotsman's weapons.

Some days earlier, he had received positive confirmation of his suspicions. His agents had told him that McPride had left from Puerto Banus by yacht in an easterly direction, and they had later observed the Scottish yacht, at intervals, passing through the Mediterranean. The yacht had been seen for the last time that day, passing through the Aegean Sea in the direction of Istanbul. At the moment, the yacht would be in the Sea of Marmara, only a few hours from Istanbul. His agents would be there when the yacht arrived.

Five hours later the Scottish yacht docked in Istanbul, on the European side of the Bosporus Strait. All the crew remained on board that night, but the next morning two members of the crew caught a taxi and travelled to the ancient Sultans' Palace on the hillside, about three kilometres from the yacht harbour. As agreed, they made contact with the Russians in front of one of the many showcases exhibiting antique golden treasures. Lapin was Salnikov's representative. The Arab agents watched the meeting from a distance, pretending to be ordinary tourists. They had followed the two crew members from the yacht.

McPride met Salnikov later the same day in a coffee bar near the yacht harbour. McPride noticed that the Russian officer seemed very pale and tired. Salnikov seemed to be quite another person now from the relatively tanned, straightforward officer he had met in the summer on the Côte d'Azur. McPride understood the weapons' delivery must have taken all the Russian's resources, while he himself felt very fit and relaxed after the pleasant cruise on the motor yacht across the Mediterranean. He hoped he would be the same when they reached Gibraltar in a few days time.

"You look tired, Igor."

"I am probably too old for such a life," Salnikov murmured with a sad, ironic smile on his lips. "But the main thing is that I have all the weapons you wanted ready for you to load."

Salnikov did not, of course, mention anything about all the people who had died because of these weapons.

The two officers agreed about some practical arrangements concerning the transport from the storage place to the motor yacht. The weapons had to be repackaged into unmarked boxes before loading onto the Scottish yacht. It would be an enormous, unnecessary risk to transport the weapons in their original boxes. If weapons, wrapped in their original Russian army boxes and marked with the symbols of the weapon depot in Kursk went astray, it would be all too easy for anyone to identify them. From that it might be possible to draw some conclusions about the delivery chain; reflections which Salnikov did not wish to invite. Therefore a small discreet warehouse, or a large garage, was needed for repackaging.

"You have, so far, done an excellent job and you will get access to the rest of your money as soon as the weapons are safely aboard the yacht," McPride said, as he emptied a cup of strong black Turkish coffee with a grin, just before the officers parted.

The next day, the weapons were transported to a garage near the famous Istanbul Bazaar. The repackaging started. Lapin carefully watched the work and guided the Scottish crew to do the repackaging correctly. Four men and two women of the crew sat on guard outside the garage. Such guards seemed completely unnecessary and totally ridiculous in the Scotsmen's eyes. Nobody knew anything about the valuable and dangerous substances that were being repackaged in the garage. Lapin, who had experienced quite another world, had demanded the guards.

"You can never be too careful in this part of the world," he had said furiously, by way of an order, when some of the Scotsmen had tried to question his instructions. The Scots were wary of the enormous, frightening Russian, and, as the Russians still were the formal owners of the goods, they reluctantly let Lapin have his way.

The guards were dressed in local clothing and completely

blended into the environment. Two of them sat at a table at a café, smoking a water pipe and talking quietly. Another two, a man and a woman, pretended to sell fruit on the street. They had placed a large blanket on the ground where they had arranged oranges, bananas, apples, dates and figs tidily in small piles. The remaining two guards, also a man and a woman, patrolled the surroundings. They walked up and down the street arguing, gesticulating wildly with their hands and pretending to wait for somebody who never came. At intervals, the man checked his large pocket watch and searched all around. All the guards behaved like professional movie stars, and would easily have got parts in cheap, gangster movies.

Nobody, though, could see the wire from the earphones, connected to small security radios hidden under their clothes, and nobody could detect small microphones hidden in the arch of their necks. The guards outside the garage were fully connected, via radio, both to each other and to their colleagues repackaging the weapons inside the garage.

The Scottish guards had for a while noted two Arabs hanging around, seemingly without any reason. They looked suspicious and did not fit in among the time wasting citizens and tourists. The Scottish guards watched the two Arabs carefully for a long time. They also detected another couple of Arabs, who were undoubtedly giving some kind of warning signs to the first two. One of them suddenly climbed onto the garage roof and tried desperately to look inside. The guards considered that there was absolutely no doubt that these bloody Arabs had hostile intent. In the garage, the Scotsmen and Lapin had already been warned, via the security radio, and they had made requisite moves to cover the weapons.

Lapin was immediately on full alert, after he had been

informed that one of the Arabs was on his way to the roof. The major decided to catch him quickly himself. He therefore climbed rapidly to the roof. He saw the Arab investigating the garage through a hole, where a window should have been. The Arab was too occupied with the inside, so he saw Lapin too late. Lapin used his traditional needle, like a tailor. The only difference was that his needle was considerably larger than the tailor's was, and he used his on human flesh, not on a tailor's cloth. Not the slightest sound escaped the curious Arab's throat before he died, like a speared rat.

"I don't like uninvited fiddlers on my roof," Lapin whispered flatly in the ear of the Arab as he killed.

Immediately, Lapin slid down to the ground outside the garage, with the speed of light, after he had dried the bloody needle on the dead Arab's clothes. He looked quickly around for the dead man's comrades. He detected one of them immediately, after receiving instructions through his earpiece, from the astonished Scottish guards. The Scotsmen had never before seen execution of such extreme and effective brutality.

Lapin observed the Arab hastening in the direction of the Bazaar and he raced after him with an Olympic sprinter's speed. The Arab entered the Bazaar area through a back door of a shop, closely followed by Lapin.

The streets of the Bazaar were filled with people; mostly European tourists mixed with local Turks, easily identifiable by their styles of clothing. The desperately frightened Arab tried to do a slalom between the amazed people, while in his speed he stumbled into them. He rammed piles of sales products and stands in the narrow streets. Jewellery, clothes and fake antiques flew into the air as he darted by. The salesmen clenched their fists and waved their arms and legs while they gazed after the running Arab, shouting all the swear words they could remember.

The enormous major followed at the heels of the Arab.

154

The salesmen and their customers had hardly seen the Arab disappear before an exploding volcano hit them. The enormous, pursuing Mongol, more than two metres tall and more than a hundred and twenty kilograms destroyed far more of the sales products than the rather small Arab had done. If they, and their customers, had not moved out of the way, when Lapin came, he would simply have run them down like escaping children trample straw in the grain field when an angry farmer is after them.

Soon, also, the sound of police whistles mixed with the rumble of the running men. Lapin reached the Arab just as he tried to hide between some coats in a temporarily empty, leather clothes shop. Once more the major drew his faithful companion, the long needle, and pressing it deep into the Arab's heart, moved it round a couple of times, and once more, a victim fell dead to the ground. This time the victim was allowed to make some helpless grunts before he finally entered through the gateway to his promised Paradise.

Afterwards, Lapin grabbed the dead Arab by the neck and resolutely hung him on a rusty peg on the wall, like a butcher might hang a cured ham. Then from a nearby table he grasped an open bottle of wine and poured the contents over the dead man's clothes. He dropped the empty bottle in front of him. The dead Arab's body swung on the peg like a drunken man, as Lapin left the Bazaar through the shop's back door.

With their hands on their hidden pistols, the patrolling Scottish couple rounded silently on the remaining two Arabs who were watching the garage. When they were close to them, they drew the pistols and pressed them discreetly into the backs of one Arab each. The Arabs were politely ordered to enter the garage and they complied without any trouble. They probably had understood there were no other possible alternatives.

By the time Lapin arrived in the garage from his successful hunt in the Bazaar, the Arabs had still not given any information to the Scots about the purpose of their presence. They claimed to be tourists, from Cairo, and did not understand why they had been taken, by threats, into a dark garage. If it was a simple hold up, they said they had no money. They were only students visiting Istanbul during their vacation from the University of Cairo.

Lapin gave them a cold smile when he heard their story. He was used to other methods of getting prisoners of war to speak the truth. He just asked them politely once more for the true story, but the Arabs kept to their explanation. They were more relaxed as they felt certain that their story was being accepted. Then Lapin smiled again very coldly and without any warning, grabbed the nearest one and killed him with his bare hands, before anybody had a chance to stop him. Lapin simply twisted the head of the Arab quickly to one side and everybody in the garage clearly heard the sound as his neck broke. Two of the Scottish army veterans threw up their breakfasts. All the others became as pale as snowmen. They had never seen anything as brutal in their entire lives.

Lapin just smiled as coldly as before at the last of the Arabs. He was completely unmoved by the incident, as he let the body drop to the concrete floor by his feet. He gave it a hard kick to move it aside, without even giving it a glance.

He then asked the surviving Arab calmly, with a violent grin: "Could you now tell us the complete, true story about your presence, my dear friend."

The Arab could not get a word out. He was standing bowed as if trying to make himself smaller. He just nodded desperately as Lapin lifted him by his throat, half a metre

156

off the ground. He was as pale as a body that had been dead for at least a week. After some seconds he finally started on his story, with a trembling, staccato voice.

The deadly frightened Arab told them about Mustafa and the Arabian organisation he belonged to, the Formation. He told about the Arabian MTB, docked in the harbour and that he was only an agent who lived in Istanbul, just doing what he was ordered to do by Mustafa. He also explained that they had tailed the Scotsmen since they had arrived in Istanbul and that there had been four of them who watched the garage, but he did not know at the moment, where his two colleagues had disappeared to. Lapin asked him further questions, to which he replied as truthfully and sincerely as possible.

After the Arab has finished his confession, he cried like a baby. Lapin gently laid his arms on his shoulder as if to comfort him, and the Arab snorted and wiped his nose. Just as he did so, Lapin killed him as quickly as he had killed his colleague, but this time Lapin used his beloved needle. He pressed the needle into the Arab's chest from beside the neck and agitated it several times, meanwhile he tried to put on an obviously fake, sorrowful look. He looked at each of the Scottish veterans in turn observing each individual's reaction. The Scots only stood shocked with their mouths half-open, saying nothing. They were silently amazed and stood stiffly like the Chinese terracotta warriors. They gazed fearfully at the huge Russian major with the strange, angular Mongol eyes. Lapin noticed their reactions and smiled warmly, like a father-in-law might smile on his future son-in-law on his daughter's wedding day, whether he wants to or not.

He said, apparently untouched by the events: "Sorry, partners, but I had no alternative."

He was actually demonstrating what would happen to them if they did not fulfil their part of the bargain.

10

The Scottish yacht again cruised across the Sea of Marmara, but this time at full speed in a south-westerly direction away from Istanbul. The Scots wanted to put as large a distance as possible between Mustafa and themselves, before he could possibly start chasing them.

The agent's confession in the garage made it very clear that Mustafa planned to capture the yacht in open sea, and seize the Scotsmen's weapon cargo. The weapon repackaging and the loading of the yacht had, therefore, been carried out extremely swiftly, once the Arab's intentions were known. Luckily, no other problems or delays had occurred after that. The customs officials in the yacht harbour had been bribed well enough to have a magnificent lunch at an expensive restaurant in town for the two hours while the loading of the yacht was completed.

The remaining payment to Salnikov had been released in Switzerland, before Lapin permitted the yacht to leave the harbour. Lapin had been very cautious about this and had not allowed McPride to board before he had received a message from Salnikov confirming the payment had been fully transferred according to the agreement. The Scots, of course, did not argue with Lapin about this, after having seen him in action. They had never seen, or even heard about, such brutality in their entire lives. Lapin had acted like the Devil Incarnate.

While the yacht had been loaded, Lapin boasted that he was one of Genghis Khan's descendants and the Scots certainly believed him. They revealed that they connected Genghis Khan's name to an extremely violent Mongolian leader on horseback leading a horde of uncivilised rapists and killers. Lapin had, after being deeply offended by this lack of knowledge concerning the great Mongol Empire, immediately and proudly given the ignorant Scots a history lesson.

The mighty Mongolian tribal leader and conqueror, Temujin, had been proclaimed as the universal leader of Mongolia with the title Genghis Khan, or the Great Khan, at the gathering of Mongolian tribes in 1206. His hordes soon raced all over Asia and gained huge territories, through their magnificent horsemanship and accurate archery, under the tight control and hard discipline of their aristocratic leaders, and Khan's own very intelligent military strategy and tactics. The Mongol Empire was created during the superb Genghis Khan's leadership. It consisted of land territories over most of Asia – from the China Sea to the Persian Gulf. The successor Khan, Great Khan Ogadai, after Genghis' death in 1227, extended the Empire further into one of the largest land empires that the world has known. He established the Empire of the Golden Horde, with the help of his army leader, Batu. In 1241 the Mongol army reached the Adriatic Sea and was preparing to make inroads into western Europe. Only the death of Great Khan Ogadai prevented the attack, because Batu withdrew all the forces to southern Russia with the intention of participating in the struggle to become Ogadai's successor.

The Grand Duke of Moscow's victory over the Mongols in 1380 marked the turning point for the swelling Mongolian Empire. A few years afterwards, religious, cultural and language differences caused the break-up of the Golden Horde Empire into four independent khanates. The Golden Horde still ruled an area, now reduced to southern Russia, till the late fifteenth century, when a later Grand Duke of Moscow finally dissolved the Empire.

Lapin had finished his elucidation of the Mongolian Empire, with the statement that he would never forgive the bloody Russians for having participated in the demolition of his ancestors' great Empire.

The Scots had been very impressed by Lapin's apparent great intellect and knowledge of his people's history. They had, till then, only considered the huge Mongol as an imbecile killing machine, but they nevertheless were greatly relieved when Lapin finally told them that they were free to leave Istanbul. The remaining payment had been received in Switzerland. They considered themselves gentlemen, and gentlemen always pay according to a reasonable agreement, and they had, of course, never considered any alternative.

When Lapin had received the necessary bank code from McPride for the Central Swiss Credit Bank to release the money, he immediately called Salnikov. Salnikov then called the Swiss bank and checked if the amount was available and immediately transferred it to his account in the same bank. Then he waited for some minutes and called the bank again and transferred the money to an account in a different Swiss bank. In this way there was no direct connection to the Scottish account, if anything happened later.

The weapons deal with the Scots was finally completed, and when Lapin called Salnikov a few minutes later, he was told to let them board their yacht. Salnikov asked Lapin to thank the Scots politely for a successful trade, achieved completely in accordance with the agreement, and to wish them a pleasant voyage home.

McPride believed Mustafa did not know that his agents had been outside the garage during the repackaging. The guards outside the garage had not observed that the Arab agents had telephoned, and examination of the bodies afterwards had shown that they wore no radios or mobile telephones. The Arab agent, who had confessed before he was killed, had also said there were only four men on the assignment. Later it would be shown to be a bad mistake to have believed him.

The Arab agents had not known about the garage before the repackaging had started. Two of them had followed the crew, and two had followed Lapin to the garage. The Scots considered it was very natural that the Arabs wanted to examine what was going on inside the garage before they made any report to Mustafa. This was correct, but Mustafa was a very experienced guerrilla leader and had naturally taken all precautions. He had more people on the Scots' track than just the four who were killed by Lapin, but the dead agents did not know about the others. Mustafa was, therefore, very well informed about all the circumstances concerning his dead operators.

Lapin had told the Scots, as they left the harbour, that the weapons delivery to Mustafa would be delayed as long as possible, to give them a good start on him. Lapin would manipulate Mustafa into being too late to catch up with the yacht. He said he would have difficulties in delaying the Arab for more than twelve hours, a day at the maximum. Otherwise Mustafa might become suspicious, because it was likely that he must have reckoned that his weapons were in town, as the Scotsmen's delivery had been accomplished. It

161

was also likely that he had been informed about the loading and the departure of the Scottish motor yacht.

After the killings in the garage Lapin had crammed the dead Arab agents into the boot of a car. The dead bodies lay in the car during the loading of the yacht, but after the Scots had departed from the harbour, Lapin drove the car on a country road thirty kilometres outside Istanbul, in the direction of Greece. He placed the bodies in the seats and let it tumble down a cliff into the sea to look like an accident. Afterwards he took a local bus back to the city and a taxi across the bridge to the Asian side of the strait. Here he booked into a small hotel, to stay, while he postponed the meeting with Mustafa.

In Cairo Salnikov and Mustafa had agreed on a meeting place in Istanbul. Mustafa had visited it at a certain time, every day since he had arrived in the city on the first of June.

Lapin had just left the reception desk of the hotel and was about to move towards the staircase, when he heard a slimy voice from behind.

"I had expected you to meet me today."

Lapin turned around quickly and saw that the slimy voice belonged to a short, black-haired man with protruding, dark brown eyes, who was unmistakably an Arab.

"You must have forgotten the meeting," the Arab continued blandly.

Lapin was a calm man who never showed when he was taken by surprise. He knew at once what the matter was, but he only feigned astonishment, as if he did not know.

He replied politely to the approaching Arab: "I'm afraid I don't know you, sir."

"I'm Mustafa," the Arab answered brusquely, "and I am awaiting your delivery of some special goods."

Lapin waited a long second before he said anything, pretending to be resorting his mind. Meanwhile, the Arab waited restlessly for Lapin's reply, like a child waits for sweets while the bag is being opened.

"Where was I to meet you?"

Mustafa told him the place for the agreed meeting, the time and an agreed identification code.

Lapin waited another few seconds, as he again pretended to think very carefully, then gave the Arab another identification code. The two men exchanged codes before Lapin suddenly grabbed the Arab on his shoulder with one hand and raised the other for a handshake, while he spoke to him as to an old friend.

"It's very pleasant to meet you, Mustafa. I was going to meet you today, but I was unfortunately delayed and I must postpone the meeting until tomorrow."

Mustafa automatically gripped Lapin's hand for an unmistakably unwilling handshake.

"It's urgent," Mustafa said, while pretending to be diplomatic, "I want the delivery to be accomplished today,"

"I'm sorry, it's too late today, another day will make no difference, dear friend. Today I'm also too tired to worry about anything but sleep. I'll see you tomorrow at the appointed spot."

Lapin started to walk slowly towards the staircase knowing that he had provoked Mustafa dangerously. The Arab did not move. He only shook with anger and hissed loudly and threateningly.

"It will, you damned bloody Russian!"

Lapin ignored Mustafa's angry utterance and did not turn around, as he heard Mustafa continue in incomprehensible Arabic. He just moved calmly upstairs, as the old staircase creaked under his huge weight. He heard Mustafa call from below when he reached the top of the staircase.

"I'll be at the appointed meeting place at six o'clock

tomorrow morning, and I expect you to be there at the same time."

Lapin had not planned to be at the place before twelve, but considered the Arab's proposal as an acceptable compromise, because he judged that by now the Scottish yacht would have the necessary lead on the Arabs.

Lapin answered the Arab loudly, while he assumed complete disinterest still without turning towards him. He continued marching towards his room.

"OK, I'll be there!"

Lapin met Mustafa early in the morning of the next day. Mustafa seemed to have completely forgotten his anger of the day before and he behaved as mildly and gently as a second-hand car salesman would have done. One hour later the weapon containers were transported from the store to the Algerian craft on the two lorries organised by Mustafa. The containers were loaded onto the craft and Mustafa's men cautiously checked their contents. The customs inspectors were again bribed to look the other way. Everything seemed to go smoothly according to plan.

All the time the loading was going on, Mustafa stayed with Lapin as a hostage for the payment. The payment was to be accomplished in the same way as for the Scotsmen. They had entered a small, dirty harbour café with a telephone and a view towards the pier where the craft was being loaded, to await Salnikov's call confirming that the payment was in order.

"You are, presumably, satisfied now you have completed your business, my dear Russian friend," Mustafa said in a smirking manner.

"I have not completed any business before the payment is in order," Lapin replied unmoved. "You have to stay with

164

me until I receive a telephone call from my partner to tell me that the money is properly in our bank account."

At that moment the craft left the pier. Lapin became outraged.

"This wasn't the deal, damned son-of-a-bitch," he shouted angrily.

Mustafa only smiled mockingly and dodged backwards as Lapin's tremendous hands lunged to catch him across the table. Lapin rose and the table overturned, cups and glasses crashed to the floor. Mustafa ran towards the door, where four Arabs suddenly appeared with drawn daggers. The newcomers looked savage and dangerous. One of them had an immense knife-scar running from his mouth to behind his left ear. Another had no left ear at all. None of them seemed to have seen a razor for days and they must have slept in their clothes for weeks, as Lapin could smell them from a distance.

One of them forced the frightened café owner into the corner by the bar, while the three remaining men headed slowly and threateningly towards Lapin.

Mustafa said sneeringly, with a baleful and malicious grin on his face: "You are an extremely stupid man – inexperienced in international business. You should never have allowed the containers to leave the warehouse before you had received payment. This small oversight will cost you half the price, and soon also your life. I have no intention of paying you the rest. I will just thank you for the extra discount."

Still with a malicious grin, Mustafa continued: "I know you killed four of my brave men yesterday, then you prepared the weapons delivery for the Scotsmen. I even know where you dumped the bodies into the sea, west of the town. You will have to pay for these killings in a few seconds, you bloody Russian."

Lapin realised that he was about to be cheated by the Arabs. He and Salnikov had previously considered just that possibility. They suspected the Arabs would not pay before they checked the containers, but Salnikov did not want to open the sealed containers in the warehouse. It had to be done on board the craft. Therefore Lapin had installed hidden remote controlled explosives in the containers. They had discussed handing over the remote control to the Arabs against the money, but had dropped this idea. The Arabs would probably say that if you blow up the weapons, you would lose the money. Likewise the authorities would detect the delivery. So the two illegal Russian weapons suppliers decided to retain the remote controls. By doing so they could activate them if the Arabs cheated them, and blow up the craft when it had reached deep international waters. In that way nobody would ever know the reason why the craft sank. This would also eliminate the possibility of the weapons being tracked back to Kursk through serial numbers and packaging. In addition it would also be a great pleasure to have revenge over unreliable customers. There was also another important matter. The value of the weapons to the Arabs was very small in comparison to the value of the weapons that were delivered to the Scotsmen. Therefore they had decided to complete the delivery to the Scots before they made the delivery to the Arabs. If everything went well with the first delivery, they could afford to lose money on the second.

Mustafa stood at the door and said rather unruffled to his men, as he gave an order to a driver.

"I'm leaving, but I am sure you will take care of our Russian friend over there," he waved his arm in the direction of Lapin, "and the owner of the café," he waved his arm again, "in a very terminating sort of way."

166

Then, Mustafa left the café with a very arrogant expression on his face and completely ignored Lapin who he already considered dead meat.

The loss of the money did not bother the major much. It was his pride that had been hurt. He had automatically taken up a defensive position as the four-man Arab assassination squad had arrived in the room. He was more than a head taller than the Arabs were and he looked down on them like he would have looked down on chickens before killing them.

The Arab to the left had approached the café owner. Lapin could see out of the corner of his eye, that the Arab suddenly made a movement with his dagger. The café owner screamed and fell to the floor like a sack of rotten potatoes. Blood poured from a slash across his throat. At the same moment the other Arabs screamed loudly in Arabic, which Lapin did not understand, and all attacked him simultaneously.

The only weapon Lapin had available was the needle. He had carried the needle hidden in the left inside pocket of his jacket, with the shaft in the pocket and the steel threaded into the lining. None of the Arabs saw the rapid movement that put it into his hand.

Lapin kicked one of the Arabs in the belly. He felt the Arab's dagger's blade being strained quickly into his kicking leg's thigh. The Arab had slashed his dagger into Lapin's only body part within reach. Another Arab reached Lapin from the side and pierced the left side of Lapin's chest with his dagger. Lapin felt the dagger's stroke as he powerfully forced the needle into the heart of the third Arab. He had no time to move the needle around. Thus the Arab's deadly wound would look as clean as if a steel mantel bullet had hit him.

The Arab, who had hit Lapin in the chest with the dagger, could not hope for any compassion. Lapin gripped his right wrist as he pulled the dagger out from his chest. He did not count the times he pierced the Arab's face and upper body with his needle, before he slung the dead body onto the assailant who came rushing towards him from the left, with his dagger high above his head in an old-fashioned attack position. This was the café owner's killer. Lapin thought the Arab looked rather ridiculous and Lapin smiled as he always found it funny when somebody fought ineffectually, but less than a microsecond later he was back in business.

The one, who had got the kick in his stomach, had regained his killer instinct and made another hopeless attack. Lapin kicked him again, but this time he hit his hand. Lapin's tremendous force made the dagger fly across the room like a large bullet before sticking into the wall. The Arab's hand was flopping like a pendulum, completely broken and he cried earsplitting shrieks like pigs in a slaughterhouse. That was exactly what was going to happen to him. He would be slaughtered only seconds afterwards. Lapin kicked a third time with full power. This time he hit the Arab's head and the neck was instantly broken. The Arab's head flopped on the body like the head on a ragdoll and he slid slowly to the floor after he had crashed against the opposite wall as if a bull in a Spanish bullring had butted him.

The only Arab still alive stopped in his tracks, astonished by the sight of the huge Lapin's handling of his comrades. He realised that quick escape was the only rational solution left, but he was unfortunate. Lapin hastened rapidly across the floor, elegant as a Spanish matador. He grabbed the terrified escaping Arab terrorist by his long dirty hair just as he reached the door and then swung the screaming man around like a hammer-thrower. When the Arab hit the wall at the other side of the room, headfirst, his skull smashed as if it were a melon that hit the ground from the top of a skyscraper.

After the last Arab had been exterminated, Lapin looked quickly through the windows to see if anyone was on the way towards the café. He saw no one and he quickly examined his own wounds. None of them was life threatening. They were only souvenirs to add to the collection on his already scarred body, he thought with resignation. He washed the wounds quickly in pure vodka from the bar and tore a tablecloth into strips to bandage the wounds provisionally. He washed off most of the blood on his clothes with cold water, and left the café.

He made a telephone call to Salnikov from a nearby public call box. Salnikov picked him up shortly after, in a rental car. They crossed the bridge over the Bosporus Strait to the European side of the city and made a short visit to a doctor to clean and properly bandage Lapin's wounds. The doctor, who was paid well to keep his mouth shut, said the wounds were not dangerous, but gave Lapin the standard medical advice: "You must stay quiet for the next two weeks."

Lapin bought a new suit in a tiny back street shop. The suit seemed to be at least ten sizes too small, even though he bought the largest size available.

"You look like a clown," Salnikov had joked with him.

Lapin could not disagree, because the suit had small yellow and orange checks and was very old-fashioned. It had obviously hung, unsold, in the shop for many years. The small size could partly be disguised by keeping the jacket open, but Lapin still looked like an American wrestler, who had been on steroids for twenty years.

The shop owner had looked rather suspiciously at Lapin's old suit, which in comparison with the clothes of a beggar in the Bronx, New York, made the beggar look as well dressed as the President of the United States at a gala. Lapin had pretended to be drunk and Salinkov had said that a car had driven over him. The shop owner had murmured something in Turkish that the two customers did not understand, but Salnikov believed it was something about drunken tourists being idiots.

After the suit shopping, the two Russian officers consumed a hot meal at an excellent restaurant, before they drove to the yacht harbour and rented a large speedboat. Half an hour later they were cruising, at high speed, across the Sea of Marmara, hunting for the Algerian craft with the two weapons containers on deck. They got their first sight of the craft after about five hours.

The antiquated craft headed very slowly, but steadily towards the Mediterranean. Its speed was no more than ten knots. The cheated weapons suppliers followed the old craft at a distance for another hour, before Lapin pressed the remote control button just as the craft passed from Turkish to Greek waters by the Dardanelles.

"If there is ever to be any investigation as to the reason why this craft sank, the Greeks and the Turks must first agree about its territorial position. Though they are both members of NATO, they always seem to have great problems in agreeing to anything," Salnikov said with an immense grin.

The craft did not sink immediately, but it caught fire. The flames lit up the night sky like a torch, reflecting yellow, orange and red on the sea's undulating surface. After nearly half an hour the craft suddenly turned over and sank quickly into the black water. Salnikov and Lapin observed from a distance, with great satisfaction, until it vanished entirely from the surface.

It suddenly became completely dark, when the craft vanished. The fire had affected the weapons traders' night vision and it took minutes to regain a proper ability to see. They calmly increased the boat's speed and they headed satisfied, in the direction of Greece. They reached a lonely harbour, near Thessalonika, the following morning. In the evening, they took a plane from Thessalonika to Rome.

Mustafa ran directly from the café to the MTB. His agents had seen the Scottish yacht leave the harbour the evening before, some fifteen hours earlier. Several of the Arab agents had secretly followed the yacht on a smaller craft that they had rented from a company in the harbour. This yacht had radar equipment and radio communications and could constantly inform Mustafa about the Scottish yacht's position and prevent possible loss of contact.

Mustafa calculated that if he cruised at full speed, and the Scots did the same, he would need about forty-five hours to catch up with them. If he reduced the speed, thus lessening the amount of smoke belching from the old MTB's engine and make it look less like an ancient steam-boat, he estimated the rendezvous with the yacht would occur during the night two days ahead. He decided that would be the best option.

The MTB overtook the Algerian craft loaded with their weapons after less than an hour. Mustafa and his men waved to the crew on the craft. Mustafa was in a splendid mood, but he was not in the same spirits when, only a few hours later he received the radio message telling him that the same cargo craft with his weapons was about to sink. Mustafa did not know for sure, but he suspected there was a close connection between the bloody, giant Russian's escape from the café that day and the sinking vessel. Mus-tafa immediately rediscovered his war temper and several times he emptied his Arabic vocabulary of swear words on his men, who huddled together terrified in the tiny MTB. Now, it became even more important to catch the Scots.

On board the Scottish yacht, the crew made preparations against a possible attack from the Arabs. They estimated the Arabs would catch up with them within forty-eight hours, but there was also the possibility that the Arabs might never catch up with them at all, if the Mongol delayed them as he had promised.

In the weapons cargo had been two, easily manoeuvrable, machine cannons, fifteen AK 70 machine-guns, in addition to pistols with extra magazines for all of them. There had also been thirty bazookas. The Scots felt comfortably armed and reckoned the odds against an old, tiny MTB to be very acceptable, unless they were taken completely by surprise. They knew the Arabs could not sink their yacht because of the cargo, which was their only reason for attack. The Arabs must eventually board their yacht and then handguns would be the deciding factor.

One of the machine cannons was stored in a front locker, easy to get at for quick mounting on the forward deck. The other one was hidden in a locker in the stern, also easy to access for quick mounting. All the crew practised during the evening, mounting the machine cannons as quickly as possible. At sunset as they did not see any other boats around, they all tried some shots with the cannons to be fully acquainted with the Russian weapons. They could confirm contentedly that they worked perfectly. The crew also tried all machine-guns, pistols and a single bazooka.

The problems with the yacht's engines occurred at about one o'clock in the morning. A few minutes before the engines stopped entirely, they behaved jerkily, coughed spasmodically and finally stopped. The yacht's engines behaved almost like car engines in wintertime, when there could be water, which froze in the fuel.

Wallace was immediately awake as the monotone sound from the engines suddenly stopped and only a few seconds later he was on the way to the engine room. He knew at once what had happened. The engine cylinders had been blocked.

"This must have been sabotage, otherwise only one of the engines would have stopped. The chance that both engines would have stopped at the same time is too small to exist," he said to McPride, who had arrived just after him. "I experienced something similar in the army, many years ago. Three soldiers were jailed for two months after they, on a drunken Saturday night, had poured two kilograms of sugar into the fuel reservoir of a battle tank. The tank's motor became completely blocked after having worked for only a few minutes the following Monday morning," Wallace added.

The crewman acting as pilot when the incident occurred, reported that he had switched on the pump to refill the engines' fuel reserve, a couple of minutes before the engines stopped. Wallace was therefore quite certain that the fuel had been polluted with sugar or a similar substance to kill the motor. At that time they had not known they were under observation by the Arabs and should have been on the alert. A lot of people had circulated around the yacht in the marina. The yacht's fuel capacity was more than twenty five thousand litres and it took time to refill the tanks completely.

"We must have been careless when we filled the fuel tanks in Istanbul and somebody must have used a minute of inattention and added the stuff to the fuel," Wallace said.

*

Wallace had reasoned quite correctly. Two Arabs had watched the yacht and suddenly seen the chance to put sugar into the fuel reservoir, undetected. The employee of the marina, who had worked the pumps, had suddenly disappeared for some minutes. The Arabs had rushed, unnoticed, towards the yacht and emptied a bag of sugar into the tank. The fuel was stored in different reservoirs to balance the weight of the yacht. The Arabs had filled only one of the reservoirs. It had therefore only been by chance the engines had been killed, because this very reservoir had been used this time, but the Scots did not know this.

The yacht was equipped with three different engines. Two of them were in use at the same time. The third was held in reserve. The yacht could therefore get one engine to function quickly, but they needed to judge which one of the fuel reservoirs might have been tampered with. The speed would also be drastically reduced with only one engine working. The polluted reservoir had also to be emptied of the spoiled fuel before the reserve engine could be started.

Wallace explained the situation to the crew, who had all appeared by now. He finished his summary and said it was a chance out of hell to select the correct tank to run the remaining engine.

McPride added after Wallace had finished: "I suggest we don't take any chances at all. We can simply not afford to take any, with bloodthirsty Arabs hanging on our tail. We must move on as quickly as possible, or we will be killed."

"It looks like we have no other alternatives," Wallace said.

McPride thought for a moment before he continued: "We must make a direct pipeline between the reserve engine and the inner reservoir, which was filled in Spain before we left for Turkey. The Spanish fuel and only one engine at moderate speed will at least take us to Malta, where we can repair the engines at the SS Group's shipyard.

I don't believe we have sufficient spare parts to repair the engines on board."

The technically experienced crewmen lost no time in making the connection between the reserve engine and the reservoir of Spanish fuel, using a provisional bypass pipeline. However, it took more than two hours to finish the job, before the yacht again could cruise rhythmically, but now very slowly, across the black Aegean Sea. The speed was reduced to nearly ten knots.

11

Mustafa observed the Scottish yacht on his radar screen just before it passed the Greek island of Sífnos situated between the Aegean Sea and the Sea of Crete. Mustafa's radar was an old, low range model, which only worked well within a range of roughly fifteen nautical miles. His agents, who had rented a yacht in Istanbul, had followed the Scots from the harbour at approximately ten miles distance. This, they believed, was outside a suspicious range. Mustafa was kept informed by radio telephone about all factors that might be of interest, including their position.

When Mustafa received the message that the Scottish yacht had come to a sudden standstill, he sent more than one thanks to Allah. He was convinced that his agents' sabotage efforts on the yacht's fuel reservoir had succeeded, even though the saboteurs regretfully had informed him that they had only managed to infect one of the reservoirs. Mustafa was aware this meant it depended completely on luck as to which reservoir the Scots chose, if their yacht was going to stop. The report said that the yacht had been drifting without an engine for several hours. Later it had continued in the same direction, but at a much slower speed. Mustafa considered that this indicated that both of the yacht's engines had been out of use for a while, but that they had repaired at least one of them.

He did not know the yacht was equipped with three

engines. However, the Scotsmen's problems had occurred perfectly for Mustafa and he happily sent the rented boat back to Istanbul. He estimated reaching the yacht twenty-four hours earlier than originally planned. The attack on it was therefore relocated to just off the island of Milos, only forty nautical miles ahead.

Meanwhile on the yacht, Mustafa's MTB had been seen on the radar screen for some time, when Mustafa discovered them on his. The Scots' radar had a much wider range. It was more powerful and the rotating antenna was situated higher above the sea's surface than that on the Arabian boat, giving it a range of twenty-seven nautical miles.

The Scots continuously observed the rented boat on the radar, but it was not unusual for boats to follow their course, as it was a normal route towards the Mediterranean. However, suspicions started to grow rapidly when the follower, too, stopped when their engine problem occurred. They tried calling it on the radio telephone's emergency frequency, but no reply was received. It suddenly had to be seriously considered that it carried Mustafa's spies. They became even more suspicious when the yacht began, again, to hang onto them when the third engine was started. The suspicion was not lessened when the pursuer turned around in the direction of Istanbul, after a second, fast-going boat was observed on the same course.

McPride and Wallace studied the radar screen in the cockpit.

"It might be Mustafa's boat that has taken the first boat's place and sent it back to Istanbul," McPride wondered aloud. "I will try to contact the second boat on the radio telephone."

This he tried, but they got no reply.

"I think the lack of reply from the damned boat only

confirms my suspicions," he said determinedly. "What do you think?"

"You might be correct. I think we must watch developments with the Hundred Eyes of Argus," Wallace replied uncertainly.

The faster boat was steadily catching up with them.

One hour later Wallace said: "All things considered, I think we should begin to prepare for a likely attack. Do you agree with me, John?"

"I think you're right, William. One might say, better safe than sorry."

The Scotsmen immediately started to prepare themselves as they expected Mustafa was approaching. All weapons were made ready for battle, the crew put on bullet-proof vests and life belts were made easily accessible.

The weather was bad and it was as dark as the black hole of Calcutta. Haze and rain reduced visibility to almost nothing. Low, black clouds covered the sky and completely prevented the moon giving any light. The visibility was frequently down to only a few metres each time the yacht disappeared into haze clouds. The helmsman was constantly dependent on radar and the electronic navigation system to steer the yacht.

Two hours went by and the approaching boat was now only approximately three hundred metres away. It steadily approached. The weather and the visibility were still very poor. Any kind of examination or identification of the approaching boat was completely impossible, even through the excellent American military night binoculars, which they had. They again tried to call up the approaching boat by radio telephone, but again received no answer.

The approaching boat was soon only a hundred metres away and suddenly an explosion in the air, just behind the yacht, pierced the dark silence. A rain of shrapnel from a shell hit the yacht.

178

"Damn hell, it must be Mustafa. Take cover at once," McPride called loudly. "It's bloody gun-grenades in the air. Hide yourselves on the floor along the hull."

Shortly afterwards he added: "Keep clear of the portholes, but the hull will withstand shrapnel."

Other explosions quickly followed and Mustafa's boat seemed to approach more slowly.

"It's an old fashioned, white painted British MTB," Wallace shouted after he carefully had looked above the fender around the hardtop.

The MTB's faint outline could be observed every time both boats were out of the thick mist at the same time.

All the Scots managed to take shelter after the first detonation. If they had not, there would have been a large number of casualties amongst them, as the shrapnel poured down like hailstones. After some minutes the detonations suddenly stopped. Instead, several machine-guns started quickly chopping. The bullets whistled and ricocheted as they hit the yacht's superstructure cladding. The machine-guns' sound was weak. It nearly faded because of the pounding sea and was not very unlike the US Marines corps' drum rolls at Arlington Cemetery, during burials.

After a short time, bullets from machine-guns started only to fly high above the Scotsmen's heads. But now and then, some bullets did hit the yacht.

"Return fire," McPride yelled several times, like a hope-less lunatic in solitary confinement.

All the Scots, except four, who quickly manned the machine cannons, together fired their AK-74 machine-guns at the escaping MTB. The cannons were already mounted and the noise from the guns was soon accompanied by the cannons' rapid, ear-splitting stuttering.

When the Scottish fire started, the firing from the MTB stopped immediately and it turned hastily 180 degrees and raced away from the yacht in the opposite direction. The two boats were moving away from each other at a combined speed of about fifty knots. The MTB became increasingly difficult to see through the darkness and the fog. The visibility was almost zero, but the Scotsmen constantly observed the escaping boat's exact movements on the radar screen and randomly swept their fire across the water, in the direction of its radar position. The distance between the boats was soon more than a quarter of a nautical mile and increased steadily. The rather useless fire from the Scotsmen's machine-guns therefore faded.

Only the machine cannon on the hardtop had clear sight backwards and could now be used in an attempt to hit the MTB. The cannon's target was tiny because the escaping boat had its stern towards the yacht, and it became smaller and smaller as it moved away. Another major problem was that the machine cannon's sight equipment was no better than that of the cannons which were used during the First World War. A hit on the MTB was almost impossible because of the limited visibility and the target was pitching up and down in the turbulent sea. The machine cannon therefore also stopped firing, as continuous shooting could only be considered as a waste of very valuable ammunition.

The Scots believed wrongly for a few moments that Mustafa had run away and quit the attack entirely, when he realised how heavily armed his opponents were. But shortly after the retreat, they observed the MTB making a quick turn to starboard, about a nautical mile away. It looked as if it were keeping that distance as it moved parallel to the yacht, like a lion guards a herd of buffaloes, just waiting for the right moment to attack.

Twenty minutes passed while the monotonous tone of the yacht's one working engine and the sound of the waves deafened the apprehensive Scottish worries with an almost calming effect.

Suddenly hand shells were detonated on the yacht's

upper level and abruptly ended the calm. Frantic screams from wounded and frightened people changed the apparent lull into a barbaric inferno. Arabs, with black-painted faces and dressed in black clothes, clambered on board the yacht like rebellious pirates who boarded Spanish gold galleons half a millennium earlier.

Mustafa knew that the Scotsmen had watched him far longer on their radar screen than he had been able to observe them on his weaker model. He believed that they did not have any information which would lead them to believe that the boat in their rear was an enemy. They would probably not be aware of any danger before he started to fire at them. Mustafa doubted that the Scots were armed with anything other than light hand weapons and maybe a couple of machine-guns. Any other weapons they might have received from the Russians were probably stored away to be undetected by a possible customs check, and so would be absolutely impossible to activate at short notice. Mustafa therefore reckoned he had to make a very quick attack so as not to give the Scots any chance to use any of the Russian weapons. Mustafa's biggest problem was how to capture the yacht without sinking it, because he wanted the weapons cargo.

He devised a simple plan. He would take the MTB as close as possible to the yacht. When they were in the right position they would fire Mecar high explosive shells over their heads. The shells only had a range of hundred metres, so the MTB had to come rather close to the yacht. The shells that were detonated would, hopefully, create panic and impair the Scotsmen's ability to act rationally. The blinding flashes in the night sky would also affect their night vision. In addition the shells would, maybe, kill a large number of them. While the shells disorientated them, Mustafa planned to send two fast dinghies with twenty of his men and attempt a silent boarding of the yacht. When the dinghies moved off, the men left on the MTB would target the yacht with machine-guns, high above the dinghies. This would divert the Scottish crew and prevent possible observation and attack on the dinghies.

Mustafa was very surprised when he suddenly realised that the yacht was equipped with machine cannons. His men, remaining on the MTB made the only possible move, when they took the boat off in the opposite direction and took up a resting position outside the range of the cannons.

Because of the loud sound of the dinghies' engines, they had to pass behind the yacht, on the starboard side, while the attack from the MTB was from the port side. They took the dinghies, at high speed, to about a nautical mile ahead of the yacht. Then with slower engines they proceeded back to the rendezvous spot with the yacht and reached it as planned.

The Arabs threw a dozen hand grenades on board the yacht, immediately they were alongside. Then, they threw grappling hooks to fasten ropes over the rail and began to climb on board like a battalion of fighting ants along a straw into a sugar bowl. The Arab surprise attack was going according to plan.

Wallace and McPride had been on the hardtop level during the entire attack from the MTB. While the shells exploded over their heads they had been lying on the floor, close to the back fenders in the cockpit, together with four other crew, who had not taken the chance to move towards the ladder to search for better protection below. They had been lucky because all the shells had detonated above the stern.

If any had detonated over the bow they would have been completely unprotected. They had been waiting for a chance to man the machine cannon on the hardtop level. No one had been seriously injured. Only one man had been hit in the shoulder by a fragment from the boat, forced loose by an exploding shell, but he could still use his gun without any problems. When Mustafa arrived with his men, the Scots thought the battle had ended, and so they were taken totally by surprise.

Three of them, Brian Cole, Daniel Folkestone and Henry Greenfield stood on the upper level's rear deck and discussed the attack that seemed to be over. Each had a whisky in his hand. Two of them were smoking.

The youngest one, Folkestone, blew a cloud of blue smoke that vanished quickly behind the advancing yacht and said, shivering with cold: "The Arabs have probably realised that we weren't so unprepared as they might have believed. They must really have been astonished at such strong resistance."

Folkestone was a bachelor who had spent almost all his adult life as a professional soldier in the Special Air Service. At the present time he had a sergeant's grade, but was not far from further promotion. He was the only son of a proud Scottish farmer. His father had a large farm in the Highlands – a farm that had been in his family for generations. The son had plans to take over the farm from his father and continue the family tradition as a sheep farmer, after he quit the army. He was an eager fisherman and used his free time to fish trout and salmon in the Scottish rivers, when he was not hunting for local girls to become the sheep farmer's wife.

"You know, nothing is like Scottish smoked salmon as a

starter and fresh Scottish girls as the main dish, or vice versa," he sometimes uttered.

Greenfield looked a bit uncertain as he said thoughtfully: "You never know about such people. They might reconsider their attack plans and be back before we know it. We'd better be extremely watchful."

Greenfield had ended his army career some years earlier and was the bookkeeper in a small Scottish timber company, when he was not a freedom fighter for Scottish independence. He was also said to be the freedom fighters' most ardent golfer. He could afford to go golfing. He was married to a business lawyer, who was well known and overcharged her clients with her large fees. They had a grown up child. A child, produced the only time Greenfield had forced himself between the law books, his friends always joked.

Greenfield had a golf handicap of minus five and could easily have been a professional golfer. It was, anyway, accepted that he was the champion at the freedom fighters' internal golf competitions, when they met to discuss future moves. He always won the whisky that was the prize, always to Cole's exasperation.

Cole was the most experienced veteran amongst them, but he was also the most serious whisky drinker. Not a single person had ever seen him sober when he had a day off. But he barely drank when he was on duty. He had lived a stormy army existence all his life. Everyone said that was the reason for his large consumption of whisky. He had fought in Africa, the Middle East and Asia.

Cole now was single, but he had previously been married

to a crazy, redheaded Irish girl who could not stand to be left home alone while he participated in all his wars around the world. One day, she had just suddenly left their flat in Glasgow, with a truck driver, he was told. He did not hear from her for a couple of years, when he received the divorce documents in the mail for immediate signing. The girl was then in the United States and had to remarry at once in order to get her residence permit. Cole signed the papers the very same day and went to his local pub and got drunk. He never mentioned the girl again.

Today, his cover, in case of enquiry by the authorities concerning any participation in the Scottish freedom fight, was as a pub owner. He owned a pub, which was absolutely unthinkable for upper-class people of the collar and tie type.

Cole thought to himself and blew smoke rings into the air, while his two friends talked, before he added slowly: "I agree with you, Henry – their attack seemed meaningless in the way it was done. It could be a cover for other actions. You never know, but we must be on full alert."

"Sure, the attack could not lead to anything. They must have further plans. We must watch out, maybe at this very moment they are approaching the yacht," Greenfield said firmly.

Greenfield was correct. These words became his last. The Arabs approached the yacht and threw hand grenades on board. The three Scotsmen were killed instantly. They never knew what hit them.

The sound from the yacht's upper level was tremendous as the hand grenades detonated.

"They're on board," McPride shouted loudly for everybody to hear, as if there was anyone who had not heard the sound of the detonating grenades.

However, McPride, as a well trained, experienced soldier, regained his self-possession quickly. He shouted orders down the ladder to the entrance section and the galley, where most of the crew was sheltered.

"Everybody out of the Arab arrival zone on the rear open deck. Prepare hand grenades to be thrown immediately."

McPride had a linguistic advantage, because only Mustafa, among the Arabs, understood the English language. Mustafa heard him, but failed to warn his men, who, without understanding English, swarmed on board.

The Scots waited a few seconds before they threw the hand grenades, in order to give their comrades, if still alive, the chance to escape from the fire zone and take cover. Afterwards, a dozen hand grenades were thrown from different positions on the yacht, in the direction of their uninvited guests.

The effect was tremendous. Seven Arabs, already on the rear deck at the upper level, had no chance. They were filled with shrapnel from the grenades and spread all over the deck in a mess of bloody body parts. It could not be worse in an African slaughter market. Viscera, legs, arms and heads, all mixed in blood, suddenly entirely covered the deck.

Three of the Arabs, who were about to climb on board the yacht, lost their grips and fell into the sea. As the yacht continued to move forward, the men disappeared at once into the dark.

Even before the hand grenades had detonated, the Scots' AK-70 attack rifles spread death, chopping fast on full automatic. Bullets swept over the rear deck and the passageway between the superstructure and the railing, along the boat's upper level. The enemy had no chance of survival on that level. The Scotsmen did not know the number of Arabs that took part in the attack, but they hoped the enemies were successfully beaten off.

Mustafa was again astonished at the Scotsmen's incredible ability to survive. The boarding of the yacht on the upper level had ended in complete disaster for the Arabs. He realised that his enemies were professionals. Ten of his men were already lost, without gaining any battle position. Seven men were killed on deck and three men must have drowned when they lost their grip.

It was, however, Mustafa's resourcefulness that had made him cut the rope attached to one of the dinghies tied to the yacht, as soon as the men fell into the sea. He hoped the men in the sea had realised this. Because of the time interval before he cut the rope, and the speed of the yacht, the dinghy would be about a quarter of a nautical mile from the swimming men.

The motor yacht had five portholes on each side of the lower level. While the explosions and the shooting had been going on, on the upper deck, Mustafa had shot the glass out of two of the portholes. It was impossible to see the dinghies and what happened outside the portholes from above, as nobody could be in the passageway without assuredly being shot. The Arabs could therefore effect almost non-risk access to the boat through the portholes.

Mustafa and his remaining ten men climbed very easily through the two portholes and into the boat without being detected. The portholes led them into the cabins in the sleeping section. Mustafa and six men were in one cabin, with the entrance connected to the staircase in the middle of the yacht. The other four were in another cabin, with the entrance connected to the staircase in the front.

Mustafa opened the door just a crack and heard whispering voices from above. There was a wide spiral staircase leading up to the upper level. After they examined the other two neighbouring cabins and found them empty, all the Arabs moved silently in single-file up the staircase with their weapons in attack positions. Thick carpets covered the staircase so they moved almost soundlessly.

12

The married couple, Michael and Mary McAllen, were kneeling beside the wall on either side of the entrance hall on the upper level, watching the doors to the passageway on each side of the yacht.

They had been married for five years, after they had met in the Army's Special Forces, but most of the time they had been away from each other, on service in different parts of the world. That might be one of reasons why they still were as deeply in love as the day the clergyman asked them if they would stay together in sickness and in health, till death did them part, somebody said. The couple had no children and considered the journey to Istanbul, from Spain and back, as their honeymoon trip. Both of them had only three months earlier finished their army service and signed working contracts with Sir Walter, as permanent crew on his yacht in Puerto Banus. Michael would work as the captain and Mary as the head of the galley. She was reckoned to be a marvellous chef, in addition to being extremely attractive.

Mary was the only daughter of a Scottish dentist from Dundee and trained as a dental nurse. When she caught Michael, she had caught one of the patients of the Army's Special Forces' Dentistry Unit.

Michael was twenty eight years old and from the northern Scottish coastal town of Thurso. He was the youngest son of one of the Stromness ferry captains. Each year as he grew up, nearly every summer, during the tourist season, he worked as a crewman on the ferry from Thurso to Stromness, in the Orkney Islands.

Both his grandfathers had been fishermen, and he had often gone with them on their fishing craft to the fishing banks and caught cod, haddock and mackerel, so he was very familiar with swinging boat decks under his feet. He had planned to follow the family tradition as a seaman, and before his army career he had taken his mate's certificate, but lack of available jobs had led him into the army.

Michael's mother's father had been the captain on a larger purse seiner, and he had sometimes gone with him on trips to the fishing banks off Iceland. Icelanders on a coast guard's vessel had once boarded their fishing craft and arrested them. They had been under arrest for nearly a week before the British authorities had managed to get them set free.

Michael was only a child at that time, and he could clearly remember the great fear he had felt of the huge fair-haired Icelandic seamen, who he was told were pure descendants of fierce Norwegian Vikings – even more pure descendants today than the Norwegians themselves.

One of the old fishermen on the British craft had frightened him greatly by telling him that the Icelanders used to eat young foreigners for supper as the only alternative to the everlasting fish. The fisherman was a real old shellback with stooping shoulders and white beard, seemingly with only one single shaky tooth and was always sucking on a crooked clay pipe. He had been on the grandfather's boat for a generation.

"Young foreigner is the only meat the Icelanders get," he had said with a grin, "and that's why they have boarded us."

Michael had been scared to death. His first days in Iceland had been horrible, but he had been somewhat

190

heartened when he discovered large flocks of sheep and understood that the Icelanders had other meat supplies. The Icelanders handled the British fishermen politely and correctly. This had given him hope that he, maybe, still would survive and not end up as a grilled meat portion on the Icelanders' table, with them sitting around, drunken and noisy, with their long fair beards and horned Viking helmets, drinking mead and chewing brutishly on his limbs.

Anyway, the Icelanders did obviously not like the British or anybody else catching their fish, and that was probably the only reason why they did not join the European Common Market.

To relieve the boredom of waiting, while the authorities negotiated the release of the fishing craft, the Icelanders invited their prisoners to visit their most famous tourist attraction – the geysers.

It was by one of these geysers that Michael first met Mary, but he did not know, at that time, that she would become his beloved wife, fifteen years later. They were the same age and they had looked curiously at each other, liked each other and played together as children always do. When they met many years later in the army's dentistry unit, they had fallen in love at what they then thought was first sight.

However, the clergyman had been quite right, when he said that the McAllen couple would stay together till death did them part.

Michael only had time to shout, "Mary, Arabs behind you," before his wife and he received a stream of bullets from the Arabs' shotguns that brutally tore their bodies apart.

Mustafa's guerrillas had shot them immediately, as they silently reached the top of the staircase from the sleeping section.

The Arabs inside the yacht were naturally detected when they killed the McAllen couple.

After the attack on the upper level McPride had climbed to the fly bridge from the hardtop level, to get a better view of the situation.

He shouted loudly when he heard the shots below and rushed down from the fly bridge to the cockpit: "Damn, there are even more of them on board – be aware and shoot!"

McPride's yelled announcement seemed completely pointless, as if any of the Scots did not know they had to shoot at an enemy that was hunting them to kill them and feed them to the fish. This was especially meaningless when the dangerous enemy was almost as close as at the other side of the table in the dining cabin and had already brutally killed their beautiful chef.

Wallace was well aware of McPride's sometimes ridiculous outcries. He remembered them vividly from the Falklands where they had fought together. If the situation had not been so critical he would probably have smiled.

The four Scots, Dave and Betsy Connoly, George Coe and Neil McNeigh, who were in the main salon in the rear of the dining cabin, threw themselves down on the floor instantly, when they heard the Arab shots that killed the McAllens. They immediately opened fire in the direction of the entrance, from where the Arabs suddenly had appeared. But their fire was too late as all the Arabs had immediately taken cover.

"Bloody hell, Betsy!" Dave Connoly whispered resignedly to his wife.

Dave and Betsy Connoly had grown up near each other in Aberdeen. They had not met during their childhood, though there were only three hundred metres between their homes. They met in the army where they both served for two years, before they started their medical training. Sweet music started smoothly between the two at that time, but it was when they met another time that the final settlement between them was categorical. Completely independently of each other, as members of the British UN contingent, they served as assistant hospital orderlies in the UN hospital in Angola. Dave was twenty-two years old and Betsy a year younger.

After the UN service, Dave started studying medicine in London. Betsy started at a school of nursing to be trained as a State Registered Nurse. Both of them were going to be employed by military hospitals. Therefore the army paid most of their education costs, but after they had finished their courses, they were bound to complete compulsory service in the army.

Betsy took additional courses in wound healing, and according to later reports, she was a lot smarter than any doctor was on that subject. Both of them were also trained in military operations as ordinary combat soldiers, and they both held the rank of captain in the Special Forces. They had experience in most parts of the world, where the Special Forces had been involved during the past decade. However, there had been some time for family pursuits and they had raised two children who were now students. As a hobby, they were eager clay pigeon shooters. This hobby served them well in their present situation.

*

193

The Connolys had just examined the results of the battle on the rear upper level deck, but they had quickly discovered that they were not needed. All the men were dead, blown into bits, spread around the whole deck. Some body parts and blood had also ended up inside the salon.

"It is an impossible task to collect the limbs and other loose parts of every person here," Connoly had whispered quietly to his wife.

Betsy had not replied. She just cried silently, and looked at him with the tearful eyes of a wounded deer.

George Coe interrupted them.

He stood nearby and said roughly, in an attempt to cover up his real feelings, but still sounded deeply affected: "Not much for doctors to do here! A slaughterhouse would not have been worse."

Coe had seen many similar incidents before, which were imprinted on his mind forever, only to be remembered every time he had oppressive moments. Nevertheless, this disaster was the worst he had ever seen.

He had previously participated in the Falklands War and the Gulf War, with the SAS's Special Boat Squadron unit – the Marines. He had been in the army since joining the Combined Cadet Force when he was only fifteen years old, although he had never gained a higher rank than commando sergeant. His superiors said he was a clever practical soldier, but not a tactical commander. He was single, but he was an eagerly practising woman-hunter wherever he went. The right one is difficult to find, he used to say, and his superiors suggested he handled that subject as he handled military subjects. He was never fully involved.

Betsy simply nodded slowly as a reply to Coe's comments, and she added dejectedly like a woman would: "It seems we have to make enormous sacrifices to reach our target. I only hope this will be the last one on this voyage."

Only a short moment later they found that their friends, the McAllens were shot.

Neil McNeigh the fourth of the Scots, who had stayed in the salon, immediately rolled down on the floor and cried loudly: "The McAllens are shot. – Bloody Arabs, they are still on board. – Take cover and shoot the devils. – They must have forced their way into the lower level through the portholes – damn bastards!"

McNeigh had been in the Royal Marines since he was only eighteen. He had never had any military ambitions. The army career had been chosen only because there were not many alternatives available for a youngster at that time, if the youngster was tired of school and had no parents to support him while he hung about in town or went to college. His military career had therefore only been to pass time, but that did not indicate that he was not very intelligent, for he obviously was. In addition to being a true supporter of Scottish independence, he was a man who greatly enjoyed nature. He was an eager sports fisherman and hunter and had very often participated in the British training camps in the wilderness, especially in Canada.

One day his military career had suddenly stopped, because of an incident where he had not conducted himself according to military rules or any other rules come to that. Not acting according to rules was quite common for him, but this time he was in real trouble, which was very difficult for his usually loyal superiors to ignore. It was during one of the annual winter training manoeuvres in Norway that it happened.

McNeigh came into conflict with some Norwegians in the valley of Gudbrandsdalen in eastern Norway late one Saturday night, over an attractive local girl. The girl had beautiful fair hair, long legs and was really an astonishing beauty, as he found most all of the Norwegian girls to be. McNeigh, though, thought this one was very special and he demonstrated his unique capabilities as a professional fighter too well with a group of large Norwegian rivals. He did not bite the opponent's ear off, like the previous disreputable American heavyweight boxing champion. No – McNeigh was a lot more rational when he fought, but altogether too designing and rational the court later decided.

In the British military court, two months afterwards, it was alleged McNeigh had sent five of the immense local fighters to hospital at Lillehammer, the famous town of the 1994 Winter Olympics. The ambulances also had to collect two local policemen, who hastily had come to arrest him after the combat.

The British military police caught him the day after and had him immediately sent back to England to prevent the Norwegian authorities catching him. They did not believe the Norwegian court would be fair, as McNeigh was a foreigner. The Norwegian court system is known abroad to have a very limited sense of justice concerning foreigners. The Norwegians have always enthusiastically talked about equality before the law and racial neutrality, but their actual conduct appears quite different.

By that time McNeigh had made the local girl pregnant. She obviously liked the grand combatant and gave herself to him as a reward for knocking out all his rivals in such an amazing way.

After the incident he loyally paid maintenance to his Norwegian daughter and her mother every month. He also maintained close contact with them. He and his child's mother planned to marry in the near future.

After the Saturday night battle in Norway, Neil was sentenced to two years in prison by the court. He served it in a British military prison and was released after eight months because of good behaviour. He found imprisonment not so very different from his ordinary army service. The only difference was the lack of freedom and that he did not have to take part in all the rough training courses for servicemen. He did not actually dislike the detention and gained a stone in weight because of a more relaxed life than he previously was used to. After his release, he was dismissed from the army, without additional pension.

McNeigh's superiors said on the day he was dismissed, that their actions were simply to demonstrate an act of precedent to their Nato ally Norway. They also said they would otherwise have dropped the whole case because of lack of evidence. It had been clearly stated that the Norwegians had started the fight, but he had been a much better fighter. Anyway, his superiors were very impressed how easily he had beaten the immense number of huge Norwegian fighters. He was a real elite British soldier. They had advised him to lie low for a couple of years, until the whole case was forgotten and then reapply to be enrolled in the forces. His superiors said they would give him the best references.

After his dismissal from the Royal Marines, the SS Group had employed McNeigh and, at present, he was one of the permanent crew on the chairman's yacht.

The gunfire, from the four members of the Scottish crew in the salon, had not surprised the Arabs as they came up the spiral staircase. Mustafa and one of his men had vaulted the hurdle on the floor, to the left side of the top of the staircase, immediately after they had killed the McAllen couple. They were under cover when the crew started heavy fire from the salon. The crew in the salon had a view through the doorway, between the dining cabin and the entrance, directly towards the top of the staircase.

Two others of Mustafa's men, who had moved quietly after him up the staircase, had tried to do the same as he had done, but at the other side of the doorway. One of them was immediately shot dead by at least twenty bullets from the crew. The dead body fell on the other one and mostly protected him from the chain of bullets, but he had still been hit in the left side of his belly by a couple. The wounded Arab rolled quickly into cover, and although he was bleeding heavily from his serious wounds, he was nevertheless able to handle his gun.

The other three Arabs, who entered the yacht in the same cabin with Mustafa, did not move when they detected the staircase being closed by the Scotsmen's fire. They wisely kept their heads below the top of the staircase. After a short time two of them hastily went down to the lower level, while the last of them stayed on the staircase, ready to shoot if the situation arose.

Wallace had stayed in the cockpit. When the last attack started he moved hastily over to the top of the spiral staircase, which was the only connection down to the level below. This staircase was connected with the staircase from the sleeping section, where Mustafa and his bunch of guerrillas had come from. Wallace quickly spotted the Arab who had taken up position in the staircase and threw a hand grenade down. This instantly killed the Arab. The two others on that level were still functioning, but in locked positions. The Scots, however, did not know of their existence.

The four Arabs, who had boarded the yacht in the sleeping section in the front, had no passage to the section that Mustafa had entered, but there was a staircase from this section to the front of the entrance, behind the galley. The galley was between the top of this staircase and the one that Mustafa had used. This cabin, with single beds four steps up from the rest of the lower level, was situated in the yacht's bow. It had two large hatchways covered with transparent Plexiglas in the ceiling and another two small hatchways, used for ventilation, and usable emergency escape ways to the front deck.

The four Arabs divided. Two of them climbed up the staircase and took cover inside the galley. They could do this without being detected by the Scots in the salon. The staircase ended a few metres from the doorway to the galley on the starboard side of the yacht.

The two others made their way through the emergency escape hatchway. They felt the cold wet wind directly in their faces when they climbed out on the front deck. The wind speed was strong because the yacht was pitched into it. This was a dangerous manoeuvre because they could easily be observed from the cockpit. However, the Scots who did not continually keep careful watch on the bows evidently overlooked them. The inner part of the deck was not visible from inside the cockpit. They crawled further along the passageway on the starboard side and observed Mustafa who had taken shelter in the doorway between the entrance and the passageway. They also saw, through the windows along the passageway, the shadows of their two comrades, who by now had installed themselves in positions to be envied in the galley. Both of them chewed enthusiastically on delicious chicken legs that they had found in the refrigerator, and swallowed them down hungrily, with some red wine.

Mustafa gratefully observed the two guerrillas, from the emergency escape hatchway, when they appeared at the front of the structure. He had previously observed the two who were in the galley. He assessed the situation and quickly designed a new plan of attack.

He whispered to the man beside him: "As far as I can see

at the moment, our force consists of us and another man at the opposite side. He is seriously wounded, but he will be able to handle the gun – do you think?"

The guerrilla beside him nodded anxiously, but it could easily be seen on his face that he was far from sure.

"Also, two men are in the galley and another two are in the passageway. In addition, I heard, a moment ago, low whispering from two men below, who still must be alive in spite of the grenade that dropped from above, but I do not know if they are wounded," Mustafa continued in a hushed voice.

Then without any further hesitation he decided on his force's next move.

He said: "I will send you and the wounded man on the other side, along the passageway to shoot through the windows into the salon. The two men in the galley will attack the salon through the doorway between the entrance and the dining cabin, just after you have started. When they have started, one or two men from the lower level, depending on their present condition will support. To prevent a repetition of the grenade attack from above, I will let the two in the passageway climb up on the outside the structure. They will shoot into the cockpit and if possible throw a couple of hand grenades. I will, however, myself remain here, as I believe it will be the best position to co-ordinate the attack."

The Scots in the salon thought cautiously about the situation after the attack through the doorway.

Connoly whispered: "Whatever we do, we can't stay here – this might be a very dangerous trap. I suggest we move silently back to the stern, below the rear deck, above the engine room. There, we will have sufficient cover and the enemy will not know where we are. We will have the same view towards the doorway to the entrance and we will, in addition, get full sight of the passageways on each side of the boat. – Agreed?"

No one replied, only nodded in agreement.

Connoly kept on talking quietly: "Betsy, Neil and I move over at once. George covers our move by burning off a short burst with his machine-gun towards the sides of the doorway after I have thrown this hand grenade into the entrance, to deafen the enemy for some seconds."

As they all took cover against shrapnel, he pulled the split-pin from a grenade and threw it into the entrance. Just after it exploded the three of them ran across the deck, which was covered in dead bodies, and jumped down onto the roof of the engine-room. Coe burned off some rounds with his machine-gun and followed. The plan had succeeded.

In the cockpit McPride and Wallace discussed their next move. The biggest problem was that they did not know what had happened below. But it was quiet at the moment, so there had to be a certain static warfare. The crew contained exceptionally brave and quick thinking people with the best experience. Thus, they believed the situation below could not be completely impossible. Anyway, at the moment they could do nothing else but concentrate on their own situation. However, they agreed to have two of the crew on the fly bridge to cover the outside of the boat structure. That would be the couple, Elise and Harry McCoy. They would have a number of bazookas available, possibly to be used against the MTB, if it came closer. Wallace and Ann Castle would cover the staircase and watch the radar screen. John and Jane Loverty would man the machine cannon if the motor torpedo boat approached. The yacht had to be manoeuvred on the auto-pilot.

Suddenly they saw that the MTB had turned its bow and was heading for them at full speed.

13

The weather had cleared and visibility had become considerably better during the last quarter of an hour. There were few problems seeing more than half a nautical mile across the sea, but there were still clouds of haze, some down to the sea surface. The wind speed had increased notably and the waves had heightened. The sea was more aggressive than earlier. The shadow-like contours of the MTB loomed into the Scotsmen's view through the dark.

John and Jane Loverty were about to rush to the machine cannon on deck in front of the cockpit, to be ready to take in the rapidly approaching MTB, but they inexplicably hesitated a short moment before they ran. This probably saved their lives.

The Lovertys were in their mid-thirties and both were working as teachers in the same high school near Aberdeen – John as a mathematics teacher and Jane as a language teacher. This year the couple had leave from their positions for further studies.

They had met approximately ten years earlier during their studies and had no children. John had sufficient weapons experience from two years in the army. Jane had a little experience from one year of army service as an assistant nurse. However, she had, during the previous evening, got a quick introductory course in being the second operator on the machine cannon.

The Scots in the cockpit could again hear the sound below of detonating hand-grenades and chattering machine-guns. Only two guns started, but a few seconds later many more were in action.

A short time later, Elise McCoy, who kept watch on the yacht's superstructure, together with her husband, suddenly yelled out desperately: "Bloody Arabs outside the window!"

The black-bearded, sooty-faced Arabs, who had climbed outside the superstructure, had appeared by the cockpit's windows. They had, as silently as possible, moved up the slimy, wet structure, like two invisible demons. The tinkling of breaking glass could be heard over the loud sound of shots.

Ann Castle, who was inside the cockpit, let out a heart-piercing shriek when the bullets hit her right upper arm and thigh. She immediately passed out and slumped to the floor.

Ann was the only daughter of a rich industrialist in Glasgow. Theirs was a very old Scottish family. She did not need to work and had mostly studied at different universities both in Britain and abroad. It was through her studies that she had become involved in the secret Scottish freedom fight. Subsequently, she had joined the army for a couple of years. Whatever she was told to do, was always carried out splendidly. She was thirty four years old, tall, and extremely beautiful. She was always a very popular guest at aristocratic banquets. Many of the nobility courted her to become their wife and producer of the next generation, but all of them were politely rejected. Miss Castle wanted a life with ordinary people and did not desire to be a protected, treasured ornament in a glass case. Another important factor was that she had become an intensely enthusiastic freedom fighter and Scottish aristocrats did not go along with her views.

The Arabs' firing positions from the slimy, wet structure in front of the cockpit's windows were somewhat unpleasant and difficult. In addition the yacht's strong vibrations as it ploughed through the large waves made it completely impossible for them to aim accurately at the targets inside. Only that saved the Scotsmen.

McPride and Wallace reacted instantly and automatically. They swung around and pulled the triggers of their machine-guns simultaneously. Streams of bullets from automatic weapons hit the two Arabs outside the window, in their faces. Their heads exploded as they were forced into the air by the pressure from the bullets. They fell in a large curve and splashed into the sea, where they at once disappeared behind the yacht, which, manoeuvred by the autopilot, proceeded steadily forward uninterrupted by the battle.

The Scotsmen below, on the engine room roof, did not have to wait more than five seconds after they had established their new positions, before they could see two Arabs, in black, running quickly towards the stern. One Arab each ran down one of the passageways that were on either side of the dining cabin and the salon. They opened fire at once, when they reached the salon's windows, which were all immediately completely shattered, and they kept on firing frantically.

A few seconds later, another two Arabs appeared in the doorway, also firing rapidly into the salon. The two Arabs in the entrance soon became four, when the two from the sleeping section ran up the staircase to join them immediately the shooting started.

They appear just like ants, Connoly thought grimly. How many might they be?

The Arabs did not realise that the salon was empty until one of them suddenly shouted indignantly in Arabic: "There's nobody in the salon! It is absolutely empty. Where in hell are the bastards?"

The Arabs stopped firing as suddenly as they had begun. For a moment they stood silently, bewildered, perhaps looking for ghosts, apparently without any plan. They just stood with empty, or nearly empty, machine-gun magazines, gazing in amazement as if they just had landed from the moon.

At this moment the Scotsmen popped their heads above the rear deck and started to shoot as fast as possible. The two of them at each side of the yacht's rails immediately killed the two Arabs in the passageways with dozens of bullets. Then they moved closer to the middle of the yacht to assist their friends with the fire towards the entrance, at the same time steadily watching the passageways.

The Arabs were taken completely by surprise, and fell dead on the deck like gassed flies. Only one of them had a mind clear enough to respond to the fire. A continuous stream of bullets was running from his machine-gun. Two bullets hit Coe in the chest. The rest of the bullets hit the teak deck in front of the defenders. Splinters flew like in a sawmill. The defenders' bullets, on the other hand, hit their target and the Arab soon looked like a damaged sieve as he fell dead on the deck.

Coe was thrown backwards by the force from the Arab's bullets. He was strung against the yacht's rear steel rail, where he remained hanging like a wet towel out to dry.

The defenders' gunfire stopped. All the Arabs seemed to

have been killed, but suddenly they saw one Arab dive into the sea.

"Don't shoot!" McNeigh said quickly. "If that bloody Arab has chosen to die by drowning instead of being killed by our bullets, that must be his own decision."

Then they heard McPride shout loudly from the cockpit: "How is the situation down there?"

He had registered that the shooting had ended and hoped fervently that they had completed their task. He was indescribably relieved when he heard a Scottish voice reply.

"I think we have managed it," Connoly replied just as loudly from below. "The last rat seems finally to have abandoned the ship."

"Dave, I hope you are right. I'm coming down immediately," McPride replied, as he started moving carefully and watchfully down the ladder.

He shook his head sorrowfully, with tears in his eyes, when he saw the young McAllen couple lying dead on the floor in the entrance.

He said sadly: "More casualties?"

"See for yourself," Connoly replied dejectedly without looking up, while he knelt beside Coe, who had been removed from the rear railing.

McPride swallowed a couple of times while he looked around, before he said in military style, hiding his feelings: "Examine the yacht for any more of those bloody Arabs."

He was silent for an instant before he warned: "Be damn careful. Shoot at once if you detect any of them, because those people will kill you if they get the chance. To kill you, will give them a much coveted ticket to Paradise, although they will be killed themselves."

The wounded, Ann and Coe, were immediately taken care of. Betsy efficiently cleaned and bandaged Ann's wounds, while her husband worked on Coe. They had been installed in the owner's cabin in the front upper level. Betsy had given Ann a pain-killing and sleeping injection. Her wounds were not dangerous. Both the hits had been by steel mantel bullets that had gone directly through the flesh in the right upper arm and right thigh, without fracturing any bones. She had been extremely lucky. Her wounds would only leave future cosmetic scars on her body. She would be completely healed within three weeks, Betsy said with relief, when she was finished.

Coe had not been that lucky, but he too would survive without any injury of a permanent nature. Two steel mantel bullets had gone through his chest and out at the back. The bullets had not touched the spine, which would have paralysed him, but one of his lungs was punctured and two ribs were splintered. He had regained consciousness after being taken down from the steel railing. However, he had been extremely lucky not to have regained consciousness before he was taken down, otherwise he would definitely have fallen overboard and vanished into the sea. Coe was also lucky that the Arabs had not used lead bullets. If they had, he assuredly would have been dead. Lead bullets would have given him fatal wounds, as they are soft and expand when they meet flesh or bone on the way through a body. Lead bullet wounds can become as large as clenched fists.

The Connoly couple were professional medical practitioners and again lived up to their excellent reputations, but they did spare some grateful thoughts for the dead Arabs who had used steel mantel bullets in accordance with the Geneva Convention. The couple had many times previously experienced terrorists using lead bullets, sometimes also with a drilled hollow, or a cross hole into the top to make the lead spread more easily in order to cause maximum damage to the victim.

*

The MTB had stopped approaching the yacht, keeping as before at a constant, but shorter distance, not far from half a nautical mile.

The machine cannons were examined. The upper ones proved to be untouched by the fighting, but the lower one had been at the centre of the battle almost all the time, and was entirely destroyed. The Loverty couple therefore manned the upper one and waited patiently for an order from McPride to start shooting at the MTB.

"The MTB remains obviously at a distance where it can see us with the naked eye, in spite of the darkness and haze," Wallace said. "They must believe that they are still at a safe distance outside the cannon's range."

"They're probably also damned right," McPride commented resignedly.

He picked up the binoculars from the floor, where they had fallen during the tumult, and carefully studied the enemy's boat for a long while.

"It's still too far away to hit them with the cannon, in these conditions. It seems we can only watch and later, if necessary, decide what to do if they come closer. I'm convinced they will not leave us before they have obtained sure indications about the outcome of their comrades' attack."

The yacht passed through a thick haze so the funeral of the dead Arabs could proceed in a way that could not be seen from the MTB. The bodies were tied up one by one on a long rope, as bait on the hooks when fishing. When the last body had disappeared into the sea, the destroyed cannon was fastened to the end of the rope and thrown overboard as sinking ballast and anchor.

Wallace considered cynically that the funeral was almost exactly like line fishing, only the flagpole with the red marker flag was missing. He thought it would be a sumptuous meal for the fishes, even if the waters were not heavily shark infested. He was convinced that the fishes that might be there, probably started on their stupendous Arabian, fresh-meat banquet long before the last body reached the surface.

Nevertheless, he said very respectfully and calmly: "These Arabs were obviously no ordinary terrorists. They must have acted for their cause, as we act for ours. By a completely random incident we have met to fight over some weapons, like two male lions fighting over a dead deer. The lions do not really want to harm each other, but nature is cruel. However, this time, the Scottish lion has won over the Arabian lion – peace be with them."

The dead Arabs got no other words to send them on their way into the deep, not because the Scots had no respect for the dead, but because of their lack of knowledge of Arabic funeral procedures. The Scots were also too exhausted after the fight, and too emotionally drained because of their own casualties, to perform anything except what was absolutely necessary. Anyway, they considered that the Arabs had probably already reached their Promised Paradise immediately they were killed in their heroic battle.

The perished Scotsmen's bodies were laid out in the cabin to the front of the engine room. The couple, Mary and Michael McAllen, had died for their cause, an independent Scotland, like Brian Cole, Daniel Folkestone and Henry Greenfield. McPride stood for a long time red-eyed and remembered those, who shortly before, had been a living part of his life. He promised himself he would do whatever he could to make sure that the Scottish people never forgot these heroic freedom fighters.

Immediately after the casualties had been taken care of, McPride and Wallace had a tactical discussion in the cockpit about further action concerning the MTB.

"Our main problem is that the crew on the MTB probably

know exactly what kind of cargo the yacht is carrying," McPride said, and took a deep breath before he proceeded, worrying about what he was going to say next. "To maintain the secret of our cargo completely, there seems no other acceptable alternative than to eliminate the MTB's crew entirely, and the only way to do that is to sink their boat."

So as not to let McPride's rather final suggestion hang too long in the air, Wallace readily took joint responsibility: "I thoroughly agree with you John, but before we can use our weapons on the MTB, it needs to be considerably closer. At the moment the Arab craft is too far outside effective operating range for our remaining machine cannon, with its antiquated sights. It is quite impossible to operate that old-fashioned cannon on a small boat rocking in the waves from another small boat doing the same. The chance of getting an accurate strike at this distance might be considered approximately zero."

Wallace pushed his right hand through his soaking wet hair. All the time the sea spray forced its way through the broken windows. He looked worried, as he continued: "The bazookas are even more inaccurate under these conditions. You know it is very difficult even to hit a moving battle tank at half a kilometre's distance, when you can at least predict the horizontal position. You can therefore only imagine how difficult it will be to hit the MTB, which is dancing violently up and down like a bottle cork in the waves. You must also consider that the marksman stands with his legs spread balanced, on this boat's deck, which is also dipping up and down, but not synchronic with the target."

"I understand, but there is also another huge problem, William. We will never get a second chance," McPride added quickly.

"Yes – of course that's completely indisputable," Wallace confirmed.

"What do you consider the maximum range for our

weapons, to be completely certain of a positive outcome?" McPride asked like a military leader in front of his men at the pre-battle briefing.

Wallace replied without further consideration: "Less than a quarter of a nautical mile, but I would like to divide that distance in two to be quite certain, especially because the MTB has a considerably higher top speed than us. If the Arabs, for instance, come closer at their maximum speed it will be exceptionally difficult, or almost impossible, to hit them with our weapons. Another major problem is that we don't know what kind of weapons they have at their disposal."

Wallace sipped from the bottle of Coke he had collected from the refrigerator, while talking. He burped loudly, in a way that definitely would have prevented any future military promotion, if there had been one of these ridiculous English army officers, recruited from the peerage, in front of him.

"Hand over the Coke," McPride said and stretched out his hand.

Wallace immediately gave him the bottle and McPride took an immense gulp and afterwards also gave a deep belch, as if to express loyalty to his companion.

Wallace smiled momentarily into his beard and continued after this break in tension: "We know for sure that there can't be many Arabs left on the MTB, because they sent about twenty people to attack us and the boat is fairly small. This will prevent them using different weapons at the same time. In their first attack they only used hand weapons and gun grenades with a maximum range of about one hundred metres. In addition they have a light machine cannon or a mitrailleuse, but I don't think that will represent any great danger if we keep our heads down."

He bent his head to illustrate, while he again wiped his wet face with the back of his hand.

"My conclusion is," he said in his school-masterly way, "that I consider their weapons not to represent any risk for us at all."

"Could you suggest any method of getting the bloody MTB closer," McPride asked, greatly impressed by his colleague's reasoning.

"I certainly can," Wallace answered with a wide smile, after he considered for a moment. "The Arabs are, of course, very impatient to get information about the result of their friends' attack on the yacht."

McPride nodded to show he agreed with Wallace's notions.

Then he asked curiously: "How would you make them curious enough to come closer, when they still haven't received any message from their comrades that they have taken control of the yacht? They must know from their first attack tonight that we carry a lot of heavy weapons. Are you going to tell them on the radio that Santa Claus has arrived, and that they must come immediately and receive their Christmas gifts?"

Wallace smiled and replied quickly: "No, I wouldn't do that. I assume the Arabs don't believe in Santa Claus. I will simply set our yacht on fire."

McPride asked, obviously astonished: "You will do what?"

"I will just set the yacht on fire!" Wallace repeated loudly as a broad grin covered his entire face."

There was a pause, while McPride stood like a living question mark and Wallace smiled brightly and knowingly, as he looked at his puzzled companion. His companion obviously believed that he had gone completely crazy.

To calm him, Wallace said: "It will of course not be as dramatic as you might think. I will simply make some small fires around the deck to produce smoke to indicate fire. From a distance it will look exactly like the yacht is on fire.

You can be quite sure that the Arabs will immediately come closer to inspect."

In Mustafa's absence the MTB's captain was Ibrahim Mahfouz. He looked distractedly through his American naval night binoculars towards the yacht on the starboard side, about half a nautical mile away. The binoculars had been bought from an American sailor on leave from a warship, on a courtesy visit to Alexandra. The sailor had no doubt stolen them from his ship, to obtain money for the harbour whores, but the binoculars were excellent and a great deal better than any other that could be bought on the black market.

"An hour ago I could hear the faint sound of chattering machine-guns and some explosions that might have been hand grenades, but now it is as silent as the tomb," Mahfouz said worriedly.

"Let me see," Naguib said, and grabbed the binoculars from him.

He directed them, at once, towards the yacht and said: "You are damn right Ibrahim. It seems completely silent, but I can see some smoke from the cockpit and from the stern and the bow of the yacht."

Pasha was one of Mustafa's oldest friends. He was not considered to be very bright, but he was vigorous and as faithful to Mustafa as an old dog.

"Let me see again," Mahfouz said, this time visibly worried. He roughly grabbed the binoculars back.

He confirmed Pasha's sighting with a slight nod and with notable apprehension said: "It seems like you are damned right, Naguib."

After a short consideration he continued rather uncertainly: "I know we have not had the agreed signal from Mustafa yet, but I think it is necessary to get closer to the

214

yacht, to examine the situation. Mustafa told us to stay away until he had given us the sign to approach, but they might be in great danger and not have had the opportunity to give us the agreed signal. We must be extremely careful because of the Scots' weapons. Would you have believed such a peaceful looking leisure yacht could be equipped like a battleship?"

He was really afraid of the yacht's weapons that had surprisingly been demonstrated during their first attack. Nevertheless, he did not wait for Pasha's reply, but turned the steering wheel harshly to starboard. With an ear-splitting roar from the engine, the MTB departed from its relatively safe position along the yacht's course, outside its expected weapon range, and moved closer.

On the yacht the Scots had lit low, widely based fires from splintered furniture, old wet clothes, wet carpets and wet curtains drenched in diesel from the fuel supply. One fire was set on the steel roof of the engine room on the lower level, outside the salon, where four of the crew had been when they killed the last of the Arabs. Two other fires were started at each side in front of the lifeboat, which was placed on the steel deck behind the teak deck at the hardtop level. The last was on the front steel deck.

McPride had ordered everyone to stay out of sight of night binoculars from the MTB. It also had to be absolutely silent on board the yacht.

14

Mahfouz accelerated the MTB to full speed and steered it in a tighter and tighter spiral around the yacht, which steadily lost its remaining speed. The oil smoke from the Arabs' boat's old engine was nearly as thick as the smoke from the burning yacht.

Mahfouz yelled loudly to Pasha between fits of coughing and the ear-splitting engine noise: "Do you see any sign of life on board, Naguib?"

Pasha, who was closely studying the yacht through the binoculars during the approach, only shook his head as a reply, while he still kept the binoculars focussed.

"I think we must get even closer," Mahfouz yelled, visibly impatient and curious.

The MTB approached the yacht closer, in steadily decreasing circles, but at a somewhat slower speed.

"The speed of the yacht can't be more than five knots and it still seems to be falling. Have they all killed each other?" Pasha speculated.

Suddenly Mahfouz became intensely suspicious and stopped the approach.

McPride and Wallace and the rest of the crew had carefully observed the MTB's movements after they had lit the fires on the decks. It slowly crept closer and closer, while circling like hunting wolves trying to steal up on reindeer on a mountain plateau, before making their final attack.

Then the Arabs' boat unexpectedly stopped approaching and McPride whispered impatiently: "Stay down and wait. They are still too far away. If they don't see anything they will perhaps come nearer."

The Scotsmen's nerves almost reached breaking point as they kept themselves hidden from the Arabs.

For a long time Mahfouz considered what he should do. Because of the Scots' weapons he felt it was extremely dangerous to go any closer to investigate the reason for the yacht's strange behaviour, but he was still curious and simply had to know. He also felt obliged to assist Mustafa or he would surely kill him at the first opportunity afterwards. Therefore Mahfouz actually had no choice. He asked Pasha for the binoculars again and studied the yacht for a long time, but he still saw absolutely no life or movements. He considered the pros and cons of going nearer before he made his resolute declaration.

"Pasha, we must go closer to examine it."

Mahfouz's curiosity and great fear for Mustafa's possible future revenge had in the end, overcome his natural innate desire for safety. He reduced the speed of the MTB immediately and approached the yacht very slowly. The distance between the MTB and the yacht was soon reduced to a quarter of a nautical mile and was steadily decreasing.

The Scotsmen stayed hidden. Their eagerness to rush out, burning off their weapons, was under control. They waited silently and obediently like trained police dogs, for McPride's order to attack.

Then McPride suddenly shouted, nearly deafening them

as he ran, together with Loverty, to the machine cannon on the hardtop deck: "Attack – attack the damned MTB – now!"

The machine cannon was already hammering death before the first bazooka missile left its tube in the direction of the MTB.

The Arabs saw the yacht come to life. They saw two people running to the cannon. On the fly bridge two others appeared with bazookas on their shoulders. The same happened on the upper level only seconds later, where four men directed bazookas towards them through the broken windows.

Mahfouz screamed desperately as a terrified horse before it sinks in a quagmire: "By Allah – the damned Scottish bastards have cheated us."

Instantly, he pulled the throttle to full speed and spun the MTB's wheel in panic to get away as quickly as possible.

These words were Mahfouz's last. The bullets from the machine cannon perforated the MTB's cockpit and the two Arabs inside. The bullets also killed the one who handled the mitrailleuse on the deck. Two bazooka missiles hit amidships and tore the steel apart. The remaining bazookas missed their target and vanished into the sea close to the craft.

An explosion in the MTB's ammunition store occurred immediately the bazooka missiles hit. The four Arabs in the rear of the craft, who handled the craft's engine, died immediately in the immense explosion. The MTB was cut in two separate parts that rose into the sky like Tower Bridge in London opening for a vessel, but considerably faster. Then the parts slid into the water and vanished in different directions, just as if the entire event took place in slow motion. Waves immediately covered the spot where the craft had been. It was as if the MTB had never existed.

Mustafa calculated, after seeing all his men being killed, that his only chance was to dive into the sea and disappear. A second later he was swimming under water to avoid possible shots from the Scotsmen, while their yacht vanished. When he breathlessly broke the surface again nearly two minutes later, the yacht was almost half a nautical mile away.

However, Mustafa had not dived into the cold sea without reflecting about his chances of survival. He knew that the yacht was about to pass a small Greek island. This island was situated about fifteen nautical miles south-west of the island of Milos. He reckoned that he was less than two nautical miles away from this island. To be realistic, he knew his chances of reaching the island were very small, nevertheless he considered himself a strong swimmer, and he had absolutely nothing to lose. The only alternative had been to remain aboard the yacht, which would have resulted in certain death from bullets from the Scotsmen's weapons.

Mustafa's biggest problem while swimming was not the distance to the island, but to keep in the right direction in the dark hazy night. Mustafa also knew he only had a short time. He calculated he could probably survive in the cold water until daybreak. He could see the yacht disappearing, far away as a shadow in the night. He knew the yacht's course was south-westerly. If he swam ninety degrees to that course, which would be north-west, he would be in the right direction. The problem was, of course, the probability of swimming in a curve, as he had no references to correct his course against. Anyway, he considered that he would be a lot nearer to the island at dawn, when the light made it possible to see, than he was at present. He considered that if he was still alive by dawn; he would reach the island.

Only ten minutes later Mustafa realised that his contemplation about swimming to the Greek island had been a waste of time. One of his men, who had been in the dinghy that he had loosened when the men fell into the sea earlier that night, picked him up from the cold sea.

The man on board the dinghy told how he caught sight of it in the wake of the yacht. He swam for his life and caught it just before it drifted away. Afterwards, he had searched for his colleagues for a long time without any result. Both of them must have drowned. After the empty search, he had headed after the yacht by tracking its wake. As he approached the yacht, he had suddenly seen the shadow of a man diving into the sea, and he decided to stop and investigate.

The only two survivors left of the large Arab attack group, headed in silence towards Milos.

The yacht sailed at full speed for the rest of the night. The Scotsmen wanted to get out of Greek territorial waters as soon as possible. They had to make the distance from the encounter as great as possible in case the Greek authorities discovered the battle. They passed between Crete and the Peloponnese islands during the night. In the morning they observed a Greek patrol boat passing at a distance, but by then they had reached international waters and were safe.

During the night they had washed down the boat after dumping the damaged carpets, furniture, teak deck and wallboards into the sea. They had tried to get rid of all signs of battle. The yacht almost looked as if it was unfinished from the fitting-out yard where the battle had been fought.

Many bullet and grenade marks were still easily noticeable in many areas. In addition windows were broken. Nevertheless, proper painting could cover a great deal of the marks on the outside structure that might not be seen from a distance.

McPride and Wallace discussed the yacht's state, because they could not sail any further with it in its present condition.

"It will be too suspicious, and will cause unwanted questions from the police, if we arrive at a port with the yacht in this condition," McPride said.

"I agree completely with you, John, but that gives us only two alternatives – to sink it and replace it with another one or to repair it somehow."

After a lively discussion they finally decided to order air freighted spare parts from the producer in the United States. The spare parts would be delivered to Malta, where the main damage would be fixed at the SS Group's small shipyard. Further repairs would be done during the journey from Malta to Gibraltar. However, to keep everything completely confidential, it was necessary to bring a reliable construction team to Malta from the group's shipyard in Edinburgh.

In the unlikely event of inspections by the authorities, the crew had rehearsed a detailed story concerning the damage. They would say pirates had attacked them, resulting in material damage in addition to the two casualties, Ann and Coe, who could be examined.

The Scots had defended themselves during the pirate attack with the two Remington rifles and the two Colt 38 pistols, which were normally always locked up in the cockpit. Weapons of this type, locked up and controlled by the captain alone, were almost standard equipment on all yachts of this size and had been customs-declared in all the ports it had visited earlier. They would say that they had been extremely lucky. First of all, the pirates had probably not expected any defence at all. Secondly, an approaching boat might have scared them off.

At noon the funeral was held for their dead colleagues, who were laid to rest in the traditional British Navy way of the sea. McPride gave a short solemn speech. Officially, it would be reported that the dead had drowned in an accident with the lifeboat, which had sunk during a pleasure trip at sea, while the yacht for a while had dropped anchor in international waters. Therefore the lifeboat on the hardtop level was removed and sunk.

The remainder of the Russian hand weapons and the last machine cannon were thrown overboard. The weapons of course, could not remain on board if there was to be an inspection by the authorities. This seemed to be completely unlikely, but good officers always take all possibilities into consideration, even though there may be only the slightest chance of this, McPride said. He and Wallace believed, as well, that it would not be necessary to have any weapons on board the yacht for the rest of the voyage. The western Mediterranean Sea was quiet and well patrolled by some of Nato's largest partners and it seemed altogether unlikely that anything would happen within their sphere of control.

The yacht arrived at Malta at dawn, two days later. It docked at the group's shipyard in Valetta. As expected there was no customs inspection by the authorities concerning a yacht owned by the chairman of one of the biggest employers on the island. Therefore the customs declaration was executed as in the usual way on Sir Walter's visits. McPride went to the customs office with the declaration documents. The Maltese authorities were used to the chairman's regular visits and never interfered with any industrial leaders that created work and activity on the island, as these people were too valuable to the Maltese society.

The yacht's producer had delivered spare parts immediately after the order was received. The Scotsmen knew they would do so, and the spare parts were already waiting at the shipyard when the yacht arrived. That is why executives always choose this brand of yachts, Wallace had cheerfully remarked, when he reported that the cargo was received as planned.

The producer had received a list concerning the necessary spare parts via the SS Group's E-mail. All the spare parts had been instantly available because they continue to build similar yachts and have a policy of always supporting their customers immediately, wherever they are in the world.

A brand-new lifeboat was rigged from a local supplier in Valetta to replace the sunken one.

The repair team had already arrived by plane when the yacht docked. The completely reliable handpicked staff worked extremely quickly and efficiently. Therefore, only four days later, the yacht was able to leave Valetta in the direction of Gibraltar with the repair team following to finish the work.

Wallace left the yacht in Valetta and travelled back to Scotland by plane, but the rest of the crew, including the wounded crew members, led by McPride, remained on the yacht to Gibraltar.

The wounded crew were under the medical care of the Connolys and could not have had better care in a private hospital. The reason they did not leave the yacht in Malta was that they wanted to be able to stand on their own legs when they left. They were expected to be able to walk by themselves when the yacht arrived in Gibraltar. If they had left the yacht in Malta, they would have to have been transferred to a Maltese hospital, where questions from the authorities would automatically have been raised because of their gunshot wounds.

The voyage to Gibraltar was extended by some days because of time needed to repair the damage while the yacht was cruising out of sight in the Mediterranean. Therefore the voyage took more than a week. The crew went ashore and took a plane to Scotland and a completely new crew took their place. This crew had arrived in Gibraltar some days earlier and had stayed at the Rock Hotel while waiting because of the delay. The yacht docked and refuelled in Gibraltar and left for Edinburgh early in the morning the day after its arrival.

From Gibraltar the yacht was under command of the newly retired Commander Stephan Hunter. His subordinate was also a newly retired Royal Navy officer, Commander Peter Ballentine. Which of them was the real commander of the yacht was only an academic question.

The two highly decorated and well known navy officers were specially selected by the Scottish Independence Organisation because they would deflect any suspicion from the authorities when the yacht arrived at the SS Group's shipyard in Edinburgh. That two newly retired, high ranking officers, both pensioners in good health, had taken a summer job on a large yacht was quite normal for such people.

After his retirement from the Royal Navy, Commander Hunter was working full time with the Scottish liberation group. The cause had deeply burned within him all his life. He was a very experienced officer, and had participated in the Royal Navy as a cadet on a British warship during the Suez crisis in the fifties, and had been the commanding officer on another during the Gulf War in the nineties, thirty-five years later.

Hunter was a tall man with a square Scandinavian face and thick white hair. His ancestors had been the historically barbarous Vikings that had come to Scotland from Scandinavia, to plunder, to drink and to rape all the women, he proudly announced at parties among the officers, especially if it were late at night and the drinks had been large and strong.

The befuddled women around him would scream pretending to be terrified: "Oh, don't rape me, brutal Viking, don't rape me, brutal Viking." Or they simply yelled pretending horny desperation, while they wiggled their bottoms worse than an old whore in the Rieperbahn might: "Rape me brutal Viking – oh, rape me – I do so absolutely need to feel a *real* man."

Hunter was, of course, very flattered, but did not always feel too happy when women yelled that, because that indicated that their husbands were not *real* men. He frequently boasted that he did not need to rape women as they always came freely. Because of this his friends called him Viking – and some of them, rather sarcastically – the horny Viking.

On duty, Viking was a man of very few words; quite different from the popular, talkative person he was at drinking parties. He was a born leader and his crew always did tasks quietly and efficiently around him. It was entirely unnecessary for him to give any orders in detail.

Surprisingly, after his many rumoured adventures with women, he was still with the same wife he had married forty years ago.

His wife, Susan, was still very pretty for her age. She was very intelligent and must have been astonishingly beautiful when they married. Susan had always been a real advantage to the Viking when they attended functions together. She

225

was always the most attractive woman at parties. A couple of times they had been representatives at naval celebrations where the queen had been among the guests. With a smile on his face, Viking had told his wife that she should keep a low profile, so as not to take the glory away from the queen. Among his friends, it was a standing joke against Viking that he had his wife to thank for his promotion.

The Hunters had three children – one boy and two girls. The boy, Hank, was a naval officer like his father. He was the captain of a minesweeper, which was stationed near Edinburgh. Both the girls had a university education. Jane was working as a teacher at a college, but her sister Kate was married to a wealthy Scottish landlord and was not working at all. All the children had at least one interest in common with their father. They were all eager Scottish nationalists, and they all worked for Scottish liberation.

Commander Peter Ballentine had a very similar style to Viking. He was also a man of few words when he was sober. He was as tall as Viking, but he did not have the same broad face. He had a more typical Scottish look. He wore a Clark Gable moustache that was now white. He was a little more of an academic type than Viking, and had by coincidence been promoted to commander shortly before him, though they were the same age. He never forgot to remind Viking about that when they had their frequent whisky battles. Viking had been his closest friend for decades, ever since they first met as cadets.

Ballentine's tall, redheaded wife, Careen and the Viking's wife had also been friends since they first met. The Ballentines had two children. The elder was a boy, who, together with his wife and their three children, had taken over the family's farm. The Ballentines' younger child was a girl, educated as a lawyer. She was divorced, as lawyers often are, and had no children.

Ballentine's name and his taste for the well known Ballentine brand of whisky, gave him the nick-name among his friends after his first week in the navy, forty years ago – Whisky. So it was that Viking and Whisky took the yacht to Edinburgh that summer. Scotland's future was again completely dependent on the Vikings and the Scotch whisky, as Scotland had been dependent earlier, many would say.

The voyage took its natural course, without any problems. They had some bad weather in the Bay of Biscay, but who does not have bad weather there?

The barometer fell the instant the yacht had passed Galicia, the western corner of Spain. One hour later the Atlantic waves thundered under the keel of the small craft. The yacht rocked on the waves like a teacup in a funfair. Many of the crew had not been aboard such a small craft in full storm and developed problems with their stomachs and vomited like young boys the first time they are drunk. Viking and Whisky, on the other hand, seemed really to be enjoying the situation.

Suddenly an intense, loud sound was heard. It sounded as if the yacht was being squeezed to pieces. Something hammered on the yacht's structure and the sound reverberated like it must feel to sit inside a drum while somebody is beating it.

"What in hell is that, Viking?" – asked Whisky, yelling because of the sound of the storm, but as calm as always. "It sounds as if we are being pulled apart."

"Yea, it really does," Viking replied also yelling but also calm. "I'd better go and look."

Viking moved along the walls from the front of the

227

cockpit to the stern, like a completely drunken man, desperately trying to keep upright. He inspected the yacht's deck outside the window and could see the new lifeboat, installed on Malta, performing like a cabaret dancer on the deck.

"The sound is coming from the bloody lifeboat that has loosened. Hope it doesn't hit the cockpit."

That was exactly what the loose lifeboat did, only half a minute later. It approached the cockpit at full speed and crashed into the wall with massive force, after hovering above the sitting area like a small plane landing with an inexperienced pilot at its joystick.

Viking was suddenly thrown back on the floor like a rag doll. The windows splintered in a roar and the lifeboat forced its way into the cockpit where it stopped abruptly with its bow nearly five metres inside the room. Stormy seawater immediately splashed through the hole made by the lifeboat. Together with the strong wind it made the room extremely cold and unpleasant.

From the corner of the room, where he had violently landed, Viking suddenly shouted loudly above the storm's noise: "I didn't ask it inside. It came quite uninvited and I had to move away rather quickly so as not to be smashed."

Whisky, who had feared his friend was seriously injured, was relieved at hearing his voice, but he did not show it.

He shouted back: "Oh, that was why you were in such a hurry. I wondered what it was all about. By the way, where did you learn to fly?"

Viking forced himself to his feet, very stiffly indeed.

By great effort he managed to inspect the lifeboat and roared loudly as he twisted his neck painfully: "It seems as if we will have to swim if the boat sinks, this lifeboat will never float again."

*

The rest of the voyage passed without any more serious incidents, but of course rather uncomfortably for the helmsmen, who had to stay in the cockpit with a large gap in the structure letting in the stormy Atlantic water. However, in the English Channel the yacht met summer weather and the rest of the voyage to the Scottish Standard Group's shipyard in Edinburgh was reasonably pleasant.

There were no customs inspections when they arrived. The customs inspectors would, of course, not risk exposing themselves to ridicule by wishing to examine a vessel sailed by two of the best-known commander captains in the Royal Navy, who for decades had taken the largest British warships in and out of their harbour.

The night after its arrival at the SS Group's shipyard, the yacht was unloaded, and the atomic weapons were freighted to their various destinations, ready to be used.

15

Salnikov arrived in Spain three days after leaving Istanbul. He had crossed the Greek border, from Turkey, in a rental car. A ferry had taken him from Patrai in Greece to Lecce in Italy, where he had rented another car. His false passport had only been briefly examined at the borders of Turkey and Greece, and again when he arrived in Italy. Afterwards, he had driven in different rental cars on the motorway from Lecce directly to Marbella in Spain.

Lapin had, with his false passport, travelled the same route as Salnikov from Turkey to Greece because there are few acceptable alternatives by road. For security reasons he had travelled three hours behind Salnikov on a tourist bus.

Before he took the bus he had equipped himself with a suitcase and clothes like an ordinary tourist. All the border crossings had been very smooth. The Turkish border guards did nothing other than wave the bus through to the Greek control, which had only checked the number of passports against the number of passengers in the bus and returned them with a broad welcoming smile.

Lapin was of course extremely relieved when he was safely in Greece. He took a tourist boat the next day from Athens to Catania in Sicily, where he took a bus directly to the ferry for the mainland and a train through to Rome International Airport.

He bought a one-way ticket with Alitalia to Madrid, where he at once bought another one-way ticket to Rio de Janeiro with Iberia. He stayed there for some weeks enjoying life, before he again changed his identity and passport and travelled on to Venezuela, where he intended to stay permanently as a real dollar millionaire. He later bought a luxurious property near the sea, in the east, not far from Caracas.

Salnikov established himself in Marbella as planned and bought a luxurious house near the Aloha golf course, for a company he had quickly established on the Caribbean Cayman Islands, on the recommendation of an efficient, but very expensive Spanish lawyer.

The establishing of the company was quite simple. It only took a telephone call to a local lawyer in Cayman and then to wire the money he wanted. A red Mercedes convertible sports car, with a very powerful engine, was also immediately bought for the same company.

A couple of months after his arrival, he bought a ninety foot American motor yacht which he registered with a Liberian post-office box company which he had established in Monrovia.

At the golf course he had, by chance, met a Scandinavian shipping magnate who had escaped his homeland some years ago, after he had been convicted for some illegal money transactions and became bankrupt. After imprisonment, the magnate had moved to Marbella and started up a well-run shipbrokers company in Gibraltar. He had recommended this way of owning the yacht to Salnikov and had quite easily established the company. The shipbroker contacted a lawyer he knew in Liberia and Salnikov sent the requested money. It was a smooth and quick operation, which was similar to the creation of the company in the Cayman Islands.

Salnikov moored his yacht, as he had planned during his first visit to Marbella, together with the jet set's yachts, in the famous Puerto Banus marina. The yacht had been sailed across the Atlantic from Miami, where it was bought.

Lapin had come from Venezuela to Jamaica by plane to help Salnikov sail. He had boarded the yacht in Kingston and sailed with it to Santa Cruz on Tenerife. "I indeed need some practical experience with yachts," he had said, and only a short time later he bought an almost identical one of his own.

Both of them had become rather capable yachtsmen during the enjoyable voyage. The weather was perfect, except for a couple of days when they really learned nautical lessons, but the yacht had been very seaworthy and they had gained invaluable sailing experience.

Lapin's participation in the sea voyage had another purpose. They had to meet in any case, to prepare bank documents, as they had made an agreement that whoever outlived the other should inherit the money.

Salnikov had organised his stay in Spain in a way that gave him no assets in the country. He therefore avoided all authorities, most especially the rather enthusiastic taxation authorities. A *gestoria* took care of all the Spanish official paper work including the taxation concerning the property at Aloha. To avoid any personal taxation he lived outside Spain on his yacht for a part of the year. In case of inspection he was very exact in keeping its log.

Sometimes he only sailed the yacht to Gibraltar and dropped anchor. Then he had technically been abroad, only little more than an hour away from the Aloha golf course and his house along the coast road. During the summer he sailed the yacht to the French Riviera, where he stayed nearly the whole season with an assemblage of new girlfriends.

After his arrival in Spain, Salnikov had laboriously improved his golf performance and successively lowered his handicap. In March, a year after he had arrived, it was as low as three and he was suddenly a very acceptable golf amateur. He relaxed frequently in the golf club's bar or restaurant, where he discussed golf and business with a growing circle of friends. Mentally he had completely suppressed his previous life and was now just a retired businessman, living out his life in Marbella.

Women were consumer goods for Salnikov at first when he arrived in Marbella. His money and life style drew women like a magnet. He really acted as one of the essential elements of Marbella's jet set and frequented the casino and night-clubs. He thought more than once that his deceased wife would have rotated rather quickly in her grave if she had known about his unrestrained behaviour. But after some months the jet set life became rather boring and he contacted Brigitte, the Danish woman he had met in Benidorm nearly a year before. He invited her to stay with him. She was most enthusiastic and immediately accepted his invitation with great pleasure. Therefore, just fourteen days later she was established as his housekeeper and mistress in Marbella.

Salnikov's life suddenly became more regulated. He always had somebody to return to after his golf tournaments and other activities. He could spend a night at home without feeling lonesome and he had a very reputable woman by his side when he was invited to dinner parties with friends. He quickly became used to her talkative ways and could soon easily read newspapers without being significantly disturbed by her non-stop chatter.

What Salnikov liked best of all about Brigitte, was that she continually increased her demands in bed. Every night she sent him wearily into a dream world where he stayed satisfied until he woke next day with his face buried between her huge tits. Nearly every morning she impatiently expected a repetition of the night's physical activity. And he often had to admit that today it was only self-charting. He was simply too debilitated. These times Brigitte always mounted him with a triumphant, satisfied smile and soon yodelled like an entire Tyrol chorus, while greatly indulging in the enjoyment. When she finally satisfied her carnal desires she would exhaustedly admit it was because she had to take the opportunity while it was there. The breakfasts Brigitte served at lunchtime these days could only be called majestic.

At Easter they went skiing in the Sierra Nevada, only a couple of hours away by car from Marbella. They stayed at the Parador Hotel. It was not a luxurious hotel, but it was in a good location above the narrow valley where most of the other hotels were situated. The hotel's restaurant was simple, but relatively pleasant, and the food was satisfactory.

Salnikov, who was a very experienced skier, believed his Scandinavian woman would be the same. But he soon realised she was not. He had to admit that she was like a cow on the skis. Brigitte explained to him that the climate in Denmark was very much like the climate in southern Britain, rainy and unpleasant in the wintertime. If it infrequently snowed, the snow would only lie for a day as a thin film over the landscape, before it disappeared. Although she had skied some weeks in Norway with her parents when she was growing up, that was not very usual for Danes.

However, Brigitte's lack of ski experience gave no problems. They took the lift to the restaurant at the plateau near the top of the slope. She installed herself at a table in the sun, while Salnikov practised skiing alone on the slopes that

234

mostly were empty because most of the visitors were inexperienced skiers and chose Brigitte's alternative, at the restaurant table. When they left for the day, Brigitte used to cow-ride on her skis down the narrow valley, before he followed more professionally some minutes later.

It happened one of those days when a haze suddenly filled the valley without warning and the visibility was reduced to only a few feet. Salnikov had slid slowly down to the centre where the lift started, but could not find Brigitte. He alerted the rescue team that found her half an hour later. She had run into one of the lift pillars hidden by the fog and seemed badly injured. She was taken to a hospital in Granada.

Salnikov had to stay alone while Brigitte was hospitalised. He became rather restless and took up his night-club visits again. It was during one of these visits that he recognised Cleo, who had been with Sofia and Mustafa in Venice.

Mustafa, and his companion, had landed on the Greek island of Milos less than one hour after he had been picked up out of the sea. The Arabs were exhausted and in soaking wet clothes after the dramatic incidents of the night. Their teeth chattered so loud with the cold, they sounded like bore-hammers on a construction site. They reached an uninhabited area of the island and undressed instantly from their wet clothes and hung them up to dry. Afterwards they threw themselves onto the soft, yellow sand on the beach and slept till the sun woke them at dawn, frozen to the marrow.

Still in wet clothes they immediately started to sail the dinghy along the island's coastline, hunting for fuel and food, which some local fishermen sold them for a bunch of wet American dollar notes. After a quick meal, the voyage continued in the direction of Athens, about a hundred and twenty nautical miles away. The voyage could be done relatively safely even with the small dinghy, as they sailed along the four islands of Sifnos, Serifs, Kithnos and Kéa, that divided the stretch from Milos to the mainland, in about five equal parts. The Arabs reached the mainland approximately ten kilometres from Athens, in the evening. Next day they departed from the International Airport after another handful of wet American dollars had been exchanged for new clothes, and a third handful, as well as their wet passports, provided them with two seats on a plane to Cairo.

Nearly two years later Mustafa landed at Malaga International Airport, together with five of his best guerrillas, in addition to Sofia and Cleo.

Since she left Venice, Sofia had joined Mustafa's army unit and had become a well-trained guerrilla soldier, though her elite weapon still was her sex appeal – her huge bust and the rest of her lovely body.

The Arabs travelled directly from the airport to Marbella and checked in at the hotel El Fuerte. Mustafa was chasing Salnikov. He desperately wanted his money and revenge for the weapons he had lost. He had never doubted for a second that Salnikov had arranged the destruction of the weapons on the vessel that sank outside Istanbul. He himself had paid him a considerable amount and he was convinced that the Scotsmen must have done the same. His only problem was finding him, as he understood, of course, he would have changed his name and tried to become anonymous. He was certain that Salnikov was in the area because the reports from his agents, who had followed the Russian after their meeting, had told him that he was looking around Marbella to find a place to settle.

Sofia and Cleo had seen him and knew his face in a way that only women do. Mustafa was therefore quite sure they would find Salnikov for him.

In the following days, the Arab women visited all the night-clubs in the area. After a week Cleo could proudly report that she had seen Salnikov at one night-club. Cleo had pretended not to know him and had therefore kept away from him when she watched him, but from that very moment the Arabs knew his every move. They mapped all his habits and also became aware of his frequent visits to Brigitte at the hospital in Granada. Later they obtained the information that Brigitte usually lived with him in Marbella, but was in hospital because of a skiing accident

Salnikov became very anxious when he spotted Cleo and so he left the night-club. He believed it was no coincidence that this girl had appeared. She is surely looking for me, he thought, frightened. Mustafa did not pay the second instalment for the weapons, and he must have plans to get back the first. He must also have worked out that I was responsible for the destruction of the vessel. The Arabs must have followed me the first time I visited Marbella and therefore knew that I would stay here. Damn stupid of me to ignore that.

Salnikov travelled directly home after he left the night-club. Mustafa certainly knows I am a marked man and must avoid the authorities. His thoughts were confused and he was really afraid – almost desperate. He was not thinking clearly and rationally. Mustafa can steal my money as easily as he can take sweets from a child. I can't contact the police. I can do absolutely nothing. When he travelled home that night, he did not know or even think that the Arabs might be following him.

The following days Salnikov was completely paralysed by

shock and was therefore not acting like the soldier he was trained to be. He realised that he had felt too safe and never reckoned on the possibility of such a situation that suddenly was a bloody reality. Till then, everything had gone so smoothly and there had been no problems in creating a new life in Spain.

He considered different alternatives to calm his fears. I might just leave Spain and flee to South America, like Lapin. The more he thought about that solution, the more attractive he found it. After some days of consideration he decided to contact Lapin in Venezuela.

Salnikov called Lapin from a phone box in Marbella, as he felt that would be safer than calling him from his home. However, he did not know that the police systematically bugged all public telephones in places like Marbella. The police know, as well as everybody else, that the Marbella district is full of criminals. Bugging public telephones was therefore only a very logical step and accepted by the ordinary citizens. Salnikov though, did not express himself in a way that would raise suspicions and would lead to police actions. He explained the situation to Lapin, in a way that definitely could not be understood by an outsider.

Lapin agreed with him that the best solution might be to travel to South America, but he said: "I'll travel to Spain first to note the situation."

This was of course not a very logical decision, considering the situation was urgent, but Mustafa had once tried to kill him and he deeply wanted revenge. Salnikov would act like bait for him to catch the damn Arab, he thought fiercely, but he did not tell Salnikov this. He concluded there was enough time available to travel to Spain from Venezuela, before anything serious could happen to his friend.

The very same day Salnikov saw Sofia at the outdoor restaurant at the golf course. She came straight towards him once she saw him. She smiled as sexily as previously and pretended to look astonished to see him there.

"Hey!" she said in amazement, "are you really here my love?" she continued without waiting for any reply. "I wouldn't have believed it!"

Salnikov did not know what to say and Sofia kept on: "Do you live here?"

Again without waiting for him to answer: "How marvellous – I am here with a friend of mine – Cleo, you know her. She is the girl you met in Venice – do you remember?"

At the same time, Sofia bent herself over Salnikov and kissed him several times all over his face.

"Oh, I love you darling. Oh, I have missed you."

She flaunted her bust in front of Salnikov's face, before she sat down on the nearby chair.

Salnikov thought quickly that maybe it was a coincidence that Cleo and Sofia were in Marbella. Maybe he still was safe. Maybe all the unpleasant and depressing thoughts that had filled his mind the last few days had been completely groundless. They might only have been thoughts without any real foundation because he was in a stressed and uncertain situation. Salnikov suddenly saw some hope, some light at the end of the dark tunnel that he felt he was locked into.

Salnikov said, pretending to feel happy: "How nice to see you, Sofia. I have also thought a lot about you."

Salnikov was not really sure if he was pretending any more. Sofia's sexy behaviour fooled him completely. Sofia whispered, and tried to look as sexy as possible. She continually wriggled her bottom on the chair like her pants were filled with ants.

"I want to have lunch with you." She rolled her eyes. "Afterwards I want to have you for myself, as dessert."

Sofia made another sexy move and waved for a waiter, without waiting for an answer from Salnikov.

She ordered *paella* and *sangria* without asking Salnikov his wishes. Salnikov smiled for the first time since meeting her. She treated him just like his deceased wife did, many years ago. His wife had never given him a chance to decide what to eat at a restaurant.

"Do you remember Mustafa?" – Sofia said suddenly, when the meal was nearly finished. "He was killed a year after you met him. It was in the Mediterranean somewhere."

Salnikov did not know anything about the battle between the Arabs and the Scotsmen in the Mediterranean, but he considered that it was not unlikely that the Arabs had followed the Scotsmen's yacht, which they had discovered in Istanbul. Salnikov knew the Scotsmen were extremely well armed with the weapons they had received from him in addition to the atomic missiles. It was therefore not improbable that Mustafa might have been killed. A hope lodged in Salnikov's mind.

After the meal Salnikov was thinking more with his head in his trousers than with his head above the collar. Sofia had done her job well. He greatly wanted her. However, his head above the collar decided that it was less dangerous to take her to the yacht than back home. The couple therefore soon left in Salnikov's red Mercedes in the direction of Puerto Banus.

Sofia undressed both Salnikov and herself as soon as they arrived on the luxurious yacht. She threw herself desperately on top of him.

"I want you – I want you," she screamed vigorously with bestial sensual pleasure, like apes in the Amazon jungle during the mating act.

Sofia at once turned Salnikov over on the bed and dipped herself hairless and wet down on his bursting manhood.

She rode him, soaked and muscular, until his eyes flickered and he was violently driven into his first climax, while she continuously screamed: "I am coming – I am coming!"

This climax was not the last one with Sofia during the afternoon. Salnikov was entirely in her hands and she did things with him that he had never imagined.

After a while Sofia said: "I want to spread you out and bind up your arms and legs to different sides of the bed and make love with you. I promise it will be a marvellous experience for you."

Salnikov accepted at once without thinking, entirely driven only by the enormous sexual desire that Sofia had created. Five minutes later she had tied him up.

Suddenly Cleo rushed through the door into the cabin, as she said huskily, with a practised sensual voice, "You have prepared him for me I can see, Sofia. I saw you drive from the golf course, and I followed you."

Sofia did not reply. Cleo undressed quickly and seemed just as impatient and eager as Sofia. Arabian women have only hair on their head. She looked stunningly marvellous without her clothes. Salnikov's desire that had been momentarily disturbed by Cleo's unexpected entrance in the cabin rose again to full length. Cleo let him taste her thoroughly before she threaded herself around him and drenched over his enthusiastic lordship. She screamed as loudly as a lioness for her mate when she reached her climax, while Salnikov made an extremely violent ejaculation inside her, accompanied by a frantic roar. He was at the same time wrenching against the ropes that firmly held his hands and legs in a stable position.

"I can clearly see that you enjoy my women," Mustafa suddenly chuckled with a malicious grin. "I knew exactly how to catch you. You damned bitch fucker."

Mustafa stood in the cabin.

16

Salnikov had not noticed that Mustafa had entered the cabin, while he had been occupied with Cleo. He panicked and became alternately hot and cold. He writhed in the ropes, which bound him. He wanted so desperately to get loose, but he could not move. He was exposed naked, and natural behaviour would be to cover himself up. He wanted to escape. He wanted to get into a defensive position. He could do nothing, but lie there exposed for all the Arabs who were streaming into the cabin. Only his eyes darted feverishly about.

Five Arabs entered to join Mustafa. All of them wore workmen's clothes. Two of them carried between them a portable gasoline driven generator of electric power. The others carried small toolboxes, which they immediately opened.

The women dressed and left instantly, without a single word, only with a compassionate smile in Salnikov's direction.

Salnikov regained a little of his senses and thought during an almost lucid moment: "I have been the world's biggest fool. I have been a tremendous, gigantic idiot."

There was no more time to think, because Mustafa said, in a simpering voice, as if he was asking a bank manager for a loan without sufficient security.

"You see, we told the port guards that we were going to

do some work on your yacht. We told them also that it would be noisy. They replied it was all right, but only during the week. On Saturdays and Sundays it had to be quiet."

Mustafa waited a moment to see Salnokov's reaction before he continued with the same smirking voice and the same unpleasant broad smile covering his face. "As you probably have already worked out, we are going to work on you, and I can assure you that we are very enthusiastic and clever workers, almost artists in our field. Years of experience have developed an artist's fantasy and creation."

The other Arabs chuckled loudly at Mustafa's remarks, as hyenas must sound over a stinking, dead cadaver.

Mustafa kept on: "I am sure the sound of the generator will cover your screams and I can promise you that you will yell more than the passengers in the loop-carriages at Disney World. However, you do not need to express thanks, although your ticket for the pleasure trip is quite free. You can only be sure that we will do the treatment on you with great delight, while we remember all our friends that you have sent early to Paradise."

The Arabs planned to give Salnikov electric shocks. They exchanged the ropes on his legs and arms for leather straps lined with rubber to prevent wounds and current leakage, and they fastened the same type of straps around both his thighs to keep them down on the bed. Straps were also fastened over his belly and his chest for the same purpose. To prevent him making a sound, they put a rubber ball into his mouth and plastered over his jaws. He had to breathe through his nose. Electrodes were fastened to Salnikov's soles and arms. Another set of electrodes was fastened to his testicles. The Arabs also fastened electrodes behind his neck at the point where the spine reaches the head. As a final act they fastened a steel ring, with rubber inside, around his head, to keep the head completely still while the operation was going on. On this ring there were some

243

electrodes connected by small wires. They shaved his head in places and fastened these electrodes to his skull.

"It seems we have finished our preparations," Mustafa said as politely as a dentist would do, with a *this won't hurt* grimace on his face.

He continued without interruption: "Now we can start on the real work."

At the same time he pulled on the generator's starter cord to burst it into action. It started with a loud roar.

Salnikov was too terrified to think clearly before he got his first electric shock. It went from his feet up through the spine into his head. Another one went through his testicles. He tried to cry out, but the ball in his mouth prevented any sound, but he shook like a pig shot in the skull. He remained conscious throughout.

The Arabs laughed loudly as if they were at a circus watching a particularly hilarious clown.

They took the ball out of Salnikov's mouth, when he had calmed down a bit, and Mustafa began his long-waited questioning: "As you probably might have guessed, we are interested in the money you got from us and the Scotsmen who you sold the weapons to. Please, tell us immediately were we can find it and give us the bank codes. In return we will stop the special treatment on you."

Mustafa did not receive a prompt reply from the completely worn out victim, so he added another lie after a pause: "You will, of course, be a free man once we have got the information."

Salnikov could not reply even if he wanted to. He was too stunned and gaped like a fish that has just been pulled ashore.

"The damned bastard will not answer," Mustafa yelled greatly irritated. "Give him some more electric shocks. I presume that will definitely loosen his damned, bloody Russian tongue."

He again pressed roughly and angrily the rubber ball back into Salnikov's mouth, and fastened his jaw with tape.

"I shall make you know how it feels to die without actually dying. I believe that will open your cussed Russian mouth very quickly," Mustafa said while he beat his clenched fists into Salnikov's defenceless face.

A second later they started the terrible electrical torture again. Salnikov vibrated once more uncontrollably like a shot pig, and his eyes turned once again inside out, but he still retained consciousness most of the time. Sometimes he had a blackout and then the Arabs stopped the treatment while they poured cold water on his face. When he regained consciousness, they immediately restarted the torture.

A couple of times Salnikov became blue in the face because he had vomited and the ball in his mouth prevented him getting rid of the substance. He could not breathe. The Arabs, who obviously were very experienced in this kind torture, simply removed the ball for a minute and then started on the torture again.

"Let him rest for half an hour," Mustafa said impatiently after a while and stopped the noisy generator. "I need a coffee-break. It's too hot in here and it smells awful. That bloody son of a bitch," he pointed towards Salnikov on the bed and made a grimace, "must have emptied himself completely. There is shit and piss all over. Clean it up. I'll return in half an hour."

Mustafa left and slammed the door behind him. He went into the galley of the motor yacht while the rest of the Arabs remained in the cabin to control the prisoner and clean up.

A second group of Arabs in doctors' white coats had entered Brigitte's hospital, in Granada and kidnapped her. Brigitte was brought into the cabin and presented to Salnikov.

Your dear darling is with us, Salnikov," Mustafa said sarcastically.

"Now we will demonstrate how Arabs handle women. Get into action men," Mustafa ordered.

"The Arabs tied Brigitte's hands together with a rope fastened to the ceiling. They gagged her and then violently tore off her clothes. When she was naked, they immediately started to rape her in turn. Brigitte tried desperately to scream, but the gag prevented her. She was soon resigned and hung by her hands from the ceiling like a cured ham, while the noisy Arabs continuously brutally penetrated her, laughing all the time.

When all the Arabs were finished Mustafa said threateningly with a barbaric smile: "If you don't give me the required information I will kill her immediately."

Salnikov whispered that he still had most of his money in Switzerland. He stated the bank's name and the account numbers with their access codes.

Mustafa hurried away immediately to catch the first plane from Malaga to Geneva.

Salnikov remained tied up in his bed, but the Arabs rigged up an arrangement to feed him intravenously. The drips should keep him alive till Mustafa returned from Geneva. They also put a blanket over him to maintain his body temperature. Brigitte was thrown down to the floor and tied up.

"Permanently available for us," one of the Arabs said leeringly.

Salnikov was as ill as he could be and only infrequently conscious. He could not think clearly any longer, but he knew he and Brigitte had only won some time before their certain death, unless something absolutely unforeseen happened.

*

246

For security reasons Salnikov had made an agreement with the bank about withdrawals from his accounts. First of all, he was the only person that could draw money from the accounts from a distance. Secondly, if he sent a fax, he had to make additional calls and speak with two bank employees who had to recognise his voice. He also had to tell them his mother's maiden name and a number code as an additional proof of being the right person. Only a small amount could be drawn in this way. If he wanted larger amounts he had to travel himself to Geneva and present his fingerprints.

Only one additional person could draw money from his accounts. That was Lapin and he could also draw unlimited amounts by presenting his fingerprints.

Mustafa returned from Geneva the following day. He was scowling with wildness, because he had realised that he would never be able to get any money from Salnikov's accounts. Thus he started on a new torture of Salnikov out of pure revenge. He gave Salnikov electric shock after shock and Salnikov vibrated like a frozen electrical cable. His eyes rolled from side to side like the eyes of a spectator at a tennis match, but ten times faster. He snorted from his nose like a horse that was being ridden to death. Salnikov was indeed experiencing what it was like to be brutally killed, hour after hour all day long, but without actually dying. When Salnikov fainted Mustafa only poured buckets of water over him to return him to unending torture.

Suddenly the choleric Mustafa got tired of the electric torture. He wanted an alternative. He tore out his revolver and gave Salnikov a shot in both kneecaps and in both elbows. Salnikov still tied up, vibrated like a compressor drill at full speed, and his eyes rotated as fast as the wheels of a racing-car. From his nose came sounds like from an old, damp locomotive.

Mustafa was not finished with the torture. He picked up a screwdriver and pierced Salnikov's ears and turned it round several times. Then he pulled out his knife and cut off Salnikov's penis and testicles. Finally he removed the rubber ball from Salnikov's mouth and one great roar could be heard from Salnikov, like the sound of the start of a Formula one race. Mustafa hooked Salnikov's tongue with his knife and simply cut it off, as he would have cut the tongue off a dead cod. Afterwards he blinded Salnikov and told his men to stop the blood from the wounds and do everything to keep Salnikov alive and conscious.

Brigitte had been forced to watch all the treatment of Salnikov except for when she had been raped.

"Well, Brigitte now it's your turn," Mustafa said like the doctor to a client.

Brigitte was gagged and twisted like a snake. Her scream could only be heard as a low repressed gurgle.

"You see the Arabians are gentlemen, we don't like to treat woman badly."

Brigitte had a short moment of hope, before she felt Mustafa's sharp knife move towards her belly.

"It's a pity," Mustafa said like a real psychopath. "Your body is beautiful, but you have seen too much and must die."

Mustafa forced his knife into her belly and let Brigitte hang twisting and gasping for air like a newly caught fish, to die slowly as her life-blood drained away.

"You must feel the pain," he said furiously and left the cabin with Salnikov's testicles and penis in his hands.

On deck he threw Salnikov's body-parts to a hungry dog on the pier. The dog ran away at once with Salnikov's genital organs in its jaws.

'It's not only the women that are satisfied with them, hungry dogs are too," Mustafa said leeringly.

Three hours later Mustafa appeared again with a lunatic,

violent grin on his face and a hammer in his hand. Mustafa loosened Salnikov from the bindings and turned him over. Then he hammered on his spine till it was completely severed. In this way he took away all of Salnikov's physical powers and if he survived he would be as a vegetable for the rest of his life, without being able to move or communicate with the world around him.

"Now he can spend his money. Take the bloody bastard home and let the *señora de la limpieza* find him," Mustafa said sadistically and vanished.

Lapin discovered Salnikov in his house when he arrived from Venezuela. Only half an hour before, the Arabs had left Salnikov as a bundle on the tiled floor in the house's salon. Lapin had never before in his adult life wept. He did now. He had never in his entire life seen such barbarous treatment of anyone, including all the dead and tortured he had discovered during the Afghanistan war.

After a while of deep consideration, he took Salnikov's head in his hands and twisted it quickly around till he heard the neck break. He had ended Salnikov's torture forever.

Lapin knew who was responsible for Salnikov's horrible treatment. He only had to find him. He decided to start his investigation with a visit to Salnikov's motor yacht. The greedy Arab would certainly steal the yacht, he thought.

Lapin was quite right. When he arrived at Puerto Banus, Salnikov's yacht was just about to leave the pier. Lapin jumped on board before any of the Arabs had a chance to react. The two Arabs, who saw him enter the craft had no weapons available, because they had not taken the risk of carrying weapons across the Spanish border. Only Mustafa and Cleo had smuggled weapons. Mustafa, a Colt revolver and Cleo, a small Browning lady's pistol.

The yacht was steadily steaming out of the harbour into

the blue Mediterranean, while the Arabs looked perplexed at Lapin. Disposing of the furious huge Russian without sufficient weapons in their hands seemed a completely impossible task for the rather small Arabs, but they courageously tried. They each gripped a ship's chair and waved it around to frighten and possibly hit Lapin, but he jumped untroubled to the side and tackled the Arabs as easily as a professional football player tackles an amateur.

Lapin caught one of the waving chairs when it was being swung. He grabbed the chair out of the Arab's hands and used it to knock the other out of the second Arab's hands. Then he quickly gripped both the Arabs by their chests and smashed their heads together with tremendous force. Their heads cracked like ripe pumpkins and he just threw their bloody bodies overboard like so much rotten garbage. He did not glance after them as they vanished in the wake of the motor yacht.

Three other Arabs came threateningly towards him with knives they had picked up in the galley. The desperately angry Lapin looked just like a gigantic wild gorilla, which frightened the Arabs who became momentarily paralysed and hesitated. This hesitation killed them. Lapin grabbed a nearby chair with his big hands and smashed all three Arabs in one stroke. Afterwards, he took them one by one and twisted their necks, to be sure they were really dead, just as he would have killed chickens, and threw their bodies directly into the sea.

"May the fishes be sick and die when they eat this infected food," he muttered miserably to himself.

Lapin would never have managed this quick action in such an extremely efficient way without the frantic anger he felt because of Salnikov's death. Salnikov had previously saved Lapin's life with great risk to his own. Lapin had never been more furious in his entire life. He had never felt such a desperate wish for revenge as this time, but he

250

had still not seen Mustafa. Where in the hell has that dirty Arab shit hidden? he thought furiously.

At that moment he was a hit by a bullet in the upper arm. From experience, he knew at once that it was only a harmless flesh wound, which would cause a pain like a mosquito bite in the days to come, nothing more. Another souvenir, he thought grimly, as always when he got such wounds. However, this time was not like always. In front of him stood the man who had brutally killed the only man in the world he respected. The only real friend that he would sacrifice his life for. Without thinking rationally, Lapin just threw himself towards Mustafa, who stood shocked, completely unable to react for some seconds. Mustafa trembled with a great fear, his revolver shaking whilst pointing in the direction of Lapin, but he was unable to pull the trigger. He just gazed in terror towards the enormous, lunatic combatant in the bloody suit.

Lapin caught Mustafa by the throat, brutally wrestled the gun out of his hand and started systematic demolition work. Lapin snarled and bared his teeth like a wolf with its first reindeer after a desperately hungry winter. He had a satisfied expression in his wild eyes, and could not count how many times he twisted Mustafa's arms around. Mustafa screamed like a wounded lion baying to the moon as his arms were pulled out of their sockets. Then Lapin started to punch him in the face until it looked like mincemeat. Then he gouged Mustafa's eyes out with his bare hands. Even his mother would not have recognised Mustafa, if she had seen him. Afterwards Lapin took the desperate screaming Arab by one leg, swung him around and punched him several times into the steel structure of the craft. He was treating the Arab as frantically as an old gold digger would use a pickaxe in a gold mine he had at last detected after having searched for it for fifty years. Lapin acted like a drunken man who was killing a cat, which he believed had

251

nine lives. The cranium was smashed and not one bone in the whole body was left unbroken. Mustafa's body became like a rag doll and was thrown overboard completely prepared for the fishes' dinner party.

After the motor yacht had been cleared of Arabs, Lapin was calmer. He checked the fuel and realised there was a lot more than was necessary for a voyage across the Atlantic to Venezuela at normal cruising speed. There was also more than sufficient food and water on board, but the food was mostly in tins. Not a large problem for an army man, Lapin thought dully, but best of all I have a collection of bottles of wine, spirits and liquor. The bottles that had supplied Salnikov and his guests were stored under and behind the bar in the salon. He realised it was not necessary even to bunker at the Canary Islands on the way across the Atlantic, if he did not want any fresh vegetables.

Lapin headed through the Gibraltar Strait and into the open Atlantic Ocean. He activated the autopilot, took a drink to calm his nerves and assuage his grief over Salnikov's death. Afterwards he examined the motor yacht properly from bow to stern. In the fore-cabin he discovered Sofia and Cleo.

The two frightened women sat in the dark trying to be invisible, while they wept quietly. Cleo had a small pistol that Lapin immediately confiscated. The woman did not try to use it. Maybe she believed her lovely body was a better weapon than a small pistol, against the huge, hairy animal of a man, who appeared in front of her.

Cleo was correct. Lapin had never harmed a woman before. He had only fucked them, but sometimes in a way that some would have labelled rape. However, Lapin was not certain what to do. These beautiful Arab women were probably forced by Mustafa to execute his dirty work, he considered, and they could undoubtedly never return home without being killed by angry relatives or friends of the Arabs that he had killed today. The women knew this. Their only chance would be to disappear to a place where they could remain without being detected by any angry Arabs. Both believed they would have no problem making a living. Their good-looking bodies would surely take care of that problem. There were always plenty of old, horny, rich men needing a mistress or a young wife.

Lapin decided to take the two beautiful Arab women with him to South America and drop them far from the place he lived. He wanted no connections to his previous life. He had already established himself as a respectable, retired businessman under the palms along the white sandy coastline of Venezuela and he would like that situation to remain undisturbed. As he thought, he felt himself become increasingly horny.

To be fucked by me several times daily and nightly all across the Atlantic Ocean will be enough punishment for their acts – or maybe it only will be a pleasure for them. I must stop my revenge activity because these women are extremely attractive and that is what matters.

He ordered them to undress and he threw their clothes overboard. The women had to be nude all the time on board his craft. His pleasures, the two beautiful, exotic women, had always to be available to him at short notice when he had a need for sex. He had no plans for a speedy arrival in South America.

17

The British Prime Minister walked restlessly across the floor of his office in Number Ten, Downing Street. The Secretary of Defence, and the top brass and Commanders of the Army, the Navy and the Airforce were together with him. He had arranged this meeting, at short notice, after he had received an urgent message about a nuclear explosion on one of Shetland's smallest uninhabited islands.

"What the hell is going on?" he said mostly to fill the time. "Had any activity been registered in the area before the explosion?"

None of those present had any additional information. All shook their heads negatively as the Prime Minister looked at them, one by one.

The Secretary of Defence had been sitting in silence while the Prime Minister spoke.

He said in a non-committal way: "I really don't believe it is any help sitting here discussing the event before we have more information."

He paused before he continued slowly and arrogantly with his precise and somewhat unnatural Eton accent. He looked with a superior air at the other participants at the meeting, who were quite astonished by his rather sneering expression.

"I believe you can track the producer of a nuclear warhead from the radiation released by the detonation. Is that right?" the Prime Minister asked, just ignoring the Secretary of Defence.

"You can of course never track any producer from a nuclear detonation, I presume," the Eton voice added self-importantly.

The Eton accent sounded rather strained and ridiculous, because anybody with the slightest knowledge of English accents could easily tell the Defence Secretary came from the working class area of Ipswich.

After his father suddenly had made a fortune in business, he had sent his only son to Eton, the traditional school for the upper classes. The son had immediately adopted distinctive upper class behaviour, including the accent, but he never managed to perfect it. Later, he only used his original Ipswich accent to flatter the electorate when he participated in election meetings in Ipswich before every parliamentary election.

The Prime Minister had never fully accepted his Defence Secretary, especially because he obviously rejected his origins, even though the people kept him on as their Member of Parliament. It was only clear political expediency that kept the Defence Secretary in his position. The Defence Secretary had a lot of powerful friends, particularly among British weapon producers.

The Chief of the Royal Air Force, Air Marshal Thomas Grantham, also ignored the Defence Secretary and replied to the Prime Minister's question very militarily, quickly and effortlessly in a broad Manchester accent, without any attempt at a fake accent: "Yes, sir, that can be done, but it takes some time and the result is very uncertain if the warhead is not produced by us, or one of our Nato allies."

The Air Marshal was a man with both feet firmly planted on the ground, and highly adored by his men as one of them, because of his complete lack of artificial behaviour.

He moved slightly in his chair and analysed all the people present for a while, before he said very quietly: "Field Marshal Charles Wield and I discussed precisely this matter in the car on the way here. It will only be a question of hours before we have an answer from our laboratories, as to whether the warhead was produced by us. It will of course take some additional time to confirm if our allies produced it, but it would take weeks or maybe months to get any proof about the origin of other possible producers."

He took a gulp of his coffee and added: "The possibility is also, that we will not get any admission of responsibility at all from other possible producers. This, because we consider it difficult or almost impossible, to make them accept that they are responsible for nuclear warheads which are out of control."

The Prime Minister brought the meeting to an end abruptly, as he said: "I will personally inform the American and French Presidents about the case, and I am sure they will instruct a quick handling of the necessary tests to get information about the origin of the warhead."

The missiles and the nuclear warheads had, for safety reasons, at once been divided and transported to their different locations for use after the yacht had arrived at the SS Group's shipyard in Edinburgh. One of the warheads had been transported to one of the Shetland's smallest uninhabited islands. Another one had been transported to one of the Orkneys' smallest uninhabited islands.

Only one hour after the meeting at the Prime Minister's office concerning the detonation on Shetland, the following anonymous message was delivered by a postal messenger, and received in the Defence Ministry. The envelope was marked "Urgent attention, only for the Defence Secretary personally!"

Inside the envelope there was a short typed message: *"By now you have received information about an incident in Shetland, which occurred at nine o'clock exactly this morning. The purpose of the incident was to put pressure on England to grant independence for Scotland. We will repeat the demonstration with another incident within twenty-four hours. This time the incident will occur nearer to you, to assure you that there is no alternative but to carry out our demands in accordance with the following instructions:*

– Our actions must be kept totally secret. Only strictly essential people, at the country's top administrative level, must be informed of our existence. The police and Secret Services must not be informed.

– If England does not comply, other incidents will occur all over England and in connection with British properties abroad.

– The same will happen if there is any leak to the press, or investigation is begun into the action or people participating.

– If the press is informed about any of the incidents demonstrating our power, the British army must officially take responsibility.

– The British Prime Minister must within a week from today, declare his support for Scottish independence.

– A referendum on Scottish independence will be held in Scotland within one year from today and only people born in Scotland, or with Scottish parents may participate.

– The announcement of the election will be made within six months from today.

– If the British Government changes within our time limit, the next Government must act in exactly the same way.

If England acts in accordance with all of the above, there will be no casualties in the action and Scotland and England will be able to collaborate in the future as two equal and friendly nations."

The note was signed on behalf of The Scottish Independence Organisation.

*

The Defence Secretary called Number Ten, Downing Street instantly and said it was necessary for another urgent meeting with the Prime Minister concerning the nuclear case discussed earlier. The Prime Minister cancelled his planned engagement and received the Defence Secretary shortly after.

The Defence Secretary let the Prime Minister read the message he had received from The Scottish Independence Organisation. The Prime Minister grew paler and paler as he read. He read the note at least three times before he looked up.

"Is this message real?" he asked, as if he hoped it was a joke.

The Defence Secretary looked snootily at the Prime Minister for a moment before he replied shortly, but without forgetting his ridiculous Eton accent: "I suppose we have to wait and see if there is another explosion in the next twenty-four hours."

After a moment's consideration, the Prime Minister asked: "Who do you advise we should inform about the Scottish action?"

The Defence Secretary was flattered by the Prime Minister's question, but he had considered this before he arrived, and could reply without any hesitation.

"The military leaders, the relevant ministry secretaries and the opposition parties' leaders must initially be informed. The information must be held on an ultra top-secret level. Only the people you personally have cleared must have access to the information, and anyone who receives it must not be allowed to pass it further."

The Defence Secretary had also reflected on the way of administering the case.

Therefore he added quickly: "I believe the best way to deal with this situation would be to establish a council of the mentioned leaders."

"Do you think it would be wise to inform the Secret Services from the start?" continued the Prime Minister.

"Of course!" the Defence Secretary replied quickly. "It is for such occasions they are paid, but I propose we otherwise follow the Scottish instructions exactly. Within one week you must proclaim that you are a supporter of Scottish independence."

He did not add that such a proclamation undoubtedly would undermine the Prime Minister's future position.

The Prime Minister probably thought the same and looked somewhat scared, when he said: "If we let Scotland be self-governing or I give my support for devolution, what will happen with Northern Ireland and Wales? Would not people in these parts of the Kingdom also demand independence? Will I be the Prime Minister that broke up the remainder of the British Empire?"

The Defence Secretary thought for a moment while he took pleasure in the Prime Minister's apparent indecision and said calmly, but rather scathingly: "Time will tell. This may be a situation where you have no choice. I also believe that Margaret Thatcher would not have let China have Hong Kong, if she had had a real choice."

The meeting was over. They only had to wait to see what would happen in the next twenty-four hours.

At exactly six o'clock the following morning, another nuclear explosion occurred. This time it happened on the Orkneys. A very small uninhabited island, far from populated areas, was the centre of the explosion.

The army was alerted, but the army commanders at once denied that the army itself was responsible. The army claimed that it was a secret test done by a secret department and the explosion would remain top-secret for everyone who might have got any knowledge about it. Everybody had to keep their mouths shut, never talk about or discuss the incident, or otherwise be arrested and accused of treason against the nation and certainly be convicted.

After the second detonation the Prime Minister's and the Defence Secretary's plan was activated. A secret council was established of the people that had to be informed because of their positions in Government. Within one week the Prime Minister had proclaimed that he was a supporter of Scottish independence.

The proclamation was made during a speech in connection with a labour union meeting in Liverpool. The announcement was hidden among others about the government performance concerning workers' conditions and improvements in its unemployment proposals for the future. Hardly anybody who was listening to the Prime Minister's speech in the open square in front of the town hall in Liverpool, realised that he had said anything about Scotland's independence. The audience was too much concerned about their own problems. In addition, the speech seemed very dull, without any exciting news, only the traditional election promises, which make nobody fat.

The television and newspaper reporters had however noticed the Prime Minister's hidden announcement about Scottish independence. The same evening, parts of the speech were transmitted on the BBC news. Next day the news about the Prime Minister's statement, was front-page headlines in most British newspapers.

The newspapers were either positive or very neutral about the proclamation. Few newspapers were directly negative, but a lot of them touched on the problem that an independent Scotland might affect the English union with Northern Ireland and Wales. Only a couple of the newspapers directly called the Prime Minister's statement treason.

Meanwhile, English nuclear scientists, together with colleagues from the United States and France, had visited the site of the nuclear explosion on Shetland. Immediately on arrival the scientists could identify that a small, tactical, nuclear weapon had caused the explosion, but they could tell nothing about the origin of the weapon. Such information had to be produced in laboratories from analysis of samples from the ground.

The scientists from the United States and France, who made their visit as secret as the English scientists, had been sent immediately after the British Prime Minister had made urgent telephone calls to the Presidents of the respective countries.

The next day, the results rushed from the English nuclear laboratory declared that the warhead had been a small fusion bomb. A relatively clean bomb with only a maximum of five per cent of the total explosive force from the fission part. The warhead had produced only small quantities of radioactive fallout and had not damaged the surrounding environment significantly. The laboratory stated that only a highly qualified producer could have manufactured such a sophisticated warhead, but the warhead still remained of uncertain origin. However, the laboratory also stated that the detonation of the warhead probably had been executed by remote control.

The American and French scientists' findings were similar to the result from the English laboratory. The warhead was not of their production and they could not determine the origin. Their conclusions were that uncommonly qualified experts had made this warhead.

The secret counsel's first meeting discussed the possible origin of the warhead, as soon as the results from the various scientists were available.

Air Marshal Grantham, who also was experienced in nuclear science, said gravely: "The results from the laboratories, that you have been presented with, do not bring us any closer to unravelling the mystery of the origin of the warheads. I believe these people, who perpetrate these actions, are very professional and must be taken extremely seriously. They are using a type of warhead which is very clean, and very difficult to develop."

He wiped the beads of perspiration off his forehead with his hand before he continued in an even more grave voice: "These warheads must have been extremely expensive to purchase. The big question is why they have bought such advanced and expensive new models, when they could have bought cheaper and older, but not such clean ones. This seems clearly to indicate they intend to make additional use of them."

The Air Marshal did not wait for any reply. He did not believe that technically unskilled politicians could add any reasonable comments. He only coughed, cleared his throat and continued slowly and rather emphatically: "Clean warheads mean warheads with a small fission part of the explosion energy. These warheads produce reasonably small radioactive fallout. The radioactive fallout is proportional to the increase of the fission part of the blast power. The larger the fission part, the larger the radioactive fallout. The problem concerning these warheads with a large fission part is that they endanger people and structures many miles away from the explosion site. The Scottish Independence Organisation's warheads do not affect the environment considerably at all. Their warheads are so clean that they could blow up Buckingham Palace, then sow grass and arrange a garden

262

party immediately the grass grows, without any radiation hazard above an acceptable level for the party's participants."

"What does this mean?" the Prime Minister asked with deep concern.

He had been sitting completely quiet while the Air Marshal spoke.

"Does this mean that we can await possible attacks on inhabited areas or towns or even Buckingham Palace, the Parliament building and Number Ten, Downing Street?"

General Wield replied to the worried Prime Minister's question with a weary smile: "I am afraid of that Prime Minister. If the Scots also use rockets, they could easily blow Number Ten, Downing Street, and us, into the sky right now. I am convinced it would be wise not to underestimate these Scottish freedom-fighters."

The Royal Navy's commander, Admiral Sir Alexander Viscount, said loudly and clearly, as an officer well used to talking: "We are all aware that the Secret Service are working on the case. Have they made any efforts to discover any transfers abroad of considerable amounts of money recently, that could be related to the purchase of such weapons?"

The Home Secretary replied quickly: "The Secret Service has worked on that matter since they started on the case, but till now they have not discovered anything suspicious."

The Lord Chancellor, who was a silent listener, nodded affirmatively to the Home Secretary's reply without opening his mouth.

The Prime Minister closed the meeting by saying: "It seems that we have to wait for progress from the Secret Service before anything at all can be done. I will, though, contact the Russians, and let our embassy in Peking contact the Chinese authorities, requesting any information about the origin of the nuclear weapons."

The Prime Minister thought for a moment before he added gloomily: "I do not expect any positive replies from these countries, even if they are the producers. They will surely not admit to any responsibility for nuclear warheads in terrorists' hands. That would ultimately be political disaster for them."

The Prime Minister sipped some water, obviously to gain time to think, before he continued: "I will also ask our embassy in Israel and India and maybe in Pakistan to make some discreet enquiries."

Afterwards, the Prime Minister rose rapidly from his chair and the meeting was over.

General Director Howard Spindlier of the British Secret Services shook his head in disbelief when group leader Bill Franks entered his office with a pile of computer paper at least fifty centimetres thick. Franks had received the pile from the Bank of England, only minutes earlier.

He placed the pile on Spindlier's desk with a thump and said informatively: "To start to investigate possible money transfers abroad that might be the source of weapons' payment, is a completely impossible task. I asked the Bank of England only to send information on transfers covering one month within the period under investigation, just to have a sample to show you. On each of these pages you see on your desk, you will find thirty-five transactions. You can yourself count how many transactions we must examine if we have to cover three years."

Franks thumped his hand on the top of the pile to demonstrate the tremendous quantity of data.

Spindlier did not reply and Franks continued, visibly irritated: "All the transfers in these papers are larger than five hundred thousand pounds. We have no guarantee that five hundred thousand will cover the possible transactions we are looking for. The transactions might, for instance, have been divided into smaller amounts. Neither have we any guarantee what we are examining is the correct method. The Scottish wish for independence is hundreds of years old. The plan they are working on might be very old, and preparations may have been made over years. Finally we have no guarantee that the transaction has gone through any English bank at all. The finance might have been made from a foreign country. There could be foreign people behind the scheme. There are, for instance, as many people with Scottish ancestors in the United States, as there are people in Scotland."

Spindlier still did not reply and Franks carried on, even more irritated: "All these transfers that you can read about in these papers . . ." Franks again thumped on the top of the pile – this time a lot harder than the first time, "have to be compared with data from the Ministry of Commerce, the Ministry of Finance and many other sources. I have not mentioned the possibility that cash might have been carried out of the country, or that the people who plan such a scheme would not make the mistake of sending money out of the country to be tracked by the authorities. If you give me ten thousand people to work on this matter for five years, I might perhaps give you a better reply. However, the result would most likely be as follows: We cannot find any source of weapons payment by examining transfers of money abroad, registered by the Bank of England."

Spindlier smiled and said: "OK, you have made your point. This line of investigation is completely useless."

Franks looked relieved and smiled for the first time since he had entered Spindlier's office.

Spindlier continued and said: "You must write a report at

once which I will present to the Prime Minister concerning his crazy idea of solving the case by examining registered money transfers abroad."

Franks nodded affirmatively and said: "I will concentrate on the case in a more traditional way, similar to how we are working on Northern Ireland's case. Examinations of money transfers must eventually be concentrated on specific likely targets. These politicians are all amateurs at Secret Services work. I hope they will not interfere with our work again."

The Prime Minister had personally contacted Spindlier immediately after the first meeting, concerning the nuclear detonation on Shetland. They later agreed on a working plan, after the second incident on the Orkneys, and after they had received strict instructions from the Scottish Independence Organisation about not involving the Secret Service.

Spindlier's biggest problem was that many of the personnel in the Secret Service were Scots. These could not be treated as reliable in this case. Any hint that the organisation was working on the case had to be strictly avoided. Spindlier therefore had to gather a group of people he believed thoroughly reliable in this situation. He had informed the Prime Minister that it was still a risk that the Scots might reveal their work on the case whatever was done to avoid it.

The Prime Minister had only replied to Spindlier's consideration: "That risk must be taken."

Spindlier had chosen Bill Franks as the leader of the top-secret group, which would work on the case. Franks had very long experience in Secret Service work. He was nearly fifty years old and had, for many years, been one of the leaders in Northern Ireland affairs. Together they handpicked all the members of the investigation group, but both agreed that it was almost an impossible task to keep the investigation secret, and they were quite correct.

Detailed information about the Secret Service work, and progress in the case, was regularly received by the Scottish Organisation.

18

The Scottish Independence Organisation's action-group, the Highlanders' Commando, had a conference in the SS Group's committee room, three weeks after the Prime Minister's proclamation in Liverpool to support a referendum on Scottish independence.

The organisation had no overall leaders. Different autonomous groups functioned all over Scotland. Each group ran its own business with the only joint goal – an independent Scotland. For safety reasons nobody knew exactly how many groups were within the organisation, and nobody knew about colleagues in other groups. If one of the groups was blown up, that would not concern the work of the others.

No new member could be added to the organisation without complete knowledge of his or her entire life history. At least three members in the organisation had to certify a newcomer and they must have known him since childhood. They had to be responsible with their own lives for the trustworthiness of new members. If the newcomer proved untrustworthy, they had to organise an execution immediately.

If British Secret Service agents tried to infiltrate the organisation, they would assuredly be detected and quickly killed. The bodies would then disappear forever. The English authorities knew this, or rather believed they did. The authorities had several times previously experienced agents' disappearances after believed connections with secret Scottish organisations, but they had never had any exact proof or any genuine information concerning the existence of such organisations.

A couple of times the authorities believed they had received reliable information from agents before they had vanished, about possible Scottish persons connected to what they suggested were illegal organisations. However, the Scots always had alibis and could give no information about the vanished agents or any organisation. Thus it became very difficult if not impossible to get any volunteers to infiltrate any Scottish secret organisation.

It was the Highlanders' Commando that had bought the atomic missiles from Russia. The SS Group's chairman, Sir Walter, led the group's operational section. His closest collaborators in addition to Wallace and McPride, were the two Royal Navy commanders, Hunter, called Viking and Ballentine, called Whisky.

Sir Walter also led the group's management section, which consisted, in addition to himself, of all the twelve Highlanders who were the members of the SS Group's board.

When the Russian weapons were divided and sent to different places for possible utilisation, nobody knew about more than one missile with a loaded warhead. There was one separate operations group for each part, for obvious safety reasons. The operators did not have to know about each other. If the authorities caught one of the groups, that would not deter the other groups' utilisation of their weapons.

Each atomic missile and each packet of plastic explosives had received a ranking number and were pre-determined to a specific target to attack. The different groups were solely responsible for planning their particular attack in detail. If the English authorities did not exactly follow the instruction received from the Independence Organisation, the groups would receive orders to attack one by one, until the English co-operated completely.

Warhead number one had been used at one of the Shetland's smaller islands, and warhead number two at another small Orkney island. The third group knew they were going to be the next ones to go into action. They also knew exactly what their target would be and had planned everything in detail. They were only waiting for the order with the exact time, if any demolition of the target would be necessary at all.

For safety reasons each operator was also covered by a back-up system, to be put into operation if he or she was caught by the authorities, or went out of business for whatever reason. If a whole group went out of business, there was an alternative system leaving the weapon to an under-study group.

All the operators were previously military trained and they all knew how to operate missiles. The fact that it was a Russian missile this time and not the usual American or English, did not concern them much. Nevertheless, some of the training missiles had been tested in safe places to give the operators confidence with the new equipment.

"They are working extremely well," one of the operators in group number three, McNeigh, said enthusiastically, after he had fired off one of the training missiles into a deep loch in the Scottish Highlands early one cold, rainy Saturday morning.

"Good the Cold War is over. I wouldn't have liked to

270

meet Russian enemies equipped with these firecrackers," he added thoughtfully.

"We have received reliable information, that the British Secret Service has got information about our action from the Prime Minister's office, and is working on a termination plan concerning the Scottish Independence Organisation. It is the TCG – the Tasking Co-ordination Group, comprising SAS, MI5, Special Branch, and military intelligence officers, which is on the assignment," Sir Walter said one day in an urgently summoned conference within the operation section.

"The TCG has previously mostly been working with the Irish problem and it seems likely the English will use all their resources on the clarification of their new Scottish problem. It will obviously be necessary to give another demonstration of our power, to get the Secret Service off our back. The management section suggests that as a commencement, we put into action atomic warhead numbers three and four and conventional demolition actions numbers one and two."

Sir Walter said *suggests*, but that was only diplomatic. What he really meant was an order to follow, without any negotiation. All the participating members knew that very well, and he did not need to express his wishes dictatorially. Sir Walter was an efficient and competent leader, trusted by all members of the organisation. What Sir Walter plainly suggested would seldom be subject for any discussion.

Sir Walter had also pursued a military career. He had ended his military service, as one of the youngest British lieutenant generals in modern times, when he took over as leader of the SS Group, after his uncle suddenly became ill and died. His uncle had led the company extremely well for fifteen years, since he took over from Sir Walter's father, who had died of a heart attack at his office desk late one evening. Sir Walter was knighted shortly after he left the army.

"Any questions?" Sir Walter asked politely.

"Only one," Wallace asked quickly: "What's the estimated time for actions?"

"At noon local time, two weeks from today, atomic warhead numbers three and four will be detonated," Sir Walter replied, businesslike and quickly, as if he gave such orders every day.

"All right – and the conventional actions?"

"All at the same time, but of course with some small adjustments to the estimated time, determined by the local operators," Sir Walter replied and rose from his chair.

"I suppose you all know what to do. It is lunchtime and the meeting is over, " he said and left without looking back.

At the English training base for the Army's elite forces, Fort Hope in north-western Quebec, west of Havre-Saint Pierre, it was a day like any other. The days were always alike. The only difference from the routine, was when a new contingent of trainees came from England to replace the previous ones. This happened every third month. It had always been like that, ever since the Second World War, on this secret base, which was popularly known as Timber Fort by the servicemen.

Fort Hope was originally established to train elite soldiers for special operations behind the German lines. The fort was in a very isolated place, far from any inhabited areas. It was in the middle of the forest, but not far from the coastline of the Gulf of St. Lawrence, where the British Navy had a small port.

The port consisted only of a pier and a small warehouse with a couple of office rooms, a sleeping area with bathroom for the guards and a small kitchen. All supplies to Fort Hope were received through this small port. The port was also the embarkation point for all the base's troops. Two Royal Navy ships were in the port on this day. They were unloading supplies for the base.

The three hundred soldiers and staff of about fifty officers in Fort Hope were not allowed to travel to the nearest town, Havre-Saint Pierre, and mix with the people. Therefore, the people in the area hardly felt the existence of the British military base at all. The commanders of the base said the reason for this was that the trainees had to experience prolonged isolation. However, the trainees always said the isolation was only instituted because the Canadian and the British authorities had made an agreement to keep the trainees out of the competition for the local girls.

The trainees at the base had gone through a 72-hour exercise that finished the previous evening. All the soldiers were, therefore, cleaning their equipment for inspection, which always followed these exercises. Weapons had to be cleaned and oiled, shoes had to shine. Everybody who has been in the military service knows how stupid these inspections often feel, but veterans who have been in the army for years, and maybe have participated in real war situations, know how important inspections are. The inspections teach the recruits to keep standards at top level, even when the external pressure is great.

*

At eleven o'clock that day, the teleprinter at Fort Hope hammered out a message from headquarters in London. The printer emitted a piercing, impatient cry as the sending operator continually pressed the alarm bell button, to inform the receiver that this was an important and urgent message, which had to be read immediately. The operator at Fort Hope therefore, grabbed the telex paper, tore it anxiously off the machine and read it.

"This is a top secret, urgent message to Fort Hope's present commanding officer. This is not an exercise. – I repeat: This is not an exercise. The base has to be completely abandoned within half an hour. – I repeat: The base has to be abandoned completely within half an hour. Everybody, including the guards, must at once travel to the two British Navy ships at the port. – I repeat: Everybody must leave for the ships. Nobody must remain at the base. – I repeat: Nobody must remain at the base. Leave all equipment where it is. The base will be totally destroyed within one hour exactly. – I repeat: The base will be destroyed in one hour exactly. You are ordered to do nothing to prevent the damage. This incident must be kept totally secret by all involved. Inform the men it is the Army that is closing the base and the information is military top-secret and part of the training. All personal effects that might be destroyed will be compensated. Confirm this message at once. Headquarters, Field Marshal, General Charles Wield."

The general had sent the message immediately he received the information about the action from the Independence Organisation. He knew, from the previous experience in Shetland and Orkney that these people were not to be ignored. The organisation had warned that they knew that the Secret Service was working on the case and that the actions against British properties at home and abroad would continue until the Secret Service stopped nosing.

*

Major Nick Murray, who was the commander of Fort Hope when Colonel Alan Bridgeton was in Ottawa, was singing in the shower, when the teleprinter operator rushed in shouting frantically.

Murray always sang in the shower when he was in Canada. He had once tried the same back home many years ago, but his wife had totally forbidden him to sing in the shower or anywhere else. His voice was horrible, she had told him in her most diplomatic way.

"It sounds like a stallion finishing his business with a mare," she had added with a satisfied expression on her face, as if she knew exactly. Maybe she did know, Murray thought reflectively when he sang. She was, after all, the daughter of a farmer.

On Fort Hope there were no mares or bitches that could stop him singing. His wife could also be certain he would not arrive back home with a dozen sexual diseases. The nearest female, except for the Grizzly she-bears, must be among the Eskimos in Greenland. So he could sing absolutely unhindered by any interruption. The base's colonel was deaf and the rest of the troops had been told to keep a very low profile, otherwise they would definitely get punishment drills. However, if anybody had any complaint, they could always use the ear protectors which they used during shooting exercises.

Murray was at Fort Hope for nine months every year. He had chosen the job because he was a man who really loved nature. He was also a very quiet man, when he was not yelling in the shower. Fort Hope was definitely in the middle of nature. Murray never felt stressed being isolated, because he had fourteen days off after every six weeks on the base. During these breaks he travelled back to England and his family.

"It's like being newly married every time I come home," he used to boast.

All his time off at Fort Hope, Murray spent walking along the nearby lakes trying to catch the biggest fish. The lakes were brimming with trout, but it was difficult to catch the really big ones. However, it was his tendency afterwards in the officer's bar when he talked about the fish he had caught, that they grew considerably after he had caught them, but nobody ever believed him.

"When you start to tell these fairy-tales about the fish you haven't caught, it's a sure sign that you've had too much to drink," were his colleagues' standard phrases.

Murray was a fly fisherman and after many years experience he was a real expert with the fly rod. Everybody that used any other type of fishing gear, were cheats in his eyes.

"As a real fisherman you have to meet the fish on its own terms and give it a chance," he often said.

During the evenings, from early spring till late autumn, the sound of his fly reel could always be heard along the rivers and the lakes. It was as if the sound belonged to nature itself.

The teleprinter operator had hastened to the bathroom and called loudly. Murray immediately stopped his howls, which he alone called a song. He quickly wrapped a towel around himself.

"It's an urgent message from headquarters in London that you must read at once."

"Has the Third World War started?" Murray replied quietly.

"I don't know," said the tele-printer operator, now calmer. "Look for yourself."

Murray read the message and became pale. He read the message again, and held the paper towards the light, as

276

British shopkeepers examine notes, to be sure they are real.

"Make the following reply," Murray said after a short moment of hesitation, but he still remained very calm.

"Your message just received, order all to leave Fort Hope immediately. Confirm the message once more. Regards Major Nick Murray, Commander-in-Charge."

"Send our message twice and press the button for the receiver's bell," Murray ordered the operator, who nearly stood on his toes.

The operator quickly ran out the door, like a desperate man with a pack of wolves after him. Murray dried himself hastily, while he prepared his future moves. He had put on his uniform by the time the operator returned.

The operator said breathlessly: "They confirmed immediately. Here you can read their message."

The gasping operator handed over the piece of paper he had torn from the teleprinter.

Murray said, as calm as before: "Tell all officers to meet me in two minutes time in the drill yard."

The officers met him in the yard only a couple of minutes later and he gave a short, but very clear order.

"Everybody, I mean everybody, including the guards, will meet here in five minutes. We are all going to abandon Fort Hope immediately, as we have received a message from headquarters that the base will be destroyed completely in a few minutes. Nobody will be allowed any time to collect personal belongings. The Army will later compensate for these."

Murray headed towards the transport officer in charge and ordered: "The truck drivers will instantly bring the trucks to be parked along the left side of the yard for the immediate loading of the troops."

The base's alarm sounded soon as a hoarse undertone

that accompanied the sound of rapidly running boots on the gravelled ground.

McNeigh had travelled to Quebec a week ahead of time for the launch of the missile. He had travelled via Miami by plane as an ordinary tourist and spent some weeks in the sun together with his Norwegian girl friend and their daughter. In Miami he had been on stand-by for the High-landers' Commando, while he was waiting for a possible message for action. When he finally received the message, he sent his girlfriend and their daughter immediately back to Norway by plane directly to Oslo. Afterwards he travelled north, apparently for a few days fishing with an army friend, before he returned to England. He travelled by car along the eastern coast of the United States to Montreal, where he met Sean Ness, another reliable and competent Scottish freedom fighter. Ness was from Inverness in the north of Scotland, but was working in London.

Ness had come to Montreal via New York, where he had done some work for a famous auction house, which sold old furniture and other items at high prices in an attempt to empty the pockets of credulous customers for the ben-efit of the company's shareholders. Ness often did business in New York and had this time especially arranged to remain there to be readily accessible, on stand-by like McNeigh.

Ness had been trained as a missile expert in the British Army, where he served for many years until his enlistment period was up. Afterwards, he had found employment in a civilian technical company, which gave him three times the wages he had received in the army.

Ness's wife worked as a buyer for a clothes company and through her he had come into contact with the general manager of the famous Scotty's Auctions. The manager was one of SS Group's twelve-man board of directors.

The English had, many years ago, arrested Ness's father. He died of pneumonia shortly afterwards in an English jail. This happened when Ness was a little boy and he could therefore only vaguely remember him. His father had been arrested because he had distributed information and taken part in demonstrations for Scottish independence. Ness hated the English deeply because of his father's death. His father had been thrown into a cold jail, soaking wet, in the wintertime, after the English had tried to disperse the demonstrators using water cannons. When his father became ill, he was ignored and he got no medical care. He did not stand a chance against the sneaking illness that soon took his life. His mother got a bald message from the local bobby at the door early one morning. Ness had by now almost forgotten his father, but could never forget his mother's anguished screams that morning.

All applicants to the army's missile department had to be carefully vetted by the military authorities for security reasons. It had obviously been a mistake when they stationed Ness at one of the most secret divisions of the British Army. The army would later pay expensively for this mistake, but they did not know it at the time.

The atomic missile was brought to Canada by a British container vessel from Manchester, together with machinery parts, and delivered to a regular receiver – an assignment that was not very difficult to execute. The missile had later been detached from the rest of the load, along the Canadian highway towards Alberta and brought to Montreal, where it waited for McNeigh and Ness. They loaded it into a camping caravan connected to McNeigh's Chevrolet estate car. Then they set off on their camping trip like two old friends, fully equipped with fishing gear and everything necessary to make a trip into Mother Nature's kingdom, feeling relaxed and successful

The English training base of Fort Hope and the surroundings were well known to McNeigh. He had previously taken part in three different courses at the base and had been in the area for nine months altogether.

Because the British troops at the base had no privilege to visit nearby towns or inhabited areas, their only free time activities were sports, plus fishing, and hunting during the season for hares and foxes. The military exercises gave an excellent opportunity to become acquainted with the surroundings of the base, but the additional free time activities allowed exceptional know-how.

The two Scottish freedom fighters slept in the caravan on their way along the Gulf of Saint Lawrence. They travelled like ordinary tourists. In the evenings they took time to test their fishing gear in the small lakes they had stopped by for the night.

The Scottish freedom fighters arrived in the area of Fort Hope on the morning of the day planned for the noon missile launch. They unloaded the missile in a wooded area thirty-kilometres south-west of the base. Afterwards, they drove away with the caravan and dumped it into a nearby lake, first removing the plates and anything that might be used for identification later. On their way back from the dumping, McNeigh dropped Ness off four kilometres away from the base, where he climbed a hill from which he could see directly into the base. He would guide the missile to an exact spot on the target using the remote target-indicator's infrared beam, after McNeigh launched it and the missile had reached the position to be covered by the indicator's control. The target would be the base's weapon depot.

McNeigh parked the car under the trees, where it was fully hidden from the road, only ten seconds walking distance from the specified launch spot. He was too occupied with the preparations for the launching, to reflect on what the results of their actions might be. However, he had been informed ahead from the Highlanders' Commando that there would be no casualties, if the British Army adhered strictly to the instructions they received in the warning message. McNeigh prayed that none of his friends would be at the base at the hour of destiny.

At noon exactly, completely loyal to his assignment and cause, he pressed the launching button for the missile. He knew he would never forget the thoughts which buzzed through his head when the missile left the launching tube and vanished into the air, leaving only a white stripe of condensed burned fuel in its trail.

19

The military doctor Dave Connoly and his wife, military nurse Betsy, had during the summer, sailed their 47 foot sailing-boat from the Brighton Marina to the British island of Anguilla, one of the Leeward Islands in the Caribbean. It had been a pleasant voyage with constant good weather and always a following wind.

The Connoly couple had decided to moor the boat in the Caribbean permanently. In Brighton the weather was seldom pleasant. It was mostly rainy and windy and always too cold to have any real pleasure in sailing the boat. The longest trips they had ever made from there, were to sail across the English Channel to Dieppe in France a couple of times, and each time they had nearly frozen to death. They had also bought one of these overpriced, grim, ostensibly luxury flats in the Brighton Marina, where they could sit looking through the window at their expensive boat dipping in the marina's silent water, without freezing to death, but that was not why they had bought it.

Connoly had sailed the boat from Brighton to Santa Cruz on Tenerife, together with his wife and George Coe, who was recovering from wounds incurred from the Arabian bullets in the Mediterranean. He was a tough soldier and the sailing activities helped him recover, day by day, until he was fully back on his feet.

*

282

The voyage to Tenerife took about two weeks and Ann Castle waited eagerly for the boat in the yacht marina in front of Plaza España in Santa Cruz. It was planned she would go with the boat across the Atlantic to Anguilla and she had taken a British Airways plane from Gatwick directly to Los Rodeos airport on Tenerife. Ann would take Connoly's place as crew, while Connoly went back to his work at the military hospital in London. He had decided not to continue on the boat across the Atlantic because it would mean he was absent too long from work.

Nevertheless, only five weeks later after a mostly splendid journey in perfect weather, the Trans-Atlantic sailors met Connoly in a town called Valley in Anguilla. He had taken a plane from Heathrow to catch up with them.

The reason why the Connoly couple had sailed the boat across the Atlantic was not only their wish to have the boat in the West Indies. That would have been too expensive, though they had sold their flat in the marina. They had simply been ordered by the Highlanders' Commando to sail it to Anguilla, with an atomic missile hidden in the keel. For safety reasons only Connoly knew this, but his wife had suspicions, although she never asked. Wives always have a complete view of a family's economic situation and she knew they could not, unless subsidised by a third party, afford to have their boat in the Caribbean. Such subsidies would, of course, not be given without some kind of return.

The missile was placed in one piece within the keel, but could easily be removed by cutting through the fibreglass in the bottom of the boat with an ordinary electric household saw. The keel was wider than necessary, because it had to be strengthened to tolerate the missile's shape. However, the boat was not a standard boat so nobody could detect the conversion of the keel from any drawings or by comparison with similar boats. When the missile was removed, the hollow could easily be changed into an ordinary storage room and filled with regular supplies and would be visible for everybody to inspect.

The landing craft HMS *Heroic*, had cruised and practised landings in the area of Anguilla for nearly two months. These months had been unforgettable for the crew and the Royal Navy's marines that had attended. To stay in the Caribbean for two months was a dream for the seamen and the soldiers who were used to exercises in the cold areas around Britain. On leave the men had drowned themselves in Caribbean rum and sexy, brown girls, who danced the calypso during the dark nights to the sound of Caribbean steel drums. The Military Police had more than once carried home dead drunken recruits from the fiestas.

HMS *Heroic* was a sister-ship of the two landing craft HMS *Intrepid* and HMS *Fearless* that had participated in the Falklands War during operation *Corporate*, as the re-taking of the Falkland Islands from Argentina had been called. The two sister-craft had played a crucial role in the battle.

HMS *Heroic* had been fitted-out in 1965 and had already been designated for scrap at the beginning of the eighties, when the Falklands War started. It was only the sister craft's great contribution to this war that had saved her from the scrapyard. However, another decision to scrap her had later been taken, as the ship had become too expensive to keep on active service in the navy's limited budgets after the end of the Cold War. She had also become too old and too outmoded for modern warfare. The scrapping would be done at the beginning of the next year.

"The Royal Navy has to be transformed for its role today. The navy cannot play an historic imperial leader's role, like a senile old lord with his staff," the navy's leader, Admiral

284

Sir Alexander Viscount, had said in a speech to his officers, some years ago.

"We have to plan carefully how to use the continuously decreasing budgets for the navy and cut all costs on everything not considered top priority," the admiral had continued.

As HMS *Heroic* was not top priority any longer, the Caribbean cruise was therefore the last mission in which she was participating.

The crew of HMS *Heroic* totalled five hundred and eighty. In addition there were pilots and service engineers for two Boeing Vertol Chinook and two Westland Wessex HU helicopters. The combat force consisted of three hundred and ninety marines, plus fifty technicians for the weapons and equipment. There was also a small military hospital on board with two doctors and four good-looking, young nurses, who all the time fired the men's sexual appetites. Many troops had become unwell only to have the opportunity to visit the hospital to catch a glimpse of the nurses, who were always overwhelmed by hopeful invitations from all sides.

HMS *Heroic* received a teleprinter message from naval headquarters, at the same time as Fort Hope, deep in the Canadian forests, received a similar message from army headquarters. The message was quite clear, but rather frightening: *"This is a top-secret urgent message to HMS Heroic's commanding officer. This is not an exercise. – Repeat: This is not an exercise. HMS Heroic must be abandoned completely within half an hour. – Repeat: Everyone must leave the craft and no one must remain on board. Leave all equipment and personal effects. Personal effects will be fully compensated by the navy. The craft will possibly be destroyed and sunk in one hour. – Repeat: The craft will possibly be destroyed and sunk in one hour. You are ordered to*

285

do nothing to prevent the damage. Go as far away from the craft as possible with all the crew. – Repeat: Everybody must move as far away from the craft as possible, immediately. You must set the autopilot on 305 – three-hundred-and-five – degrees and leave the craft at a speed of 7 – seven – knots per hour. Everybody involved must keep this incident completely secret. You must tell the crew only that the Royal Navy is responsible. The incident is ranked as top secret military information. You and the rest of the crew must never comment on or give data about it. Military authorities will deal with any information about it eventually picked up by the press. Confirm this message at once. From British Royal Navy headquarters, Admiral Sir Alexander Viscount."

The message was sent to HMS *Heroic* according to the instructions of the Defence Secretary who had received them from the Scottish Independence Organisation only minutes before. The Organisation had ended their instructions as follows: *"We hope you take our instructions seriously. To assure you that you are dealing with a legitimate group, we refer to two similar previous incidents on the small Shetland and Orkney islands. We do not want to hurt people unnecessarily, so we give you the chance to remove all your staff before another demonstration of our extreme power. This time we will detonate an atomic warhead to destroy one of your largest warships. The demonstrations are executed to inform you that you must terminate all investigations, including the TCG's investigation, of our business. You must follow our previous instructions exactly. If you do not immediately stop all your investigations completely, closer demonstrations will be executed without warning."*

Commander Edward Stanford at HMS *Heroic* received the message, while he stood bent over the chart table together with three other officers on the bridge. He followed the exercise plan exactly and he considered it as a must, always to be absolutely perfect. The retired commanders Hunter and Ballentine had worked out the plans for the exercise and these commanders had also always put their vast experience into precise work

Both Viking and Whisky had previously been commanders on HMS *Heroic*'s sister craft, HMS *Intrepid* and HMS *Fearless*. Viking had been commander on HMS *Heroic* on two occasions and he had set the standard for all commanders to follow. Stanford was therefore trying to operate as a perfectionist, always to be in the right place at the right time. He was hardly a minute too late or too early at a position according to a plan.

Everybody in the navy knew Stanford's way of working and considered him obstinate. He was a very unpopular commander. His officers were always completely exhausted after they finished their shifts on his bridge.

Stanford came from an old family of naval officers that had always lived in Grimsby, and where he too had grown up. Many of his ancestors had ended their lives at sea in heroic battles for the English throne. Somebody even said that Admiral Nelson was related to a branch of the family, but definitely some of Admiral Nelson's commanders were Stanford's ancestors.

"I am representing a very old tradition in my family," he said. "To follow the tradition is the only way Mother England can keep her dominance at sea."

Stanford's only son had also continued the family tradition and become a naval officer.

Stanford had been commander on various large craft. He had had the reputation at navy headquarters of being an extremely competent, efficient and reliable commander of any vessel, since he had become captain on his first motor torpedo boat thirty-six years ago, but in the later years he had become rather mulish, they said. At sixty-three, he was one of the British Navy's oldest commanders on active service. That would end after this cruise.

HMS *Heroic* had by this time moved into position according to Hunter and Ballentine's exercise-plan. The two retired commanders had been given the job of planning the final exercise for the old landing craft, as a nostalgic gesture. The plan had, until now, worked perfectly and the two commanders would probably get high distinctions for the excellent work they had done for a whole generation. They would probably be knighted, their colleagues suspected.

One of the telex operators had run to the commander with the urgent incoming message. Commander Stanford stood astonished for some seconds when he read it, before he turned alternately red and white. He was a large man. The telex operator moved slowly away from the Commander to gain sufficient distance from the possible volcanic eruption that seemed to be building up inside him.

Stanford was about to scream with frustration and prove that he also knew some English swearwords, but he suddenly changed his mind and asked loudly, but surprisingly calmly, as if it was a routine message, which was not welcomed: "What are these damned idiots at headquarters doing?"

He did not swear, though he really wanted to. He fought desperately to achieve equilibrium for a moment before he continued brusquely: "Are they about to become bankrupt at headquarters, so accelerating the reduction of the old fleet – to save money?"

He turned unexpectedly quickly on his heels and looked violently at the telex operator who stood tight against the wall in the shadows and tried to become invisible.

"I will of course follow the orders in this message. Confirm the message at once and report that we have started to abandon the craft instantly."

The telex operator slunk away like a stoat. Stanford turned again quickly on his heels, to give orders to the officers, who stood questioningly beside the chart table with him.

"We have received a message that the ship will be sunk within one hour, and are therefore to abandon ship immediately. Presumably the last exercise for this ship," he said with a pardonable sneer. "Press the alarm-siren at once and make all necessary preparations. I want everybody away from the craft within twenty minutes."

The officers stood as if they had been caught with their pants down for a few seconds, before one of them said confusedly: "What's the matter, sir?"

"Didn't you hear my order?" Stanford yelled uncompromisingly.

A second later the alarm-siren sounded all over the craft. It gave a hoarse, repetitive, frightening sound.

Stanford pointed to his second-in-command, Kirk Ludlow, who hastily crossed the bridge to the chart table, when he observed that something special was about to happen.

Stanford said sharply: "I order you to take with you in the helicopters a minimum crew in order to stop the craft if this message is only another damned exercise to test our reaction capability. Nevertheless, keep well away from the craft for one hour and fifteen minutes from now."

"I am not fully aware of the situation. Please inform me," Ludlow replied gently, but undoubtedly quite bewildered.

"Sorry – of course you are not," Stanford said and handed over the telex message, that he still kept in his hand, like a priest holding the Holy Bible on his deathbed.

"Sorry," Stanford repeated politely. "I did not realise that you were absent when I received this message."

Ludlow read the message carefully, twice, before he said: "This seems strange, there must be a mistake. I will investigate."

Ludlow hastened away to the communications room before Stanford had a chance to react. Two minutes later he returned crestfallen.

Ludlow was fifty four years old and had been second-in-command on the craft for one and a half years. He had been in the navy for thirty-four years and expected to be a commander of his own large ship within one year. He was short, but broad and athletic. It was easy to see that he was from Wales. He had grown up near Swansea, a fishing boat's skipper's son. He gained his sea legs at an early age and had never had any doubts that he belonged to the sea.

"Headquarters confirmed the message," Ludlow said sorrowfully, as if he just had received a message that his house had burnt down.

"I will execute your orders at once," he added, and snatched a telephone.

Stanford heard Ludlow talk loudly to the disbelieving helicopters' officer, while he rushed to the pilot's section and ordered: "Set the auto-pilot to three hundred and five degrees exactly and at a speed of seven knots and then all of you leave for the lifeboats at once."

Afterwards, Stanford grabbed the intercom microphone and switched on full ship coverage.

The hoarse alarm siren stopped while he spoke with a calm measured voice that could be heard all over the craft's intercom system: "This is the commander speaking. All crew including the engine and galley personnel, the medical staff and their patients, all helicopter pilots and the service personnel, together with all the troops and their officers, must abandon ship immediately."

Stanford could of course have said, everyone, but he was a perfectionist and mentioned all different groups of personnel on board, so as to be sure that everybody had understood him quite clearly.

Then he said with heightened emotion: "This is not an exercise! – I repeat: This is not an exercise! Everybody must immediately go to their emergency stations, man the lifeboats and leave the craft. No panic, we have sufficient time. – I repeat – no panic, we have sufficient time."

Stanford knew the behaviour of crew on board, when they had to abandon ship.

So he hastily added: "You are not allowed to take with you any personal belongings. Lost belongings will be fully compensated by the navy."

The hoarse siren started its monotonous wailing again.

Coe had been in the Royal Marines for many years and he had also participated in landing operations from HMS *Fearless* during the Falklands War. At the moment, he sat restlessly in a small rubber boat dressed in diving equipment, only waiting for HMS *Fearless'* sister-craft, HMS *Heroic*, to appear. Below the rubberboat was fastened a miniature submersible that could pull him through the water below the surface at the speed of five knots. In his hand Coe had the steering mechanism, which produced the infrared laser-beam that would lead a missile to its target. After days of calculations he had decided where to hit the craft to obtain maximum effect. He knew these craft from top to bottom after he had served for many years as a marine.

Inside, in the rear, HMS *Heroic* had a dock for the small landing craft, which were floating in seawater. These craft could each carry more than a hundred tons, accommodating two tanks or several smaller transport vehicles. They could alternatively carry thirty six fully battle-equipped soldiers. The landing craft could easily be launched from the mother craft only by opening the rear ports. The tanks were placed in a hold on the deck in front of the small landing craft. HMS *Heroic*'s engine room was situated in the middle, under the depot for light vehicles, which was below the battle-tank depot. Three decks with storerooms and the ammunition arsenal were in front of depots that contained tanks and light vehicles. This was right under the craft's bridge. Coe had decided that site was the weakest part of the craft and the best location for the forthcoming missile attack. He planned to aim the laser-beam exactly on this spot and hit it on the waterline, right under the bridge.

Connoly had taken the sailing boat from Anguilla to the coast of the Dutch island of Saint Eustatius, to the southwest. There was a narrow strait between these two islands, which HMS *Heroic* would pass through. Connoly had planned to sink *Heroic* when she passed out from the strait into deeper water. Beyond the islands, the sea had depths up to seven thousand six hundred metres. Because of possible detection from over-flying planes, satellite photographs or randomly passing ships, he had decided to launch the missile from the Dutch Island, not from the sailing boat. Using diving equipment and a miniature submersible similar to Coe's, he would be able to quickly reach the sailing boat that was anchored far off the missile's launching spot.

Connoly had reckoned it would become very difficult for the Dutch authorities to hunt those responsible for the launch if it originated from the island, because they also had to consider the possibility that those implicated might remain on the island. The fact that Saint Eustatius belonged to a nation other than Britain would also delay any efforts to find those responsible.

After Connoly had launched the missile, it would be guided by Coe's steering mechanism and led to the target. Coe would, immediately after the attack, sink his rubber boat, and with the help of the miniature submersible, reach the sailing boat in the same way as Connoly.

The moment had come. The submersible was anchored within easy reach, just off the beach of Saint Eustatius. Connoly pressed the button and the missile immediately left the launch pad with a loud roar. He could follow with the naked eye, the white vapour trail behind the missile fading far away in the distance. The missile was on its way to end HMS *Heroic*'s long service in the Royal Navy. Connoly hoped, as a responsible doctor of medicine, that nobody would be killed or injured by his actions.

20

The Boeing 767 jumbo jet belonging to British Atlantic Airways – BAA, steadily approached Miami International Airport. The plane had left Heathrow just after eight in the evening and had crossed the Atlantic during late night Greenwich time, or during the evening, Miami time. The passengers, who mostly were tourists, would arrive late in the evening local time, where they could go to sleep and wake up restored the next day after an extended night. There were never problems with jet lag when flying with the sun. The problems with the diurnal rhythm would only occur on flights in the opposite direction, towards the sun, from America to Europe.

The pilot on board was Captain James Rotting, and his co-pilot was Ralph Saxon.

Captain Rotting was a very experienced pilot and had crossed the Atlantic frequently during the last twenty-five years. He had landed hundreds of times in Miami and knew the airport thoroughly.

Because of the pleasant climate in Florida, Rotting had bought a small house in Fort Lauderdale, where he and his wife lived in the wintertime, when the weather was grey and cold in England.

He had reached fifty four, was of medium height and was bald. He looked distinguished in the way plane passengers generally wanted their captain to look. He was trained as a fighter pilot in the Royal Air Force – RAF.

"The fighter pilots of the RAF are always the best," he used to proclaim proudly when he was participating in discussions about pilots' ability on education and experience.

The captain had been a pilot of different small jet fighters in the RAF for many years, before he became a civil airliner pilot. He had enjoyed taking the jet fighters into steep dives and actually feeling the G-force, almost fainting as he reached the bottom of the dive. Then he would employ full throttle and pull the stick back to take the plane into a steep climb towards the sky, with a loud, magnificent roar. Meanwhile the plane constantly rolled around on its axis while climbing. That made him really feel as free as a bird and a true pilot.

When test pilots did the same manoeuvre during the time of the aircraft's infancy, many pilots calculated incorrectly the loss of altitude, when the plane reached the bottom of its dive and turned its nose for climbing. The planes very often smashed on the ground in a sea of flames and the pilots perished. Another great resulting problem, especially during this time of the planes' newness, was the loss of speed at the turning point, if the turn was too steep. The planes with often relatively weak engines, sometimes had too low a speed and did not get enough lift to carry their weight, and so dropped helplessly to the ground like twisting stones. This was not such a large problem for a modern jet fighter with enormous power compared to its weight, but it would be a significant problem for a heavy jumbo jet if a dive and rise situation occurred.

The captain was remembering his happy days in the RAF as he approached Florida's East Coast. He was a lot younger then and full of speed and spirit.

"The speed and spirit have not completely left me," he thought and smiled contentedly to himself.

"You still react as quickly as a young man," the doctor had told him last time he had his periodic medical check-up to keep his pilot's licence.

However, co-pilot Ralph Saxon was quite a different type. He was trained as a civil pilot and had not had the same experience as his captain. BAA always paid their co-pilots significantly less than other airline companies, while paying their chief pilots considerably more. It was BAA's policy to recruit the best top officers from their competitors, but still keep the total wage bill at the same level as theirs.

The co-pilots were never promoted to captains. They knew this and only second rate pilots, who could not find better positions elsewhere, applied for BAA. Opponents of this claimed the quality of the co-pilots might be danger-ously reduced and thus the company's general level of safety. It was also more expensive over time. Nevertheless, the company management assured shareholders this was a great advantage because it allowed BAA to compete in the airline business in an exceptional way, and the company was continually updated in development, safety and all new trends in the business.

Captain Rotting had not flown with Saxon much. He could therefore not tell much about the co-pilot's flying abilities. The co-pilot was in addition, somewhat unusually silent and uncommunicative and Rotting could not form a clear picture of him.

"Anyway, the fact that he is not talkative can only be an advantage," Rotting had said to one of his colleagues, "then he will not disturb my thoughts during the flight."

Almost anyone with minimum experience can take down a jumbo jet, Rotting reflected, while he glanced indulgently at the motionless and quiet co-pilot. Everything is almost automatic these days. It is only when exceptional circum-stances occur, that it is necessary to have a really experi-enced and qualified pilot. The chance of anything disastrous occurring exactly at the same time as a captain might be indisposed, is unlikely.

Purser Maryanne Maywood emptied the passenger cabin of used plastic glasses, napkins and everything that might be strewn around, ahead of the landing in Miami. She and her eleven colleagues looked forward to a good night's sleep, after they had served two hundred and sixty eight passengers for nearly seven hours. Although night flights were a lot more quiet and relaxed than stressful daytime flights, with all passengers awake. Most of the passengers had dozed the time away or had fallen sound asleep. Though the passengers were mostly completely unknown to each other, some were sleeping and snoring noisily with their heads towards each other as if they had been friends for years. The crew always found the passengers a bit ridiculous at this stage of the flight, but soon it would be a lot noisier in the passenger cabin, when the captain informed them that the airliner was approaching landing.

Captain Rotting got a radio message from Miami International Airport, nearly half an hour before he was to land.

A voice crackled in his ears that sounded particularly uncertain, but still calm and monotonous: "Miami International to Bravo, Alfa, Alfa, flight 273 from London, Heathrow, do you hear me?"

"Bravo, Alfa, Alfa 273, from London to Miami International. OK, I hear you loud and clear!" Rotting replied routinely.

The crackling radio voice continued in a tranquil monotone: "Miami International to Bravo, Alfa, Alfa 273. An urgent message has been received from Heathrow, London, that all British aircraft in the air at the moment have to choose alternative arrival destinations, because of a general threat that has been received. The threat is that British aircraft in flight all over the world will not be able to land according to their flight schedules. If these instructions are not followed, they run the risk of being destroyed on landing."

At the end of the message, the voice faded away as the radio frequency was disturbed for a moment, apparently because of the weather.

Then it came back and sounded strong and completely clear: "Miami International to Bravo, Alfa, Alfa 273 from London, did you comprehend the message?"

Rotting considered the message for a moment, as he was not sure what to do.

It took him a short time before he replied: "Bravo, Alfa, Alfa 273 to Miami International. Read your message once more please."

The voice read the message once more, clearly and slowly, then said: "You must, if possible, select an alternative landing place if you consider the threat serious enough to be reckoned with. At the moment Tampa International Airport would be your nearest alternative, because of the heavy traffic situation."

The voice that most of the time sounded like the message concerning an ordinary weather report, disappeared again for a moment, before it returned as clear as before: "Miami International to Bravo, Alfa, Alfa 273. Do you hear me?"

"Bravo, Alfa, Alfa 273 is listening!"

"The weather situation at Miami International airport is relatively good. Visibility: *Cave OK*. Wind: 10 knots, from 270 degrees, west. Air pressure normal and temperature eighteen degrees Celsius. – Confirm."

The voice disappeared and Rotting confirmed. Afterwards, he thought carefully about the received message. The co-pilot had heard the same message as the captain, but made no comment. He only looked questioningly at the captain and remained silent. The captain took no notice of him. He had reasoned that he could not expect any logical help from that direction. He checked the fuel reserve. There was sufficient fuel to extend the flight from Miami to Tampa, if it became necessary, and if the consumption of fuel was kept at a normal level.

He spoke into the microphone: "Bravo, Alfa, Alfa 273 to Miami International."

"Miami International – Listening."

The sound was distinct and clear.

"Threats are common in the airline business and there is no threat directly to our plane, so the threats potentially only concern the airport."

Rotting hesitated for a couple of seconds before he continued: "The question can simply be directed to the airport and our decision depends therefore fully on you only. Is it safe enough to secure our arrival?"

After a moment or two, the reply came loud and clear: "Miami International to Bravo, Alfa, Alfa 273 from London. The airport's management confirm that Miami airport is safe and secure. We await your landing as normal in twelve minutes. Descend to six thousand feet. Follow normal landing procedure. Final on runway two – your arrival has first priority. Welcome to Miami!"

"Bravo, Alfa, Alfa 273 to Miami International. *Roger* – I confirm new altitude 6000 and landing within twelve minutes."

The radio was silent for some minutes. Then it said: "Miami International to Bravo, Alfa. Alfa 273. Descend to three thousand feet and follow normal procedure to runway two. Weather situation unchanged – *Cave OK*, 10 knots, 270 degrees, pressure normal, eighteen degrees Celsius. Confirm!"

"Bravo Alfa, Alfa 273 to Miami International. Confirming;

altitude 3000, weather status quo, approaching by standard signals, final on runway two. Thanks. Over and out."

The landing lights of the BAA's jumbo jet from London could be observed from the control tower at Miami International Airport, when the plane came closer and closer to final landing.

Three weeks earlier necessary periodic repairs had been completed on the airport's drainage system. The work had to be completed before the rainstorms started in September. The regular construction company, Miami Construction and Maintenance, had, again, given the lowest quotation for the assignment. The chief engineer at the airport said that the company had given the lowest quotation only because it was clever enough to send additional invoices concerning the work later. The invoices covered tasks the company did not mean to include in the job. They were not presented ahead of the quotation and must be calculated in addition.

The airport's administration had great problems accepting the company's additional invoicing, but the airport's chief engineer said that they had rather unwillingly given the assignment to the company before and would do so this time: "There are a couple of important factors we have to consider. The company knows the work from previous experience and has always executed the work well and within the agreed time. We know what we have, but not what we might get if we change to another company."

The company workmen and engineers were all dressed in the company's blue uniform with the large letters MCM on the back. On the airport they were also equipped with special identity cards issued by the airport, in addition to the company's standard identification.

The second Monday of the work period, two additional

workmen passed through the security control, smiled and showed their ID cards, which were hardly checked. The two workmen were Harry McCoy and Michael Samson.

Michael Samson was a very reliable Scottish Highlander. He was an industrial worker's son. His father had worked with the SS Group all his life. This year Samson would be fifty. He was hairy, short and very vigorous. He had grown up in the working-class district of Glasgow. Because of extremely good results at the secondary school, he had received a scholarship from the SS Group's labour union and had been trained as a machine engineer. After college he had, for many years, worked with British Special Airforce Security, where he had been trained as an expert on explosives. He had joined Scotland Yard's bomb disposal squad when his service with the airforce ended. Here he, more than once, had risked his life, disarming bombs in the City of London.

A full, dark red beard had covered Samson's face for the last twenty years. The beard had been there since he was injured in an accident in Ulster, while he and two colleagues were about to disarm a sophisticated bomb. His two colleagues died instantly, but he was saved, only because he had walked away from the bomb to collect some special tools, a few seconds before the explosion. The bomb had obviously been created for one purpose only – to kill the disposal team. Afterwards, Samson was hospitalised for nearly six months, while the doctors put him together as best as they could.

"I am a handmade man. When I walk through the scanner at an airport, I always have to undress because I set off the alarm system. The scanner reacts to all the steel inside me," he once said over a beer in a pub, but only people who did not know his real story laughed.

301

Samson was not married, but he was assured that the accident had not reduced his ability as a husband. It was just not possible to work in Scotland Yard's bomb disposal group, with daily risks of being killed and at the same time have the responsibility of a family.

"It may also be difficult for me to get a bonny lass to marry me, with all these terrible scars all over my face and body," he joked when anyone touched on the subject.

People who knew Samson very well did suspect that sometimes he felt quite differently about the subject. These times he was exceptionally angry when anyone mentioned it, and his connection to the police had helped him more than once, when he had settled his exasperation by violence.

However, Samson continued to work for the bomb squad for nearly ten years after the accident, until the SS Group employed him as the senior security officer for installations at the Brent section in the North Sea. Later, his tasks had been extended to be the overall security advisor for all oil installations of the group.

Samson was officially with Harry and his wife Elise on a swimming holiday at Long Beach, when they had received a package containing Russian plastic explosives, by regular freight-boat from Southampton via Jacksonville in northern Florida. The package was smuggled in, hidden among chemical supplies, sent from a company in Manchester to a company near Mobile in Alabama.

The Highlanders' Commando had considered the transport to be safe, first of all because there were not many products that could be smuggled with any benefit from Britain to the United States. Secondly, the British Customs control was known to be extremely effective. The US Customs inspectors were aware of that and relaxed their control. As calculated ahead, the chemical supplies with the hidden package of plastic explosives, had therefore not been examined.

McCoy and Samson had followed the lorry that loaded the supplies in the harbour to Crestview, in a rented car. When the lorry-driver finally stopped to get some food, McCoy guarded the hungry driver, while Samson effected a break-in on the lorry and retrieved the package.

"That worked very well Michael."

McCoy panted heavily and seemed as relieved as if he had just been saved from certain death, falling from the top of the Empire State Building and had been gripped by strong hands one metre above the street. He had felt enormous stress when they passed the control by the workmen's gate at the airfield.

"You had not expected anything other than a safe and easy entry, had you?" – Samson asked shortly, seemingly completely unaffected.

McCoy did not reply. He knew his colleague was used to stress through his previous work with Scotland Yard's bomb squad. His colleague had an experienced mountain climber's relaxed attitude – does it work or does it not work – anyway I have done my best. McCoy just stared straight ahead like a hungry dog at his master's dinner table, watching the beef pieces disappearing from the fork into the master's mouth.

Samson looked obliquely at his obviously terrified colleague and laughed silently. It was correct that he had not been stressed at all when passing the guards. From his experience as security chief, he knew guards' normal behaviour. Therefore he was entirely certain that they would never check them properly.

He continued talking to McCoy, almost as a psychiatrist

to a patient: "The airport guards' behaviour was perfectly normal, because when something becomes routine, security procedures often become neglected. If you ever become the manager of a security company, one of the first tasks you have to impress on your employees, is to keep the alertness and the control at a constant high level."

McCoy still did not reply and Samson kept smilingly on: "It is unlikely that anything would be detected here. In my opinion, to pass that control was like disarming a harmless hand-grenade with the security-pin intact. I would have fired those guards immediately, if they had been under my command. They made every mistake possible and were probably only looking for terrorists with black, greasy hair, Arab manners and manicured hands."

The Scotsmen took one of Miami Construction and Maintenance's small motor vehicles that was parked just inside the control-gate and drove towards the west end of the runway. They parked and entered a drainage tunnel, about a kilometre from the end of the more than three kilometre long runway. The drainage tunnel passed under the runway and had recently been cleaned during the work on the system. While McCoy watched the surrounding traffic, Samson fastened plastic explosives in a long sausage along the left bottom corner in the drainage channel, under the grating that covered the base of the tunnel. The tunnel was built in such a way as to make it possible to inspect it without getting wet, but the whole tunnel would drain water when there was flooding after a heavy downpour. The dirty water that continuously flowed in the channel covered the explosives completely, until the next cleaning the following year. Samson finally fastened a detonator to the explosive sausage and rolled out an almost invisible thin wire along the bottom of the channel, from a small reel. The wire ended just beside the runway's asphalt, well out of the lawnmower's area, and was covered by sand.

The wire was connected to a small remote receiver with a short black antenna, which was placed along the asphalt and partly covered with sand and dirt, so as not to be discovered. The explosives could hereafter be controlled by remote control, outside the airport.

The two Scotsmen left the airfield at once. Their job was finished, and they celebrated a successful result, so far, with a glass of cold beer at Long Beach.

When BAA flight 273 crossed the Atlantic from London, Elise McCoy walked smilingly through the departure hall of the terminal building at Miami International Airport. She carried her small red Samsonite suitcase, her red beauty box of the same make, and was dressed in a BAA's purser's light blue uniform. She was an ample-bosomed beauty and she knew it. Her uniform seemed almost to explode, as she tripped across the floor on her long, tanned elegant legs on high heels, to the crew's entrance door. The men around in the entrance hall glanced dreamily at her and the women envied her. Elise had been an airline purser for many years and knew how to tackle any situation. The guard by the door to the crew's section smiled and gasped for air, as she sent him an inviting sexy smile. She only hoped he would not die of a heart attack where he was. He would not dream of asking her for her fake security card.

This woman would have been a catalyst for my decreasing sexual life with my always tired and colourless wife, the guard thought longingly. My wife is only interested in watching television and eating hamburgers, while the flat becomes more and more filthy and she becomes fatter and fatter. The guard took a deep breath, as he looked longingly after the beautiful purser who soon disappeared into the crew area.

Elise walked through the crew's section to the terminal.

305

To the right of the terminal building, she could see a BAA Boeing 737 parked. This plane had arrived about an hour ago from Manchester, with tourists. She walked resolutely to the plane, which was unlocked because it was to be cleaned during the night. Once inside the plane she immediately opened the door to the inner, upper cupboards in the pantry, behind the pilots' cabin. She had hidden a packet with plastic explosives in her suitcase together with her bras and briefs. She opened the suitcase, took out the packet, which she placed in the cupboard behind napkins, straws, plastic cups and paraphernalia for serving passengers on an airliner. She pressed the button to activate the detonator's time trigger, after she had carefully adjusted the time corresponding with what she had read on the flight-information board, when she passed through the airport's entrance hall.

Then she retraced her steps, leaving the airport unnoticed.

21

A top secret telex message was received from the Canadian air force's headquarters in Ottawa, at the air force base, Déboisement, near Havre-Saint Pierre in Quebec. This message arrived shortly after the evacuation order had been received at Fort Hope.

It was a copy of a message which just moments earlier had been received by headquarters from the British Royal Air Force. The message was short, but unmistakable: *"We have received a warning from terrorists about a possible attack, with nuclear missiles, on our training base at Fort Hope, in north-western Quebec. The attack will take place within half an hour. We have therefore given all our troops at base the order to abandon. The threat is combined with other very pressing threats aimed at the Canadian authorities and their power to investigate. The terrorists have previously demonstrated their tremendous force, and have shown themselves to be able to execute all their threats. We require you, primarily, to make a survey from very high altitude with photo-reconnaissance aircraft. We want the observation of the surroundings of the base – not directly over it – and in a way that the aircraft can not be connected to any prior warning we have received from the terrorists. Do not provoke the terrorists while our troops still are ashore. The troops will leave Canada from our port close to the base in two British navy craft. What you do afterwards will mainly be up to you, because the terrorists must accept that the Canadian authorities will react, when a nuclear missile is deto-*

nated on their territory. However, withhold any actions against the terrorists until at least one hour after our craft have departed. It is conceivable that the two navy ships and the troops will be in great danger, if you take any action that can be detected by the terrorists and connected to the warning we have received from them. – For that reason we repeat: Postpone all actions against the terrorists till one hour after the departure of our craft. More information will follow later. This message is highly confidential. Inform us about possible assignment you will activate. Best regards Air Marshal Thomas Grantham, Commander British Royal Air Force."

The Canadian commander at the air base, Colonel Henry La Fontene, ordered two General Dynamics F16XL Fighting Falcons launched for the assignment. The aircraft were on stand-by alert, with the most modern photo-reconnaissance equipment. The pilots, who, when on stand-by alert were always completely kitted out in flying gear ready for action, ran immediately from the rest room across the asphalt and climbed hastily up the ladder into their planes. The ground maintenance officers followed closely, fastened the communication cable to their helmets and slammed the cockpit covers over their heads. The planes' huge engines were started at the same time by starter mechanisms and radio connections were tested. The two Fighting Falcons left a minute afterwards from the runway in aligned formation and climbed quickly, in steep curves, into the sky. Shortly afterwards ear-splitting booms from far away could be heard by everybody in the area as the two jet fighters broke the sound barrier.

F16XL Falcons have a double surface to the wings in comparison to ordinary F16 Falcons, which increases the aircraft's action time by nearly fifty per cent, in addition to permitting it a much higher altitude.

Only twenty five minutes after the colonel had received

the telex message, the planes had reached the actual area and were circling at an altitude of thirty eight thousand feet.

Demonstrations of rapid actions like this are certainly very good for my future promotion, La Fontene thought with pleasure, while he drank hot coffee in the operations centre, bent over the current radar commander's shoulder, carefully following the planes' movements on the radar screen.

"This must be the first hostile mission ever for the Canadian Air Force, on their own territory. We had better send an urgent message to headquarters informing that both the aircraft have achieved the target area," La Fontene undoubtedly satisfied, said to the present radar commander, a confused, young inexperienced lieutenant.

A quarter of an hour later the pilots detected a vapour trail from a missile fired from about thirty kilometres from Fort Hope. They could follow the trail with their eyes, as it expanded in the wind. The missile looked for a long time as if it was about to miss the base by several kilometres. Suddenly it changed direction entirely and headed directly for the base, like a puppy unexpectedly discovering a scared cat to chase. The pilots were certain the missile hit the base at its weapon depot, as they observed a sudden huge explosion that formed a mushroom cloud, and rose several hundred metres into the sky. They had never actually seen such an explosion, but they knew instantly what it might be, and understood they had witnessed America's first hostile nuclear explosion. The pilots reported the sombre incident to their base immediately and continued their surveillance, which included heat detector photos of objects in the firing

309

area as well as tracks of a car that drove towards the coastal road and south-westwards shortly after the missile was launched.

The Falcons returned to base with their collected information for the photo laboratory, as their operation time ran out and several colleagues had taken over their task.

Colonel La Fontene walked restlessly around in his office, while he considered the incident and waited impatiently for the results from the photo laboratory.

He came from one of the oldest French families in Quebec. The family had lived there, near Montreal, since his ancestors had fled from Rouen, in France, after they had opposed the French nobility early in the seventeen hundreds. In Quebec the family had started trading with the other early immigrants.

The La Fontenes had always married French, so La Fontene considered himself as pure French.

"Had my ancestors accepted another fifty years under the monarchy's slavery, till after the invention of the guillotine, which shortened most of the French nobility during the Revolution, we would never have been in Canada," his French-looking father once said to his son.

"Then you would never have been born, and that would have been a great disaster for the French cognac industry," his son had added quickly, and they both laughed.

La Fontene's father had also been an army officer, but had openly been against any British involvement with Canada.

"Britain is historically France's enemy. Canada, and specially Quebec, should have joined the American War of Independence," his father had expressed loudly and clearly from the rostrum during a private celebration of the French national day, the 14th July.

His father was also a supporter of an independent Quebec, separate from the rest of Canada.

"Quebec should have been an independent state. Tell me, why should Quebec support the whole economy of the rest of Canada that mainly consists of Englishmen? The English have undeniably always lived by other people's work," his father also said in a speech.

La Fontene's controversial and colourful father had many friends, but his non-diplomatic expressions did little for his military career so he ended up only as a major when he retired.

Colonel La Fontene also looked very French, like his father. He was not short, but he was not very tall either. He had thick black hair, brown eyes and was always smiling. He was certainly not as outwardly frankly controversial as his father was, although he was a very enthusiastic supporter of the same ideas.

"You could have had an excellent career as a diplomat," several of his superiors had said during his many years in the Air Force.

La Fontene had started his career as a fighter pilot and had then advanced very quickly. He had reached fifty-three, and was married to a dark-haired French beauty whom he had met in Paris during his service in Nato's Southern Command.

Who in hell are using nuclear weapons against a secret British base in Quebec? La Fontene kept walking around in his office, like a tired horse in the circus ring. Was this an action by Quebec's separatists, to close down the last British base in Canada? Anyway, the terrorists had this time managed to accomplish within seconds a task, which his French ancestors had fought for, without any success, during more than two hundred years. La Fontene was as curious as a stoat. He stubbed one cigarette and lit another, emptied one cup of coffee and poured another. He sat down on a chair, but rose immediately as he was too restless to sit still for a second.

The terrorists had, by their action, succeeded in throwing all the British off the base, which actually meant that they had lost their base forever. The old agreement, which was made between the British and the Canadian authorities, during the first days of the Second World War, was formulated in such a way that, if all British left the base, it would then be closed forever. This was because it was anticipated that the British would only need the base for the duration of the Second World War, but they had never left. They had steadfastly kept their legal right to remain; though a lot of diplomatic effort had been made to expel them. The British have, in theory, after this incident, to apply for a new contract for the base, which surely will never be sanctioned by the Canadian Parliament, because of the tremendous public opinion against any British military presence on Canadian territory. One might almost accept the use of a nuclear weapon to produce such a desirable result. Anyway, the radiation danger would disappear within fifty years, according to the United States' analysis on Bikini Island, even in the worst cases, but the British might have stayed at the base a lot longer than that. La Fontene had become considerably calmer after his reflections and his discovery that the British base had finally been closed forever.

The nuclear explosion had immediately been reported to the Canadian government, the Defence department and all the different units of the Canadian defence forces. There was continuous contact between the British authorities and the Canadians, who waited impatiently for further information, but no information turned up.

La Fontene was also still waiting for information, but from the laboratory as well, while he steadily and restlessly moved around in his office deep in thought.

Perhaps the responsibility for the incident was connected with one of all those endless independence struggles the British authorities had fought for centuries: – Battles against subjugated people in territories all over the world that had given the rather negligible English country her wealth. Historically included among all those fights, had also been the fight against the American settlers that established the United States. Later there had been diplomatic battles against the Australians, the Canadians and Indians, who all wanted to eliminate their previous colonial masters and their unjustified exploitation of their territory.

La Fontene left the history and reflected on the world situation today. The perpetrators of the attack could possibly be Spanish rebels, who wanted Gibraltar back for Spain, Irish IRA rebels who want Northern Ireland out of the union with England and independence fighters from Wales or Scotland, who want the same.

More and more questions filled La Fontene's head as he thought about the matter. Why had the British decided to leave the base so quickly without any resistance at all? The only answer to that question could be that they must have known exactly what was going to happen. They had known precisely that nuclear weapons would be put to use against them. Otherwise, it would have been completely illogical to withdraw the large force that the base contained, just because of a threat of a terrorist attack. Threats of a nuclear attack against a military base in the middle of Canada's deep forest would normally have been considered only as a simple joke, without any real foundation at all, and coming from completely lunatic people.

La Fontene had speeded up his walk around the office while he was thinking, but suddenly he slowed down, walked over to the chair behind his desk and sat down. He was convinced he had reasoned out the correct answer to the question. No terrorists would of course have been so stupid as to attack such a large force of specially trained soldiers, which the British had at the base, without knowing that their force was considerably stronger. The terrorists must simply have informed the British beforehand that a nuclear attack was going to happen in order to save lives, and the British must have known the threat was real. They had therefore actually received no threat, but only received concrete information. The incident must logically have been a demonstration of force in order to put political pressure on the British authorities. Very responsible people could therefore have perpetrated the attack, which must also be the reason why a target, so far from inhabited areas, had been chosen, in the middle of the forest, where they expected nobody to be injured.

La Fontene poured another cup of coffee and took a large gulp, while he gave a satisfied smile. This political pressure must only concern the British, not Quebec – not Canada. We must keep a low profile and not become involved, otherwise we can reckon with possible similar attacks against Canadian properties, and maybe without any warnings. La Fontene suddenly froze in a cold sweat, when he thought about the consequences of such an attack on a Canadian city. I must have a meeting with those in command at Headquarters immediately, he decided just as the telex operator knocked on his door.

"Come in," La Fontene said.

"We have just received an urgent telex from Headquarters," the operator said and handed a piece of paper to Fontene before disappearing.

It was concerning Fort Hope – an extract of a message

314

from the British Defence Ministry to the Canadian: *All British troops had left Fort Hope only minutes before the base was completely destroyed by a nuclear detonation. No messages about casualties have so far been received.*

McNeigh did not lose any time after the missile was launched. He threw the launching attachment into the boot of the car at once. He also checked the ground carefully for any items that could have been dropped, and other tracks that could lead the authorities later to make a connection between him and the launched missile. Then, he drove quickly down the road till he reached the place where he had left Ness. Ness had taken cover in the forest near the road, and appeared, with a broad smile, when he saw the Chevrolet.

"Completely successful hit," Ness boasted satisfied with a large grin, while he quickly got into the car, after he had wiped the sweat off his face with a dirty handkerchief that he conjured up from his pocket.

He continued enthusiastically: "We hit the base's weapon depot exactly as planned. The deserted base was entirely demolished. It is really good stuff in these Russians missiles. The Russians have definitely superb quality nuclear weapons, which can be compared to Western equivalents. We had better keep the peace with them in the future, I think."

To calm down Ness' mood a fraction, McNeigh said thoughtfully: "Our most important task at the moment is to get out of here without being discovered by the Canadian army or police. Turn on the military radio and search through all the frequencies, to find if they use the ordinary frequencies on military radios for communication. Find out if they are looking for us. The British might have alerted them before the attack, after they had received our message which saved their lives."

Ness turned the radio knobs, and shouted loudly after only half a minute: "They are here, we must change our plans, because they have already put up a roadblock between Moisie and Sept-Îles."

"I had reckoned with that," McNeigh said calmly and quietly. "It seems as if we have to use the alternative getaway plan and make a forest excursion for some days." He considered silently for a second. "It will surely be too risky to make an attempt to get through the roadblock. If they have any suspicions about us, we are finished, because we cannot escape with the police hanging on our wheels. That only happens in movies. The police radios are always quicker than the cars and their colleagues do not need many seconds to roll out nail mats."

The Scotsmen drove for another half an hour along the coastal road, then they turned off, stopped for a few seconds at a suitable place to throw the missile's launching attachment into the sea.

"The attachment will never be found," Ness stated determinedly, as he looked down nearly two hundred metres below towards the cold waves that continuously battered the rocks in their efforts to destroy them.

Later, the Scotsmen stopped at intervals along the road to make fake tracks, which might confuse searchers into believing these were dumping places for the missile's launching attachment, in case they were observed from the air.

They turned left and drove off the coastal road by Mingan, onto a country road that ended in the forest, half way to Waco. The road became narrower and narrower and was soon only a rough timber road intended for trucks. The Chevrolet was not constructed for forest driving and it soon danced up and down on the suspension like a rodeo horse.

"The road ends about twelve kilometres from here,"

316

McNeigh said informatively. "I have been here many times for hunting and fishing."

He paused before he continued: "It would be very stupid to park the car at the end of the road. That will give us away if anyone follows us. You can be sure they will have dogs on the track at once, so we must get rid of the car before the end of the road."

McNeigh drove quietly for another kilometre and said suddenly: "I propose we dump the car into the lake you see to the right – over there." He pointed at a small, idyllic lake that could hardly be seen as it was hidden by the forest about two hundred metres from the road. "Make the camping equipment and the fishing gear ready. This will be the end of our vacation in civilisation, as car tourists. From now on, we will be tramps hiding in the forest. We have no alternative, but to walk unless," he tried to look frightened for a moment, "we find a bear to give us a ride. There are a lot of large grizzlies in the area."

Ness giggled silently.

A small narrow path went from the road to the water's edge. Many cars had used the path earlier, though it looked only wide enough to walk on. There was a small open space at the end of the path that seemed to be a place where the weekend anglers frequently put up their tents. This was a great advantage for the fugitives. The tracks from the car could not so easily be discovered. The disadvantage was that the car could be discovered a lot sooner, because of the fishermen.

The Scotsmen drove the Chevrolet to the edge of the lake, to a spot ideal for fishermen in the light North Canadian summer nights. They removed the number plates and all other marks that could easily identify the car if it was discovered. All places on the car where they could have left their fingerprints were wiped. Then they loosened the hand brake and pushed the car into the water. It floated some metres before it filled with water and sank front first. It quickly vanished entirely in the deep water. Only a couple of tiny oil spots on the surface showed where it had sunk. The Scotsmen carefully swept, with spruce branches, where the car had been dumped from, in order to cover up the tracks of the wheels.

"Well done," Ness said with a broad smile. "If they find the car in the future, they probably will think it was an insurance fraud."

McNeigh breathed deeply in the air. He enjoyed being in the forest. He felt he was at home and thought with pleasure that he was surely a child of nature.

Ness looked at him and said shortly, while he chuckled softly: "The wild animal is awakening I can clearly see."

McNeigh did not listen to Ness, because he was too occupied by his own thoughts. Anyway he did not notice. He only pointed to a spot on the map that he had taken from his rucksack.

He said, as if instructing a troop: "We are here, and have to walk south-west to get out of the area."

He moved his finger along an imaginary route on the map, before he continued: "To make problems for any searchers, if they have dogs to help, which I surely believe they will, I would suggest walking towards the north-east for a while, till we reach this small burn here."

McNeigh used the Scottish dialect word *burn*, as the name for the brook. He pointed at a brook on the map that meandered in a narrow valley, and passed under the road they had just been driving on.

"We will follow the burn to the other side of the road," he said informatively, "and we will walk in the water all the time to make it impossible for dogs to follow our tracks. In this way we will increase any pursuers' tracking area radically, and have a considerably better chance of making a successful escape, supposing they find this spot and the car."

Colonel La Fontene at Déboisement had waited until the laboratories had developed the films that had been brought back by the two Falcons. Afterwards, he had flown a two-seater Phantom Jet to Ottawa, where he had a meeting with the area commanders from various military branches. General Franc Lyon was the highest-ranking officer present. He led the meeting.

Lyon was a large, sixty four year old, robust man whose family originated in Normandy. He had grey hair that had been fair in his youth, which proclaimed he was descended from Scandinavian Vikings who settled in Normandy a thousand years ago. He had obviously planned to continue the family's Scandinavian line, because he had married a fair, tall Swedish woman from Uppsala when he attended university in the town, nearly forty years ago. Like La Fontene, he was a fervent, but silent supporter of a separate Quebec.

Lyon said very determinedly: "I suggest letting the navy patrol the coastline from the Strait of Belle Isle to Quebec. The army must work together with the police to cover the search for the terrorists on land. The airforce must be at the disposal of the army, making aerial searches, if necessary. I also suggest ordering Colonel Henry La Fontene to be in command of the entire operation." The general pointed quickly at La Fontene with his pen. "He will report to me directly."

Lyon paused, looked around at the officers present, who all nodded in agreement.

La Fontene smiled briefly. He had, prior to this meeting,

had a short meeting with the general. He had told the general about his thoughts concerning the motive for the attack on the British base. He was one of very few people who knew that the general, like he, was an eager supporter of the French Quebec's separation from the rest of Canada.

"Colonel La Fontene will brief you on the information we have about the situation at the moment," Lyon said and sat down.

La Fontene went to the overhead projector at the end of the large, long conference table and placed a transparency on the projector's light disk. He dimmed the ceiling light, cleared his throat and began.

"This is Fort Hope before the attack." La Fontene changed the slide. "This is Fort Hope after the attack. It was taken from one of our high altitude aircraft. One of them we sent over the area immediately we received the threat. Not much *hope* for the base on this slide," La Fontene said cleverly with an indication of a smile on his lips that he tried to hide with one of his hands, while the other changed the transparency for a map. "This is a map of the actual area. The missile was launched from this site."

He pointed with a pen to the place on the map where McNeigh had been standing. The audience could see the shadow of the pen on the wall-screen.

He continued: "I will now show you some shots of the missile's flight. You can follow the vapour trail." He placed six photos in quick succession in the projector without any comments.

"The missile took this route," he said and moved the pen along the assumed missile track on the last photo.

La Fontene paused a few seconds and looked at the audience for any significant questions or comments.

They said nothing and he continued: "At this point the missile changed direction." He pressed the pen roughly down for a moment on a single spot on the plastic sheet that lay on the projector. "Somebody must have been standing in this area with an infrared laser remote control pointing towards the base's weapon depot." He made a circle with his pen and looked up for a short time. "Here you can see something that might be very interesting concerning the possible future arrest of the terrorists." La Fontene placed another photo on the projector. The photo gave a thermograph presentation, which showed variations in ground temperatures. "You can see the launch spot. This is the temperature shadow of the person who launched the missile."

At first he pointed at the shadow with his pen for a while, but then the audience observed that the pen slowly made a circle around another shadow on the wall-screen, as La Fontene was suddenly pondering over something else completely.

However, he obviously ended his disturbing thoughts swiftly, because he suddenly continued talking quickly as though nothing had happened: "Here you can see where the person had parked his car. The motor is hot and leaves a shadow on the photo."

He made a new circle and hastily placed new photos on the projector as he said: "We can, on the other photos, follow the car moving towards the base. On this photo the car is evidently picking up another person." La Fontene carefully highlighted the spot with his pen and followed the movements of a shadow, as he changed the photos rapidly. "By following the shadow on the different photos backwards, the movement of the person who got in the car can be tracked exactly. He stood here when the missile was launched, which corresponds precisely with what I said about where we presume the target indicator must have been." La Fontene made a small circle with the pen to indicate where the person stood, and quickly showed some other photos. "The other shadows you see are probably animals."

"This equipment must be great for hunting," one of the listeners muttered loud enough for everyone to hear. Everybody laughed, breaking the tension.

La Fontene smiled and continued after this welcome break:

"From this spot we are following the car along the coastal road," he said while he continually pointed with his pen as he constantly changed photos on the projector. "But we might already have lost them because it is very difficult to track temperature shadows of a car, when cars are overtaking each other. There is always a lot of traffic on the coastal road. However, we will be able to be more specific later when the laboratory has ended their work, but at the moment we have a lot of alternatives."

La Fontene mentioned roughly more than twenty possible alternatives, including the car that had driven along the forest road, in the direction of Waco and then completely vanished.

"Probably drove into a garage," La Fontene said shortly.

22

The missile quickly reached maximum speed through the air heading towards HMS *Heroic*, across the Caribbean Sea from the island of Saint Eustatius, where Connoly had launched it. The vapour trail drew a straight, white line in the perfect blue sky. The straight line expanded by the wind into a curve. The wind speed changed at different altitudes and the curve became irregular and twisted till it presently floated into nothing but haze that soon disappeared.

Connoly wore a diving suit and oxygen tank on his back. Immediately after the missile was launched, he hastened swiftly, with the missile's aluminium launching attachment in his hands, towards the miniature submersible that he had left at the water-edge. The submersible's electric engine was idling softly and rhythmically, ready for immediate departure. Dave pulled the submersible into deeper water and hung himself on its rear, while he twisted the throttle. It accelerated and towed him towards deeper water, where he vanished completely from the surface.

Commander Stanford on board HMS *Heroic* stood alone on the bridge with his hands behind his back and inspected the organisation of the abandoning of his craft. He concluded, with satisfaction, that his crew was well prepared in emergency procedures. The crew could see him through the window. They felt a sort of pity for him, because he looked so grave and utterly lonesome where he quietly stood alone, unmoveable in his duty.

All the lifeboats and the small landing craft that left from the port doors, sailed quickly one by one in the direction of Anguilla as HMS *Heroic* steadfastly and precisely retained its course and speed. The ship had been checked and double-checked for any remaining people. Almost all the helicopters had flown, taking off high-ranking officers and the medical staff and their patients. The three remaining helicopters would soon leave. These contained a skeleton naval crew who could quickly return to the craft if it proved to be a false alarm.

The second-in-command, Commander Ludlow, who was going to leave in one of the remaining helicopters, climbed quickly up the staircase to the bridge. He saw Stanford standing alone in the same place, looking sadly towards the last lifeboat, as it slowly moved away from the ship, fading away as a smaller and smaller spot on the blue sea.

Running up staircases was not a usual exercise for Ludlow and he was rather breathless when he finally reached the top.

"You are the last one, and we are just waiting for you," he shouted exhaustedly.

Stanford made no reply to the information.

He only said, tranquilly, but clearly, like a wise old judge reading the outcome of a criminal case to an unfortunate, young defendant: "Kirk, I'll tell you, I'm greatly impressed with your organisation of the abandoning of the ship. You have trained your crew very well."

Ludlow became visibly flattered, and replied very politely: "Thank you, sir. Thank you."

"Are you sure you have checked the whole ship suffi-

324

ciently? Are you quite sure there is nobody who accidentally might have been forgotten?"

Ludlow confirmed: "She has been thoroughly checked – completely sure, sir."

Stanford added shortly and sharply: "Excellent, Kirk!"

"We are only waiting for you, sir."

Stanford looked seriously at Ludlow for a short time before he replied rather harshly: "A captain never leaves his ship!"

"I feared that reply, sir," Ludlow said with a sad smile. "One of the officers, who has sailed with you for many years, told me that I could expect such a reply. You are too obstinate, he said."

Stanford did not comment, but smiled bitterly through cold, tight lips.

Ludlow continued apparently angrily: "That would be refusing to carry out an order. You will be court maritalled."

"Maybe," Stanford said sincerely, "but I don't want to be the first captain in my family, with its long tradition at sea, to leave my ship when it is in difficulties."

"That's nonsense," Ludlow said in great agitation. "Not to leave the craft will only be treated as what it really is – a refusal to obey an order. You will be punished, dismissed and possibly end up as an able seaman. You will be denied all honours and spoil forty-five good years of service. You would suffer loss of your pension and status. It has been suggested that you are in line for a knighthood."

"Sorry, Kirk," Stanford said very determinedly. "There is one matter we have to consider. If we leave the ship to be like the *Flying Dutchman*, without a single person on board, anybody could board her and claim a salvage reward. I'm remaining on board. And you must leave at once. That's an order, Kirk."

"OK – you're the captain," Ludlow grumbled rather

annoyed. "I have no choice and will follow your order and leave, but I wish you good luck, Edward."

He added softly, but with a slight sign of a bright smile and a blink in his eyes: "I would probably have done just the same myself, in your position. I believe you are thinking just like me. This ostensible destruction is not rational, – probably just nonsense. You know it was only my plain duty to try to convince you to follow Admiralty orders. I'll see you in one hour!"

"I know," Stanford replied with a melancholy smile, when he saw his second-in-command close the door silently behind him.

The last three helicopters left shortly afterwards and flew towards the sun, led by the one with Ludlow. The group on board the helicopters could see Stanford watching them from the bridge like an unreal ghost, absolutely still.

Stanford had never believed that anything would happen to HMS *Heroic*. The international community would never have tolerated destroying a large naval craft, filled with weapons and oil, in such a way. Those things could not happen in peacetime. It was completely illogical and absolutely unlikely. This was an exercise. He was thoroughly convinced that he had analysed the situation correctly. Stanford knew he had done exactly what was expected of him. He had also prevented HMS *Heroic* becoming a *Flying Dutchman* by remaining on board, although he definitely did not believe that anybody would capture a British warship cruising in the Atlantic, apparently in perfect order. He felt quite safe on board as he walked resolutely towards the automatic coffee-machine.

Coe sat silently in his dinghy wearing a diving suit with two oxygen tanks on his back. He looked at the large landing craft that approached slowly, but steadily on the horizon. He observed three helicopters leaving the craft in the opposite direction. Previously he had observed lifeboats and small landing craft leaving. Everything seemed be proceeding exactly according to plan. He checked his scuba-watch and waited tranquilly. Fifteen minutes later he again checked his watch. HMS *Heroic* was about to reach its determined position. He fastened the infrared beam to the spot where he had decided the missile should hit and waited, but he did not see the missile until it hit the ship five minutes later.

The missile hit exactly. The explosion created a mushroom-shaped cloud that billowed hundreds of metres into the sky. The ship's magazine had increased the explosion. The ship broke into two parts that rapidly started to sink.

Coe did not wait to examine the result of the explosion after he had seen the hit. He just grabbed his knife, made a quick gash in the dinghy at sea level and threw himself into the sea, where the miniature submersible's electrical motor was idling. The submersible was quickly on its way into deep water with Coe towing the destroyed dinghy. The dinghy had been previously filled with lead, and it was towed on a thirty-metre long rope. When the rope became horizontal in the water, Coe knew the boat was emptied of air and he cut the rope. The boat sank to the bottom of the ocean and would never be seen again.

Connoly climbed on board the sailing boat with the help of his wife and Ann Castle. He gave them the thumbs up, and a broad smile covered his entire face. He did not have to say anything, because the women understood clearly what he meant. It could only be concluded that the mission had been a success so far. He was too exhausted to talk. After he had sent the miniature submersible away, he had swum for a quarter of a nautical mile at his top speed and he was fully aware that he was no longer a trained athlete.

Long before Connoly got his breath back, he took off the diving suit and dumped it into the sea loaded with a lead diving belt to sink it. He raised the anchor and ran up the sails with the aid of the women. The boat shuddered restlessly. The sails flapped frantically a short while before the wind filled them and the boat became steady and started to accelerate.

Connoly became at once more relaxed when the sailboat moved. Ann poured whisky into a glass and took a gulp herself, before she handed it over to Connoly who emptied the rest in one single gulp. He shivered as the strong whisky ran down his throat, and he placed himself on the bench in the rear, behind the large steel steering wheel. His wife was seated at one side of him and Ann at the other. Then he started to talk after making some grimaces and coughing a couple of times.

"A good scotch makes a man quite new," he said with a broad smile. "Everything went exactly according to plan. We only have to wait and hope that George had success as well."

"You do not have to wait and hope," Betsy quickly answered her husband. "I don't believe you saw the huge explosion. We saw the top of it. The missile must have hit perfectly."

"Fine – very fine" Connoly replied, but not as enthusiastically as his wife and Ann had expected.

He was too concerned in case anyone had been injured or killed.

He continued: "I was under the water the whole ride back. I didn't see a damn thing except fish. Let us hope nobody has been killed."

Without waiting for any comments from the two women, he said: "We must accelerate towards the south-west, to get as far away from the missile's route as possible and get into the agreed position for picking up George. We must also prepare for possible inspection by the Dutch navy or police. You can be sure they will examine the sailing boat because it has been so close to the explosion."

Dave was quite right, because only half an hour later a small Dutch patrol-boat appeared on the horizon. It came slowly and silently towards the sailing boat. The patrol-boat's motor was just humming quietly. The three on board the sailing boat pretended not to have heard it until the young commander aboard the patrol boat shouted to them in perfect English. He had seen the Union Jack on the boat's mast.

"Hello, anybody there?"

The Scots pretended to be suddenly disturbed and stood up. All of them were quite nude. They were pretending to have been sunbathing and relaxing. They were so surprised they did not notice they were without clothes for several seconds. The men on the patrol boat grinned rather horny, taking in the spectacle of two good-looking nude women. Suddenly Connoly pretended he had just discovered he was nude.

"Sorry," he said pretending to be embarrassed. "Sorry – we forgot. You normally don't expect visitors in the middle of the ocean." He took a towel and wrapped it around him. "What's the matter?"

"Sorry to disturb you, sir," the officer said stuttering, even more embarrassed than Connoly. "You haven't seen a missile above your head recently?"

"Not even a damn common gull. Why are you asking? Have the Americans and the Russians started low altitude flights with their satellites?"

"No, we just wanted to know, that's all," The commander replied shortly. "By the way – who are you?" – he asked without a pause.

"I'm Doctor Dave Connoly from London and this is my wife Betsy," he turned around and pointed at his wife who by now had covered herself up with a blanket. "She is a state registered nurse and this is her friend, Ann Castle."

He waved with his right hand towards Ann, who had pulled on the tiny bottom of her yellow bikini and shot her huge tanned breasts demonstratively towards the Dutchmen.

"Very well," the officer said resignedly. "We have work to do." He gave a quick salute. "Excuse us for disturbing you. Have a nice voyage!"

The patrol-boat slid carefully away from the sailing boat and the frequencies of its motor increased. When it was two hundred-metres away its motor gave a huge roar and it disappeared in the direction of the launch curve of the missile.

Betsy had been very nervous while the patrol-boat was alongside. She was exceedingly relieved when it left. She squeezed her husband. She let the blanket that covered her, fall to the deck and pressed her unprepared husband down on the bench at the rear of the cockpit. She threw his towel into the sea. He became confused and did not know what to do, but Betsy geared him, and soon he not only enjoyed her attack, but also participated completely. Betsy mounted him as soon as he had got an erection. She rode him till they both loudly cried in orgasms together.

Betsy had not noticed or simply had forgotten Ann who was standing behind her. Ann moved discreetly away to the front deck. She had become extremely horny watching the erotic lovemaking of the couple. She immediately lay down on the front deck and comforted herself, and soon she too cried out frantically in ecstasy, when a deep, tearing orgasm came over her. She did not care, or even consider, if the two in the rear of the cockpit saw or heard her. She was only too desperate and incredibly horny.

The two in the cockpit did indeed hear her. How could they avoid it? They blinked, smiled happily at each other, pleased that good friends had nothing to hide from each other hereafter.

After the successful destruction of the British ship, Coe headed, towed by the miniature submersible, towards the appointed meeting position with Connoly's sailing boat. The estimated time for the voyage under water was about two and half-hours.

The submersible functioned perfectly the first hour, and then it started misfiring. Coe worked desperately to keep it going. Sometimes it even stopped and floated towards the surface. Once it took nearly fifteen minutes before he got it started again. He was terrified of being discovered in the calm sea as he had twice seen low-flying aircraft in the distance, while he worked to start the stubborn submersible. He also saw a couple of grey navy patrol boats sailing in the direction of the explosion site.

After approximately two hours the miniature submersible absolutely refused to go. The batteries seemed completely burned out. The continual starting efforts had probably entirely finished them. Suddenly Coe was lying in the sea with no other option but to wait or swim. The situation was desperate. He decided he would stay by the submersible till a boat rescued him. He hoped optimistically that Connoly would suspect mischief and sail the boat along his anticipated course to the meeting point. There was also the problem that he did not want to be detected by any of the British authorities' boats. He had already observed several of these during the last hour.

Coe had been drifting in the sea for about half an hour after the engine gave out when he observed a grey naval craft on the horizon coming in his direction. The craft kept a high speed. He realised that, if the craft did not directly run him down, it would be close enough to detect him. He had to sink the submersible that floated to the surface when the propeller did not force it down. Coe immediately twisted off two plugs to open inlets in the flotation chamber. One inlet at the bottom to let water in and another at the top for air escaping. The chamber gradually filled with water, but very slowly. The naval craft continued to approach. It came directly towards him. The craft was no more than half a nautical mile away and the submersible was still afloat. The distance decreased, but the submersible would not sink. The sound of the craft's engine and the water forced from its bow increased. The craft would hit him head on. Coe condemned the submersible loudly to hell, but it did not help. It floated on the surface, but low in the water, so it could not be detected at a great distance. There was no more time to lose. Coe left the submersible and dived. He heard the loud thundering of the huge craft's propellers over his head, but he also heard the sound of the submersible as it smashed into the craft's hull. The crew must have heard the same sound, as the engine's speed was immediately reduced.

The sailing boat was well ahead of the agreed time at the meeting point, but Coe did not appear.

"He must have been delayed in some way. We must sail towards him," Betsy said optimistically after they had waited restlessly for twenty minutes after the estimated time for the rendezvous.

"We can't leave the appointed site. It's the only reference we have to meet him," Connoly remarked worriedly.

When Coe still did not appear after one hour, the Scotsman became more and more concerned that something could have happened to him.

Connoly said grimly: "It seems, as if we must sail the route he should have taken and try to find him. Something must have happened with that damn submersible. The engine, for instance, could have stopped."

The sailing boat left the position and the three Scots on board carefully watched the surface with binoculars for Coe, as the boat sailed towards the site of the destruction of HMS *Heroic.*

Coe decided to stay under water for a long time while he swam quickly away from the position at which the submersible had collided with the naval craft. Half an hour later he cautiously stretched his head above the surface. He saw the navy craft was just about to vanish over the horizon. Otherwise there was only the empty sea blinking in the sun.

He dropped the divers' lead belt to swim better on the surface. He lay on his back and swam using flippers, towards the agreed meeting point with the sailing boat. He reckoned on reaching the meeting point within less than three hours swimming. He was too far out at sea to consider other alternatives like swimming towards shore. The sailing boat was his only real chance. The Caribbean water was agreeably warm. The nearly empty air bottles on his back gave him a high, relatively relaxing position on the surface, and the sun which was about to go down, warmed his wet suit. He was, therefore, not very uncomfortable. The only problem was that he could not decide on his position and course exactly and he was afraid of missing the sailing boat. He had a compass fastened to his arm, but he could not calculate correctly the deviation and the distance that he swam

After about two hours Coe saw a sailing boat on a course opposite to his, about one nautical mile to the right. He quickly recognised the boat to be Connoly's and waved desperately with his arms. Can they see me? He thought hopefully. Yes, they can, he believed for a few moments when the boat corrected its course, but it then proceeded forward and faded in the haze that was about to cover the sea, as the sun went down. It became dark. Coe became completely dejected. He stopped swimming and only floated like a bottle on the calm water, waiting for whatever would happen. He could not influence the course of events anymore.

On the sailing boat the atmosphere was very strained. They had watched the sea as they sailed, but Coe had not been discovered. The boat was near the site of the destruction of the navy vessel when a British MTB approached at high speed.

"The navy is exercising in this area. You must stop," could be heard from a metallic voice over a megaphone.

The MTB came close and a young officer in a perfect white uniform, stood by the rail looking with a grin down at the people in the sailing boat.

He said very civilly: "Sorry, you must change course. The navy is exercising in this area."

"OK, where can we go?" Connoly asked politely.

"To the right or to the left as you choose and a minimum five miles before you change course."

"Then we would rather turn completely and sail back," Connoly replied just as politely. "We are only on a sailing holiday and our direction doesn't matter."

"As you wish, sir," the officer added with a smile. "What are your names?"

Connoly told him the same story he had told the Dutchman earlier.

Another officer joined the first. He whispered something in his ear.

The first continued politely: "May we inspect your boat? As you are in international waters you are within your right to refuse."

Connoly thought for a second before he replied. Here they can detect nothing. The only problem is that they possibly can detect that another man is sleeping in the boat, but that is not a big risk as the women have made everything tidy. If we do let them look us over, it may allay any suspicions, if not, they might examine us more closely later or even ignore international laws and arrest us. We have no choice.

"No, there is no problem, if you want to inspect the boat you are very welcome."

A rope ladder with wooden rungs was thrown over the rail. The two officers climbed down onto the sailing boat. Connoly assisted them when they reached the boat's deck, and all three of them went into the cabin.

Connoly said gently: "In any case, here are our passports if you need to examine them, and here are my and my wife's official certificates as officers in the British Army."

The two officers were taken by surprise and looked at the documents.

The first one was visibly amazed and saluted as he said quickly with great embarrassment: "Sir, we didn't know."

"It doesn't matter," Connoly added softly. "It was a pleasure to see the British Navy doing its duty." He smiled comfortably, while he watched the two officers standing like tin soldiers, because he had the higher rank. "What's your real problem?"

"A British warship has sunk, but we don't know why."

"Why are you examining small leisure craft in that connection?"

"I don't know, sir. It's only an order we have received. And we shall also keep all passing boats out of the area."

"Very well," Connoly said in his military manner. "We will not disturb you. We will return to Anguilla."

The two officers saluted again and returned hastily to the MTB, which a few moments later speeded quickly away.

Betsy asked her husband worriedly: "Do you think this incident will throw suspicion on us."

"Not at all," Connoly replied assuredly. "It might rather be an advantage, as we previously have been checked by the Dutchmen who will certainly report us to the English. Nobody will believe that anyone would be so stupid as to visit the site where the navy craft has sunk, if they had any connection to the incident."

The mood on board was completely resigned. Ann sat weeping and Betsy tried to comfort her, as best as she could.

"I loved him," Ann wept, "and I did not tell him. He was so cute. Oh, I loved that damn bastard."

The sailing boat followed Coe's expected course in reverse. Connoly still had a small hope that they would find Coe. He knew Coe was equipped with red emergency lights similar to those that can be found on life-vests.

All of them used binoculars constantly to scan the sea and more than two hours later Ann cried desperately: "I can see a light – I can see a light." She jumped up and down like a spoilt child who gets its wishes from Santa Claus. "Look back about a mile to the left."

Coe lay on his back dozing in the waves. He had completely given up all hope. Psychologically, he prepared himself for the end. He saw the sailing boat disappear westward against the slightly coloured night sky where the sun had set. A last hope had just been created, but had only lasted for a few minutes. He had desperately waved with the red emergency light, but obtained no response. They had definitely not seen him. He felt great pity for himself and believed by now there was absolutely no hope.

However, suddenly the sailing boat turned and came towards him. Coe waved his arms again wildly and cried loudly in relief, while the tears were streaming down his face.

He was received on the sailing boat like the long lost son and Ann overwhelmed him with her expressions of love and gave him her special treatment before he properly came to his senses.

23

McNeigh and Ness had decided to become backpackers in the Canadian forests to escape the authorities. After they dumped the car, they had walked north-east for half an hour, until they met the stream that they had seen on the map. The stream meandered down a narrow valley in a westerly direction. They followed the stream's bed until it crossed the same road they just had driven along, about three kilometres down from where they had dumped the car. To avoid leaving any traces for tracker dogs, they waded in the centre of the waterway.

The Scotsmen approached the road very slowly and carefully although they expected no pursuers to be on their track so soon. Anyway, they knew that they could never be too careful, avoiding making mistakes, and taking no chances. This proved to be a very sound precaution, as they suddenly heard cars in the distance. The cars were approaching quickly. The Scotsmen took cover in the forest, before crossing through the tunnel, which carried the stream beneath the road. Only minutes later they observed a police car followed by an army jeep. Both vehicles contained two people.

"Our route must have been detected," Ness whispered. "What else can explain these vehicles being here?"

"It might, but I doubt it," McNeigh replied thoughtfully. "I reckoned with aircraft observations from high altitude, after the Canadian authorities had been informed about our attack by the English. However, it is almost impossible to follow a car based only on ordinary photos or thermograph photos taken by these aircraft. It would have been quite impossible for the Canadians using other methods, because we would have detected them. Low flying aircraft are easy to see. The warnings about our future counter actions were intended to scare them. That must definitely have had a positive influence on their actions, as our warning contained clear information about automatic release of counter actions in consequence of any detected investigation. They were also clearly informed that the counter actions would be executed without further warning. The authorities would therefore not have dared risk taking any chances. Reconnaissance planes must have been told to operate at altitudes that made them entirely invisible from the ground and therefore their observations will be very inaccurate and questionable."

Ness added worriedly: "I am, of course, fully aware of what you say, but it is unreasonable to believe that the Canadians would sit on their bottoms, totally paralysed, if someone detonated an atomic bomb on their territory. Even if the English had not warned them, they would of course immediately have started a full-scale investigation into the circumstance."

"I agree with you, but unilateral investigation by the Canadians would certainly have led to the instant setting up of roadblocks around the base, not far away as we heard on the radio. I rather suppose that the English must have warned them ahead of our attack, as soon as they received our message to keep them out of the way. Exactly as we calculated during our planning. The Canadians were told to delay the start of the investigation because of our additional threats."

The cars had vanished up the road and the Scotsmen

examined the surroundings thoroughly, while they listened carefully.

Ness said quietly: "I can't hear or see anything. I think we now can safely cross under the road."

They moved soundlessly and quickly, as trained guerrillas, through the water tube. They did not speak until they rested after wading hastily in the middle of the stream, half a kilometre away from the road.

"So far so good," Ness said smilingly, but quite exhausted.

"If we were two hundred kilometres further south-west, I would agree," McNeigh replied, equally exhausted.

"The patrol has not returned yet. I believe they are probably wondering where the hot spots on their damned photos have disappeared to," Ness said, while he was still breathing like an old steam engine.

"Maybe," McNeigh replied, also breathing heavily, "but there are lots of possibilities for errors on these photos. They probably need to examine them further in their laboratories to discover what might have happened to the car. Then they will have to locate the car in the lake. That will not be very easy, but of course it all depends on the number of people they might put on the job and a degree of luck."

McNeigh gulped for air a couple of times, like a fish on the shore, and considered for a few seconds before he hastily continued: "The recognition aircraft could also have been forced to terminate the assignment because of the fuel situation. It is very questionable if they have planes that can stay in the air continuously for such long periods and they don't have so many planes equipped with a thermostatic photo capability that could have taken over the assignment. If such temperature locating photos are to be of any use, the photos must be taken in rapid succession."

Ness did not comment. He only lay silently on his back, looking at the tops of the nearby spruce trees.

340

Maybe he is looking for satellites, McNeigh thought bleakly and kept on: "Our car is probably only one of many they may be examining at the moment. All cars which have passed us, or we have passed, during our travels from the detonation, will be suspect."

"I noticed several times that you often drove the car in an unusual and strange way," Ness said.

"Just so," McNeigh remarked quickly. "I had to drive erratically in a way that would create difficult situations for possible recognition from above. For instance, I speeded up pretending to pass the car in front and then slowed down. We would then be so near the car in front that the hot spots or shadows on the temperature separation photos could not be separated. The car in front that pulled away from us might possibly be thought to be our car and confuse their analysis. They suddenly have two cars instead of one to investigate. In this way and others we have created a lot of confusion. All the cars we have involved could later unintentionally add new confused situations on their journeys, and in the end, the number of possible cars involved will be multiplied. I believe they have many hours' work or maybe many days' work to separate and examine all the suspicious cars first in the laboratory and afterwards in the field. Our car is probably only one of many cars under suspicion, otherwise there would have been a complete army on the road by now, not just a couple of patrol cars."

McNeigh proceeded without any further interruption from Ness, after a small break: "Then I believe they will not find the car for many hours. Afterwards, they will need to organise a search. They will have also to examine the car they find dumped in the lake in connection with an insurance fraud for instance. There could also be many other reasons. They can't start a very considerable search based on probabilities, without any real definite facts."

McNeigh stopped talking for a moment and became

341

grave and completely silent, as if something serious had suddenly hit him. Ness still lay in silence on his back and only seemed to count the satellites on the tops of the spruce trees in a world of his own, only half listening to McNeigh's musings.

He turned his head and looked enquiringly at McNeigh, before he asked silently: "Is something wrong, Neil?"

McNeigh looked perplexed at Ness for some long seconds before he replied: "There is still a probability that a search could have been started sooner than we estimated. It is a possibility I have not considered earlier. We are in Quebec, the French part of Canada. In this part, the British are not very welcome. The possibility is that a search may have been started just to show the damned British that the Canadians can manage their own affairs, of course completely immaterial to the outcome of the search. The Canadians have tried diplomatic ways to get rid of the British base for decades, but the British have arrogantly refused to close it down. They have only referred to the long established agreement. Our attack has probably closed the base forever. I don't expect any Canadian support for our action, but I am sure they don't care too much. The environmental effects of the bomb will disappear entirely in a few years and they will have received a very long-awaited reward, finally being rid of the British for ever."

"I don't understand," Ness said rather bewilderedly. "That must only be an advantage for us."

"No, it absolutely isn't," Neil replied sharply. "The bloody Canadians will of course choose to start a search in the forest, even if they have other, more rational alternatives. They are, as said, only moderately interested in the search's actual result and will, if it is possible, not want to disturb the rest of Canadian society. So we have to expect a search in the area even if they have only detected the slightest clue."

342

Ness, who had not such an insight into local conditions and opinions in Canada as McNeigh, said shortly: "I presume you are right."

The Scotsmen suddenly heard the sound of cars driving back down the road.

"It's probably the patrol cars, coming back," Ness said. "Though your reasoning is correct, it will probably take hours before they can return and start a search. By that time their search-area will be enormously increased, because we will steadily move away from this area. In twelve hours we will be more than forty kilometres away and the search area will theoretically be four hundred times larger covering a circle around the site of the car. That is, of course, if they don't find tracks that can indicate our direction. In twenty-four hours we will have moved a further forty kilometres away and the search area would have increased dramatically. The trackers' chances of finding us will be decreasing proportionally with the time they are behind us, and they must know that."

McNeigh added quickly: "An additional large problem for them will be that they don't know for whom they are searching."

At Déboisement, Colonel Fontene had returned from Ottawa. He had scheduled a staff meeting with the appointed representatives – from the army, Lieutenant Colonel Charles Gouzon and from the navy, Commander Kirk Nelson. The police were not represented. Not only because they did not belong to the Canadian armed forces, but because they were not fully informed about the case. It was a military top secret, and would remain like that. The police were completely independent of directives from the armed forces. The government had taken this decision, and the Minister of Justice had informed the Canadian Police

Force's commander. The police had to concentrate on setting up roadblocks and examining suspicious cars, which the laboratory at Déboisement was continually discovering on its photographs.

"I believe you have been informed that this case is a strictly top-secret, military matter?" La Fontene asked.

Then without waiting for any reply he continued: "We shall not inform the searching troops or anybody of the reason we want to catch the fugitives, and we shall keep the press completely out of the case. If it is leaked to the press in some way, the information must at once be spread that it concerns only an ordinary military exercise."

"Do you have an up to date estimate of the number of suspect cars, discovered by the reconnaissance planes?" – Gouzon, asked very lazily as if the reply was of no great interest.

He was extremely relaxed, leant backward in the chair and he constantly flicked the top of his pen at the papers in front of him. The pen made a faint, rather irritating, ticking sound. The two others waited only for him to put his feet on the table.

"Yes," La Fontene replied, while he looked at Gouzon with an impatient smile. "We had forty three cars on our list, but the police patrols have been out checking most of them. We don't expect the terrorists to be parents with three or four noisy kids in the back seat. Neither do we expect the terrorists to be old, retired couples, that have only blown up the base just to have some excitement during their outings and to make their boring days pass quicker."

La Fontene took a short break while he lifted his water glass to drink, but suddenly changed his mind and lowered it without drinking.

He continued: "At the moment there are seven suspicious cars that are unchecked. One of these seven cars has disappeared into a blind road in the forest in the direction of Waco. The last thirty kilometres of the road is only a rough timber-truck track, but a lot of people use it for week-end trips, because there are a lot of marvellous fishing lakes in the area. I have been fishing there myself several times." La Fontene looked dreamily at the ceiling for some long seconds. "The car in the forest has vanished completely and that's very suspicious."

"Cars don't fly, do they?" – Gouzon asked sarcastically, and looked at the other two questioningly, as he waited for a serious reply from them. No reply came. Gouzon leaned forward for a moment over the table, before he again fell back into his established, apparently very comfortable, position.

"If the car is not parked or has not returned to the road," he said in a way as if the damned matter did not concern him at all, "it must have been dumped into the water. Isn't that the only logical explanation? I believe there are no garages up there in which the car might have been parked. Don't you agree?"

"We have of course considered that," La Fontene replied quickly with a diplomatic smile.

He had been sitting, wondering how the lazy Gouzon ever got out of bed in the morning. It took a moment before he believed he had found an adequate answer to that question. Gouzon must have an extremely forceful and demanding wife, he thought maliciously, while he smiled triumphantly. Neither La Fontene, nor any other of his army colleagues had ever expressed negative remarks about Gouzon's work. Gouzon was a very efficient and intelligent army officer and would surely reach the top of the Canadian army within a very few years. The best soldiers always rest when they have the opportunity, La Fontene concluded philosophically.

Gouzon continued sleepily, while he blinked his eyes: "To get into action at once I suggest that I order a company to fully examine the area where the car has disappeared, to get an answer as to why it has vanished. We can possibly be in action early tomorrow morning."

Both La Fontene and Nelson reacted to Gouzon's remark about *early morning*.

Gouzon observed his two colleagues' questioning expressions and added, while he chuckled loudly: "I will of course not participate myself early next morning, because then I will be sleeping. You see my wife has a day off tomorrow, and then I am allowed to sleep a little longer."

La Fontene nodded with a flush all over his face, as if to confirm he was quite correct in his assumptions about Gouzon's wife, then he, together with Nelson, roared loudly with uncontrollable laughter.

Gouzon rose from his sleepy position in the chair and went to the window and looked for a moment in complete disinterest at the usual slow army movements outside, while his colleagues tried to stop their uncontrolled roars.

When they became silent Gouzon turned around and said with a broad smile, apparently unaware of any humorous incident: "Anyway, if this action doesn't lead to any discovery, the troops will get some experience in the organisation of a search. They will also be readily available to be moved to other areas, if other alternatives show up."

La Fontene had finally regained his self-control.

He dried the tears from his eyes and tried to say seriously: "I believe we have agreed about what is to be accomplished. This first of all, because there are no better proposals at the moment and our superiors desperately need to have something to report to the British, to show them that we really care."

Gouzon had a broad grin all over his face as he bent over the table.

While he gesticulated rather impatiently with his pen, he said in mock seriousness: "I agree with the colonel, and I believe the troops will love the assignment. It is a very nice time of the year to be on a picnic in the forest."

La Fontene thought the lieutenant colonel doesn't care a shit if the terrorists are caught or not. He is obviously only satisfied because someone has at last thrown the British out of their base. The grin on his face says that clearly, and I agree completely with him.

La Fontene looked at Nelson and asked: "Do we all agree this to be the start of the search in the absence of better alternatives?"

Nelson was alone among the meeting's participants with an English name and English ancestors. He too had observed Gouzon's grin, but he knew he was in the minority.

However, as he was an intelligent man and knew exactly when he was beaten, he nodded in affirmation of a positive reply before he said slowly: "Yes, there seems no better plan at the moment."

At dawn next morning a small company of three hundred and fifty troops, mostly recruits with less than three months' army experience, arrived from the nearest military base, at the forest road by the lake, where the Scotsmen had dumped their car. In addition to the soldiers, ten navy divers also appeared, equipped with oxygen tanks and diving suits.

They organised the search by dividing the twenty upper kilometres of the road into eighty stretches of about two hundred and fifty metres and let two soldiers examine the stretches on each side of the road. The divers were available for examining possible dumping places for a car. They found the Chevrolet at the bottom of the lake within three-quarters of an hour.

"The question is only, is this an insurance fraud or is it

the car we are looking for?" – Lieutenant Glen Batholm asked doubtfully.

"We have to wait for experts to do a full examination of the wreckage," the company leader, Major André Durand replied shortly, as he arrived somewhat exhausted.

Experts from an army weapons laboratory, close to Havre-Saint Pierre, were included in the search group, and arrived soon after with a large, dark green Mercedes van containing a small mobile laboratory. They had been roughly interrupted in their morning coffee chat in the sun, further down the forest road.

The experts knew exactly what to search for and could very soon confirm that there were fragments from burnt jet fuel in the back of the car, where the missile's launching attachment had been placed after the missile had been launched. The search group definitely concluded that they had discovered the car.

The search group's dogs were brought into the area and soon their brilliant noses found the trail of the fugitives in a north-east direction. The dogs lost the track in the stream. The handlers understood what had happened. The fugitives had walked up or down the stream, to escape sniffing dogs. The search group had five dogs. They decided to examine both sides of the waterway in both directions.

It took four hours before the dogs found the trail again. The reason why it took such a long time was because the dog that examined the right side downwards passed across the track, but missed it. The dogs and their handlers went many kilometres further downwards before they changed sides and returned. The other dog detected the track immediately it passed it. That it was the right track that had been detected was without any doubt. In addition to the dog's positive reaction, footprints moved away from the stream and into the forest. The dog's handler, a native

Indian from Nakina in the middle of Ontario's forests, could also easily detect the prints.

McNeigh and Ness had headed in the direction of the Manicouagan Réservoir two hundred and fifty kilometres away, according to the map. They estimated about a five-day march. From the Réservoir, they planned to walk in the direction of Chute des-Passes, crossing the river from the Réservoir and the river Rivière aux Outardes. They estimated it would take another five or maybe six days. The distance was about three hundred kilometres. Chute des-Passes was a minor, but very busy town in the wilderness, filled with hikers at this time of year. The Scotsmen hopefully considered their arrival would pass unnoticed. From Chute des-Passes they planned to hitchhike to Montreal.

Both the Scotsmen had taken part in survival courses and were trained to make meals out of readily available resources in the forest. They could easily live in the forest for a year if necessary. Because of the possibility of being caught they carried no arms. They could never use them because of the noise, which could be heard over large distances in the quiet forest. If they were searched it would also be very difficult to explain why they carried unregistered weapons. They would, without doubt, be arrested for that if nothing else. Anyway, weapons would only represent additional weight to carry.

They had been on the run in the forest for two and a half-days before they discovered something that might mean pursuers. They saw a helicopter far away in the west. The helicopter flew back and forth at a low altitude, as if the crew were looking for something. It disappeared after half an hour. Later the same day another came from the south-west and did the same thing. That helicopter also disappeared after some low passes.

The Scotsmen caught some trout in a small, isolated lake that evening.

"Nobody might ever have fished in this lake before. The nearest road is three days away," Ness said enthusiastically, while he prepared his fishing gear.

It was a time when fishes swallowed whatever came their way. Within half an hour they had caught trout enough to eat that evening and for breakfast the next day. They even had an additional supply for lunch. The trout had beautiful, red flesh and were exactly grill size. They tasted marvellous with salt and a dash of black pepper from the rucksacks. They sat in front of a small fire, hidden by a rock and impossible to see from far away. They picked the bones, while they told stories, just like ordinary hikers enjoying a fishing trip. The night sounds from the forest accompanied them and made the idyll almost complete.

"We only need a couple of women," Neil said gloomily.

They drank coffee. Coffee is easy to carry in rucksacks. They also had a variety of dried soups, sauces, dried milk and sugar.

"Hollandaise sauce is excellent for trout," Sean said, as if he were the chef of the Grand Hotel in Paris, when they had bought the supplies in an ordinary supermarket, on their way by car, along the Gulf of Saint Lawrence, towards Fort Hope.

They had of course, tea. No British traveller goes far without tea in his supplies. It always had to be Twinings' Earl Grey tea for the morning. All the products in the Scotsmen's rucksacks could be bought in any supermarket, but all products had the same common elements. Low weight, easy to cook and containing a lot of calories compared to the weight, of course not counting the tea and coffee. The fugitives did not carry any tin cans or food that contained water. Water was heavy to carry and not necessary in Canadian forests, where clean water was readily available. The only water they carried was the water content in two small pocket bottles of whisky.

"A Scotsman doesn't make a trip in a forest without whisky," Ness proclaimed gravely when he bought the bottles, but McNeigh told him to consider the weight carefully.

For dessert that night they ate blueberries until they looked like children with blue fingers and faces. After a cold bath in the lake, they slept soundly all night and woke up, fully rested, at dawn.

It was a beautiful morning, with blue sky and a red-orange sun rising in the east. The deciduous trees beside the lake, that had begun to change to the red and yellow autumn colours, threw long shadows across the quiet water, between the gleaming reflection from the sun and ripples from feeding trout. It was cold and fresh, even though it was nearly two months before the winter would arrive. Their breath became white condensation. A couple of ducks left the water and their wings drummed through the air. Small birds suddenly started to sing in chorus while the sun lifted higher above the horizon. The start of the day was exactly as it should be. A bright new day absolutely without any serious problems to think about, a day without any special assignments to finish and a day that could be a rest for the mind.

It was nearly noon when the idyll in the forest was broken. The two fugitives did not see it before it appeared from behind a low ridge in west. A nearby stream had covered the sound. They threw themselves into shelter under some small bushes, where they lay completely still as the helicopter passed right above their heads. They could feel the strong turbulence from the rotor, the trees shivered. The altitude of the army helicopter could not be more than fifty metres.

24

BAA's flight 273 from London had started landing procedure at Miami International. Captain Rotting worked
carefully through the plane's checklist and co-pilot Saxon
confirmed successively as the captain read the questions.

"Landing wheels in position?"

"Confirming, landing wheels in position," Saxon replied
monotonously and disinterestedly, as he checked the indicators on the panel in accordance with the questions.

The jumbo jet had received priority clearance from the
airport's traffic control tower, for final at runway two. The
captain had, as usual, already talked informatively to his
passengers about the weather conditions and the temperature at their destination. He had also, as usual, wished
everybody a pleasant stay and hoped they would choose
BAA next time when flying.

In addition, his passengers had been given the standard
landing instructions: "Fasten your seat belts and raise the
back of your seats. We are going to land in a short time.
Please remain with seat belts fastened until the plane has
stopped."

The airliner rapidly approached the airport's runway,
coming closer and closer to the final touch down. Meanwhile Rotting checked the air speed, the flaps and the air
speed again, the position towards the centreline of the

runway and the plane's levelling. The stress on a pilot when landing is huge.

"To land a small plane always feels like cycling," Rotting said amusingly to the co-pilot. "You have to keep your balance. You have to keep the flaps in the right position, while you constantly press the rudder pedals to keep the heading of the nose towards the middle of the runway. At the same time you have to use the control stick to keep the plane's crosswise axle through the wings horizontally, and the lengthwise tipped forward in the correct position. The wind constantly tries to move the plane out of position. Meanwhile you must keep the correct air speed by pulling or pressing the throttle, otherwise you can lose the necessary air under the wings and stall. If you're flying low when that happens you will drop like a stone to certain death. Of course only if you don't have a special agreement with fate." Rotting said with an ironic grin. "But landing a big jumbo monster by comparison, is just like running a large factory. You only need check dials and make corrections. The craft's own large computer works itself."

Saxon did not comment. He acted as if nobody had spoken, although he must have understood that Rotting talked to him if only to be pleasant at the end of a long flight.

The co-pilot must have psychological problems, Rotting thought irritably. I must write a report on the damn fellow as soon as I have the slightest concrete evidence to put on paper. However, it is, of course, very difficult to get anything that is concrete against fellows like him, especially on an airliner, where everything is almost automatic. You need never show that you can handle the plane manually and you only need perform designated tasks.

Rotting was very upset. He had already formed a clear opinion about the co-pilot's capability as a pilot. Saxon was absolutely not appropriate.

I will never take the chance of letting him handle the plane alone, because that would be bound to end in disaster. Saxon completely lacks any confidence in people around him, and he positively lacks any confidence in himself. He would without doubt have a lot of problems selling a loaf in a bakery. It looks like he is going through the motions, entirely without any interest in the pilot's work, purely to get his rotten salary. Anyway, there would probably need to be a disaster to get sufficient conclusive, negative evidence on him concerning his work, to get him discharged without any risk of the company being sued by him afterwards in court.

As Rotting saw the runway approach in front of him, he suddenly also saw the flash of an explosion near the terminal building. It seemed quite a small one as seen from the plane at that distance.

"Bravo, Alfa, Alfa 273 to the tower. What was the explosion beside the terminal building?" – Rotting immediately asked the tower.

"Don't know yet," the voice from the radio replied. "You will be informed as soon as we know anything."

It was quiet for a few seconds, before the radio spoke again: "You can continue landing as normal, but remain at the end of the exit-lane for further instructions. Please, be aware of other aircraft that are following you in the landing queue."

Flight 273 was soon only metres above the runway and slid slowly to a smooth and silky touchdown. The people onboard could hardly feel the plane touch the ground, but soon they felt as if they were hanging in their seats-belts, as the plane's brakes were automatically pressed on, the plane's engines were reversed and the flaps were turned up to catch the air stream. The sound of rubber wheels braking against asphalt could be heard clearly, together with a moment of increased engine sound that soon decreased.

The plane reduced speed before it turned off the runway into the exit-lane, clearing the runway for the next plane from a growing landing queue – planes waiting filled with business people and tourists for Florida's beaches, Disney World, Sea World, Cape Canaveral, The Everglades and whatever else would be of interest.

Suddenly, a tremendous explosion threw gravel, stone and asphalt into the air on the runway in front of the airliner. It was unquestionably on its way towards certain disaster from which nobody had the slightest chance of survival.

Possibilities ran at the speed of light through Rotting's head. – What to do? – Do we have any chance? – At Tenerife in Spain five hundred and eighty five people burned to death in an airport accident. – No possibility of turning off the runway. – The aeroplane will undoubtedly collapse into the crater left by the explosion and will burst into flames. As different thoughts swirled around, he reacted completely automatically in accordance with the reflexes that he had developed during his time as a Royal Air Force fighter pilot. He cut the brakes, drew the flaps down, pulled the throttle to full speed and bent back the control stick for quick takeoff as soon as the speed had increased sufficiently.

The aircraft accelerated with all its power towards the crater with ever increasing speed. Would the speed increase be sufficient for takeoff before the plane hit the crater, where it was sure to explode into a horrible and deadly inferno of flames? Rotting was not religious, otherwise he would have prayed. He only desperately hoped.

Meanwhile he heard the traffic controller's desperate voice on the radio shouting madly: "273 take off! – Take off! – 273 take off! – Take off!"

*

In the cabin, the passengers and the cabin crew were completely unaware of the drama that had suddenly begun in the cockpit. Stewardess Maryanne Maywood had, as usual, unfolded her own seat and put on the belt before landing. She was sitting facing the passengers. The nearest male passengers looked longingly towards her beautiful tanned legs in her short uniform. She was used to this male behaviour and did nothing to cover herself. She only smiled naturally and happily, letting the men whet their appetites on pleasures they never would obtain.

The crew and the passengers always became very restful in a relieved way, when an airliner had touched down on the runway, to make its final stop. Both the passengers and the crew were greatly fatigued after the long flight across the Atlantic. They were looking forward to a good night's sleep, except the men occupied by the air hostess's long legs – so near but yet so far.

The sudden acceleration of the plane came as a shock for everybody in the passenger cabin. They were pressed back into their seats by an invisible force.

Many passengers let out loud and nervous screams: "What's happening? – Damn, what's happening?"

The passengers and cabin crew gripped the arms of their seats and held them desperately, as if to give them some kind of protection. People became pale with intense fear.

"What in the hell is happening?"

People looked at each other as if they were asking questions, though without knowing what about. Some people began to cry silently, some cried loudly and some simply screamed desperately. The sound in the passenger cabin was like a pigsty at feeding time. Loose objects fell on the floor and tumbled noisily backwards in the cabin.

"We unfortunately have had to make a quick takeoff," the captain suddenly said on the intercom.

He seemed stressed, but concentrated. His announcement seemed unnecessary because everybody had indeed realised that they were going to make a quick takeoff.

The crater came quickly closer and closer to the accelerating aircraft. Rotting felt like he was standing over a cliff and was forced to dive into the rocky hillside hundreds of metres below.

"We won't make it! – We won't make it!" Saxon suddenly screamed without warning.

He hammered fervidly on the control stick and the instruments in front of him, while he roared like a lunatic in a straitjacket.

Rotting had not noticed Saxon since the explosion and the co-pilot had, as expected, not contributed any suggestion as to how to deal with the situation. Saxon's panic-stricken behaviour greatly disturbed Rotting's effort to save the aircraft. Rotting could only hope the lunatic co-pilot would not destroy any essential equipment, because it was completely impossible to stop him at this moment.

Rotting pulled the control stick backward with all his force, to raise the nose of the plane, before it reached the rocky surroundings of the crater. Sweat was pouring from his forehead down into his eyes. He felt the force of the acceleration on his back as the horizon disappeared when the nose of the plane finally rose from the ground just ahead of the crater, but the main wheels were still on the ground. The whole plane was shaking as the main wheels tumbled over the stones on its way to what could possible be one of the largest aircraft disasters in America.

In the passenger cabin, screams increased notably when the passengers felt the shaking of the aeroplane and heard the sudden roar of friction between the aircraft's metal body and the ground. They trembled uncontrollably in their seats, as the plane tumbled and jumped. They were then completely sure they were going to die.

Rotting felt the same as the passengers, but he was too occupied to notice. The rear end of the plane had rammed the ground. The plane's front tilted down again towards the runway with colossal force. He felt the front wheels' pillar bending. The craft was over the crater, but its speed was too high to stop before it reached the end of the runway. Rotting still kept the control stick backwards with full force and the plane's nose rose once more above the horizon. Suddenly he felt the plane leaving the ground. Immediately it became considerably quieter, without the rumbling noise of the wheels rolling on the asphalt. Rotting swept his forehead of sweat with the back of his hand. He looked angrily towards the co-pilot's seat and discovered that Saxon had become quite silent. He had simply fainted.

What luck for us all, but this is definitely Saxon's last flight in a pilot's seat, Rotting thought furiously. These privately trained fellows lack the necessary experience to be adequate pilots and their nerves cannot withstand any pressure. They probably also think too slowly, in comparison with a trained and experienced fighter pilot.

Rotting had achieved the first part of his task to prevent the death of two hundred and sixty-eight passengers and crew. He had realised that he could not have managed to do the same, with a fully loaded craft. The craft had been emptied of the fuel, which had been consumed over the Atlantic, and was a lot lighter in weight now than at takeoff at Heathrow. This had made it possible, to shorten the takeoff distance sufficiently to avoid the crater, but Rotting knew the craft could not have been closer to total wreckage.

So far so good, Rotting thought worriedly as he turned the plane and suddenly became aware of the sound in the radio. The sound might have been there all the time, but he had not heard it while he had been completely concentrating during the takeoff.

It was the control tower at the airport: "Bravo, Alfa, Alfa. Congratulations – congratulations on a remarkable and impressive manoeuvre. Few pilots would be able to duplicate that one."

Rotting did not reply, and the tower was on the air again: "Any casualties on board?"

Rotting replied, calm and controlled: "Bravo, Alfa, Alfa to the tower. I have no information from the passenger cabin yet. You will soon be informed."

Rotting broke the connection with the tower and said on the plane's intercom: "Sorry we had to abort the landing because of an explosion which had destroyed the runway in front of us. Don't be worried. Stay calm and seated. Everything is under control and we will land in a few minutes. You will be kept informed."

Rotting switched to the crew phone. He did not know who answered, but he said calmly, in a good captain's way: "Will somebody from the cabin crew come immediately to the cockpit."

A few seconds later Maryanne opened the door and entered the cockpit. Rotting could hear the passengers applauding in the background.

"Anybody hurt back there?" – he asked at once.

"Not as far as our survey at the moment shows," Maryanne replied quickly.

"Good," Rotting replied visibly relieved and continued without pausing as he pointed forcefully at Saxon, who sat hanging with his head in the seat belts. "Get three stewards at once to remove that lunatic before he regains consciousness. – Luckily he has fainted."

Some seconds afterwards Saxon was removed from his seat and given an injection of a tranquilliser from the craft's emergency supply. He was placed in a vacant seat in first class, out of sight of passengers, with one male member of the crew on each side.

Maryanne appeared again in the cockpit with many thanks from the passengers, although they had not been completely informed about what really happened.

They do not know how near death they have been, Rotting thought crisply, but without telling Maryanne.

"Bravo, Alfa, Alfa. All other incoming aircraft have been directed out of the area," the traffic-control suddenly broke in informatively on the radio. "You alone have air over the airport and permanent radio connection with us. You must fly near the tower as low as possible for inspection of the damage to the plane. It looks like you have serious damage to the tail, where it hit the ground, when you actually hovered over the crater."

The flight operator was silent for some time, while he anxiously conferred with somebody beside him.

The discussion was obviously finished as he abruptly said: "The technician beside me, says you might have also damaged the steering wheel pillar. The damage occurred when you crashed down again after you had passed the crater. He also believes that you might have damaged the tyres on the main wheels' carriages, as stones and gravel were spread when the aircraft passed the crater like a tornado. I suppose it is unnecessary, to tell you to keep the landing wheels down for the rest of your flight."

"Yes, it is," Rotting replied shortly.

The radio was silent for a while. The jumbo jet set about to make a wide slow turn, so as not to stress the hull of the craft more than necessary, for fear of possible damage. The plane flew over the western part of Miami and passed over The Everglades before it turned south of the town and out over the Atlantic, where the nose of the plane again pointed in the direction of Miami International Airport.

The control tower could once more hear the aircraft's captain on the radio, when he said calmly: "All the passengers seem to be physically in order, but some of them appear to be suffering from shock. Medical people amongst the them are taking care of the worst cases."

Rotting reflected as he manoeuvred the aircraft into position for the inspection from the airport's control tower: Had the narrow escape from the crater just been a postponement of the final execution of all the passengers and crew? Was the damage on the plane so substantial, that a crash-landing was likely to be the result of the next landing attempt? Was the damaged aircraft only a death trap? Were the grateful thanks he had received from the pleased passengers completely undeserved? Would they die anyway? Maybe I have only given them false hope and a few extra, short minutes to live.

The aircraft came lower, parallel with the runway in front of the airport's control tower for the inspection, after making its turn. It flew as low as Rotting had decided was advisable. They would receive the verdict if they were going to live or die, Rotting thought gloomily and nervously. They were, in a short time going to be condemned, as a defendant in the court, to life or death. Rotting thought he by now knew exactly how a defendant felt when he sat in a prison cell and waited for the final judgement from a jury of twelve men and women.

The control tower was on the radio. Rotting was as excited as a child that waits anxiously for the visit of Santa Claus at Christmas. He could hardly sit still in his seat.

The voice said slowly, after the craft had passed the tower: "The damage seems to be in accordance with our short

362

briefing some minutes ago. There seems to be nothing wrong with the craft's ability to fly and manoeuvre in the air. The rubber on the main carriages seems mostly to be in order, but three or four of the wheels seem to be punctured. You will have to land manually, without lowering the front of the plane before the speed is much decreased. The front pillar is damaged and will probably collapse if it carries any weight. You will get further information when we have analysed the video-films that have been taken while you passed."

The radio became totally silent for a minute, before it crackled again.

"It has been decided that you had better make the landing at the airport in Palm Beach. They will be well prepared to receive you. – Good luck."

The captain confirmed the new landing order and headed in a northerly direction, along the coast of Florida.

Rotting was not satisfied with the verdict of the inspection, but he was a lot happier than before the inspection. It could have been a hell of a lot worse, he concluded partly pleased, although he pondered worriedly about the coming landing attempt. Had they sent them to Palm Beach so as not to thicken the polluted Miami air with the additional smell of burned flesh from passengers from this craft?

Anyway, when he started on the landing procedure before Palm Beach, Rotting just hoped that he could manage the landing successfully. He was an optimist, however bad the situation really was. This time he started on the landing procedure completely alone, without any distraction from the lunatic co-pilot.

Maryanne carefully opened the cockpit-door and with a smile she asked if he wanted to have something to drink. Rotting replied he only wanted a glass of pure cold water. He enquired about the condition of the fainted, removed co-pilot. Maryanne replied that he was awake, but squirmed in his seat like a worm. The crew kept him firmly under constant watch.

Rotting said briefly: "Saxon probably had a shock when he saw the explosion on the runway in front of the craft, and suddenly realised that he was not sitting in a flight simulator."

Maryanne only lifted her beautiful shoulders as an unspecific, but diplomatic reply.

Rotting smiled and said provocatively: "Do you remember anything from the BAA's short introduction lessons about flying a Boeing 767?"

"I don't think we learned anything about flying the planes, but it is correct that we were briefly instructed on some essential things concerning flying."

"I know," Rotting replied gently. "After you have collected a glass of water, can you please sit in the co-pilot seat and keep me company, reading the checklist while I'm checking."

"I'll be delighted," Maryanne lied with a beaming smile.

Flight 273 soon approached Palm Beach airport, only seventy kilometres north of Miami. The captain repeated the standard phrase that they would be landing in a few minutes and the passengers were told to fasten their seat belts, but he forgot to bid his passengers welcome to another flight with BAA. He also missed out the hope that they had had a pleasant flight, as he understood the passengers' nerves were at breaking point.

Maybe there was a psychologist among them who has lifted them out of their morbid thoughts and shortened the time till landing, Rotting hoped as he could hear them sing loudly through the open door.

"We shall overcome, we shall overcome, some day . . ."

"It sounds like Martin Luther King is leading them,"

Rotting said dully. "Let's hope that we all shall overcome, but today I'm really not sure."

Maryanne immediately became pale.

"Oh – that was just a joke," he added and smiled calmly.

Darkness embraced the flat landscape below the plane. Only a faint stream of light could be seen above the horizon towards the west, where the sun had disappeared. On the ground, to the left of the plane's course, lights could be seen from the highly populated area north of Miami. The coastal road twisted like a glow-worm along the coastline. The craft kept a course about two kilometres over the Atlantic, parallel to the coastline. The altitude was only five thousand feet, because the plane had lost pressure when a hole was made in the rear end of the body as it punched the edges of the crater. This made the cabin cold and unpleasant.

Rotting looked through the left window and said rather dejectedly: "Down there somewhere," he waved his hand as he pointed, "is my house in Fort Lauderdale. My wife is waiting for me to return, right now." Rotting impulsively checked his watch. "She does not know that she probably never will see me again."

Maryanne again became white as a corpse.

"Sorry it was just another joke," he said rather apologetically.

Such talk was nonsense, only a slip of the tongue. I must for a moment have become completely morbid with this large responsibility on my shoulders, he thought, as he knew their chance of coming down alive was only marginally better than nil.

He was rudely brought back to reality by a loud voice on the radio.

"Palm Beach control tower to Bravo, Alfa, Alfa 273. Good

evening. You have priority flight. No external traffic will disturb you. We are on full alert to receive you. You must drop some of your spare fuel into the sea to reduce weight and fire-danger. You must make an entirely manual landing because of the craft's grounding angle, which must be abnormal to reduce the danger of collapse of your damaged steering pillar. You must also consider that as many as five of your wheels on the main carriages have been punctured according to information we have received from Miami International. Three wheels on the right side and two on the left side. You must therefore touch down as lightly as a mosquito. We await your final run on runway two, that's from east to west, if you don't know our airfield."

"You must do this, and you must do that," Rotting said irritated. And turned towards Maryanne, while the connection to the tower was switched off a moment. "However, the damned bastards in the tower have not yet mentioned that they await me to make a bloody cock-up!"

Rotting thought for a short moment. He regretted his expression and added shortly: "Sorry – I must really be irritated."

"You are definitely allowed to be angry," Maryanne said to gloss over it. Also this time she spoke with a wide, reassuring smile, although she was extremely nervous.

There was a short break on the radio before standard information about the weather situation followed, with a request for confirmation and finally a wish about good luck.

"Thanks," Rotting said mechanically. "I do really believe we need all the good luck possible to bring this scrap-heap to the ground and creep out from it alive."

The tower made no reply to Rotting's last remarks. Rotting observed the lights from the airfield approaching quickly as he continued with the descent of the craft. The automatic indicators showed him the right direction, the correct descending schedule to reach the landing site of

366

the runway and the speed he had to keep, but the flight control was altogether his and completely manual.

"I have never done such a landing with an aircraft of this size before," Rotting said informatively to Maryanne with a weak smile. "Let's only hope that the flight simulators had programmes not too far removed from hard reality."

However, Rotting had got back some of his fighter-instinct from the old days, when he was behind the stick in a Freedom Fighter, during the Cold War, and was on cutting missions when Russian zombies came along the British coastline. He had started to react like a true professional fighter pilot does. Nerves were suddenly completely unknown and an irrelevant factor. His mind was concentrated only on his task at the moment, to get this infernal airliner safely to the ground, soft as a mosquito sets down.

The plane actually touched the ground slowly and smoothly, piloted by the extremely able captain. He kept the plane's nose up from the ground as the craft rolled along the runway, when he suddenly felt the right carriage support break. The craft immediately started pulling to the right, but not as quickly as a smaller plane would have done. The jumbo was too heavy. The friction between the asphalt and the carriage was heard for a moment as a shrill noise and the flying sparks from beneath the craft looked like fireworks. The nose was roughly thrown down towards the ground and the front pillar collapsed. Rotting cut the engines immediately. The engines' braking force was of no use anymore and the fire danger had to be reduced. A half-second later and the other carriages collapsed. This stabilised the direction of the craft's movement. It headed forward on its belly on the grass beside the runway. A furrow was made in the ground, like a farmer using a gigantic plough, before the right wing caught the ground and the tip was wrenched off. The remaining fuel from the

367

destroyed wing poured out onto the ground. The craft stopped completely only a couple of seconds later, after making a violent turn to the right.

Now, for the huge explosion, and then our end will come, Rotting thought cynically, but he said to Maryanne: "I really think we managed it. Get the hell out at once!"

There had been complete panic in the passenger cabin when the sound of the violent friction between the asphalt and the metal reached the passengers. They shouted and roared like trapped inmates in a burning asylum with no way out.

"Not again, – to hell, – not again."

When the plane stopped, the sound stopped too. It was completely silent for a moment, before the sound of dozens of fire engines and ambulances racing towards the stricken craft filled the air. The aircraft's emergency doors were immediately opened and the passengers streamed out, like slithery herring from a fish barrel, on the rubber slides that automatically filled with air. The passengers ran desperately away from the plane as soon as they touched the ground.

Rotting was the last person to leave the plane. He had not walked ten metres when the first explosion occurred. It was the inner engine on the opposite side of the plane, where the wing tip had been ripped off. The firemen pumping foam on the plane to prevent explosions, and everybody else near, recorded Olympic sprint times to get away from the huge aircraft. Only a few seconds later it exploded into a burning inferno.

It was certainly a very relieved group of people that left BAA's flight 273 from London. Luckily, nobody had been seriously injured physically, but doctors at the airport said that psychological damage would probably show up later. Previous medical experience had shown that people who had narrow escapes from certain death developed mental problems years later. An army of medical people with equipment for an expected much worse catastrophe took care of the passengers fortunate to have only superficial injuries.

Experts stated that only the ability of the competent pilot, Captain Rotting, had saved the people aboard flight 273. The true situation was that Miami International had not given him all the details about the serious damage that they had discovered. They had not wanted to take hope away from the unlucky people on board. The craft was actually given no hope, and they had been sent to Palm Beach to die.

25

At that moment, McNeigh believed they were definitely discovered. It was not until he saw the helicopter make sweeps over the nearby area that a small glimmer of hope filled him. Might they still be undiscovered? They had been directly under the helicopter when it passed. That must be the only reason why the helicopter's crew had not seen them. They would not have had a chance, if the helicopter had been just ten metres to either side.

The rest of the day McNeigh and Ness saw and heard neither helicopters nor people who pursued them. They walked as quickly as possible to increase the distance from the disposal place of the car. They realised that the car must have been discovered. The helicopter search they had observed gave sure indication that the hunt for them was on. The helicopters had been seen further to the east and behind them. This indicated luckily, anyway, that the hunters must believe they had chosen another route, closer to the coast.

Autumn had already given indisputable signals that it was about to arrive with the transformation of the leaves to all the spectrum's gorgeous colours. McNeigh watched the wide forest below the ridge where they rested after a very fatiguing climb up the steep hillside. He saw the green spruce trees and the pines covered the whole area to the horizon as a green carpet. In the middle of the carpet were spots of deciduous trees with a wide variety of changing colours. From a distance they looked exactly like colourful flowers. These flowers were mostly concentrated in the bottom of the valley around small lakes that looked exactly like blue eyes staring through small hollows in the green carpet, twinkling with excitement in the bright sun.

"Why in the hell are we fighting? We could just settle here and live by hunting," McNeigh said fascinated, while he listened to the sounds of the birds from this year's brood singing jointly with the previous generation. They were only waiting for the exact time, incomprehensibly decided by nature, to gather together for the lengthy flight to a warmer climate for the winter. A small hare ran swiftly across the small clearing in the forest in front of them.

"Be careful," McNeigh suddenly said loudly to the young hastening hare. "Always be aware of danger or you will soon end up as dinner for the fox. Life is too short to be spoilt by only a second's lapse in concentration."

Ness laughed: "I think you are getting a bit melancholy. I believe you would change your opinion completely about being a hunter in the Canadian forests, when the cold winter storms start."

"Major André Durand, our field commander for the search, has up till now reported no contact with the fugitives after the location of their car," Lieutenant Colonel Pierre Vienne said resignedly, during one of the frequent operational meetings in the briefing room at Déboisement.

Colonel La Fontene, who was the leader of the meeting, did not comment on Vienne's remarks. Vienne, who was the slothful Gouzon's deputy, represented the army. The calm Commander Nelson attended as usual for the navy.

Vienne continued to explain that he had done everything possible: "We can only present a negative result; nevertheless seven helicopters have trawled the search area up and down for more than two days. In addition fifteen-hundred men have searched methodically a strip of the area, more than seventy kilometres wide, from where the fugitives' damned car was detected towards the town of Manicouagan."

"I simply think you utilised the resources wrongly," La Fontene said and shook his head resignedly.

Then he raised his voice and continued resolutely: "There is only a very small chance that you will find the escapees in this way, such a long time after they vanished into the forest. Realistically, I would consider there to be no chance at all of finding them."

"Have you a better idea?" – Vienne asked rather caustically and sounded more than a fraction doubtful.

"Yes, gentlemen, I believe I have a considerably better proposal," La Fontene replied promptly and undoubtedly very self-confidently.

He smiled brightly for a short time, while Vienne looked querulously at him with deep disapproval.

Then he said: "I suggest you should consider the fugitives' possible destinations, instead of running after them in a haphazard way." He pointed on the map in front of them with a steel pointer. "Concentrate the search in these possible destination areas."

He continued after a sip of a glass of Canada Dry ginger ale: "You are probably correct if you surmise their destination will be in the neighbourhood of the town of Manicouagan." He studied the map a few seconds. "However, I believe they will pass that area in secret on their way to more crowded, inhabited areas."

"You mean they may be trying to reach one of the cities in the Dolbeau area?" – Vienne asked shortly.

"Exactly, sir," La Fontene replied very self-assured, "because the only chance the fugitives have to succeed in

372

their desperate escape, is to come into a densely inhabited area and disappear among people. They are probably banking on that."

He paused for a moment before he continued: "Another important point is that the fugitives probably are town people or people from crowded areas. People of that type wouldn't stay for long in the forest before they need human contact. A psychologist would probably say the maximal time such fugitives would manage to stay in the forest on the run, would be," La Fontene considered for a second before he added, "a maximum of fourteen days."

He waited to see if his colleagues followed his reasoning. Vienne said nothing and the colonel considered that as an acceptance. He kept on with his argument.

"Let's estimate a daily walking distance of a maximum of sixty kilometres for trained people. The walk in the forest would be at least twenty per cent more than on the map. That will make less than fifty kilometres progress per day. You can therefore make circles around the place where you discovered the car with a radius dependent on maximal, daily walking distances. You know the direction the fugitives have walked and you can thus limit possible destination areas by drawing a sector, let's say fifteen degrees from the centre of the circle, and see which towns this sector includes."

"That seems reasonable," Commander Nelson, said nodding agreement.

His only wish was to make some contribution to the discussion on behalf of the navy. Until now, he had been sitting completely silent listening to Vienne and la Fontene.

"Just a moment gentlemen," the colonel said, "I am not finished."

He rose from the chair and walked towards a large briefing map of the actual area, which hung on the opposite wall, to better illustrate his detailed orders.

"You!" La Fontene said loudly, as if he were briefing a flight squadron ahead of an exercise whilst pointing at Vienne with a steel pointer.

Vienne smiled.

"You!" La Fontene repeated, a little more quietly this time, as he suddenly remembered that he was not talking to a complete squadron, but only to two colleagues. "You must concentrate your forces here and there." He pointed with the steel pointer firstly at the town of Gagnon and then at the town of Manicouagan. "By now, the fugitives have probably passed the road to Gagnon or will pass it in the near future. I would say within a maximum of twenty four hours, if they have walked in the direction of the town." He motioned with the steel pointer between the different alternatives on the map. "So I believe it is of little use patrolling the road with a large force the day after tomorrow, but rather concentrate a small force in the terrain around the town of Gagnon. Because the town is small, all strangers will be quickly recognised. If our fugitives enter the centre of the town, I am sure we will get news at once. I believe the best recourse will be to let the local police cover the search in the centre of the town. The traffic police should carry out the establishing of roadblocks where the road from the town meets the coastal road. If the fugitives are trying to hitchhike or steal a car to get out of the area they will probably go in that direction. In this way there will also be fewer questions about why the army is around, than if army personnel establish the roadblocks themselves."

The colonel smiled to himself after a short pause and a gulp of ginger ale.

He burped silently, pointed again with the steel pointer towards Vienne, and said: "You must concentrate your forces from here to there." He pointed at the Manicouagan Réservoir and drew the steel pointer down to the town of

Manicouagan and further along the road towards the coastal road. "Along this stretch the fugitives most certainly will appear within a few days."

It was silent for some seconds, before La Fontene pointed at the river to the east of the road from Manicouagan to the coastal road.

"The river from Manicouagan Réservoir will help us a lot. The fugitives must search for bridges to cross the cold river. It would be very difficult and dangerous to attempt to swim across. You must therefore watch all bridges carefully," La Fontene said and pressed down on the steel extension pointer, till it was about an ordinary pen's length.

Satisfied he put it into his inside pocket and concluded: "The longer the fugitives stay in the forest the more careless they will become and the greater chances they will take. They are as far as I can see, completely trapped."

Colonel La Fontene's prediction concerning the fugitives' movements was accurate. The two Scottish fugitives were just about to enter the exact area that he determined for the main search. Early the following morning after the meeting at Déboisement, the two Scotsmen approached the road connecting Gagnon to the coastal road. They had planned to traverse the road at half past four in the morning, because they knew the guards' alertness at that time of the night was at a minimum.

On the stretch where he expected the fugitives to cross the road, Major Durand had placed his main force in small groups hidden in positions along the road with continuous patrols between the positions. Durand considered the frontier he had established along the road was as secure as the border between East and West Germany during the Cold War, or at least as secure as a shark net outside an Australian beach.

However, where the Scotsmen actually reached the road the distances between the guards' positions were significantly longer, as Durand had placed his main force further to the south-east or nearer to the coast. This section was mainly patrolled by cars and only a few groups of guards threaded themselves silently between the spruce trees along the roadside.

It was one of these groups Ness discovered when he and McNeigh sneaked, like Indians, towards the road. He suddenly heard somebody whispering nearby and he raised his arm to warn McNeigh who was walking only a few metres behind him.

"Get finished Peter, we can't stand here waiting for you to irrigate all the forest."

Another voice replied louder, in mock irritation: "You know I must roll up the whole length before I am finished and that will take some time. It is of course easier for you, if you haven't lost your tweezers."

All men in the group laughed loudly until somebody with a weak voice said: "Shut up, I think I heard something."

"That must be a large female grizzly which has smelled that fellow watering over there."

Everybody laughed again, and the Scotsmen could hear the patrol start moving, as their laughter faded, eastwards along the road. They waited silently for ten minutes before they carefully approached the road. They stood out of sight, hidden in the shadows when a car came from the west.

"We run now," McNeigh said hastily, after the car had passed, but was still only ten metres away.

The Scotsmen ran quickly over the road behind the car. They hoped the car's lights would dazzle the guards, if they turned their heads and looked westwards along the road. They were quickly across the road and the small trees that grew tight along the roadside waved crossly as the Scotsmen hastily forced their way through them. That went well, Ness thought satisfied a moment before he heard the shot. The Scots threw themselves down on the ground and lay completely still. They could hear loud voices not very far away. The guard group had stopped and was seated by the roadside smoking, when the car passed.

"What in hell are you doing?"

"I think I saw somebody disappear behind the small trees on the other side of the road, just after the car passed," an uncertain voice replied.

The first voice said: "I saw nothing and I saw the car passing."

"I know," Peter's voice added, full of self-importance suddenly, pretending to be very important, as if declaring that the Second World was finally over. It was he who a short time before had rolled up his irrigation hose. "It was the same female grizzly you heard ten minutes ago which ran over the road to smell the aroma of my excellent piss. She was obviously so eager that she could not wait till the large piss stream had crossed the road."

"To hell, I saw something," the uncertain voice repeated steadfastly.

"And we believe you didn't," the first voice replied, "and I am in charge."

There was silence for a short time as the soldiers listened. The Scots could see the soldiers' cigarettes light up, every time one of them took a draw. Meanwhile, they lay completely quiet on the ground, as pleasantly as fakirs on needle mats and waited deadly curious for what was to follow.

Then the first voice spoke again: "I know you will have a hell of a job tomorrow explaining your shot."

"Don't be cruel," Peter's voice said. "If there is nobody coming, nobody has heard the shot. He can get one of the cartridges I stole on the shooting range last week, and have a complete set to deliver after we have finished guard duty. And tell me, can we expect any of these fugitives to come

377

in this direction, if they heard the damn fool's shot? I suggest we just move on and forget the whole damn incident. I am sleepy and I would rather be in my sleeping bag."

The group moved slowly eastwards, while they talked loudly, but the marksman with the uncertain voice, turned his head and looked back every few seconds.

"That was a really narrow escape," Ness whispered very relieved.

"It was my fault," McNeigh replied morosely, "I should of course have checked more carefully before we ran, but the car disturbed me. The guards sat on the slope and smoked only a hundred metres down the road. I should of course have seen them. It was an inexperienced amateur's mistake. I believe our concentration probably is being reduced because we are getting tired."

He sat quietly for a moment regaining his breath, before he added nasally, with a slight smile, to imitate how a sergeant speaks to recruits: "Never run into open terrain before you have double checked or you will definitely be killed."

In the morning, the soldier with the uncertain voice spoke to his troop commander about the incident that his corporal had refused to believe or check. The young lieutenant, who was the troop commander, immediately drove over to the place where the shot had been fired, together with the hapless soldier. He detected the tracks of two men at the place, and immediately contacted Major Durand on the military radio. Durand told him at once to secure the road completely, for twenty kilometres in each direction from the spot where the crossing might have happened. A special force would come later in the day with tracker dogs and examine the area properly.

Afterwards, Durand ordered three helicopters to comb the area. The helicopters started a systematic search at about ten o'clock in the morning, but detected nothing that day. The tracker dogs were at the place at three in the afternoon and made positive findings. Durand did not raise a search party because he considered it was too late in the day and the fugitives would have gained too big a head start. Anyway, he had received categorical confirmation that the fugitives were walking, as expected, in the direction of the final trap along the river from the Manicouagan Réservoir.

He did not want to scare the fugitives into heading directly west to pass north of the Réservoir, or making some other unpredictable movements. If the fugitives passed north of the Réservoir, the search area would have to be extended enormously, and it would be well nigh impossible to catch them. He ordered the whole area between the river, from the Manicouagan Réservoir and the road where they had crossed, completely sealed. To seal it thoroughly he had to order a company to patrol the stretch of about eighty-kilometres between Gagnon and the Manicouagan Réservoir. Helicopters were also ordered to inspect the borders along the entire sealed area, which formed a large trapezium. It was two hundred kilometres long, from the coastal road to Gagnon and about 100 kilometres wide, from the road between Gagnon and the coast, to the river from the Réservoir. Durand told his colleagues they only had to wait patiently, because he was quite sure he finally had the fishes in the trap.

The Scotsmen reached the cold and wide river from the Manicouagan Réservoir at the end of the following day. It had been a very exhausting trip after they passed the road between Gagnon and the coast. They had to reckon with the possibility that the place where they crossed the road would be under surveillance, because the soldiers had almost certainly detected them. So, after the crossing, they headed westwards. They believed that had helped them avoid the helicopters they had seen in eastern and southerly directions later the same day. They had waded in streams, never able to take the shortest route, in order to leave no tracks for any tracker dogs.

It would be too difficult to cross the river at the place they encountered it. Therefore they decided to walk downstream, to find an easier place to cross or perhaps find a bridge. After three hours they did come upon one. Very slowly and watchfully they approached it. Unfortunately they did not see anybody before they were at the edge of the bridge and about to cross.

A soldier at the other end suddenly shouted loudly: "Halt, or I will shoot!"

26

In Glasgow, the leaders of the Highlanders' Commando had assembled in a meeting of all its five members. The leader, Sir Walter Bruce, was the first to speak as always.

He said in a businesslike manner: "All three targets have been destroyed successfully, without any casualties, but for the old and ambitious commander of HMS *Heroic*, who died, only because of his refusal to obey a naval order. Refusal to obey an order is a very serious charge against a naval commander. If he had survived, he would have been court martialled, punished and dismissed. The old lunatic was probably only hunting for another medal, in spite of warnings from his second-in-command. But the navy probably does not consider his death as the end of their involvement. The commander will no doubt receive a posthumous medal, despite his insubordination. The navy of course does not punish the dead."

None of the meeting's participants had any comments on Sir Walter's contribution. They were all fully aware of the successful result of their actions.

"The Caribbean operators have reported that everything is in order. The same report has been received from our Miami operators, but we have not received any information from Canada yet," Sir Walter added, before he gave a nod towards McPride to continue.

McPride took the hint and said: "The operators in Canada are probably walking back through the Canadian forests. Fort Hope was a very difficult target. It was too far away and very isolated in the wilderness. The only possible escape was by car, along the coastal road. We had reckoned that the Canadian police would quickly block the roads. We didn't anticipate a complete paralysis of, and therefore no retaliation by, the Canadians, though we had given the English strict orders not to investigate our action. We knew before the action that the Canadians would be forced to react in some way when an atomic bomb was detonated in their territory."

He changed his position in his chair, cleared his throat and continued without waiting for any comments: "We also considered using a small one-engined plane, as both our men on the assignment have pilot's licences, but that would have exposed them if they had been detected. So we decided on the least risk. The most discreet way would be to walk through the forest and then hitchhike; possibly use public transport for the last stretch to Montreal, in case of a car being too risky or completely impossible to use. From Montreal the operators had planned to cross the border to the United States as ordinary tourists, before they finally return home to Scotland."

The colonel coughed discreetly and lowered his voice before he added: "It may take more than a week before we have any contact with those operators, but by now unconfirmed reports tell us there has been a massive search launched to find them in the forest. We will have to wait for some time until these rumours are confirmed or disproved. If the rumours are confirmed, we will have to give the English a rough reminder to effect an immediate termination of the Canadian authority's investigation."

"I suppose all of you agree about giving the English another reminder?" – Sir Walter asked shortly, when the colonel had finished.

382

Everybody nodded in agreement.

Wallace said: "The incident at Miami International airport could have ended in a real disaster. The damned pilot ignored the threat, though we blew up a plane by the terminal building to warn him and the control tower, when he was about to land. Luckily for him, he was an extremely capable pilot and saved his passengers by exceptionally clever manoeuvres at the last moment before a disaster happened. Afterwards he was ordered to land in Palm Beach, where he again performed another brilliant manoeuvre, but I suppose you have read about all of this in the newspapers."

Nobody commented and he continued, after a short break: "The pilot has almost become a national hero in both England and the United States. The Americans have released to the press that they believe the Arabs were responsible for the action. Lucky for us that the Americans generally accuse the Arabs of everything they can't explain any other way."

He took a gulp of Coke before he continued and appeared somewhat relieved by the thought: "However, at least ten different guerrilla and terrorists organisations, including the Formation and the IRA have claimed responsibility for the action. There seem to be many people *working* for us." He suddenly grinned somewhat uncertainly. "Although, despite all the enthusiastic claims of responsibility, we have just been informed that the Americans have started a huge investigation into the case."

He looked quickly at each of the persons present as he drank some more from his bottle of Coke.

Then he said determinedly: "We must have that investigation stopped immediately, as it may expose us. We must remember that they probably have Elise McCoy on their videos as she walked through the airport departure hall. I therefore suggest we press the English to tell the Americans to stop the investigation and to inform the press that the explosion on the runway was simply caused by leakage from gas tubes. Pipes cross the runway and an inexplicable concentration of gas had unfortunately been created in one of the drainage pipes. The explosion in the parked plane before the dramatic landing, must be deemed a fault caused by the electric system in the plane, combined with a fuel leakage, or something of that sort."

Wallace took again a short rest while he looked inquiringly at the other meeting participants for a moment, before he said politely: "Do any of you have any better proposals for a credible explanation of these happenings in Miami?"

McPride cleared his voice like a politician before a long speech, but replied very shortly: "One ridiculous idea is probably as good as an other. I think the public opinion will, probably, believe none of them anyway, as two disasters of that sort, by chance, normally will never happen at the same time. The only things to interest us are that the Americans stop the investigation immediately and that passengers all over the world, for safety reasons, will abandon all English aircraft. The Americans will certainly find their own reasons, as they have always been clever in doing. I suppose, especially this time, they will do it when they see the possibilities of filling their airliners with passengers who otherwise would have chosen British competitors."

"I presume the English want the Americans and the Canadians to investigate the cases to use them as buffers, as they are instructed not to investigate by themselves at all," Sir Walter said. "A strong reminder is necessary and soon, before the investigations disturb or damage our plans. I will send the damned foolish English a special message tomorrow morning that will turn the whole of London Town upside down."

Wallace added: "The action against English air traffic all

384

over the world is working extremely efficiently after the incident in Miami. Foreign competitors have taken over most of the English airliners' world-wide routes. English airline companies are meanwhile losing a hell of a lot of money."

"Excellent, gentlemen," Sir Walter said shortly, while he turned his head, looked at Viking and Whisky and asked: "How about our activists in the Caribbean. Are they back in yet?"

Sir Walter Bruce had always been concerned about his personnel.

Viking answered, and as always with a broad smile on his face. He never seemed to suffer any great problems.

"Our agents are still in the Caribbean, celebrating the successful outcome of their action. The last report we received from them was that they had delayed their return for a couple of weeks. At the moment, they are very busy in Martinique dancing calypso to the music of steel drums and drinking rum from coconuts."

"I have heard something about them also becoming very horny," Whisky suddenly added and laughed loudly.

The others present, with the exception of Viking who only smiled, looked at him with disbelief and questioning expressions.

"That's correct – my dear gentlemen," Viking said laughing, with an understanding grimace. "Castle and Coe have unexpectedly married during the voyage. They are now said to be on honeymoon in the sailing boat with the Connolys. It is also said that the sailing boat is rocking like it is in a full storm, even though the sea is calm as a bathtub."

"It's cramped in these sailing boats, I suppose," Sir Walter said quietly, but sarcastically and chuckled as he added: "This is really good news for the creation of the next generation of native Scots."

Wallace smiled too, as he said: "Samson and McCoy with

his beautiful wife, Elise, have already returned to the United Kingdom. They booked a tourist boat to Nassau from Miami and a plane back to Manchester via Paris."

"Excellent," Sir Walter commented, then said shortly: "I believe you all know what to do to execute our next plan?"

All nodded to confirm and rose from their chairs without a word.

The day after the meeting, a large explosion took place west of London, on the connecting link between Heathrow airport and the M4 motorway, where the motorway runs alongside the airport parallel to the A4. A second explosion happened on the A4 at Cranford. A third explosion occurred at the intersection between the M23 motorway and Gatwick airport, south of London. A fourth explosion damaged Victoria railway station and a fifth went off at Hammersmith subway station, both in the centre of London.

The authorities received information ahead of all detonations, telling them to evacuate the areas. Consequently no casualties were recorded, except for a paparazzo photographer who wanted to earn a fortune by getting a firsthand photo of the explosion at Victoria.

He had been ordered to leave the station area immediately, together with everybody else, only minutes after the authorities had received the warning of the bombs and their locations. Despite the clear warnings over the station's intercom from the police, the paparazzo had hidden himself in the station's lavatory. He sustained serious injuries, whilst Victoria station was out of action for days.

The damage to Hammersmith took that station out of use for almost two days and created severe problems for the subway transport.

The traffic situation in London became horrendous

especially in the centre, when all the tube and railway stations had been emptied and closed. Travellers mostly had to remain where they were, because all the taxis were immediately occupied and then trapped in traffic jams. People felt the whole pulsing city had stopped. The only people that might have been a little satisfied with the situation, were possibly the taxi drivers, the restaurants and pub owners, plus all the hot-dog and fish-and-chips vendors.

The information received at Heathrow and Gatwick before the explosions was sketchy. It told of large explosive devices on some roads normally used by the airports' travellers, within a one-mile radius of the airports. All roads to and from the airports were blocked at once and cleared of traffic by the police.

The traffic situation on the roads round Heathrow was, after the detonation, relatively quickly redirected, because alternative roads could be used while the damage on the A4 and the connecting link was repaired. The traffic was led into the A30 and the M25, which reached Heathrow airport, on the A4, from the opposite direction. However, traffic jams occurred widely over the whole area, because the M4 was also the main road to Reading, and west to Bristol and Cardiff. The traffic was completely blocked for an hour and a half, and the incident affected almost all travellers to Heathrow and people just passing the area in other directions for the next four hours.

The situation at Gatwick airport was similar to that at Heathrow because the service link between Gatwick airport and the M23 motorway had become completely unusable because of the large crater left after the explosion. It took more than an hour before provisional arrangements were in place to divert the traffic from the M23 for the A23 and Gatwick airport. The total traffic jams in the area turned out to cause considerable hardship because the M23 and the A23 are also the main roads to the south coast towns, including Brighton and Worthing. Through traffic going south and north was completely blocked on these roads and on all other smaller roads in the areas. The police had, ahead of the explosion, blocked the roads from Redhill in the north to Horsham and Handcross in the south, for more than one and a half hours, including the waiting time before the blast, after the bomb threat had been received.

Experts reported afterwards that there must have been considerable quantities of plastic explosives used in each of these various bombings that day.

The English Secret Council that was established specially for the Scottish case had a meeting at Number Ten Downing Street only one hour after the explosions, while the whole of London was one large traffic jam.

"England has participated in many wars," the Prime Minister said resignedly, "but this one must be one of the worst, because we really don't know who our enemy is. It could be you or it could be you."

The Prime Minister pointed vaguely at the participants of the meeting, but was careful not to point at anyone directly.

He continued: "There is more chaos in London today after these bombs, than on any of the days when the Germans emptied their bomb loads over our heads. At least then we knew who our enemy was. Today we have no idea. We only know, or rather suppose they must be of Scottish origin. Do you have Scottish ancestors?"

The Prime Minister again vaguely waved with his arm pointing at no one in particular. Nobody replied. They just stared suspiciously at him.

The Prime Minister saw the expressions in their eyes and said with a grin: "I have Scottish relatives, as you know, but I am certainly not responsible for blowing up England."

"We never know," the Defence Secretary said with his comical, affected Eton accent.

The Prime Minister hated that man even more. He considered him to be a disgusting son-of-a-bitch, but he laughed loudly, together with everybody else at his absurd remark.

Immediately afterwards the Prime Minister dried the perspiration from his forehead with his handkerchief, before he said with a lowered voice, as if reading fairy-tales for children, and now he had come to an exceedingly exciting paragraph: "Our enemies seem to be rather clever and extremely dangerous."

The Defence Secretary's slimy voice was again heard: "The reason why the Scots have caused these explosions today, is that they want the United Kingdom to put pressure on the Americans and Canadians to stop their investigations on the destruction of the BAA's planes and our base in Canada. In addition they have directed us to inform the press that the bombs today, were executed by, at present unknown, terrorists. The bombs should only be connected to similar incidents accomplished by the IRA in recent years."

The Defence Secretary looked around, but nobody made any remarks or raised any questions. They sat waiting patiently to be presented with more facts.

He smiled his foolish smile whilst he continued and seemed extremely satisfied not to have been disturbed during his presentation of the account of the course of events: "Anyway, I don't think the last part of the terrorists' requests should be especially difficult to comply with because various terrorist groups have already begun to fight over the responsibility. The first part of their requests could

389

be a considerably more difficult problem to tackle because the Americans and Canadians are unlikely to acquiesce with any British requests automatically, especially the Americans."

Field Marshal Charles Wield had listened to these opinions in silence.

A successful officer with more than 40 years experience behind him, he considered quietly before his rough, loud voice was heard: "These terrorists, who I rather will call our counterparts," he placed great emphasis on the word *counterparts*, "have always executed their actions with great precision. They also always give proper warnings to the authorities ahead of each action, to avoid any casualties. They have really demonstrated their power in a way that shows we are dealing with people with influence in nearly all levels of our society. It seems as if they always get the necessary information. We probably made a very wrong decision when we told the Americans and the Canadians to catch the saboteurs. Our counterparts have obviously discovered that we are using the Americans and the Canadians as fronts for our own investigation. They have discovered that we are trying to approach their organisation via these third parties, because we ourselves can't investigate properly due to their threats. Our counterparts have again today, simply and easily, demonstrated that they know everything that we attempt to do, and that they can easily stop English society if we do not follow their directions to the letter."

Wield made a short break before he continued, even louder and more militarily, as if addressing a bunch of new recruits: "You must know!" He looked indulgently around at those present, who all sat quietly wondering what they should know. "You must know – we always received information ahead of our honourable counterparts' actions. This has prevented almost all possible casualties. I can't imagine the number of dead and injured there would have been if they hadn't warned the authorities beforehand or if they had used the terrible atomic missiles against our towns. If we put any pressure on them, I'm sure they also will be forced to demonstrate their power without warnings and the situation will quickly slip completely out of control."

"This means that you suggest we give the Americans and the Canadians instructions to drop all the investigations of the cases? Simply throw in the towel," Air Force Marshal Thomas Grantham asked rather incredulously.

"Yes. You have understood me quite correctly, sir," Wield replied quickly.

"Do you all agree with that conclusion?" the Prime Minister asked quietly, as he felt he was being completely taken over by the situation.

"I really don't," the leader of Secret Service, General Director Howard Spindlier, said loudly, seemingly deeply offended. "I believe that if we now throw away these superb chances to investigate our counterparts," he expressed the word *counterparts* in a very sarcastic way, "we will never get another chance to detect the sources of this blackmailing organisation. We will have lost the battle for ever, even before it has begun."

"I really think the battle has begun," Admiral Sir Alexander Viscount said, irritated. "Never before has anybody sunk a British battleship so easily. Never before has a hostile atomic missile sunk a British ship. Worst of all, is that our counterparts have done this without leaving any positive tracks at all to investigate. They are acting just like demons."

The admiral looked around to see the reaction to the word demons, but the meeting's participants, with the exception of the self-satisfied military men, only sat waiting for him to continue, like schoolboys waiting for their end of term reports.

Viscount decided that he was almost enjoying the situation and took an extra drink of water to extend the artificial break, before, with a smile, he continued severely: "We don't know how our counterparts managed to hit the naval vessel so damned exactly spot-on to create maximum damage. If they used the same type of atomic warheads they previously demonstrated on Orkneys and Shetlands, they would not normally have damaged the ship so completely as to sink it. Only because they hit her very accurately in the ammunition magazine, was the ship's fate entirely sealed at the bottom of the Atlantic. The second-in-command followed the vessel at a distance, in a helicopter, because the captain disobeyed our order to abandon it. The second-in-command made a video of the craft that shows the detonation."

Viscount took another short break for another gulp of water before he continued: "It appears that somebody on board the ship must have collaborated with the counterparts, because they knew her exact position and the location of the magazine. I don't believe for a moment their missile's target was chosen entirely by chance. Interrogation of all the crew would obviously be the right place to start an investigation. Another step would have been to examine all previous crew from this ship and her sister ships, such as HMS *Fearless*. We are almost sure they didn't have a submarine. Therefore, we consider that the information about the ship's exact position could have been obtained by one or several of the many leisure yachts in the area, equipped with modern long range radar, if they had followed the ship from day to day during her exercise."

Wield suddenly interrupted: "We have a similar question concerning the destruction of Fort Hope. How did they hit the ammunition depot so exactly? This fact would be a very strong indication that the action was planned by somebody who previously had stayed at the base."

Wield made a break to let the facts be absorbed, before he said: "Sorry to interrupt you Viscount. Please continue."

Viscount resumed: "The only really certain facts we have at the moment about the missile in the Caribbean is that it seemed to have been launched from the Dutch island of Saint Eustatius. But this fact raises another essential question. How in hell," he added with a short excuse because of the language, "could they direct the missile to make such an exact hit?"

Viscount took a fresh swallow of water and leant over the table where he had placed his elbows. He observed that all the other participants, except for the Field Marshal, also had leant over the table, as they sat still, absorbed and excited, waiting for what he would say further.

Viscount took a deep breath and said quietly: "I consider the battle is lost if we don't want to have any casualties. The counterparts have carefully informed us ahead of any of their actions. This means we must have very committed counterparts. They run the business with military-like precision and we have only to follow their steps like well trained dogs."

"If they run the business with military precision, then I am obviously entirely beyond suspicion," the Prime Minister said unexpectedly, trying a joke with a forced smile and glint in his eyes.

"Don't tell us," the Defence Secretary added sneeringly, without looking up, while he bent over his documents.

How I hate that damned slimy fellow, the Prime Minister thought, as he looked at his Defence Secretary with real loathing in his eyes. Everybody in the room easily detected this, except for the Defence Secretary himself who was still busily shuffling documents.

That greasy individual will certainly be removed in the next government reshuffle, the Prime Minister reflected grimly.

Viscount continued as if nothing had happened: "The counterparts continually demonstrate that they want to achieve their aim, an independent Scotland, without any bloodshed if possible. But they know very well that they cannot change a country's way of government without a revolution, if elections are denied. It looks as if at the moment they only ask for the right to hold free democratic elections, while they use atomic power to be certain of obtaining this right. If the demonstrations so far appear not to be sufficient, they will assuredly attack with appalling consequences."

The Prime Minister had listened carefully to the admiral's monologue and he asked him: "What action do you propose?

Viscount sat down gripping his glass, without drinking and replied quickly: "I suggest we act according to the counterparts' instructions, but delay the date of the election. Meanwhile I suggest starting a political campaign to change the Scottish people's wish to leave the Union. This is a matter for politicians, not a matter for the army. The army doesn't want to shoot at its own people. The Scots are too integrated in English society for the English to have them as enemies. The only problem is that if Scotland goes, Northern Ireland will surely follow quickly, and maybe Wales, but this seems to be the way of all colonialism in our modern society."

"Then the next step is crystal clear if no one has any better proposals," the Prime Minister concluded.

Nobody replied and the Prime Minister continued with the utmost seriousness: "I will travel to Washington to negotiate with the President of the United States to stop the investigation on the Miami bombing exactly as our counterparts direct. I will also travel to Canada and ask the Canadian Prime Minister to do the same and stop all investigations in his territory. The largest problem is of course that these incidents occurred in their countries and that they alone must decide what to do, absolutely independently. Bear in mind they must consider what serves them best, concerning winning their next elections. Therefore, I hope I don't have to mention to them that, if they refuse, they must themselves reckon on a possible atomic attack by the terrorists – correction – I of course mean, our honourable counterparts. Attacks directed at the White House or the Capitol in Washington, and the Parliament in Ottawa."

The Secret Service's general director's driver let him off outside his club, not far from Number Ten. He told the driver to take the rest of the day off and went by taxi to a secret office in the City of London, where the investigation group for the Scottish problem had established their exclusive headquarters, among large banks and finance companies.

"No use saving money by using a dark, unpleasant flat in a squalid street in East London, when you have a direct line into the British Prime Minister's special account for official matters," Spindlier had said to Bill Frank when they rented the office.

Frank had been appointed leader of the group, which handled the Scottish case.

"If you don't withdraw anything from an official account, it will never exceed annual grants," Spindlier had continued.

Frank had nearly forty of his handpicked men and women on the assignment and they needed a lot of space. He felt that the expensive office in the City was justified.

"The Prime Minister told me today to lay off the case," Spindlier said angrily to Frank. "He wishes to let the terrorists escape. Terrorists that have nearly blown up the whole of London, stopped all our airliners and blown military bases and naval craft to hell."

"What kind of threats have the Scottish fanatics presented now?" – Frank asked. He was a lot more balanced and calm than his superior was.

"Nothing specific," Spindlier replied, "The military leaders and the Prime Minister are afraid we won't get any warnings next time they make an attack."

"Have you thought about closing down our activities before we really get started?" – Frank asked curiously.

"Not in hell," Spindlier replied brusquely, "I don't need to do what those scared military leaders with uniforms like decorated Christmas trees, and the weak Prime Minister, obviously afraid of his own shadow, tell me to. It was different when the Iron Lady ruled. In those days there wasn't any room for remission of sentence for terrorists. The Prime Minister obviously doesn't know the instructions for the leader of the British Secret Service. My instructions are clear, to do whatever I find necessary to secure the country against internal and external enemies. I find it very necessary to do what the Iron Lady would have done, to catch these Scots who are playing cat and mouse with us and blowing our beautiful city to hell."

"You are my boss," Frank added shortly, "and I obey what you think best."

"Good," Spindlier replied. "I want you to examine the crew lists for the last ten years on HMS *Heroic* and her sister ships, to find every damned Scot and especially Scotsmen that have been trained in the use of mobile hand held missiles. I believe you wouldn't find too many suspects with these diverse skills. Then examine where those Scotsmen were at the moment of detonation for each of the missiles. Do the same with Fort Hope's troop-lists. And now – I am leaving for an extended dinner at my club."

Spindlier turned on his heels and left without further ado.

27

Several other soldiers appeared quickly behind the soldier who was shouting from the other side of the bridge.

McNeigh said, astonished and lost: "Damn. They have discovered us. What can we do?"

Without thinking, Ness replied completely confused: "Run, what else?"

The Scots heard the soldiers shouting as they ran back into the forest at the eastern side of the river: "Stop or you will be shot."

They did not stop. McNeigh heard the shots. He turned around to see Ness with outstretched arms as if he was going to give him a bear hug, before he tumbled down to the ground with a guttural, pulpy cry and remained absolutely still. Ness had been hit in the head by one of the warning shots. He died instantly never having had the feeling that he had left the living world. The marksman had probably not seen them through the leaves and had certainly not realised he had just killed a man.

McNeigh did not think for a second about what to do. He reacted automatically. He lifted his dead friend on his shoulders and ran, but quickly became completely exhausted by the heavy burden. After only three hundred metres his strength was gone. He could not carry his friend a metre further and stopped in the cover of a high stone ridge. To the right was a small tarn with a tiny brook, which flowed into it on the west and out on the east side. McNeigh moved slowly along the stone ridge with the heavy load of his dead friend. He had moved about twenty metres along the tarn when he found a narrow strip of water along the stone ridge. The strip was half a metre to one metre wide and four or five metres long. There was a narrow stony path between the water-filled gully and the tarn.

McNeigh lowered the dead body carefully to the ground. He heard the soldiers' voices coming closer. He picked up a stone and dropped it into the water. It was very deep. He quickly filled his dead friend's rucksack with stones, fastened the front straps of the rucksack over his chest and dumped him into the gully. Tears streamed down his cheeks as he completed the funeral with indecent haste.

McNeigh could hear the shouting from his pursuers close by. They had no dogs. He had only seconds to decide what to do. He was too exhausted to run and saw the brook flowing into the tarn. The decision was easy because there were no alternatives. The brook cascaded into the tarn over a two metre wide fall from an overhanging stone ledge. Under this ledge there was a ten-centimetre clearance to the water surface. McNeigh jumped into the water and hid himself behind the waterfall. He could breathe in the small clearance between the stone ceiling and the water surface if he bent his head backwards. The turbulence caused by the waterfall hid his shadow.

He had not waited for fifteen seconds in his wet and uncomfortable hiding place before his pursuers appeared by the eastern end of the tarn. They were five young soldiers. They were obviously not professional hunters. They talked loudly about the two desperadoes they had just seen running into the forest and vanish. One of them urinated right on the spot where McNeigh had dropped his friend to the ground.

He has destroyed any possibility of a sniffer dog tracking me, McNeigh thought.

The pursuers disappeared after a few minutes. McNeigh remained in the water for another quarter of an hour then he sneaked out, but he did not leave the place. He was extremely cold, though the sun, about to set, was still warming.

Half an hour later he again heard voices. He once more slid silently into the hiding place behind the waterfall. Three men with a dog appeared. The dog smelled the urine of the soldier and dragged its handler back the same way it had come – obviously hunting for the soldier who had urinated.

McNeigh stayed at the same place that night, the next day and the night that followed. He slept in some thick bushes behind the waterfall, only five metres from his hiding place in the water. Nobody came. Hopefully, they believed the two desperadoes had disappeared into the forest. Four times he observed helicopters flying low over the area, but he was sheltered and could not be discovered from the air.

The British Prime Minister travelled in secret to Washington following the resolution of the last meeting of the committee concerning the Scottish question. He met the President in the White House. The President received him with his usual unnaturally wide, election smile. This was the very smile that had provided him with all his electoral victories during the past years.

After the heads of state had exchanged the standard diplomatic phrases and the staff had left them alone in the Oval Office, the President asked nonchalantly, like a cowboy might ask for a whisky in a saloon: "I understand you want us to close down the investigations concerning the explosions at Miami International airport. Is that correct, sir?"

The Prime Minister replied, completely ignoring the world's self-confessed leader's indulgence: "Yes, something like that, Mr. President."

"Do you know that the plastic explosives used in Miami originated in Russia?"

The President crossed his legs and sat with his hands behind his neck, quite relaxed on the sofa in front of the Prime Minister and waited curiously for his reply.

"No, I didn't. However, we have received indisputable indications that those responsible for the explosions were Scots. Therefore, I had assumed the plastic explosives had a British source."

"You see," the President said, as he pulled his feet nearer the sofa and lowered his hands, "the origin of all plastic explosives, detonated or not detonated, can be tracked by their composition, just like you recognise fingerprints. We presumed the bombs in Miami had been placed by Arab terrorists because plastic explosives of that Russian type are exactly similar to what Arabian terrorists have used several times around the world. And now you tell us the detonations probably were made by Scottish independence activists?"

"That's true. The Scots also have missiles with atomic warheads. We are afraid the activists will use these against our towns and . . ."

The Prime Minister intentionally stopped to keep the President on edge for a short while. The President waited for him to continue.

The Prime Minister cleared his throat, before he carefully continued, deliberately enunciating every word, "– maybe even against the White House in Washington."

"Do you have any proof?" – the President asked and sounded quite astonished.

He had become pale.

"I had understood your efficient intelligence services – CIA externally, and FBI internally, had updated you about that fact."

The President shook his head negatively. The Prime Minister knew he had him on the edge of his seat. The Americans run policy as if they are selling hamburgers, he thought smugly. They have not developed the same efficiency in negotiations as we English with our long diplomatic experience.

The Prime Minister described the Scottish demonstration of atomic weapons on the Shetland and Orkney islands, against the battleship in the Caribbean and at the secret training base in north-eastern Canada. The President became more and more astonished, but the Prime Minister observed he had regained the colour to his face.

The President said: "I really didn't believe it, but it seems like you have worse enemies now than you had two hundred years ago when the American rebels fought for independence."

The President continued after a short pause, as the Prime Minister wisely did not reply. This time, he said, with a small smile and knowing manner: "The Scottish independence fight at the moment is perhaps not very different from our fight then, but they have only changed to more modern sophisticated weapons, instead of the old muzzle loaders and knives."

It was obvious the President did not dislike the situation when he considered the possibilities of Scotland gaining its independence. The Prime Minister knew that some of the President's own ancestors had left Scotland because of poverty caused mainly by high English taxation.

The President suddenly rose from the sofa and went to his famous desk at the end of the room, thus giving himself time to think. The Prime Minister remained silent.

"You are quite right," the President suddenly said. "We must stop the investigation immediately. Anyway, now we know the cause. We must stop the investigation for political reasons, otherwise your royal family may have to move into a cottage when the activists blow up Buckingham Palace and all your MPs may have to move out of Westminster into an empty whorehouse in Soho when the activists destroy your Parliament."

The President waved his arms like an old lady, who pretends to be very sorrowful when she finally gets the message of her unlamented husband's death.

"And what about the dear lords? Where should your precious lords sit when the Upper House's comfortable red seats have vanished? That would be a real tragedy," the President said with a taunting glint in his eyes.

The Prime Minister did not comment. He only laughed loudly at the President's performance. He could see the President was full of good humour and that was probably his best weapon in this situation.

"What do you think?" – the President asked with a self-deprecating smile. "You understand, it is a tradition to have actors in this chair."

The Prime Minister mimed applause as he kept on laughing.

"You would have made an excellent figure in a comic movie," he said, his eyes filling with tears.

"OK, we agree my dear British friend, but don't say anything," the President said in his paternal role, even though they were about the same age. "You have got what you wanted. I know we are playing on the same side of the table and I shall, of course, immediately order a halt to the investigation."

He did not say that in obeying the Scottish demands, he would automatically help the Scots towards their goal. He was well informed of the British Prime Minister's Scottish origins.

The President, who was half a head taller than the Prime Minister, rose from his chair and went towards the Prime Minister who had also risen.

He slapped him on the shoulder while he said with slightly flippant laugher: "Now, we must hurry to the dining room and have lunch. You see we have employed some beautiful waitresses. Let's start some new scandals so as not to disappoint the press."

Early, before dawn on the third day, McNeigh started to walk downstream in the forest on the left bank of the river towards Baie Comeau, on the coast. His clothes were dry and he was physically rested, but he was very lonely and certainly psychologically unbalanced. He greatly missed his friend. It is quite different to be hunted together with somebody who can share your thoughts and hopes, from being hunted when you are completely alone. He was mentally tired. He felt entirely fed up with the dark forest. After his friend's brutal death he had subconsciously decided to run any risk to get out of there as soon as possible. Therefore he changed his escape plans drastically. Now he planned to cross the dam at the power station above Baie Comeau and either hitchhike or travel by public transport along the coastal road to Montreal. In this way he considered his chances a lot better than trying to get through the strongly guarded border that he understood had been created to catch them. This was a thousand times better than following the previous plan of walking through the forest on the other side of the river towards Chute des-Passes with the entire Canadian army on his track, he thought depressedly. The distance to Chute des-Passes was nearly equal to the distance he had already walked in the forest. He had decided that was far over the limit of his remaining strength.

The next day he was almost discovered by a patrol of soldiers. He observed nothing but helicopters far away and was not thinking of his pursuers at all. The patrol consisted of six soldiers who were not talking or making any sound. The soldiers were simply taking the chance of relaxing. They lay on their backs in a clearing in the forest and dozed the time away, thinking about everything but the army.

McNeigh came silently through the forest and discovered the soldiers, luckily, just seconds before he walked directly into their arms. He was hardly thirty metres away from the nearest of them. He stopped immediately and bent down. He moved backwards as silently as possible. He stepped on a twig. It broke and he heard the sound just like a shot. He stopped breathing. Did the birds also stop singing? Was he discovered? Which possible escape routes were available? Thoughts ran through his head like they must run through the head of a man who knows he has only seconds left to live.

Suddenly he heard hushed comments from one of the soldiers: "Did you hear that?"

"Probably an elk looking for a mate," another soldier said, "don't disturb me, I am sleeping."

A third soldier added: "Shut up – damned fools!"

McNeigh kept on moving, silent as a churchyard ghost, backwards, when he heard the first soldier get up and say: "I'll go and look to see what it was."

The soldier grabbed his rifle and went in the direction where he thought the noise had come from. McNeigh threw himself down as fast as possible behind the first rock he saw. The rock did not cover him completely. He lay quite silent while the soldier started to play Indian hunting. The soldier had bent his back and was sneaking through the forest, with his gun in the attack position.

"If he sees me, the bastard will assuredly shoot me," McNeigh thought, almost dead with fright.

The soldier came to the place where the twig had been broken. He looked to left and right. He was obviously no track trapper. There might have been tracks from McNeigh's shoes. He probably did not look for any tracks at all, only for possible movements.

"If he chooses to walk to the right, I am a dead man," McNeigh thought frantically, shivering like a leaf in an autumn storm.

The soldier chose to walk to the left. He disappeared from McNeigh's sight. McNeigh moved quickly in the opposite direction. Shortly afterwards he heard the soldier coming back to the clearing, where the others still lay undisturbed by their friend's lonely hunt.

The intrepid huntsman said: "You were right. It must have been an elk looking for a mate."

McNeigh reached the dam with the electric power plant, just before sunset the following day. The power plant was enormous. On top of the large dam was a road. He carefully studied the dam from two kilometres away, for a long time. He decided to cross it during the night between three and five o'clock. He reckoned that the guards would be most sleepy and less watchful at that time of night.

McNeigh had slept for a couple of hours when his watch showed two o'clock, although he had tried to stay awake all the time. It had been very nice to sleep, but he knew it was quite risky in his situation. He could easily have slept too long, which would have lead to postponing the crossing till the next night. He moved quickly and quietly to where the dam started at the eastern side, and decided to cross on the upper side, outside the railings, along a concrete walkway for workers, just above the high water mark.

He advanced slowly and silently, close to the dam wall, like a shadow. The moon periodically shone, as the clouds were moving in the wind. He could hear the sounds of the waterfall cascading down to the turbines becoming louder and louder as he approached the centre of the dam. He passed the first set of water intakes for the turbines.

The intake was just below the water surface and he could see a strong current of water on the surface. About two metres out, in the dam, he could also see bars in the water that prevented floating items reaching the intake. The baffle walls were closed, because the dam collected water for the winter after a dry summer. The water level was low. All the water left the dam through the turbines, which generated electric power. He felt the whole dam vibrate with the waterfall and the spinning water turbines. He knew any sound he made would be completely covered by the sound of the dam. The sound was similar to the sound when water pours into sewage pipes from an enormous bathtub or an enormous creature gasping for air while its stomach rumbles. McNeigh approached the next water intake.

Along the road at the top, the guards had made a barrier just outside the western dam house. Two men were always on watch, while the rest of the patrol was sleeping inside. The soldiers also kept watch over the workers' walkway along the upper side of the dam. Frequently they looked over the railings along the road, down at the pass. The moon was hidden behind the clouds. A soldier, who had crossed the road and looked down at the walkway, waved suddenly to his colleague at the other side of the road. His colleague ran over to him.

The first soldier whispered: "I think there is somebody down there."

The clouds moved and the moonlight was like a spotlight.

McNeigh, who had just passed under the place where the soldiers were standing, heard both of them cry: "Halt – stop – or we will shoot!"

McNeigh again automatically started to run. He was too astonished to think properly. The soldiers fired warning shots over his head to get him to stop. McNeigh could hear the whistling sound of the bullets above his head before they hit the concrete and ricocheted with a deeper whistling tone. No sound is worse than the sound of bullets whizzing around when there is no cover. Suddenly a bullet hit him in his left shoulder. He was swung around to the right by the force of the bullet. He tumbled directly into the water between the dam and the bars protecting the water intake for the turbines. He had no chance. He felt the grip of the strong current pulling him into the feeding pipe for one of the turbines. The next second he was spinning inside the pipe together with the water, completely out of control. He reached the turbines, which in no time pulverised him like an enormous mincer, into molecules mixed with water. Nobody would ever find his remains.

The British Prime Minister travelled directly to Ottawa, after his successful meeting with the President of the United States. The Canadian Prime Minister similarly agreed to stop the investigation and the search for the activists in the Canadian forests. It was late in the evening, but the Canadian Prime Minister at once contacted General Lyon and asked him to come to his office.

Afterwards Lyon immediately contacted the investigation and search's leader, La Fontene, at the Déboisement air base.

"It seems it was Scottish independence activists who closed down Fort Hope. The Prime Minister has, for some unknown reason, agreed with the English to stop all investigations and all searches immediately," Lyon said, evidently relieved, over the telephone. "The Scots seem to work more efficiently than we do," he continued ironically.

La Fontene replied, also rather relieved: "We have not caught anybody yet, but we think we had close contact with the fugitive three days ago, near the city of Manicouagan. I will suspend the search early tomorrow morning."

However, by then it was too late.

28

"Information has been received from Canada, which probably confirms that Neil McNeigh or Sean Ness was killed at an electric power plant dam above Hauterive, along the river from the Manicouagan Réservoir. The man, who was shot there, fell into the water and was immediately caught by the stream, which led to the turbine intake. No remains have been discovered to make any identification," Sir Walter said angrily with tears in his eyes. "The same source also reports that blood was discovered in the forest near a bridge further upstream. The Canadians believe shots from the guards at the bridge fatally wounded one of the fugitives. They also believe that without any proper treatment he later died of his wounds, and was buried by his comrade. They reckon that might be the reason why the man at the dam was alone."

None of the other participants in the Highlanders' Commando's meeting, held one week after Neil was killed, commented on Sir Walter's information. They only registered the news with ashen, sorrowful faces.

"This means," Sir Walter continued, raising his voice greatly, so that he could be heard by the whole company, "– this means that the damned English have cheated us. Our two companions have been killed because we warned them before our attack, in order to save their bloody lives. This means," he repeated loudly, "that more Scotsmen have been killed to help the rotten English. Note especially that our countrymen have been brutally killed even after we made our successful offensive in London as a warning against further investigation concerning the demolishing of the base. The damned English took no notice of our warning. They simply ignored it completely and continued using the Canadians as buffers even though our message on that point was crystal clear. We must now give the bloody English a final shock lesson before we let loose a strike they will remember for a thousand years."

Sir Walter took a short break while he looked at everybody in turn to observe reactions. Still nobody interrupted the furious leader as he carried through his ever louder diatribe.

"I have decided to launch new attacks that finally will make the bloody English understand for ever that they can never ignore the Scottish independence fighters' strict directives," Sir Walter concluded determinedly.

It was just before dawn two weeks later. London was not awake and it was still dark. The city was wet and cold. Autumn had squeezed it in its cold grasp. Only a few lonely cars were driving in the empty streets. The night watchmen were on their way home, walking slowly, tired and sleepy. The paperboys and the milkmen were about to start their rounds.

Nobody seemed to observe the grey missiles flying high in the sky over London that morning. Nobody seemed to observe that these missiles suddenly changed their direction and went into a nearly vertical dive down towards the central part of London.

The army's radar stations, which watched the sky over London, had though, just a short time before observed, altogether, four zombies on the radar screens. The altitude radar made blips and determined the altitude of the zombies to be six thousand five hundred feet, climbing eastwards from different positions below radar range. Civilian radar operators, at different airfields around London, had, at the same time, also made similar observations of unidentified flying objects on their radar screens.

It suddenly became very noisy in the sleepy observation room at the RAF radar station north-east of London. The blips on the screens were clear and could not be caused by any radar clutter. Supersonic aircraft could possibly have made such blips, but the computers had not stored any corresponding flight plans. No pilots would fly over London without a proper flight plan and still be certain to keep their licence. Not even by the wildest coincidence would there be four such lunatics who would act together at the same time. Either the RAF or its allies were out of control of their planes at that moment.

All replies to the question: "Were the zombies friendly supersonic planes?" were completely negative.

That the zombies could be hostile planes was another question. The Russians had, as early as 1972, for instance, completely fooled the Norwegian radar warning system.

The Norwegian Air Force was, in the early seventies, about to convert its radar system to Nato's new electronic one, which covered all the western European countries' borders from eastern Turkey to Hammerfest in northern Norway, against the threat from potential eastern European enemies during the Cold War.

Russian fighter aircraft had suddenly, late one night, without any warning, appeared over Bodø. This town in northern Norway was also known to be the base for Powell's

U2 spy plane, which was shot down by the Russians in 1962. The radar was out of service at the town's air force base, because of the rebuilding programme.

The coastal naval radar, which was ordinarily intended for ships and vessels, could possibly have discovered the Russian planes, but the rotating radar antenna had a lower position and, as radar beams go straight, the radar did not cover the area below the horizon out at sea. In addition, the naval radar only covered low altitudes, the sea's surface and just above. Between the naval radar range and the neighbouring aircraft radar's range was an uncovered section. The Russians obviously knew this detail exactly and sent two MiG-25 Foxbats from Murmansk, a few kilometres beyond the Norwegian border, towards Bodø, to test Nato's new warning system. The Russian fighters flew under the naval radar's range towards the Norwegian coast. When the planes reached the naval radar area, they climbed steeply to reach an altitude above its range, but below the neighbouring aircraft radar's range.

The indication on the old fashioned naval radar screen would only be a couple of blips, nearly at the very same place, depending on the planes' angle of ascent. The operators probably read the radar blips as only being clutter, especially because of its slow movement in a horizontal direction. To sum up – the naval radar station was not equipped with any altitude radar as ships follow the water surface. It, of course, influences the situation that tired operators manned the radar screens during the night. Thus the blips were not thought to be important by anybody.

By this clever manoeuvre, the speedy Russian fighter planes patrolled the entire length of northern Norway without being intercepted. The Norwegians, of course, officially claimed later that they had made an interception, so as not to lose face. However, an interception would obviously have been quite impossible, as the Russian fighters could easily reach a speed of mach 3.2 if necessary, and they had a cruising speed of mach 2.8, or approximately 3 thousand kilometres an hour. The few Norwegian Freedom Fighters available at that time could not approach speeds anywhere near the Russian fighters, and they needed time to become airborne.

It was considered that human error at the radar stations had allowed the Russians to execute their very impudent, but very clever operation. There had not been the correct reaction when the Russian zombies suddenly disappeared over the Norwegian Sea outside the territorial border. The zombies had previously been observed in daily repeated passes along the Norwegian coastline, well away from the border.

"It can't be Russian aircraft that are testing our radar warning system like they did in Norway," said the night shift leader, Captain Paul Bradford.

"No – absolutely not," confirmed the operator at the nearest radar screen, a grenadier in his early thirties. "Not a sparrow can pass us undetected."

"We will inform all aircraft within the area immediately, to keep them out of the zombies' path," Bradford said calmly.

Meanwhile he nodded an instruction towards the senior operator, Second Lieutenant Gloria Hove, who was seated to his right, at the third row of radar screens.

She immediately pressed the buttons for a direct phone link to the air traffic control towers at the main airfields in the London area. Heathrow, Gatwick, Luton and Stanstead all received the emergency message only seconds later. However, all the control towers reported they had made similar observations themselves and had already warned all civil air traffic in the area.

413

"The zombies are certainly not Russian," Bradford's superior, Major Harold Lynn said quietly.

Lynn had come, by coincidence, from another room behind the observation room, where he was testing equipment during the night, while all was quiet. He usually worked only during daytime.

Lynn had previously been a fighter pilot, but was permanently grounded by the RAF after a second parachute jump from a crashing fighter plane. Later at the investigation he was not fully acquitted for committing catastrophic mistakes.

He was a splendid technician his colleagues said, but a completely incompetent pilot. However, Lynn was a lone wolf and had never adapted completely from the diurnal rhythm of a pilot to working within normal office hours as technician and radar supervisor.

"I am working when my wife is angry," he had said once.

Lynn was nearly always at work so always received the same comments: "She must always be angry then."

"The distance from Murmansk to London, is too far for the Russian supersonic fighter aircraft's operational radius, if they have planned a return. It is only their long range, slower speed ones that reach our coastlines and frequently are intercepted by our fighters," Lynn continued quietly. "The Norwegians are neighbours of Russia and observe Russian aircraft over the Arctic Ocean and the Norwegian Sea nearly every night. If the Russians had planned to attack the United Kingdom, they would certainly have used intercontinental missiles. Such killing machines operate ten times faster than these zombies you see on your screens."

414

"The Cold War is over, so I am quite sure the zombies can't be Russian," the shift's comedian added with a laugh.

"This is too serious to laugh at, but – no, that's correct and they can't be V-2 bombs either," Bradford said. Then he became very serious. "These bastards are coming from the west, the opposite direction of the original V-2's, which whistled over British heads during the Second World War's blitz against London."

"Perhaps the zombies are flying objects from Mars or somewhere. You know, small saucers filled with small green men – you never know these days. The blips on the radar screen can't tell us the size of the objects," the operator at the nearest screen added to keep the conversation at the level he decided it ought to be. "I'd better rush home at once and take care of my wife. You see, she is stuck on small green men. She might be kidnapped – or she might rather leave me voluntarily and follow them back to Mars."

"You might be correct," the shift's comedian continued enthusiastically, "I must also rush home to protect my girlfriend. She tells me she is always dreaming blissfully about small green men when she gets an orgasm."

"She's obviously not dreaming about you," Bradford added sarcastically.

All laughed loudly, but for Lieutenant Downfield, Bradford's second-in-command, who had very long radar experience. He immediately occupied a vacant screen when he heard something unusual beginning to happen.

He shouted loudly: "What the hell, it seems like the bloody zombies are going into a nearly vertical dive, directly onto central London."

Director Spindlier was an incorrigible workaholic. It was this very addiction, combined with his obsequious, ingratiating nature that had propelled him through continuous promotions towards the top position in the Secret Service. He usually slept for a very short time, mostly only four hours a night, and sometimes took short after lunch naps on his office sofa. This morning he had woken as usual at half past four and quietly sneaked from the bedroom where his wife snored loudly.

His wife was generally sleeping when he came home late in the evenings after work or representative assignments, and was seldom awake when he left early the next morning. He usually only saw her awake at the weekends.

His wife was the only daughter of a former Conservative politician and newspaper magnate in Fleet Street who had great influence in the running of the Secret Service. She was not especially attractive and Spindlier had often wondered what had induced him, forty years before, to marry her. He would never admit, even to himself, that he married her only to serve his career and income. Soon after the wedding he concluded that his wife was no use for anything other than giving him social status and money to spend.

He had a man's normal needs and his wife's lack of sex appeal had led him, more than thirty years ago, to start an affair with a fellow civil servant, the daughter of one of his chiefs. The father had rapidly pushed his career forward as he may have expected that sometime Spindlier would become his future son-in-law. The association with the daughter of a high-ranking member of the Service had also guaranteed that the affair would remain as a well-hidden secret. It became a very confidential secret for nearly everybody, except for his closest colleagues who gradually, one by one, were deployed to different assignments abroad or simply quit the Service.

*

The chauffeur collected Spindlier from his home in the neighbourhood of Regents Park. He was driven in the back seat of the official dark blue Bentley towards the secret office for the Scottish operation, in the City. It was on the top floor of a new office building at the east end of High Timber Street. The street was a short, blind alley parallel to and close by the River Thames, east of the City of London School.

Spindlier got out of the car in the locked garage under the building and told the chauffeur to pick him up three hours later and drive him to his office at headquarters. He smilingly greeted the guard by the lift and went up to the office at the top. Two police guards remained in the office. Spindlier dismissed them immediately, before their duty was ended. This was, of course, completely against regulations, but he was the boss. He waited for Frank to arrive.

At Number Ten, Downing Street the Prime Minister finally had fallen asleep and slept deeply, but rather uncomfortably. The evening before, he had represented the United Kingdom at an official function for ambassadors. Till late into the night he had been listening to boring speeches, full of uninteresting nonsense and the usual diplomatic phrases. This part of his job was what he disliked the most. He had strenuous work to do the next day and had not felt well as the wasted hours at the engagement passed. Therefore he had been really exhausted when the car took him back to Downing Street, after he had made his final handshakes with the diplomats in their elegant, black suits.

Before he went to sleep, he gulped his glass of whisky like one of his predecessors, Margaret Thatcher, had always done to keep her in good health and make her sleep well. However, this Prime Minister did not sleep well. It was exactly as if someone was telling him to wake up. He twisted in his bed like a worm on a fisherman's hook. He had not been asleep many minutes when the missiles crossed the London sky.

The royal family had finished with its quarrels for the night and was sleeping, in apparent peace, at Buckingham Palace. They all enjoyed their privileges in the broad soft beds in the glorious royal palace, but they never thought for a moment that all the luxury surrounding them had been squeezed, through generations, from poor people all over the British Empire. The Royal family's only problem was to think about how to preserve its wealth and old-fashioned privileges while keeping the press and paparazzi at bay. They certainly did not reflect on, nor had the slightest idea about, those hostile missiles that, at the very moment, were making vapour trails high above in the sky, in the direction of central London.

Charley, a vagrant, had periodically been sleeping for the last two decades alongside the wall of Westminster Abbey, straight across from the Houses of Parliament. This night he had, as usual, slept on old newspapers, in his black plastic garbage bag that he always used to protect himself against the cold and wet weather, not to lose all his body heat. Two Bobbies had passed Charley some minutes earlier. One of them had given him a hard kick with his heavy boot and told him laughingly to find another, more suitable place to sleep. Charley was therefore awake now, freezing and shivering, while he knew too well that he could never relax sufficiently to fall asleep again. The bloody Bobbies had destroyed another quiet night for him. He was cursing his bad luck when he looked up and observed in surprise a missile from the sky on its way downward towards the centre of London.

The radar station at the Royal Air Force base east of London had immediately alarmed the stand-by group when the zombies appeared. Four supersonic fighter planes were rapidly launched. However, the pilots had barely got the Plexiglas cockpit covers closed for take-off, before the first missiles hit their targets.

The commander at the nearest Royal Air Force missile base, without hesitating, launched four Bloodhound MK2 ground-to-air defence missiles to no avail, when the radar operators detected the zombies on their radar screens. He had at once recognised the zombies' flights to be those of smaller missiles. Though the Bloodhound had double the speed of the incoming zombies, they did not reach them fast enough as the zombies' suddenly changed course and started to dive towards central London. The Bloodhound's flight path was fixed on the zombies, but this had immediately to be changed, otherwise they would follow the same course down to the zombies' targets on the ground, and increase the damage. The course of the Bloodhound missiles was therefore quickly changed to safe spots in the English Channel, where they would be dumped without either fulfilling their tasks or causing any damage. One of the Bloodhounds failed to respond to its change of course command.

The newly married couple, Coe and Ann, had parked their car in a narrow road near Borehamwood, north-west of London, close by the M1 motorway. They did not see a soul in the neighbourhood. It was too early in the morning. Nobody was out jogging, and nobody was out walking their dogs. It was totally quiet. The birds had not started to sing yet after the night in silence and it was still dark. Only an owl hooted plaintively far away.

Coe carried two missiles with their light aluminium launch attachment container to a position about thirty metres from the car in the field among some low bushes. Meanwhile, his wife kept careful watch for anyone coming. Coe aimed the weapon in a south-east direction. He fixed the compass direction exactly and the tilt of the launching container in the sight unit. He also carefully examined his watch and when it showed the appointed time he pressed the button.

The front cover of the launching container violently blew aside and the force roughly threw the rear lock back, as the missile left the launch container, with a loud roar. The missile climbed quickly out of sight. Only a stream of exhaust gas and condensation, which quickly narrowed, showed the missile's route. The vapour trail was quickly spread by the wind, but at the firing point the smell of jet fuel still hung heavily in the air.

Without hesitating, Coe grasped the other missile and repeated the operation. Afterwards he quickly collected the loose parts from the ground and placed them, together with the launch containers, on an old woollen blanket. Then he took off the boiler suit and the gloves he had worn, and placed them on the same blanket. He quickly wrapped it all up and carried it back to the car, where he threw it into the boot that his wife had already opened. The car left rapidly and drove to the M1 motorway and headed north.

Mrs. Coe was dressed in a yellow dress that gave no limit to the imagination. No police patrol in the world would suspect this couple to be linked with a missile launch towards central London as Ann swung her long, beautiful, tanned legs out of the car into the bright morning sun when they stopped for breakfast. They stopped at Stapleford, near Nottingham, along the M1 motorway, in the direction of Scotland.

The Coes had come back from the Caribbean only a few days previously, after the successful action against HMS *Heroic*. They had been married on the British island Anguilla, after they had discovered their love and need for each other. Afterwards they had spent an unforgettable honeymoon cruising between the different Caribbean islands in the sailing boat, together with the Connolys. They felt as deeply in love, as if they had just met, though they had known each other and been close colleagues for many years. They happily awaited the birth of their first child in eight months time.

Elise McCoy let her husband, Harry, out of the car just after Egham, close to Windsor Great Park, west of London. Then, she drove around the park towards Ascot, where they had agreed to meet. Her husband hurried with a missile container in his bag into the park and stopped at the west-end of Virginia Water, a small, narrow lake about two kilometres long. He carefully checked his surroundings for people. Somebody might be out jogging in the large park instead of taking his physical exercise with his wife in bed, he thought sourly. He had checked the area several times in the last week at the same time of night, and knew that the first jogger would appear in about one and a half hours. However nothing could be left to chance and he therefore made a careful check to be completely sure he had no witnesses to his activities.

Under cover of some bushes, McCoy put on a blue boiler suit and rubber gloves. He took the missile container from the large white and blue Reebok sports-bag and took careful aim with it towards the agreed target. He checked the angle of elevation before he pressed the button at the appointed time. As the missile left with a roar he did not waste any time. He twisted off the boiler suit, picked up the loose parts from the ground and put everything into the sports bag.

Under the boiler suit he wore a black Adidas tracksuit with three stripes on both sides. With Nike trainer shoes on his feet, it was only the large sports bag that distinguished him from the other crazy, morning joggers, whose ambition was to participate in the London Marathon – or die.

His wife waited nervously for him in the car at the agreed site. After the large sports bag was thrown into the boot, the car smoothly set off at an ordinary speed.

They passed Ascot and drove onto the A322 at Bracknell and proceeded further out to the M4 in the direction of Bristol. Elise's old aunt and uncle lived near the sea at Clevedon. Clevedon was a small town across the Severn Estuary, just opposite Cardiff, approximately ten kilometres from Bristol. The old couple had invited the newly married couple to stay with them over the weekend.

Whisky to his friends, but still Commander Peter Ballentine to the rest, had left the hotel early that morning. He drove on the M3, the same motorway that he had driven all the way from Southampton, where he had participated, the evening before, in the annual meeting for retired officers, at the town's Royal Navy base. It had been a successful meeting, except for the main speaker. He had met a lot of old friends and they had been served superb food and drinks. No restaurant could outclass the kitchen at the Royal Navy's officers' mess at the Southampton base.

A former American Foreign Minister had been the main speaker and the attraction of the meeting. A very well paid one, Whisky thought, irritated. The former minister's speech did not contain anything of interest. It was only a collection of meaningless sentences strung together in a way that only the minister himself might have believed was elegant, but the speech did not fool any of the professional Royal Marine officers. It was an absolutely typical politician's speech, which would only be a success, when given to the uninformed. The subject for the speech was the changes within Nato because of the changed political situation in Eastern Europe. Whisky considered, rather irritated, it was completely absurd to pay that old cast-off American politician such an enormous amount for the presentation of such nonsense.

Whisky had chosen to launch the fourth missile from a park area near Farnborough, south-west of London. He parked his car only a few metres from where he was to make his launch, behind some thick bushes, well away from possible spectators.

To launch the Russian missiles was almost the same as firing bazookas. Only they were larger. Whisky had fired tens of bazookas for exercise purposes during his forty years in the Royal Navy. He had also fired some Blowpipes, ground-to-air missiles, which were not very different from the Russian version, though they were a lot smaller and did not have the same range. A Blowpipe had a range limited to four kilometres and maximum altitude was about seven thousand feet.

Whisky was only away from his car, an old fashioned Rolls Royce, for a few minutes before he continued his aristocratic drive at slow speed, as if nothing special had happened. He was going to have breakfast in London, near Piccadilly Circus, at Old Lords' Club, together with his close friend, Viking. He would drive on to Glasgow later the same morning.

29

Sir Walter had travelled to London for business meetings a week previously, all of them especially prearranged by him to explain his presence in London today. He was deeply furious about the way the English appeared to have ignored his strict prohibition against investigations when they always received sufficient warning before each action. Their investigations had resulted in the deaths of McNeigh and Ness, and those simply because of the warning. All his life he had cared greatly about the consequences of his orders on his staff. This time he felt personally guilty and responsible. He therefore decided to take a personal role in the execution of the punishment on the English. He had chosen to be the one responsible for the missile which was to destroy the Secret Service's special office concerning their case.

The Scots had always been thoroughly informed about the development and running of the secret office. They had received information from a variety of sources, as the Scots were deeply integrated in British society. Among the 40 selected collaborators at the office for the Scottish case, three of them had daily leaked information to the independence organisation. One of the other collaborators, a very talkative and boastful man, revealed everything he was working on to his Scottish girlfriend in bed, and she passed it immediately on to the organisation.

During the past week Sir Walter had, several times visited

the neighbourhood of the office in High Timber Street, near the banks of the Thames. This to decide on the best location for him to stand when activating the steering laser beam for the missile, in order to execute a perfect hit on the office. He had decided that the best place would be to the left of Southwark Bridge, in front of the Shakespeare Globe Museum, at the other side of the Thames. From that location he had perfect visibility to the office roof.

Sir Walter was in place ten minutes before the appointed time, after having spent the night in the SS Group's company flat in Bayswater Road, near Hyde Park. He was quite calm, as a former high-ranking army officer would be. He sat quietly in his dark grey Mercedes, patiently waiting for revenge time.

Spindlier had hardly filled his cup of coffee before a rather worn out Frank arrived. He had worked till late the night before.

"I can see you are timing your arrival well in the early morning," Spindlier said with surprise while he stood and raised the coffee cup to drink with one hand, and held the saucer with the other.

He had not expected Frank for another hour. "How did you know I was here?" he asked.

"Seriously, I had not expected you to be here before me," Frank replied politely, "but I understand you have not changed your morning habits recently."

"I always work best in the mornings, and old habits die hard at my age, but I have noticed I am not alone in being an early morning bird"

"I am not only a morning bird. I work day and night. Before she divorced me, my wife said that I was married to my work in the Service." Frank paused before he continued. "Anyway, I received all the files you advised – the last one,

426

late yesterday evening. I verified the files on the computer immediately, although it was after all my colleagues had left the office. I got some very interesting results. I suggest we go to the computer room immediately to have a look."

Both men walked quickly into the computer-room, which was situated in the centre of the office complex. It had no windows, but had an excellent air-conditioning system. Frank showed Spindlier the lists where he had cross-checked the crew lists for HMS *Heroic* and its sister ships, to find all Scotsmen that had recently been trained in the use of portable missiles.

"As you can see there are six possible names. I immediately called the Navy's computer centre and received information only an hour later about them. Five of them are still in service, but one has quit. That is George Coe. He had been in the Royal Marines for many years and had also participated during the landing operations from HMS *Fearless* – one of HMS *Heroic*'s sister ships – in the Falklands War. I made a call to the Scottish police station in his hometown and let them check where he was at the moment. Can you guess what reply I received?" Frank asked smugly without stopping talking.

"I think you would have guessed correctly. He has been in the Caribbean together with a married couple, called Dave and Betsy Connoly and a woman called Ann Castle. She is the only daughter, and sole heiress, of Lord Benjamin Castle, the owner of the international Castle Enterprises. Incidentally, Coe married that woman on Anguilla a couple of days after the destruction of HMS *Heroic*."

"I presume he will be reasonably well supported for the rest of his life," Spindlier commented with an sour smile.

"The local Dutch Coast Guard and a British Navy MTB had both observed Connoly's sailing boat in the neighbourhood of the demolition site."

"Impressive – you have done superb work," Spindlier said

quietly while he was thinking hopefully. At last I have got a hook to catch these damned Scottish bastards.

"That's not all sir," Frank said proudly. "I also cross-checked similar variables concerning Fort Hope, after I received sufficient data from the army's computer centre. I got several more names to work with on that case, concerning possible suspects. Yesterday I made random investigations. The rest of the names will be checked today. I checked a person called Neil McNeigh, who frequently had been on the base, but had been dismissed from the army after some fighting trouble concerning one of the *Winter Express* manoeuvres in Norway, some years ago. I made another call to another Scottish police station. After a couple of hours they informed me that McNeigh was in North America on vacation. He had travelled with his Norwegian girlfriend, who he has a child with, to Miami. Another short telephone call to Interpol's British branch and only an hour later I was informed that the Norwegian police had been in contact with the Norwegian woman, who was back in Norway. She had not heard from her boyfriend since she had left Miami, but she said that he had travelled to Canada by car on a fishing trip together with a Scottish friend."

Spindlier slowly released a breath, and looked at Frank, who continued even more smugly.

"And that's not all sir. The data I received was too interesting to call it a day. I started to examine any possible links between Coe and McNeigh. I soon found that the Scottish Standard Group in Glasgow had employed both of them. You know the company is one of the main builders of the installations on the Brent Oil Field in the North Sea.

"I know that very company," Spindlier nearly shouting with eagerness, "and I also know the director of the company. His name is Walter Bruce – Sir Walter Bruce, if I remember correctly. He was once a general in the British army. Actually one of the very youngest in modern times.

428

He was a tough fellow who was believed to be destined to reach the top. Suddenly he quit and took over as managing director of the company when his uncle unexpectedly died. Bruce was knighted shortly after he quit the army. As far as I know, the company has increased its turnover enormously under his leadership and has probably become one of the largest in Scotland. However, there are rumours that Bruce is an enthusiastic Scottish nationalist."

Spindlier did not tell Frank that he absolutely hated Bruce because he had used his influence to stop one of Spindlier's early promotions. He had suggested to influential sources that Spindlier was absolutely incompetent for any positions of great responsibility, because he was a wheedling sort of person only interested in feathering his own nest. Spindlier had calculated that Bruce's interference had caused a five-year delay in his promotion prospects. Spindlier was suddenly completely blinded by the possibility of long awaited revenge on Bruce. He did not consider logically if the simple coincidences concerning the two suspects' employment could have occurred incidentally.

However, Spindlier was a very smart fellow, and he asked: "Are there any connections between Bruce and the Connoly couple?"

"I raised the same question, and many police and MI5 agents had an extremely busy night's activity."

Frank smiled slyly as an embezzler, and continued: "Dave Connoly is a medical doctor and his wife is a nurse. Both are working at a military hospital in London, both of them are officers in the British army and both are capable of launching hand-carried missiles. I was, by the way, also informed that the Connolys were on a vacation on Sir Walter's yacht from Marbella this summer. I immediately checked where they had been and very soon confirmed that they had been in Malta. This information was received from the Customs office's computer concerning declarations.

The same computer also confirmed there had been a large delivery of spare parts to Bruce's yacht from the manufacturer in the United States. SS Group has a shipyard on Malta where the spare parts had been used. Pirates in the Northern Mediterranean had apparently attacked the yacht. Some members of the crew also had apparently been killed. Do you believe that? Do you believe that could happen without the incident being fully described in all the newspapers in the entire Western world?"

"Hardly," Spindlier replied quickly.

"This is exactly what I thought, and I asked the agents to examine where the yacht had been during its whole voyage. Therefore they sent urgent requests to all Nato members and searched for where the yacht had made customs declarations. This showed the yacht had been visiting Istanbul before it had been to Malta. After leaving Malta the yacht had appeared in Gibraltar, where the crew had been changed. Then it had proceeded directly to SS Group's shipyard in Edinburgh captained by the two retired commanders – Peter Ballentine and Stephan Hunter. I must mention that the time the yacht arrived in Edinburgh coincides perfectly with the detonations of the atomic missiles. I therefore suppose the yacht had freighted the missiles from Istanbul, after having been delivered by some Russians. It could be of importance in that connection that a Russian weapons depot in Kursk was demolished just a couple of weeks previously. I presume the missiles came from there and the demolition of the depot must have been some sort of cover up action. I also believe that the pirate attack on the yacht must have been a fight between rivals over the cargo of weapons and that the Group must have been the financing source for the weapon trade and the actions. I have planned today to examine the company's foreign transactions. You remember the immense pile of lists I previously presented to you?"

Spindlier nodded in confirmation.

"This time I will not have so many promising transactions to examine. I can promise you the required information within one hour of the banks opening."

Frank took a short break while he studied Spindlier's pleased expression. Spindlier said nothing. He was thinking that this was his greatest victory ever in the intelligence business. The evidence was simply formidable.

"Do you have any idea who previously commanded HMS *Heroic* and who planned the vessel's last voyage in the Caribbean?" Frank suddenly asked with a satisfied grin.

Spindlier did not reply to that, but asked instead: "I presume nobody else but me has received all this information?"

Frank replied smirking, as he expected immediate promotion: "I have been very careful. The information has been assembled from quite different unrelated sources. Only we know the full story."

"Excellent," Spindlier said, silently registering Frank's fawning, whilst still deeply considering plans for the future handling of the case. "It seems there is no time to lose, as we expect a new attack from the Scots at any moment. I will therefore immediately order the arrest of all of your afore-mentioned persons, because of investigations concerning the cover up of the pirate attack in the Mediterranean. That will give us time to inspect the yacht and interrogate the suspects to prepare further evidence. Then we can present it before a magistrate's court to claim custody while the case is under investigation. I will, at once, contact one of our reliable lawyers to prepare the warrant to be executed immediately – long, long before the bloody suspects have woken up this morning."

*

However, Spindlier did not know that at the same moment Sir Walter was standing on the opposite bank of the Thames with the Russian laser target indicator, pointing towards the office roof, while a missile hastened down from the sky. The missile hit the roof only seconds after Spindlier had taken his decision to arrest him.

After the mission was completed, Sir Walter calmly placed the indicator under his coat on the back seat, and drove eastwards along Park Street, turned right and was soon driving on the A2 eastwards. The highly respected Scottish industrialist was on his way back home, after a week of successful business meetings in London.

McPride had numerous problems concerning how he should hit Number Ten, Downing Street with the laser beam. Number Ten was well protected by surrounding buildings and particularly difficult to reach. On the south, the Foreign and Commonwealth office protected the house for the full length of the street. To the north the Old Treasury building bordered on Whitehall, but there was one small space between the old Treasury building and Horse Guards Road. There was a large open square along the road – Horse Guards Parade.

McPride finally decided that would have to be the acceptable location for the sight of the laser beam, from the south corner of the Old Admiralty building, along Horse Guards Road, with a view over Horse Guards Parade.

The only problem was that he could not park a car along that road in the middle of the night because of frequent police patrols. In addition, the police obviously kept constant security watch over the square. McPride had therefore chosen to use a van, without windows, that could pass along the road between the square and Saint James Park, without creating too much suspicion, as the street had little normal traffic.

A plumber's van had been his choice, because such vans would not be unusual in any London street, even in the middle of the night, as plumbers are always doing emergency repairs. However, this road would of course not be considered as a natural choice for that kind of traffic. In order to use the laser beam it was necessary to keep the van's back door open a few centimetres. That was not a problem because plumbers very often transport pipes that are longer than the van. The pipes only jutted out through a narrow opening in the doors and had a white cloth tied to the end, warning other cars from driving into them from behind.

Fifteen minutes before the appointed time for the arrival of the missile, an old, white Bedford van with a large company sign *Central London Plumbers* on each back door and on the sides, drove down Victoria Street. The van drove at a moderate speed. Inside sat two plumbers with dirty hands and faces, dressed in boiler suits. The unshaven plumbers had dirt even under their fingernails and smelled revoltingly of drains. It was the plumber boss, Doctor Dave Connoly, who was sitting at the steering wheel. His assistant was Lieutenant Colonel John McPride. Nobody would ever doubt they were real plumbers. The company signs had been fastened to the van some days ago. They were of plastic and easily removable – a type that could be bought in nearly every stationery shop. After the van had been decorated, it had been driven on muddy ground to get a natural layer of dirt on the new signs and the rest of the van. Central London Plumbers gave twenty-four hour service. This could be read from the signs. That would explain why the van drove through London in the middle the night.

The van turned left when it passed the Queen Elizabeth II Conference Centre and proceeded up George Street, as Storey's Gate was blocked at the end. It turned right where a roadblock narrowed the road and drove into Horse Guards Road at very slow speed.

A police car passed the van shortly afterwards, without showing any signs of suspicion that the van did not belong to plumbers working all day and night to feed their families. The two tired officers in the police car had no intention of checking the plumbers' van, until a voice over the radio ordered them to do so. The officers were at this time more interested in ending their night patrol and getting home to their beds. It was the security guards located in the area that had noticed the lonely van, found it suspicious and wanted it routinely examined.

The police car stopped approximately one hundred and fifty metres in front of the van. The younger police officer got out of the car with a stop sign in one hand and a torch in the other.

In the van, the plumbers' hearts nearly stopped, because of the possibility of being delayed for the arrival of the missile, which was only a few minutes ahead. Dave stopped by the police officer and wound down the right side window.

"What's the matter, officer?" he asked with a strong Cockney accent, pretending to be tired and peevish.

"Nothing really," the police officer replied politely," only doing a routine check."

The police officer flashed his torch into the van a second before he continued: "You have been on a job, I suppose." He grinned, as he smelt the awful aroma of the drain water.

"Yea," Connoly replied lazily, "and we took this shortcut

to have a minute more in bed. We have been working non-stop since seven this morning."

The police officer looked again into the van with the beam of his torch. The second it took felt like hours. Then the police officer smiled.

He saluted quickly and said: "Sorry to disturb you, sirs. Have a safe drive home. Good night!"

Afterwards, the officer got back in the police car, which at once moved off.

"That was close," Connoly said, while he looked at his watch and tried to regain control of his racing pulse.

He smiled at McPride, who jumped into the luggage space behind the front seats. McPride at once picked up the target indicator and sighted the roof of Number Ten, Downing Street, through the small opening between the back doors. It was almost the appointed time and he turned on the laser beam at once, while the van moved slowly forwards.

Shortly afterwards, their mission was complete and the van moved faster. They turned left and reached Trafalgar Square less than three minutes later. From Trafalgar Square they drove up Charing Cross Road and about ten minutes later they arrived at a garage near Hampstead Heath. At the same time, a full alert was issued to all the police patrols in central London. The order was to find the old Bedford van that had been seen in the vicinity of Number 10, Downing Street.

In the garage Connoly and McPride cleaned the van. All marks and fingerprints were removed. They had used gloves during their activities so identifying fingerprints would appear only on the steering wheel and the door handles. The number plates were changed and the sign was transferred to a flower shop's. It would be driven from the garage a couple of weeks later, directly to a scrap yard.

They shaved, washed themselves and put on business

suits. Every loose part, including the target indicator, they put into the boot of Dave's green Jaguar that was parked near by. Afterwards, exhausted they headed north for Scotland in a very satisfied mood.

Wallace had arrived in London three days earlier. He had officially travelled to London on business, but most of the time he had been looking for the best and safest place to be, when he marked the missile's target with the laser beam. He had been considering several different places, but he quickly realised that the best position would be on the east bank of the River Thames.

He had carefully examined the riverbank from the Fire Brigade Headquarters, near Lambeth Bridge in the south, to Waterloo Bridge in the north, where the river made a ninety degrees turn eastwards. Straight across from the Houses of Parliament was St. Thomas' Hospital. The hospital covered an area from Lambeth Bridge to Westminster Bridge. The best place would of course have been in the hospital area, but the problem was that it was heavily guarded and therefore would be too dangerous a position. The hospital buildings prevented the direction of the laser beam over Archbishop's Park from a location along Lambeth Road. It was only from one house at the east side of Lambeth Road that the roof of the Houses of Parliament could be properly seen, but it was quite impossible to gain access to it.

At the other side of the river by Westminster Bridge, opposite Big Ben, was County Hall. This was another potentially superb location for the laser beam, but this area was also under constant surveillance and could therefore not be used.

There was a one-way street around the Royal Festival Hall, close to the South Bank Pier in the eastern bend of the river. The road had to be entered from Belvedere Road to the northern side of the Festival Hall, close to the Hayward Gallery. The street ended by the entrance to the Shell Centre in front of Waterloo railway station. To the right of the road, there was free visibility from Jubilee Gardens, directly to the Houses of Parliament.

Early that morning the missiles were forcing their way through the air, high above central London. The missiles gave grey hairs to everybody who saw them on their radar screens. Wallace drove slowly into the one-way street passing the front of the Royal Festival Hall. He arrived ten minutes earlier than the appointed time and parked the car in Jubilee Gardens. Only a police patrol or somebody that had to take the dog out might disturb him, but it was unlikely at this time of night, he hoped.

Wallace's hope was unfulfilled. An old, grey-haired woman, old enough to walk safely around London by night and be absolutely certain not to be interfered with, appeared with her terrier dog on a leash. The woman was not poorly dressed, but not well dressed either. She lived in one of the houses near Waterloo station and had been woken up by the dog's squeaking because it needed out. She let the dog loose. It ran around in its newly gained freedom and lifted its left back leg to mark its area wherever there was a chance.

Wallace checked his watch. The appointed time for the missile came closer and closer. The old woman did not seem to be in a hurry. He checked his watch again and again, but she remained. He realised that he had to act quickly.

He opened the car door, got out and shouted loudly to the lady: "Madam, I am a police officer. It is forbidden to let dogs foul the park. Leave with your dog at once, otherwise I will take you to the police station and summons you. There is a large fine."

The old woman leapt into the air and called desperately for her dog: "Honey – Honey, come to mummy. Honey – Honey, come to mummy – dear."

She called to the dog as if it was a child. After some unsuccessful attempts, and nearly weeping, she managed to fasten the leash to the dog's collar. She almost ran across the grass pulled by the dog.

Without having time to think further about the old woman with the dog, Wallace opened the left back door of his car and quickly picked up the target indicator from his golf bag on the back seat. Afterwards, he jumped into the front passenger seat and placed the front end of the target indicator through the open window of the right door. He turned on the laser beam and sighted on the roof of the Houses of Parliament, to the left of Big Ben. The old woman would have seen him if she had turned her head, but he had no time to wait for her to disappear. She would, hopefully, never know what had happened. He only prayed she was as lunatic as she looked.

Wallace grinned when he suddenly thought about the annual burning of Guy Fawkes, the man who had tried to blow up the Houses of Parliament. He slowly counted down the seconds until the estimated arrival time for the missile.

Immediately afterwards, he started the car and drove carefully, but quickly, into Belvedere Road. When he turned left he became aware of police sirens.

The old woman had turned her head. She had stopped a police car passing on Belvedere Road.

The police officers saw Wallace's car come from Jubilee Gardens and switched on the sirens to stop him.

Wallace did not stop. He speeded up as if he was driving a racing car and drove under Waterloo Bridge. The police car was following. Then he turned right almost on two

438

wheels and drove up to the roundabout where he chose Stamford Street to the left. He followed Stamford Street till he met Blackfriars Road, where he turned left over the Thames. The police car hung steadily on his tail. Now he could hear sirens from several cars. He felt trapped.

Viking had booked a room on the top floor of Lanesborough Hotel, by Wellington Arch, with the corner of Buckingham Palace Gardens at the one side, and with Hyde Park at the other side. He had a beautiful view towards Buckingham Palace from his window. Many times previously, during the last twenty years, he had stayed at the same hotel and was well known to the staff.

This morning Viking's alarm clock went off early. He had shaved and dressed long before the appointed time when the Russian missiles would make their way through the air high above the heads of the sleeping Londoners.

For some minutes Viking was sitting in one of the two easy chairs in the room, relaxed, like an experienced hunter before the day's chase. Then he rose and collected the target indicator from his golf bag. He opened the window slightly and inhaled the cold air mixed with the smell of the city, as the traffic sound now gained free access to his sound insulated room.

He looked, with a grin, down at the nearby police station in the middle of Wellington Arch, to the left of the hotel. There is not a lot the police can do for the Royal family if somebody is gunning for them, he thought sardonically.

Viking personally had no special thoughts about the Royal family. He did not like them and he did not dislike them. He had always held that the Royal family was simply part of the deep-rooted English system, more difficult to get rid of, than keep in position – a system that would exist for generations, unless something drastic happened. Anyway, it

439

would be very expensive to change Royalty with, for instance, a President, as almost everything in England has the name *Royal* included in it. Tourists like the Royal family. There must be something exciting about this old fashioned institution. Perhaps there even are some ordinary English people who like them.

Gallup polls report there are many. People are strange, Viking thought, but these people are probably old women who only read stupid weekly magazines. Anyway, the newspapers and magazines do like Royalty as they sell many extra copies every time pictures of Royal scandals cover the front pages. Articles about other society clowns never sell so well.

Viking considered further, rather surprisingly, that he felt true pity for the Royal Family who lived in the building he cold-bloodedly was about to target with a deadly missile. They had not themselves chosen to be born and they had not chosen to be Royal.

Viking placed a high backed chair at the window and placed the front end of the target indicator on top. He tested the sight. He had previously chosen the target spot on the Palace roof. The site was chosen so that there would be no indication where the missile had been directed from, when it was investigated. It could have been from one of a thousand suitable places.

It was still some minutes before the appointed time for the missile's arrival. Viking took a can of soda water from the fridge and some salt biscuits from the coffee table and seated himself again in the easy chair. He was still quite relaxed, and did not at all seem affected by the forthcoming event. He kept a close eye on his watch, which was exactly synchronised with Whisky's watch.

When it was a minute before the estimated arrival time, he rose and made a careful sight towards the roof of the Palace, while the indicator lay steady on the back of the

440

chair. He turned on the laser beam and waited as patiently as a hunter in the forest waits for an elk while the dogs chase it towards him.

He observed with satisfaction the missile's hit, immediately dismantled the target indicator and put it into the golf bag. With the bag in one hand and his old Samsonite suitcase in the other, he quickly left the room for the lift, as if nothing unusual had happened. The receptionist greeted him with a broad smile.

"You are up early as always, Commander."

"No man's work can be done by lazy fellows," Viking replied smilingly. "I'm checking out."

A new guest entered the lobby from outside and said: "London seems to be at war again. There are police everywhere."

"Their exercise season has probably started," the receptionist said with a smile, without looking up from his computer screen.

"These people were certainly not exercising," the new guest replied, visibly irritated.

"They might have let loose the foxes for the autumn hunt in the wrong place" Viking added with a grin, "or they might be hunting for somebody who has broken into the Bank of England. Everybody needs a lot of money with these ever increasing prices nowadays," he said while looking at the hotel bill.

The new guest did not reply, just grinned and left the desk pointedly and walked over to a leather sofa beside the wall at the other side of the lobby, where he quickly and deliberately disappeared behind a newspaper. The receptionist checked Viking out of the hotel, while he chuckled at his remarks. Viking left the hotel by taxi. He had an appointment with Whisky for an early breakfast at Old Lords' Club near Piccadilly Circus.

441

30

With the police on his tail, Wallace sped across Blackfriars
Bridge as fast as the Jaguar was able. The car belonged to
the police and had been stolen late the previous evening,
from one of London's Police Stations by a local Scottish
independent supporter with the necessary knowledge. To
avoid its absence being reported before it was to be used, it
was taken as close to the time of the operation as possible.
It was equipped with fake registration plates. The original
plates were hidden inside the car. It had a police radio and
even a blue light to put on the roof.

Wallace passed Victoria Embankment and drove up New
Bridge Street with the police car hanging on. He heard on
the police radio the officers in the tailing car ask for
assistance. They would block the road in front of him.
Therefore he turned left at Ludgate Circus into Fleet Street,
on a red light. The sound from passing cars' wild horns
made a loud atonal symphony. In the mirror he could see
that the police car behind him had received assistance from
two others. They were catching up with him quickly and he
had to make a wild manoeuvre to get rid of them.

After four hundred metres along London's famous newspaper street at maximum speed, the police cars were only a
few metres behind. Suddenly he jammed on the brakes just
before he passed the Royal Courts of Justice. He turned
quickly to the right, up Chancery Lane. The car swung

around with a screeching sound from the wheels, but he managed to get it into the correct position to enter the street.

The sudden braking surprised the police drivers, who immediately pressed their brake pedals to the floor. But the second one was not quick enough and hit the first one. Wallace could see them both in the mirror spin around in the street. The third car managed a narrow escape and accelerated after Wallace, who took the first street to the left, around the corner of the courthouse, into Carey Street.

On the radio he heard another police car was on its way down Kingsway, being directed into Portugal Street in front of him. A few seconds later Wallace saw it as it passed the London School of Economics. He did not brake, but drove at full speed towards it. The police car behind was only a car's length away.

Just as he was going to pass the one from the opposite direction, he wrenched the car into its path. I believe I have the stronger nerves, he thought grimly. He was right. To avoid him, the oncoming police car turned desperately into the opposite lane, where their colleagues were driving. They had no chance, but crashed into each other like two male rhinoceros.

Wallace entered Kingsway at high speed. He decided to drive in a northerly direction and had to drive against the traffic flow for some metres because of permanent roadway barriers at the intersection. He could again listen to the angry atonal music from oncoming cars, which he just managed to avoid by using the pavement. He slowed down when he was able to return to the left hand lane, but soon after, he met a police car that turned just as it passed him. The hunt was on again.

Wallace pressed the accelerator and drove up Southampton Row, but turned left at Russell Square and passed between the University of London and the British Museum.

The police car was hanging on. He took a right, with wheels screaming, down Bloomsbury Street, passing New Oxford Street, right again at Princes Circus and down Shaftesbury Avenue, in the direction of Piccadilly Circus.

Another police car had joined the one on his tail. Suddenly, Wallace turned left down Charing Cross Road. By this manoeuvre he was for a short moment, out of sight from his pursuers. He quickly jammed on the brakes and turned rapidly into the short Litchfield Street just down from the intersection. He barely managed it. The car skidded along the road. Half of the tyre-tread was left behind. The police did not see him and believed they still followed him when they continued along Charing Cross Road.

Wallace stopped the car and dashed out. He changed to the car's original registration plates, threw the fake ones into a nearby dustbin, and put the blue police light on the roof. Again he drove into Shaftesbury Avenue via West Street, but above the intersection he just had passed. He put on the siren and drove this time along the street towards Piccadilly Circus. He was passed by several police cars. On the radio he could hear they were looking for the vanished fugitive. They saluted when they passed him. A Jaguar police car indicated an executive officer. He smiled and saluted back.

Relieved, Wallace parked the car in Archer Street, a small street near Piccadilly Circus, and with a satisfied air took the suitcase with the missile attachment in his hand and walked to the tube station.

The missile that hit the Secret Service office was equipped with a conventional warhead developed by Michael Samson but based on Russian plastic explosives. He had tried to estimate the exact force necessary to demolish only the top floor of the building, but he had calculated incorrectly. The

444

Russian explosive was too powerful and all the three upper floors were completely destroyed. Afterwards, the building burned to the ground.

Spindlier and Frank were killed instantly and all the information collected about the Scottish action was completely destroyed. Luckily, nobody else was in the building or in its immediate neighbourhood at that time of night, except for three police guards in the lobby, on the ground floor, who narrowly escaped any significant injuries.

All the other missiles that were used for the attack on London were without warheads. They therefore caused little damage, but frightened the English leaders in the intended direction – especially after they received information that another missile had detonated an atomic warhead in Dartmoor National Park, near Whitehorse Hill, exactly at the same time as the four missiles had rammed London. Nobody died from the unloaded missiles, but a police officer was slightly injured.

To avoid casualties, McPride had targeted the wall of the Foreign and Commonwealth Office building instead of the roof of Number Ten, Downing Street. If the missile had impacted the roof, the Prime Minister could have been killed in his bed. The Foreign and Commonwealth Office building, however, was empty at that time of the night. If it had been an atomic warhead on the missile, the result of the explosion would have been completely fatal for the Prime Minister anyway.

The injured police officer guarded Number Ten. Fragments of concrete, forced loose when the missile impacted the neighbouring building, injured him. He was extremely lucky because only seconds earlier he had been very close to the target spot. His injuries kept him in St Thomas's Hospital for a week. Afterwards, he received a medal for heroism in the line of duty, with a handshake from the Prime Minister in person, a rise in salary and a month's vacation with full pay.

The missile that landed on the Houses of Parliament went down into the patio behind Big Ben. It caused some damage at the roof-edge, where it first rammed, but it forced itself further down to the bottom of the patio, where it disintegrated. All the windows in the surrounding rooms were shattered either by fragments from the destroyed missile or flying concrete and stones from the building.

At Buckingham Palace the intention was for the missile to hit the patio in the Queen's Gallery. However, the target indicator's position made it impossible to ram the patio directly. Therefore the missile went through the roof.

The unloaded Russian missile would not have caused much damage, but the Bloodhound missile following it caused serious damage. The explosion that followed entirely demolished the interior and the building structure A fire started, but was soon brought under control by the Royal staff and members of the fire brigade. The Royal family slept at the other end of the huge building and hardly noticed the incident.

EPILOGUE

As directed by the Scottish Independence Organisation, the attack on London was kept completely out of the press and all investigation was closed. The Prime Minister announced shortly afterwards, in a live television speech, that a referendum for Scottish independence would be held in a short time.

He said the reason for the government's decision was that the world had changed, and the period when England ruled territories, other than its own, was finally over. The same process had been observed all over, especially after the Second World War. Recently the Soviet Union had also been dissolved. Developments, which once had given South Ireland its independence, would probably soon give Northern Ireland and Wales the same.

He also said that British membership of the European Common Market was of major substantial consideration when the government had made its final decision about Scotland's independence. The European Union meant all members would become integrated, so borders in Europe in the future would become increasingly insignificant matters. Scotland was a neighbouring country and England would evidently be its largest trading partner in the future.

"In the future, Englishmen must prepare themselves to buy Scottish oil and Scotch whisky from abroad," the Prime Minister said with a statesman's smile, but with tears in his eyes.